To-Do Him List

by

Denise Marie

The Lipstick Diaries, Book One

This is a work of fiction. Names, characters, places, and incidents are either the product of the author's imagination or are used fictitiously, and any resemblance to actual persons living or dead, business establishments, events, or locales, is entirely coincidental.

To-Do Him List

Contact Information: info@thewildrosepress.com

Cover Art by *Diana Carlile*

The Wild Rose Press, Inc.
PO Box 708
Adams Basin, NY 14410-0708

Visit us at www.thewilderroses.com

Publishing History
First Scarlet Rose Edition, 2015
Print ISBN 978-1-5092-0267-6
Digital ISBN 978-1-5092-0268-3

Published in the United States of America

Fighting Against Love...Fighting Against Time

"Wait. You do drink, right? I mean, you're not some kind of recovering alcoholic or anything, are ya?"

She couldn't resist. "You know, admitting you have a problem is the first step."

The charade couldn't be maintained with the panic on his face. She turned her head away from him; the laughter bubbled over.

He hip checked her and moved on. "You're gonna fit in here just fine, beautiful."

Her fingertips drained of color as she gripped onto the counter beside her. She didn't want to make anything of what had to be an error in words.

"Pfft." She waved her hand in the air and urged her feet to follow him. "How do you think I concocted the list? Alcohol can be as therapeutic as it can be damaging."

"Very true. I often lie back on the couch and sing my woes out to Dr. Jack Daniels." He opened a narrow door and took a quick peek inside. "Yes." He flung it agape and pointed in. "The bathroom isn't big, but does have a shower. I hope you are familiar with short showers. The supply of hot water sucks. If you want hot, you will need to beat me to the shower." He winked and raised his eyebrows with all kinds of suggestion as he strolled away.

She stopped at the doorway and stared at the radiant white shower with a clear glass door, no longer empty. Her skin warmed.

Cole stood under the stream of water and tipped his head back to wet his hair. The blond strands darkened to a rich shade of brown. She stood in front of him, and splashes of water from his movements sprinkled her bare skin. She smoothed her hand up his muscled chest. "Touch me, Cole."

Dedication

It is very easy, as a wife and a mother, to become the one who supports others ambitions and say, “maybe one day” to her own. Without my husband and children becoming my cheerleaders and encouraging me to follow through with writing this novel, something I once referred to as a “pipe dream,” I would not feel the remarkable sense of pride and fulfillment I do now.

There are many people, along with my family, who have supported this amazing journey—friends, coworkers, and editorial assistance from afar. You all know who you are. Because of the love and reassurance you have offered me, I can say with confidence to all hard-working wives and mothers, there are many crazy wonderful things out there for you too–go for it. Dreams do come true.

Chapter One

Dear Diary,
If it's written, it's there for all to see. To know.

Isabelle Chambers closed her eyes, and let her head fall back to the passenger seat. What next? The sun's rays through the window warmed her face—a little too much considering the wave of heat from the driver. She tapped the stack of medical papers in her lap, loud enough to tune out the bluster of city traffic and her guilt. Springtime weather in Tampa, Florida lured in the tourists, and offered lots of distraction.

"Thank you, Katherine." Izzy tipped her head in the direction of her best friend since college and opened her eyes.

From the anger on Katherine's face and refusal to make eye contact, this wasn't going to be an easy sell. "Don't mention it. If you had told me three days ago when you were admitted to the hospital for the damn biopsy, I would've been there sooner rather than just when called for a ride home."

She scooted sideways with her leg bent in the little beat-up Ford Tempo, which had seen many sketchy paths given Katherine's career as a Tabloid Reporter. "The tumor is benign, Katherine."

"But you still need surgery, Isabelle."

She put both feet back on the floor and crumpled

the papers. Her friends called her Izzy; they only used Isabelle when mad.

Uncomfortable silence reigned the rest of the way home. Katherine pulled into the driveway, close to the house. The well-groomed neighborhood screamed, “safe,” “family-oriented,” and “working-class,” but she too had endured many reprimands from Isabelle’s mother as well.

“We single women need to protect ourselves at all times, girls. I feel like I’m teaching my young and naive teenagers at the high school sometimes with you ladies,” she would always say, her sternness reducing them to little kids once again.

Isabelle unlocked the now trendy, on account of the several similar homes down the street, cerulean blue door on her white bungalow. She threw her car keys on the antique entryway table like any other day, and trudged into the living room.

“Ahem.”

She glanced back at Katherine, bent over to pick up the keys that landed on the runner that covered the dark brown hardwood floor, not the table.

Huh.

As per usual, she collapsed onto the cushy, gray sofa with a sigh and let her eyes drift closed. “Please don’t tell anyone.”

“What are you going to do, Izzy?”

Instant regret hit her when she dared to open her eyes and glance at Katherine, leaning against the doorjamb with her arms crossed. She closed her eyes once again and resumed avoidance. The glare in her direction pierced her eyelids. “I’m not too sure yet, but I know how I can decide.”

The fake expression of happiness she'd mastered over the years, in attempt to ward off Katherine's lectures, never worked, but she tried again. "The same way we always make decisions."

"You just had a hole drilled into your head, dumbass. You are not getting drunk."

She bolted from the couch and stuck her tongue out at *mom* on the way by. "A couple won't hurt if you help me hide the rest." Abigail and Taryn, also best friends and roommates from college, could be swayed to her dark side of recklessness. Okay, recklessness might be an overstatement, but she needed it now more than ever.

Katherine's chastising glare stung her back while several items women can't seem to live without soared in every direction from her over-sized purse. A least *it* had dropped beside the table like usual. Yes, her unusual heightened mood would appear bizarre to most, but Katherine would, when she calmed down, understand her wish for uncomplicated distraction.

She pivoted to the mess around her, waved if off, and headed back into the living room. The slight bounce in her step faltered when she stepped on something sharp. "Naturally."

Focused on the task at hand, she ignored Katherine and scrolled through her phone.

My place, seven o'clock. Bring booze…lots.

Send.

****

The front door flew open at seven o'clock sharp. Each girl's house was like an extension of their own, no knock required.

"We have margaritas," Taryn sang out in her usual

confident voice.

She laughed, already angling for the appropriate glasses from the oak, cottage-style cupboard when the tall bombshell and successful bartender, Taryn Scott, strode into the kitchen. She carried in a large blender filled with green slush, also known as stress relief.

A tall, beautiful redhead paraded through the door and set her designer briefcase on the table.

"What a day. Taryn, whatever concoction you made for us, make mine a double and keep them coming." She sauntered over to the island, dragged out a stool to sit, and relaxed her arms on the stone top. Their common place to gather.

Isabelle leaned against the counter with the margarita glasses in her hands and listened to the effortless banter of her best friends. Her shoulders relaxed, but not quite to the point of the comfort she needed.

Taryn ripped the glassware from her grip, causing them to clink. She stuck her tongue out and gave Isabelle a hip-check on her way back to the 'island of entertainment' to fill them. The woman swept about the room with style, her familiarity with preparing drinks and snacks for a night of companionship apparent. Cocktails made by the notorious bartender, Taryn Scott, and food had solved many problems over the years, even made the toughest decisions achievable.

"Oh, was it a tough day in the marketing world, Miss Money Hungry Abigail Jameson?" Taryn rolled her eyes.

Abigail sighed, plucked a cocktail umbrella from Taryn's bag of supplies, to throw at her, and glared in Katherine's direction. "Katherine, honey, you are the oldest and bossiest, spank her for me, would you?"

Taryn threw her hands in the air to surrender. Katherine's pointed glare in her direction hushed everyone for a split second, not long before they used shovels of food or their hands to hide their chuckles.

"So Izzy, spill."

Isabelle observed the pretty, salt-rimmed, drink in front of her. She needed to pace herself, make her actions believable, normal, even though Abigail's request made the margarita taunt her. She picked up the liquid balm in one hand, a tray of food in the other and headed to the living room. "Let's save the heavy stuff for later, okay Abby?"

She tucked her drink away on the end table, set the tray of food down, and waited on the couch with her legs folded underneath her. Katherine and Abigail followed with trays of goodies while Taryn arranged all of the alcohol off to the side. Katherine sat next to her and dropped a bottle of water into her lap.

She scrunched her nose at Katherine. The movement made the tiny incision on her head, hidden by her hair, sting. "Thank you," she whispered, for Katherine's ears only.

Katherine tipped her head, silent.

Her phone beeped, preset at the highest volume in case the night got a little rowdy, as it always did. She held her best and most observant friend's gaze, and dug in her pocket.

She had no clue what the beep could be; everyone was in front of her. The notification indicated a response to her earlier tweet, from before the biopsy.

Liquid courage is a must today. Isabelle

Her heart raced. She couldn't explain her sudden

interest in this site, or the responses she got, possibly from the *real* Cole Davies.

Bad day? I could recommend some music to go with your beverage. Cole D.

She tucked her phone away, but the corner of her mouth rose, just a little. The girls settled into their usual seats throughout the modest, decorated with pastel colors to make it appear bigger, living room. From their desperate hoarding of goodies and booze, tonight's get together couldn't be better timed, and soon she'd add to their stress.

After several margaritas, or what her friends believed were glasses emptied by her, Isabelle gripped the water bottle in her lap and laughed at Taryn's latest gossip about the bar. Heat lingered in her cheeks since she read his message, and made the little white lie about her so-called intoxication much easier to pass off.

The painkillers prescribed by the doctor for the headache she might endure after the procedure, which she was, could knock anyone on their ass. She didn't need the alcohol.

Abigail stood on unsteady legs and held her glass in the air. "It's later, Izzy?" She scoffed, as if she'd never overlook an unexpected reason for a *girl's night*.

Isabelle peeked up from her empty water bottle. The two drinks Katherine *allowed* didn't offer much courage; her tolerance for observing her friends' enjoyment while she pretended, wore thin about five drinks ago.

She put the bottle on the table beside her. "I'll be a lot lighter yet, when they cut a chunk out of my brain."

She closed her eyes and sighed. The sudden silence meant she hadn't said that under her breath.

"Izzy?"

She boosted her tired in every way body from the couch and dragged her feet to the large bay window that faced the front yard. Taryn's somber voice struck hard. This wasn't going to be easy. She stared at the darkness outside and crossed her arms to keep the tremble at bay. It *should* have been an ecstatic pregnancy announcement.

"Here's the thing. Life sucks." They would agree. When one of them experienced pain, they all did. It'd been that way from the start.

"I had it all—a husband, rewarding career, and friends anyone would consider themselves lucky to have. Well, a drunk driver killed my husband a month ago. April was my happy month, our anniversary month. Not any longer."

She stiffened her stance, couldn't handle their comfort just yet, and they'd swarm her if she didn't make that clear. "I've just recently gotten my shit together enough to return to work. Being a teacher once brought joy. Now, I only see something I won't experience myself. I was late…and nauseous, fatigued. Early signs of pregnancy."

Taryn and Abigail gasped, Katherine didn't.

"I'm not. I do, however, have a brain tumor." Her voice shook. She eyed the ceiling to keep her tears away. She had to tell them and be strong for them. "Surgery is a must. It's not cancer, but it's complicated, and the odds of me surviving are not good."

The air weighted her down, and she couldn't explain anymore without giving into it. Goose bumps formed on her skin. They needed to say something. A dropped pin would echo in the room. "Guys—"

She spun around and before she could finish her sentence, several arms surrounded her. They squeezed so tight it would have taken her breath away if she weren't already choked by fate.

"So, when is the surgery scheduled to take place?" Abigail stood back and crossed her arms.

She shimmied through their embrace, flopped down on the couch, and snatched a cushion to hold tight in front of her. A shield for what came next? The three women sat and faced her but didn't speak.

"This is where it gets difficult for me, guys. I don't even feel like I've truly lived life. How can I get on the operating table and tell myself if *that* day was going to be my last, I would die satisfied with the things I've done? I'm not."

Everyone concurred, even though they were hesitant about it. The knot in her stomach loosened, just a little anyway.

"I have always been a cautious, dependable, boring prude. I tried so hard to be an easy to raise child for my mother, avoided any situation destined to cause trouble. I want to get in trouble." She threw the pillow to other end of the couch. "I want to have sex with more than one man before I die. Earth shattering, wild sex."

The girls giggled and reminisced about their own sexual experiences, Isabelle stared at her laced fingers, caught in the past. The night before David died.

"David, we need to talk." They sat in bed, like every night in their two years of marriage. Her, in her faded Jake Owen concert T-shirt, not a sexy look but comfortable, and David with his laptop in his lap. He placed it off to the side.

"Sure, babe. What's up?"

She shut off the television and faced him. He was so tall, even while he sat. She'd never get tired of ogling his toned, olive skin, shaggy hair, and green eyes that captured your attention. He turned her on. "If I strolled in here swaying my hips, naked, would you feel so overwhelmed with hunger that you'd storm up to me, pin me against the wall and only lower your pants enough to fuck me senseless?"

"Are your girly porn novels giving you ideas, darling?"

Her brave posture gave way, and she slumped. "Never mind."

He pressed his hand to her bare knee, but didn't slide it any further. Did he resist, or just not feel the same urge to lose control? "Isabelle, I'm sorry if I've offended you, but where's this coming from?"

She dropped her gaze to her twining fingers. "David, I want to explore with sex. I'm not the prude everyone sees—there's more to me. God, the places we could lose control." She bit her lip. "The not so typical things we could do."

"Are you saying you're not happy with our sex life?" His tone was clipped, and he yanked his hand away.

Ugh. It wasn't playing out the way she'd practiced in the bathroom mirror earlier. "No, no. That's not what I'm saying. I love having sex with you. So much so, that I think about all the different ways we could *have sex."*

"Like?"

"Like...somewhat hidden, in public. Or, with me...tied to the bed. Have you ever fantasized about taking me from behind, anally?" Excitement rose in her

voice, but she crashed down to reality when she met his uncomfortable, wide-eyed glare.

"Are you serious?"

"Yes."

He leaned over and closed his laptop, flicked the switch on the lamp, and lay down in the dark. "Can I have some time to think about this?"

"Sure." She placed the remote on the nightstand, snuggled under the covers, and rolled away from him—wide-awake.

"Izzy? Where'd ya go?" Abigail crouched in front of her and touched her knees.

She met her gaze and smiled. She didn't want her friends to see the sadness she hadn't been able to let go of yet. "Just remembering my last night with David."

She leaned over, snatched her hidden drink from the end table, and chugged. Relief didn't come at the bottom of it. She spun the empty glass by its stem. "If I told you there would be no surgery," she held up her free hand when their backs stiffened, "*until* I did a few things, would you understand?"

"Like a, err bucket list?" Katherine teetered into Isabelle's side and slurred her words.

Her stomach knotted with guilt as she admired a friend she couldn't imagine her life without. One so supportive, she drank her own margaritas and Isabelle's when no one paid attention, so the others wouldn't prod too soon.

Isabelle tapped her closed lips with her finger and made eye contact with each friend before a framed picture captured her attention.

David.

"Yes Katherine, that's exactly what I'm going to

do." She jumped from the couch and stood firm, with her hands on her hips.

She scoured the room for a pen and paper, without a care for the things she knocked over in her haste. The girls followed her lead, yanking cushions from the couch, and gathered around the coffee table she'd found, abandoned, on the side of the road. Magazines supported its uneven legs. A temporary fix until she could refinish it to the potential she imagined. Her weakness for unwanted items no longer made them giggle.

The girls placed a cushion on the floor for her too, and she sat with a huff. "So where do I start?" She scribbled at the corner of the paper to make sure the blue pen worked.

"Well Izzy, this could get as interesting as you want it." Taryn winked and bit her bottom lip. The booze, beyond a doubt, impacted everyone's ability to be subdued.

"No laughing?" She scanned the empty paper but could see their heads shake in her peripheral vision. She placed her free hand on her stomach to ground herself. In no way did her desires match the person on the outside.

"We know there's a wild woman in there somewhere Izzy, do your worst."

Abigail sparked her inability to ignore childish persuasion—games like truth or dare—at any time. She used her fingernails to make sure the two white sheets were tucked together, the pen in place but not quite touching.

Start with the easy ones.

1. Get a tattoo

2. *Bungee jump*
3. *Sing karaoke in front of strangers*
4. *Dance in the rain*
5. *Eat caviar*

"Come on girl, these could be done in one day. What happened to the woman who craved bold adventure?"

She gripped the pen tighter after Katherine's not so gentle, nudge, a quality in her best friend that always helped, but pissed her off too.

6. *Learn how to fly a plane*
7. *Shop on Rodeo Drive*
8. *Drive a Lamborghini*
9. *Learn to dance the tango*

A tequila shot slammed down in front of her. She raised her head to see everyone with their own, held out in her direction. The room temperature liquid spilled over her fingers as she raised it in the air, unable to keep it steady. In one quick motion all shots disappeared, and she focused on her list, no longer fearing their judgment.

Cole's responses on Twitter surfaced in her memory, and urged her on.

10. *Go on tour with a band*
11. *Experience a knee-weakening kiss*

She set the pen down on the table and wiped her sweaty palm on her thigh before she continued.

12. *Have multiple orgasms during sex*
13. *Try anal sex*
14. *Be tied up during sex*
15. *Have sex in a public place*

In slow motion, she put the pen down and raised her head to see their shock. Instead, they high-fived one another like they'd finally corrupted her.

"Damn Izzy. Goodbye prude, hello girl gone wild." Taryn shouted and threw her fist in the air.

She fell back onto the hard floor and breathed deep. Her heart raced with a new release—freedom.

"This could take some time, Izzy. Are you sure putting off the surgery is such a good idea?" Not even alcohol could keep the concern from Katherine's voice.

"Katherine, I love you, all of you. I know this means asking you guys to have patience, but I've made up my mind. The surgery will wait until after this list is complete, it has to." She braced her hands on the floor and shoved upright. The room spun from getting up too fast, of course. She held onto the table to stop the motion.

Taryn and Abigail gossiped about an unrelated topic like her breakthrough was no big deal, but Katherine's glare challenged her will. "I'm gonna need some help with this list. Any suggestions, ladies?"

Katherine's stubbornness dissolved, and she joined the fun once again. She swayed and held her finger up to quiet them.

Isabelle clutched her arm to support her, still wracked with guilt. "Here we go."

Abigail placed her hands to her hips. "Whatcha got, Miss Investigative Tabloid Reporter?"

Katherine's day job always made secrets near to impossible, but the suggestions she could come up with were most often valuable.

"You still have a Twitter account?"

She squinted, not quite aware of where Katherine was going with this. "Yes."

"Go viral."

Chapter Two

Dear Diary,
If you put it out there, it will come back to you.

"Scandals! Scandals! Scandals!"

The short distance back to the bus always involved rowdy chants from stragglers who refused to let the night end. It was a show in itself, with shrieks, invasive gestures, and camera flashes in your eyes until you couldn't see straight.

Catcalls could get a little sadistic. Most nights it fueled their adrenaline rush and on others, sheer hell. Though, as part of the business, the fans would never know any different. Annoyance masked by graciousness, they maintained the "devoted, rock stars who appreciate their entire fan club," image. At least until they got on the bus.

"Atlanta kicks ass!"

"Give me something to jack off to, ladies!"

"Look at those tits!"

Cole stomped through the roped-off path from the arena with his arms at his side, jaw tight, and gaze focused straight ahead. The nighttime chill of Georgia cooled his overheated skin. He punched the bus door left ajar, not in compliance with the *fan appreciation*, and without caring that Derek would give him shit for it later. Nothing went right for him in tonight's show. Not only was he forced to improvise through broken microphones, he neared a face plant when he slipped on a drumstick that got away from Brett. He trudged up the steps and stripped off his sweaty T-shirt on the way to the shower.

He let go of his foul mood, for a second anyway, and chuckled under his breath. Bass guitarist, Zander Wells, begged their very responsible driver, Derek McRae, to hold off leaving until he got a little ass.

"The drive to the hotel will only take thirty minutes. Get your ass in here." Derek scolded, as he did every night. But invitations to party always took place before, during, and after a show.

Cole rolled his eyes and didn't bother to get involved. That piece of ass would make an appearance in their hotel later anyway. The instant the hot water massaged his tense muscles, he sighed. He leaned forward and rested his head to his forearms, up on the shower wall.

The water that trickled from his back and over the sliver of a tribal tattoo wrapped around his side, held his attention. He was in great shape for thirty-five, but adrenaline pumped through him like a drug and his breathing labored. He tipped his head back in the water and closed his eyes.

Many years of experience on the road with the Scandals and long-time friends led daily events, present shower included, to evolve into predictable routine. Tonight wouldn't be any different. Alcohol consumption passed the time; women relieved certain needs, and when time allowed, they'd finally sleep. Living on the road as a musician fulfilled a lifelong goal, but he longed for a passion absent from his life—a woman to go home to.

A woman. That scared him more than any performance on stage in front of thousands of fans. Love was fragile. His mother taught him that lesson the day she left his father to raise Cole and his three younger brothers on his own. Relationships were fantasy, not reality, and his ex-girlfriend had confirmed this the night he caught her in his college dorm room, on her knees in front of his roommate.

Loud thumps at the door forced him out of his misery.

"Hurry the fuck up, Cole."

Just like home.

He shut the tap off but didn't respond. The hot water had run out long ago, and his greediness always irritated them. He wrapped a towel around his waist and whipped the door open to a young, pissed off drummer, Brett Young. His last name reflected his position in the band, since he was only twenty-three years old, and they never let him forget it.

"Zander is going to kick your ass if you used up all the hot water again. You should see the groupie he invited back to the hotel." Brett nudged past him into the tiny three-piece bathroom, frustrations from moments ago already forgotten.

"I'm sure a little cold water would do him some good." He nabbed his deodorant on his way out.

Brett rubbed the back of his neck and glanced back over his shoulder. "You okay, man?"

He waved back over his shoulder and strolled to his bunk, muscles tensed once again. The guys took turns in the cold shower and cursed him out in the process. A night in a hotel rather than the bus had evolved into a novelty everyone enjoyed on the road. It gave them time to party with select fans, choose a date for the night, and actually enjoy some privacy or take the opportunity to sprawl out in bed alone.

Or, have a warm shower.

"It's party time. No diseases, boys, cover 'em up." Derek McRae, long-time driver for the Scandals stopped the bus, swiveled in his seat, and gave them the usual "I'm not your father, but don't mess with me" stare. Back up drivers came and went, but he'd stayed for the long haul.

Cameras flashed outside the tinted windows. The four men flung overnight bags on their shoulders and adjusted ball caps to shield their faces, along with sunglasses. Long-sleeve shirts and pants hid the visibly tattooed parts of their well-defined bodies. The piercings and tattoos drove the women wild and often drew crowds the hotel management didn't care for. They were foul mouthed at times, partied hard daily but always composed themselves around businesses that could make or break their stay.

Customarily, Cole stepped off the bus first. After years of being together, the strangest of routines developed, but this time he waved at his best friend and lead guitarist, Drew Michaels, to take point.

"You and I are having a talk later, Cole." Drew stomped down the stairs and just like the rest of the men, kept his eyes on the ground until inside.

Cole threw his bag over his shoulder, sighed, and trudged to the bus door.

"What's up, Cole?" Derek grasped his arm and held firm.

"Nothing a little Jack Daniels can't take care of,

Derek, don't worry."

Derek shook his head and spun back around in his tall, leather seat. His gaze roamed to the picture that never left his side, his deceased wife and daughter.

"Shit." Cole stepped off the bus with his head down.

****

The walls vibrated when the elevator doors swooshed open, and loud music filled the dimly lit hall. Cole smiled and tapped the wall with his fist on the way to Brett's room. It had started out as a rookie ritual, being forced to put up with the never-ending party. That backfired. Brett liked it.

Cole took a deep breath and joined the always-predictable after party.

Hoots and hollers welcomed him in the enormous luxury suite, along with a bottle of Jack Daniels shoved at his chest by Drew. "Loosen up, buddy, leave the heavy shit outside."

He swiped the bottle and drained a large amount into his mouth. He held it there until he couldn't take the burn any longer and swallowed. "Since when do you dipshits need me to get the party started?" He gave the bouncer a high-five," Please don't let the beautiful ladies down. We have a reputation."

He relaxed when the familiar warmth of the alcohol entered his bloodstream. The crowded room, with lots of lounge areas meant to entertain, offered typical rowdiness, with the odd girl who could get his attention. He scanned until the first, somewhat attractive one caught his interest.

The pretty brunette, huddled in a group of underdressed women over by the long, wall-mounted fireplace, blushed as he neared her. The group parted with schoolgirl-crush ogles when he put his arm around her and led her away. He stared ahead while she rambled.

The lack of challenge sucked.

The young woman, whom he was quite sure had mentioned her name in her blabber, sat very close to him on the oversized, brown-leather sofa. He eyed the bottle of amber-colored liquid in his hand. The urge to indulge didn't strike him. He used the bottle to slide the cluster of empties out of the way on the table next to him, and set it down. While she continued to chatter, he leaned his head on the back of the couch and observed the rather typical evening. Her slurred words didn't hold his attention, but the advance of her hand up his thigh to his cock—that got his attention.

He flung her hand away. "Don't. Go find one of the other guys. I'm not in the mood for sloppy sex."

His attitude sucked, and she deserved better, but he didn't have time to apologize before she scrambled up on unsteady legs and staggered away with a snarl.

Cole huffed and leaned to the side so he could snag his phone from his pocket. Social media contact with the fans was a part of being famous he could take or leave, but there were always comments on Twitter that caught his interest enough to respond. The group tended to get a lot of sexual offers, words of fondness or hate, but anyone and everyone had an opinion.

He used his finger to swipe at the screen, scrolled past the negative comments, and responded to people who showed commitment to their band. With his finger on the power button, he lowered the phone back toward his pocket when a tweet caught his attention.

Need help with my bucket list.

It was from her, Isabelle. He'd responded to a couple of her tweets and even sent a private message but she never wrote back. It had become a challenge to get her attention. A woman who didn't fawn over him felt new. Her profile picture and the innocent, untold story in her eyes captivated him enough to go back for more. He opened the attachment, too curious not to read further.

1. *Get a tattoo*
2. *Bungee jump*
3. *Sing karaoke in front of strangers*
4. *Dance in the rain*
5. *Eat caviar*
6. *Learn how to fly a plane*
7. *Shop on Rodeo Drive*
8. *Drive a Lamborghini*
9. *Learn to dance the tango*
10. *Go on tour with a band*
11. *Experience a knee weakening kiss*

After he read her list several times, his heart raced along with the twitch in his leg. The noise in the background faded, and desire for her overwhelmed him. Warmth that'd become difficult to kindle, traveled farther down to the bulge now straining against his zipper. He claimed the pillow beside him and placed it in his lap, not interested in what the easy to impress women would try to do to *help* him out. With his head still down, he scanned the crowd to make sure no one paid him any attention before he gawked back down at the screen again. He enlarged the picture.

Beautiful

"Your knee tells me your mood has either

improved or will soon. What's got you worked up?"

He jumped when the tall, dark-haired man sat next to him.

"Fuck, Drew. You've scared the shit out of me since we were kids. Will you fuck off already. Remind me again why I always ran away to *your* house?"

Drew punched him in the shoulder, but hidden underneath the scruff of his dark goatee, was a childlike dimple he would poke at if he needed to. This wasn't one of those moments.

He handed his phone over to Drew and leaned back to gaze the room. Already intoxicated groups of people blabbed on about trivial matters, roughhoused, or over in the corner, had sex.

Drew read the list and stared at him, his eyebrow still raised. "So?"

He scrubbed his face with his hands and huffed. "I know I've been an ass today."

"Yep."

"I'm living my dream, but I can't shake this twist in my gut. There's still more out there for me."

Drew maintained his perplexed expression. "And this ordinary girl is the answer?"

He threw the pillow at Drew; he no longer needed shelter. "I can see why you would say that. No, she doesn't appear to be anything like the women we hang with but there's something about her. I can't explain it, just check out number ten?"

Drew stared at the phone and counted out loud to be an ass, before he landed on the item Cole referred to. The smile on his face didn't agree with the concern in his eyes. "Cole, you know one of the reasons why people make these so-called, *bucket lists,* right?"

He shrugged his shoulders and jerked the phone away, "I know, idiot, who cares. Why couldn't we help her?"

He scrubbed his jaw with the palm of his hand and leaned his head back like Cole. "If doing this will get you out of this funk, man, by all means do it. I have to warn you though, if this is what I think it is, don't get attached. Go crash for the night since this party sucks anyway. If you're still drawn to this chick in the morning, do something about it. You know we won't give you too much of a hard time."

A very attractive blonde prowled up to Drew and held out her hand. He laughed, jumped up, and let her guide him away. Within seconds, he glanced over his shoulder and flicked his tongue between his fingers. Cole broke out laughing when his older, not so mature friend, ambled right out the door with the well-endowed bombshell on his arm.

****

Cole stretched out in the "much more enormous than his bunk" hotel bed. The sheets slipped down from his chest, but the chill it generated didn't elicit the readiness required to start the day. With his eyes closed, he rolled over, away from the faint light of day he could see through his eyelids. He opened one eye and squinted at the red numbers that glared from the clock on the nightstand. "Ugh."

There were so many unused pillows around him, he tugged one and covered his face with it. One hour until bus call, to make it in time for their interview with a local radio station.

Conversations from last night surfaced and he laughed; it'd become normal not to remember a damn thing after a hotel party. He threw the pillow across the room. It swooshed when it hit bare floor. No random person's clothes thrown about or furniture bumped from its usual position in the throes of ecstasy for him. He slid his phone to the edge of the nightstand with his fingertips until he could take hold of it and groaned. His leg up, knee bent and already revved up with a twitch, he set the phone down on his chest and rubbed his eyes.

"Ugh. Okay."

He picked up the phone and enlarged the picture again, shocked his reaction remained the same and wasn't an alcohol induced attraction. With two things on his mind now, he copied the email address on Isabelle's account into his contacts and typed a message he prayed would make his life a little more enjoyable.

Hello there Isabelle Chambers.

I got your email address off your Twitter page, hope that's okay. I read your tweet and was intrigued. Seems we both may be in need of a change, or something new, right about now. My name is Cole Davies, lead singer for the rock band Scandals. As you read this, we are somewhere...on tour. You didn't specify any preference in music on your list. If you can handle a little partying—okay a lot of partying—we have an empty bunk with your name on it. Interested?

Cheers, Cole

Send.

Now that that was taken care of, another issue required the attention of a firm hand. No bandmates, roadies, or groupies could interrupt this moment—or the fantasy that inspired his body last night in the crowded room.

Her beautiful blue eyes stared at him as he placed

the phone down on the bed. When he closed his eyes and leaned back into the pillow, Isabelle was there. She straddled him, and ran her delicate fingertips down his body as if she hungered him in every way imaginable.

"I need you, Cole," she begged in the most seductive voice.

He slid his hand down his body and used his palm to smooth the pre-cum that already leaked from his swollen, sensitive crown. The silkiness coated him, just like her heat when he raised his hips to thrust into her.

"Yes." She threw her head back and moaned.

Her blonde hair fell back and tickled his thighs in the most erotic way. "God…Isabelle." Every muscle in his body clenched. He kicked back the covers and pumped into her. "Take it all, baby."

"Cole. I'm going to come, please." She pleaded like she needed a push over the edge, and only he could get her there.

She leaned forward, gripped onto his shoulders and rode him, her touch firm yet delicate. He pumped into her hard. A shockwave of lust coursed through his veins and he swelled to an unbearable length. "Isabelle."

"Oh God, Cole, yes."

All sound faded, and their orgasms became one. He slid in and out of her with ease as she coated him.

A loud pound on the door startled him out of his euphoric state much too soon.

"Stop stroking it and get your ass up, Cole, time to go," Zander shouted from the other side of the locked door.

He opened his eyes and inspected his empty, untouched except for his lone bag on the luggage rack near the door, hotel room. A quick glance made reality crash down on him. It wasn't her cum that coated him; it was his, all over the place. He wiped his hand with the sheets, got up, and flicked the lock on the door. With little desire to listen to Zander rib him about his condition, he continued into the bathroom. "My hand is a lot safer than what you left with last night, asshole."

The cold shower didn't wash away her image, though. With the towel around his waist, he braced his hands on the counter. The reflection in the mirror was one he'd seen for years. Would she really be interested in the pierced ears, tattoos, and muscles?

Familiar banter from the guys, already helping themselves to his room, snapped him out of his one-man pity party. With a cocky grin on his face and sure to cause a scene, he tugged at the towel and let it drop to the floor. If they haven't learned by now, they never would.

He whipped the door open and joined the men who didn't seem to understand the word "unwelcome," with a little added strut to his step. All the guys groaned and threw pillows at him. He tipped his head back and laughed—he needed that.

"Cover that shit up, man. We all know you're hung, doesn't mean you have to flaunt it." Brett held up one hand and searched in his pocket with the other. "No, wait. Maybe this Twitter chick will be impressed and won't say no to coming on tour with us. Let me just send her a picture, so she knows what she's getting herself into, or *onto*."

Cole tugged on a pair of faded, ripped jeans and glared at Drew. "Just couldn't keep your mouth shut about it, could ya?"

Drew held his hands up and shrugged. "Hey, I told

you they'd be okay with it. What did you decide anyway?"

Cole yanked a shirt over his head, smoothed his hair back with his hand, and placed a ball cap on backward. He didn't want to miss their reactions when he spoke. "I sent her an email not long ago and invited her to come with us. I haven't checked to see if she responded."

Drew laughed and threw Cole's phone in the air, short. "Check it."

Cole lunged and managed to snag the corner of it only inches from the floor. His heart raced at the possibility of a response. He dragged his feet to the bed, so focused on the phone he tripped. A quick glance down revealed nothing but bare, ugly-patterned carpet.

Get it together, Cole. Since when do women make you nervous?

With his back to the guys, he sat on the edge of the bed and let out loud breath.

"It's a girl, Cole, not the end of the world. Give it another hour, and there will be *more* begging for your attention. Don't get your panties in a bunch."

He shook his head, ignored Brett, and searched his email. The immature comment sparked a conversation about some chick from last night, but he tuned it out. His hand froze when he landed on it.

RE: *Bucket List item #10*

"She responded—"

Before he could finish, Drew stole the phone from his hand and read the response so everyone could hear.

"Dear Cole, if this is really Cole Davies, although this may sound like a joke, I am truly committed to the completion of this list. Have another drink. Cheers,

Izzy."

"Ha. Feisty little thing isn't she, I like her already." Brett laughed at the shocked expression on his face.

"How can I make her believe me?" He wasn't used to this; women never brushed him off. They were irresistible to women 'cause of their fame, even on their worst days. That part of his lifestyle he struggled with, never knowing whether a woman liked the real him or the fame linked to him.

Zander yanked the marker clipped to Cole's bag; they all had one in case of ideas, and spun around to search the room. He hurried to the table and ripped a paper out of the hotel directory binder and scribbled on the back of it. "What's her name?"

Cole shook the nervousness from his free hand, and made his way over to Zander. "Isabelle Chambers, or Izzy, why?"

He jolted backward when Zander slammed the piece of paper into his chest.

"Hold that up and smile." Zander wrestled the phone from Cole's firm hold. "Where's the fucking camera on this thing?"

Brett peeked from behind. He elbowed him, "Every group has a genius."

Zander winked. "You know it."

He yanked his phone from Zander before he could snoop any further, and attached the picture to another email. This has to convince her.

Believe me now Isabelle—Izzy—Chambers?

Chapter Three

Dear Diary,
The pain will travel with me, to new heights.

Isabelle sat at the kitchen table, covered with odds and ends that she didn't bother to put away, since family meals no longer took place. Well, meals for two. She held onto her coffee with one hand and poked at her car keys with the other while she gazed her favorite room in the house. The chiffon-colored paint, which David had picked out and her mother helped apply, still streaked around the edges of the white ceiling and taunted her attention. Today was a Memorial Day holiday, which meant no work, a bonus to being a teacher. She took a deep breath, scooped up the keys, and strode for the door. Just as she gripped the knob, her gaze drifted to the picture on the wall, a close-up of her on her wedding day, caught in an emotional embrace with her mother. She frowned, two years had passed, but it was still like yesterday. Not able to put off the inevitable any longer, she opened the door and stepped out.

****

"Isabelle, you are my daughter, which also means you are a strong young woman. You will be the one person in my life to defy the odds and come out stronger than you went in." Carol smiled at Isabelle, perched on the stool in front of her. If she timed her reaction right, the anger that bubbled inside her would stay just that—inside. Flashes of the little girl her daughter used to be crossed her mind. Izzy on that very stool with icepacks and Band-Aids. She couldn't fix this one.

She placed two mugs of hot tea on the kitchen island and paced. Water welled up in her eyes as she glanced at the tiny space. The refrigerator no longer revealed her little girl's artwork, the oven she didn't use much anymore, and the sink never filled after meals for one. Food. That she could do something about.

"We need something to go with the tea. Biscotti?"

She didn't wait for an answer. The well-organized cupboards fell apart, much like her as she sifted for a box she wasn't quite certain even existed anymore. Empty-handed and angry, she clamped her hand to the powdered sugar, and squeezed until her fingertips pierced the pliable plastic. No food could replace the loss of their husbands or the potential for more heartache.

She let her shoulders fall and fixed the boxes of crackers tipped over in her haste. Isabelle waited in silence and no doubt expected some kind of release or emotional breakdown, but no. She'd vowed to her dying husband she would remain strong; she wasn't going to let him down now.

She closed the cupboard and ambled out of the galley kitchen, lost. When she'd cleared herself from Isabelle's view, she braced her hand on the tiny wall and let a tear slip down her face.

"Mom?"

She wiped the tear away with the back of her hand,

straightened her back, and forced her feet to move. She cleared her throat. "Yes, dear?" With her gaze locked in front of her, she dragged a stool closer to Isabelle, slid the tea into her daughter's cold hands, and sat.

"Mom, I have to tell you something."

She peeked out the corner of her eye. Isabelle's attention remained glued to the inside of her mug.

"I've made a list."

Her stomach fluttered at the uncertainty in Isabelle's voice, leery, as if what she had to say would disappoint. Not possible. Carol sipped her tea and waited for its effect to calm her. It didn't.

"There are things I would like to do…before surgery. Yes, the doctor would like me to have the surgery soon, but this diagnosis has sparked something in me. A need for fulfillment." Isabelle swiveled on her stool.

She copied the movement, needed her daughter to witness her strength, and acceptance. Isabelle was clearly struggling to mask her doubts and fears in her tone, not actually call it a "bucket list," but she imagined the words, and it hurt like hell.

All the years she'd allowed her daughter to be so reserved, compliant, no longer gave her the peace of mind she treasured as a single parent. Isabelle's life would not be perfect, no matter how hard she shielded her.

Isabelle handed her a piece of paper with a list. It wasn't very long, and not what she imagined. *She's got to want more than this. Is there something missing? I could add to it for her. Would that be awkward?* She stared at it, and listened to her reasons for doing this. She didn't need any. Carol folded the paper when her daughter's voice trailed off to silence. She glanced up, and the tears she'd held back slipped down her face.

"You're right, Isabelle, you haven't lived. As your mother, I have to try and persuade you to act now, but as your friend, I won't let my needs come before yours. Do what you need to do, honey."

She hugged her daughter tight. The day of Isabelle's and David's wedding flashed before her. Isabelle had glowed as she walked down the aisle in her beautiful, white-satin gown. Happiness spread across her face, content with her choice. Not the troubled way she does right now.

Carol let go, grasped the handle of her mug, and marched back into the kitchen. She set it in the sink and stood still with her back to Isabelle.

"Thank you, Mom."

She wiped her face with both hands and spun so her back rested against the counter. "No need to thank me, Isabelle. You deserve this."

Isabelle's shoulders slumped as she released a breath, consoled by Carol's unconditional support. She wrapped her arms around herself and rubbed. She'd seen her daughter do that for years when overwhelmed with emotion. The corner of Isabelle's mouth rose and she stared back at Carol, but not really at her. Eagerness brimmed in her eyes.

****

For the first time ever, she pulled into her driveway and parked not so close to the house.

Typical Isabelle would traipse into the living room, plop on the couch, and allow her red-rimmed eyes to become watery once again. Instead, she sauntered in with a newfound lightness and aimed straight for the curtains to let the sunlight in.

A beep interrupted her endeavor to start different routines. She threw her hands in the air and growled. "Seriously? I was having a moment here." With her hands on her hips, she spun until she spotted the computer she'd left on, and froze.

"Nah, it can't be. Right?" In the short distance to check, her throat dried, so she veered toward the kitchen. "A drink would be nice."

Way to be a coward, Isabelle.

She opened the fridge and held the door ajar. There had to be something that would calm her nerves, but she lost focus every time she glanced back at the living room.

Could it be?

She nabbed the first cold bottle and started back for the computer. Yes, it was a little early for a beer but hey, she was on the path to a bold life unlived to date.

She sat at the desk, next to a floor to ceiling bookshelf that'd been neglected for some time. Unable to go explore the possibility just yet, she set the bottle down and shuffled bills around. She even opened them, but her attention wandered to the black screen. She held her finger out over the button that could send life in a new direction, squeezed her eyes shut, and pressed it. Not quite brave enough, she opened one eye, but it was enough to see.

Him.

He smiled at her and held onto the proof she needed. Her pulse raced as she admired him with both eyes—stared more like it. Maybe even drooled a little. She grinned in return. The silly expression on his face eased her doubts, no more worries about a joke at her expense.

Cole Davies was famous and from what she'd seen in the news, displayed a great stage presence. But this picture of his clear-blue eyes, and hair held back by a ball cap was real, no façade. It represented more than a sign or a single piece of paper; it was her new path in life. But why? She leaned back in her chair and tapped her leg a moment before she dug in her pocket for her phone and sent a text to Katherine, Abigail, and Taryn.

You have to see this. My place ASAP.

Within seconds, the replies blew up her phone.

On my way. Katherine

'Cause I am sooo not busy. Be right over. Abigail

Shift starts in an hour, gotta be quick. Taryn

She tapped her fingernails on the desk, and glanced around the room at anything other than the man in front of her. No one had ever pursued her before, and the foreign rush it created baffled her, but the pleasant tingle of arousal was something she'd missed.

She sat up straight and then slouched, many times. Every back and forth motion bunched her clothes, so she'd fix them. The girls needed to hurry. A picture of David popped up on the screen and she startled right out of her chair, knocking it over too. She flung it back upright, raised her hands in the air, and wandered to her bedroom. A tirade of rational explanations escaped her in the short distance.

A need for comfort consumed her. The half-empty closet made the search for her yoga pants and tank top very easy. She stared at the open space, didn't like *easy* anymore. Time to shop. The room spun around her and a cold sweat broke out over her body. Familiar with the sensation, she ran to the bathroom.

She sat back on her haunches and wiped the tears that streaked down her face. The pregnancy test in the trashcan next to the toilet—the one she'd convinced herself was false—still lay in plain sight. She cringed. Wasn't she supposed to be living her dreams? She wasn't even thirty yet.

On unsteady legs, she rose from the cold tile floor and braced her way to the sink. It didn't seem to matter how much she wiped her face or pinched her cheeks for color. The mirror, and florescent light above it, didn't lie. The mint of her rinse replaced the acid-like burn in her mouth, and she held it there for as long as possible. When she glanced down at her watch, she winced and spit it out. She needed to get it together fast, or they would see.

She opened the door to leave with much less determination than going in. Two familiar hands greeted her, with a glass of water and tablets.

"A little something to take the edge off?" Katherine held out pills and shook her head. "It will take a lot more than pinched cheeks to convince me, honey."

Both women laughed.

She took the tablets but only sipped enough water to get them down, not wanting to relive her earlier moments.

"Time's a ticking." Taryn demanded with as little patience as usual.

Katherine latched onto her hand and gave it a quick squeeze before they made their way out to the living room.

"I am still feeling hung over, and it's been days. Please tell me this will not require booze, Izzy." Abigail placed her hand over her stomach and sat down with a sigh.

“Check this out, and tell me if you think its bullshit?” She clicked the email from Cole and leaned back.

They stood behind her in record time; wind breezed along her back from their rush to spy. Curiosity about their reaction clawed at her. Nothing. Their silence forced her to spin around in her chair. Katherine, Abigail, and Taryn stood side-by-side with their hands over their gaped open mouths.

“Isabelle Chambers. Is that what you responded?” Katherine scolded her with flare in her eyes and pointed at the screen.

“I didn’t believe it to be true. I still don’t. Why would he want to help me? Me?” She spun back to the computer, and slumped in her chair. She was an ass. “Fuck me.”

Taryn laughed. “If I remember right from the gossip Katherine reports, he may be able to help you out with that too.”

A moment of snickers filled the air behind her before nothing…a distant buzz. Her head wobbled. Her body became the string attached to a balloon that’d lost too much air. She opened and closed her eyes but the screen still blurred.

“Breathe, honey. You’re going to pass out.” Katherine placed her hand on Isabelle’s shoulder and squeezed.

The words sharpened and she jumped. Deep breaths, strong enough to cause her shoulders to rise and fall in an exaggerated motion, stopped the room’s spin. “I…um…What?” She leaned forward and dropped her forehead to the desk; the girls laughed when the sound echoed.

"A man who doesn't put up with your stubborn side. I like him already. It also doesn't hurt that he's hot." Taryn rubbed Isabelle's back. "Oh my God, maybe you will get to see where Drew Michael's tattoo goes under those perfectly molded jeans. I am *so* jealous right now."

"Think the country girl can handle a little rock and roll?" Abigail placed her hands on her hips and raised her eyebrows, always able to spur everyone's madness.

She forced her head up off the desk, touched what she assumed to be a very noticeable red spot on her forehead, and glared at Abby. "I can be a wild woman too, ya know. Well, I will be."

She raised her eyebrows and cocked her head, not sure who she convinced. Back straightened and not able to back down now, she swiveled to the computer, and slumped.

"Well then, get typing, *wild woman.*"

A supportive hand touched her shoulder, and she didn't have to double-check to know it was Abby.

She opened a new email before the courage faded and typed.

Subject: Re: Bucket List item #10

Dear Cole, I'm in.

She ended the message with her cell phone number and hit send before she changed her mind; still not quite sure he would contact her.

"Well, now that that's settled, I have to get back to work. Let me know when he calls you." Abigail strode out before the girls had a chance to respond, or see her face.

"Me too." Taryn wrapped her arms around Isabelle from behind and squeezed tight. She placed her hand over Taryn's arm and squeezed back before Taryn tore hers away, wiped her face, and marched out the door.

Now that the room held less intimidation, she directed her uncertainty to the friend who wouldn't break down. "Katherine, I'm scared." She traipsed over to the couch and sat with a pillow stuffed in front of her. "I'm trying to pretend like I'm not. I don't want pity."

"Izzy. There is a difference between pity, and sympathy for someone you love who has just been dealt the shittiest hand in their life, which might I add, is usually the case when you lose your money to us on poker night."

She waved her hand in the air and grabbed her purse. Tears pooled in her eyes. "That Gravol should help you relax for a while. Take advantage of it and get some rest while you can. Something tells me after the next time your phone rings, you won't get much rest, day *or* night." She winked and opened the door to leave, a little more hurried than usual.

Isabelle fought it, but Katherine was right; what else was new? Not long after the girls left, her eyes drooped and she snuggled back onto the oversized couch.

****

She stretched out and yawned. Nothing hurt.

Thank God.

After what she imagined only a moment's rest, Isabelle glanced back and forth, disoriented at the darkness outside and the time on the clock. Midnight? She sighed and scrubbed her face.

"Yep Abby, I am a wild woman."

A little more alert, she tossed the pillow to her side and locked up the house. Long gone were the days of unconscious slumber on the couch, too lazy to go to bed. A comfortable night's sleep trumped all. Steps away from her bedroom door, her phone beeped, and she startled. "Yes, ladies, I'm fine. Give me a minute." She ran back to the living room. If she didn't respond to whichever one of her friends texted her, she would be in trouble.

Though, a little more comfort before a longwinded conversation took priority. She grabbed her phone, ran back to her room, and changed into the concert T-shirt she slept in every night. "Yep. Country girl gone rock and roll, that's me."

She lit up her phone, and climbed into bed. "Let me guess, Mother Hen?" When her glance landed on his name, she dropped the phone. When he included the number in his email, she'd programmed it into her phone, but didn't expect it to be real.

Hi Isabelle, Izzy, which do you prefer? It's Cole. Now a good time to call or is there a husband I might piss off?

Deep breaths prevented another spell like earlier. She picked up the phone, didn't have to hear his voice yet, so why not dare to test the *new* wild side? The corners of her mouth rose slightly as she bit her lip and replied.

Just me keeping this bed warm. Sure

Clearly Cole wasn't one to text and get distracted, the next text bounced back, instantly.

Shame. Give me a minute to find somewhere quiet to talk.

****

Drew stood stiff in front of the bathroom door with a cocky grin. It was the only place on the bus for privacy and when someone rushed toward it with a phone in their hand, it meant one thing. A girl. "Fuck off, man." He shoved Drew out of the way and glanced over his shoulder. "Knock on the door and you'll get Nair in your shampoo." He slammed the door shut.

Hoots and hollers from the guys echoed, and even the dramatic moans vibrated through the door. He put the toilet lid down and sat, but his knee bounced with force while he stared at the screen with her number on it. He ran his fingers through his hair, touched the green icon, and held the phone up to his ear.

"Hello?"

Even her voice is beautiful.

He cleared his throat and held his knee down with a firm hand. "Hi Isabelle, or Izzy, you didn't say which you prefer. So I guess this means you really do believe me?" He played with the roll of toilet paper, giddy like a little kid, and grateful for Zander's brilliant idea.

Not that he'd mention it.

Her quiet laugh calmed his nerves, and gave him a hard-on impossible to hide.

"My friends call me Izzy. I have no preference as I like both. You got my attention, Cole. I apologize for my apprehension. If I had to guess, not many women play hard to get in your world?"

He could hear the smile in her voice along with another noise; did she bite her nails? The image of her scoring his chest with those teeth and going down, further, made his pants feel a bit tight. He leaned against the back of the toilet and lowered his zipper.

The added room didn't allow for the relief he needed. He scanned back and forth between his free hand and his cock. Now wasn't the right time.

"You're right. It was refreshing to be challenged for a change." A deep chuckle escaped him before Drew's earlier words replayed in his head. *You know why people do these so called bucket lists, right?*

Cole frowned. He hadn't fallen for anyone since Alexis and his reaction to Izzy shocked him.

"So, your band is on tour? Where are you right now?"

He creased his eyebrows. The tone in her voice had changed from flirty to, serious. "Yes. We're on the road right now, but we're on our way to the recording studio back home, just outside of New York. We'll be back on the road in a couple of days though, for a show in Columbia, South Carolina this Saturday. We'll be stopped about a half hour away from the airport there Friday afternoon, so Brett can visit with his…*parents*."

He glanced over to the door and winced, didn't want to explain that further. "Anyway, we have a rule. No driving through hometowns without a stop. Do you want to meet us there, or do you have to make some plans first?"

He hit himself in the forehead; he sounded desperate. "I assume you are interested? Actually, do you even like our music?" He bent forward, elbows to knees and clutched his shaggy blonde hair between sweaty fingers to stop the rambled words that spilled from his mouth. It was so quiet he couldn't even hear her breathe. He held the phone away a brief moment and inspected the screen.

Still lit up. "Izzy? Are you still there?"

"Yeah, sorry, I'm here." Her voice sounded pained. "I can speak with the principal of the school I teach at in the morning to request an immediate leave of absence. I'm sure he will understand. I haven't taken time off since—"

Cole caught it, the inhale of breath right before what he imagined was her hand over her mouth.

"Since?"

"Nothing. I have to be honest, I am more of a country music fan than rock, but I am very familiar with your group. My closest friend is a reporter for our local tabloid. She often tells me the latest gossip. Provided I can get a flight out of Tampa, yes, I think I could meet you in South Carolina, if you don't mind. I assume it really shouldn't take more than one week to get the feel of what life is like on tour. I'll be out of your way in no time, I promise."

He rose and leaned his butt against the counter. A familiar edginess simmered inside him, and he didn't want her exposed to it. He tugged the towel that hung on the wall and threw it.

"I talked to the guys, and they're cool with it. You can stay on for however long you like. Our manager on the other hand, will only find out after I get off the phone." He kicked the toilet and the lid bounced loudly. He held his hand out in surrender to the toilet. He didn't want to have to explain his current whereabouts yet either. Ugh.

"We like to keep him running in circles. Keeps him out of our hair, but I am sure he will come up with some kind of legal document for you to sign. I hope that isn't too much to ask?"

She shuffled around on the other end of the phone,

and her breath became heavy. He liked the sound of it.

"It won't be possible for me to make things difficult for you or your band's future."

She coughed a little to clear her throat. He raised his eyebrow. She was trying to avoid something. After all, he was a man with baggage and knowledge of the many tactics of avoidance, that one included.

"I have no problem signing any nondisclosure agreements, or anything for that matter. I can book my flight right away and text you the details. I'll let you know when I land, so you can tell me where to meet up with you."

Her words were fast, rushed, but pain still lingered in her tone. He scooted back to sit on top of the small counter. His foot shook, and his mind raced with it, trying to decipher the hidden message in her voice.

Is it awkward if I offer to pay for the flight? She said she's a schoolteacher; do they make good money?

Her laughter caught him off guard. "Okay now it's my turn to ask. Cole, you still there?"

His leg stilled and he relaxed. She couldn't see the calm affect her voice had on him. "Still here. I can't lie. I debated if it would be too forward of me to offer to pay for your flight. I don't want to offend you but my dad taught me to always provide where a woman is concerned." He rubbed at the stubble on his chin when she shuffled around again and groaned.

"I have money in savings. You've already offered more than imaginable, so please, I will take care of my flight, and no, you didn't offend me. I should let you go though, so I can make arrangements. It's late."

He didn't want the call to end, if it did, she might not follow through with this. Something about the hurt in her voice made the desire to reach through the phone and hold her so intense he ached. She couldn't get to him soon enough.

"Of course. Please let me know if you need anything. I look forward to meeting you in person." He punched at the wall beside him with very little force, but it didn't offer the same impact his fist through it would.

A loud thump vibrated the door. "Stop the phone sex and get your ass out here, I gotta take a piss." Zander might be smart from genetics, but his timing sucked.

Although a lot remained the same, the tour just veered from its usual routine, and lightened his mood. "Stock up on ibuprofen, you're going to need it."

"I have all the pain meds I'll need, trust me. I'll text you soon."

The air went silent before he could ask if she was okay. He tightened his fist around the phone, clenched his jaw, and whipped the door open.

****

Not able to support herself anymore, she fell back onto the bed with the kind of ease only shown by someone in undeniable pain, and let the phone slide out of her hand. She glimpsed the bottle on the nightstand, closed her eyes, and sighed. Those pills offered a relief she longed for, but her plans required attention.

She huffed and forced her way to the living room to switch on the computer, but needed something to calm her tired chills first. A mug filled with hot tea did just that. She held it to her chin and let the steam warm her face. Her mother claimed it was a panacea for all ailments, which would be nice for the current throb in her head.

A flight to South Carolina for Friday only took minutes to book, a lot easier than expected. She sent him a quick text message.

Hey Cole, it's Izzy. Flight booked, arriving 6:30 pm. Will text you when I touch down, so you can let me know where to meet up.

She jumped when his response appeared right after. "Doesn't he have better things to do?"

Perfect, I can't wait. Now get some sleep, you will need it. Sweet dreams…

She stared at her phone. Her shoulders relaxed, comforted by his words yet unsure what to make of them. Once again, she flicked off the lights, and dragged her feet to her room. Would it be possible to complete the list without hurting anyone in the process?

Chapter Four

Dear Diary,
Today I toured the unknown...

Isabelle managed to get things in order, a process that went a lot smoother than she anticipated. Honesty with Principal Harris about her diagnosis netted an open-ended leave of absence, well wishes, and a job to return to after surgery. She neglected to inform him the latter might not be necessary.

The key slid into the old deadbolt as rough as any other day, but it wasn't any other day. She placed her hand on her stomach and dropped her forehead to the door. Butterflies always sprang to life with new adventures but never this many, and her friends who waited in the car more often than not took the adventure with her.

She checked the lock one last time, and squeezed the handle of her suitcase. Her determination slowed with each step down her front porch. The soles of her feet were like lead, and encouraged her undivided attention on every aspect of life around her. Fathers and sons played road hockey between bouts of traffic, and the elderly couple two doors down sat out on their swing and sipped what she assumed to be tea.

Her gaze stopped on Katherine's car and a single tear spilled over. The girls were animated but she could still see the worry in their faces. She wiped her cheek in haste and continued to the car. No regrets.

The luggage for one that she placed in the large trunk launched *her* solo adventure. She made a conscious note of her home one more time, and wasn't offered any excuse to stay, so she climbed into the now quiet car and avoided eye contact. Be brave.

The girls resumed their frivolous banter on the way to the airport, maybe to prevent tears but she sat there, quiet, and gazing the traffic.

"Umph"

A journal thrown into her lap jolted her attention forward. Abigail waved as if she'd said something gone ignored. "Stop your worrying. You'll have the time of your life, and I'm jealous of you for a change." She laughed. "So, use that book to write because we want to know everything."

"I'm a grown woman, Abby. I haven't had a diary in years." She set the book down on the seat, and stared at Abby with a tilt to her head. The mood in the car shifted. Giving light to the nervousness also gave it strength.

"Izzy, shouldn't every bucket list be written about? We expect you to text us, trust me, but you are going to be on a bus with a bunch of really hot guys. You will need some way to get your girl moments out of your head. And stop lying. We know you keep a diary under your mattress." Abigail grinned with confidence and snapped her attention to the front window once again, but removed her sunglasses from the top of her head to cover her eyes. Her shoulders slumped.

Tears formed in the corner of her eyes when Abigail's words sank in. She reverted her attention to the window, took a deep breath, and willed her heart rate back to normal.

"Did you pack something for headaches? I can't imagine rock music will be too soothing."

She eyed Katherine in the rear view mirror, and acknowledged the subtle message that lay beneath. Not many people were aware of the migraines she suffered because of the tumor. "Yes, thank you."

The shuffle at the airport provided a much-needed distraction from the weighty, unspoken, emotions during the drive. People passed, speeding to their terminals without a care in the world other than being somewhere on time.

"Now boarding flight 425 to South Carolina," echoed over the intercom. The girls stood up in unison and grabbed their purses off the chairs around them. It was habit for them to take up as many chairs possible, a demand for privacy wherever they were. The angry glares from others no longer fazed them.

She gave her friends a quick hug, and marched through the terminal. Impossible to follow through dry-eyed given the loud sniffles she left behind.

A box of tissues and a beautiful woman's smile greeted her at the entrance of the plane. "Let me know if you need anything."

She flopped into her first-class seat, up-grade courtesy of her friends and hugged herself. The world outside of the small window moved, and would continue to do so without her. The observant and well-trained flight attendant offered a selection of beverages, sure to calm her nerves. She sighed, and then accepted the drink. The clear liquid burned as she reclined the seat and blared the music in her ear buds. She let her eyes drift closed and ignored the bustle around her. Country twang bellowed in her ears, and she laughed out loud for all to hear but didn't care.

The descent jostled her. The combination of migraine medication and alcohol worked wonders for the sleep deprived. A little foggy, she texted Cole while she steered her way through the crowd to the baggage claim.

Hi Cole, I'm here. Let me know where you are so I can catch a cab. Izzy

She shoved her phone into her pocket and waited for the carousel to reveal Taryn's, impossible-to-miss lime-green suitcase. *Geez, Taryn. Really?* She extended her hand to catch the handle. A rather large male hand beat her to it. She jumped.

"Please, allow me."

****

Cole glanced from Isabelle to the floor as he paced. Wear marks were sure to become visible soon, but his knee bounced if he sat.

"Someone special?"

He stumbled toward the cheerful woman's voice. With caution, he twisted in her direction and frowned at her. He couldn't recall her approach, but the lust in her eyes for a "bad boy," he'd seen right away given his years of experience. "I think so."

He'd help Isabelle with her bag, but the idea to check her out from a distance crossed his mind first. Stupid idea. He glared at the man who, by the grin on his face, enjoyed helping her.

"Goodbye, then."

He glanced to his side. The young woman's sullen words hit him a little too late. She fled with her head down.

"Ahem"

He waved off Derek and lowered his ball cap over his face. Otherwise, they wouldn't make the quick in and out Derek lectured him about on the car ride to the airport. After a deep breath, he stepped toward her and froze when a flush on her skin appeared for the other man. With rigid arms at his side, he balled his hands tight enough to feel the indentations of his fingernails. He tightened his jaw. Her first blush might've been for him, if it weren't for his brilliant ideas.

Lots of time, Cole. He shook his arms, tilted his head from side to side, and got out his cell phone. The corner of his mouth rose when the slight challenge to compete hit him hard, and not just in the chest.

That is some blush Izzy. I'm a little jealous over here.

Send.

The front of his pants tightened, and he scrambled to adjust himself before his condition became apparent to the observant eye. He held up the paper, guaranteed to get her attention.

Believe me now Isabelle—Izzy—Chambers?

Cole rocked front to back with stiff feet, to ease his itch to fidget without her missing him. The paper shook in his hands. She scrambled things around in her arms to search for her phone, and the spasm that tormented his body eased. He stood still for the first time since he'd arrived.

They were both a mess, a perfect mess. When she found her phone and read the message, she popped her head up, right at him. His pulse raced. For a moment, she dropped her gaze to the floor and back up, before she did it again, blushing.

"Yes." Her gaze lowered to the paper and the lust in her eyes disappeared as she bent over in hysterics. People stopped and giggled at the beautiful woman before them.

He lowered the piece of paper, shook his head, and laughed with her, so hard he had to clench his lips together to prevent a scene. He let out a breath, and a weight lifted from somewhere deep inside. There was a difference between the laughter he experienced every day with the guys and this.

With the paper tucked into the back of his jeans, he strolled in her direction, thumbs hooked in his pockets. He raised an eyebrow at the ugly green suitcase she picked up. Every inch of her creamy skin sparked desire as she drew closer with a sway of her hips. Her beautiful blonde hair, held back in a ponytail, swung with each step.

His libido, suppressed for many years with alcohol, sparked to life at the sight of her navy-blue tank top. Well…more so, the beautiful cleavage beneath, enough to be a handful. He bit his bottom lip at the faint evidence of the blush still on her skin, hidden by material he longed to peek under. The tent that formed in his pants made proper introductions difficult, so he closed his eyes and pictured the most repulsive thing. His mother. That did it.

He stretched his arm out, prepared to take her bags when she stumbled. Sarcastic comments about her clumsiness duly noted, he scooped up her bag and lead her to the private exit, "We better get out of here before people recognize me, Izzy."

She placed her hand over her chest and inhaled.

"Okay."

****

A tall, older gentleman with silver-streaked hair appeared out of nowhere and placed his hand over hers. She jumped.

"Please. Allow me."

He winked, removed her carry-on from her grip, and rushed them to the car.

Cole opened the door and raised his hand for her to go ahead. She tensed from his gentle touch on her lower back along with the scent of cologne, anything but scared.

When the door closed, flashes from cameras blinded them. The car bounced with the slam of the trunk. The nice man hustled in behind the wheel and secured the locks. He extended his arm over the seat. "I'm Derek McRae, driver for the Scandals. Seems you two managed to dodge the paparazzi…somewhat. It's nice to meet you, Isabelle." He winked again, shook her hand, and glared at Cole. "Have a hard time with instructions, don't you." He rotated back to the front of the car, his attention shifting from mirror to mirror.

Puzzled about Derek's anxiousness, she surveyed the commotion out the windows and held her breath. A swarm of people, most of them women, rushed with the car when they drove away. The door handle and seatbelt, secured tight around her, doubled as anchors to grab onto. "Wow, this is a little crazy, hey?"

Cole shrugged, and she squeezed her thighs together. His presence affected her in the same way, if not more so, as the night she creeped his Twitter profile.

"I hope you aren't shy, Izzy, this is nothing. We'll

drive around for a while before we make our way back to the bus. Don't want to lead the pack home."

Derek's concentration remained on the road while he spoke. Cole sat with his hand fisted on his knee. She focused on Derek in the rearview mirror. Although well aware of the traffic ahead, he glanced in Cole's direction every few seconds and shook his head. Cole mouthed the words *fuck off* back at him.

With her brows furrowed, she gazed out the window. The landscape that passed by was a similar green to Florida, only green though, no other color. At least in Florida there was an array of color added to the city by flowers. Really, Izzy? Unsure of how to start the conversation, she sat as quiet as he was for most of the drive, which dragged out the distance. She rubbed her crossed arms and continued to watch, but couldn't track where they were going.

"Cold?"

She startled back to his curious smile. Her body heat rose in reaction to the provocative excitement it stirred in her. She shoved her laced fingers between her legs. He raised an eyebrow.

"What? No. Just a little nervous, I guess."

When the tour buses in the parking lot ahead came into view, she swallowed hard but the ramble still bubbled up her throat. "Will all the guys be there? Are you sure this is okay? Maybe I shouldn't have come."

He laughed and wiped his palms down his thighs. "Breathe, Izzy. See?" He held his hands in the air and pointed his finger down at his legs. They bounced faster than she'd ever seen before. "You rub your arms, I do this. You're not the only nervous one. And to answer your question, the guys went out to eat but should be back any minute. We have to get back on the road. They are more than okay with you being here, but I have to warn you, the grown men you see on the outside take a back seat when we're on the road. It can get a little immature in there."

He got out of the car first, rubbed his hands down his pants and took her hand. "Derek will get your bags. Come on, I'll give you the grand tour."

He opened the door to the bus and stepped aside so she led. The possibility that he struggled with something nagged at her. When she peeked back over her shoulder, he held his hand an inch away from the small of her back without the actual follow through of physical contact. Their gazes locked and he jerked his hand to scratch the back of his head. He didn't fool her.

"It may seem big, but it gets claustrophobic really quick."

He climbed the steps behind her at a safe distance. She held back her sarcasm. They didn't know each other well enough yet. At the top of the stairs, he pointed to the tall, gray leather driver and passenger seats. "Derek is very much like a father to us on the road. He gives us shit all the time, but there is usually one of us sitting up front getting some type of advice from him. He is our Yoda."

"Good to know. Does his wisdom work well on women?"

His expression changed when he glanced over the seat at a picture of a woman, and a young girl who could be in her early teens. "I'm sure Derek would enjoy some female company again."

Sadness covered his face. She bit her lip; it wasn't her place to ask.

They continued forward, and he showed her the small lounge in the front. The walls of the bus were cream colored and the furniture a light gray with dark hardwood flooring. It really didn't appear as small as he'd let on. Still caught up on the elegant, yet manly bus, she was somewhat tuned into his emphasis on the well-stocked bar.

"Wait. You do drink, right? I mean, you're not some kind of recovering alcoholic or anything, are ya?"

She couldn't resist. "You know, admitting you have a problem is the first step."

The charade couldn't be maintained with the panic on his face. She turned her head away from him, the laughter bubbled over.

He hip checked her and moved on. "You're gonna fit in here just fine, beautiful."

Her fingertips drained of color as she gripped onto the counter beside her. She didn't want to make anything of what had to be an error in words.

"Pfft." She waved her hand in the air and urged her feet to follow him. "How do you think I concocted the list? Alcohol can be as therapeutic as it can be damaging."

"Very true. I often lie back on the couch and sing my woes out to Dr. Jack Daniels." He opened a narrow door and took a quick peek inside. "Yes." He flung it agape and pointed in. "The bathroom isn't big, but does have a shower. I hope you are familiar with short showers. The supply of hot water sucks. If you want hot, you will need to beat me to the shower." He winked and raised his eyebrows with all kinds of suggestion as he strolled away.

She stopped at the doorway and stared at the

radiant white shower with a clear glass door, no longer empty. Her skin warmed.

Cole stood under the stream of water and tipped his head back to wet his hair. The blond strands darkened to a rich shade of brown. She stood in front of him, and splashes of water from his movements sprinkled her bare skin. She smoothed her hand up his muscled chest. "Touch me, Cole."

He met her gaze, stepped forward with one arm around her lower back, and guided her until the cold tile wall met her heated skin. He used his free hand to raise her chin, and lowered his mouth to hers. "My pleasure."

The air of his breath drifted against her lips before he consumed her with his need. She pressed her body into his and he responded. He massaged his hands down her body and cupped her behind to lift her higher and braced her against the wall. At that height, his swollen crown touched her opening. He inched forward.

"Something interesting caught your attention?"

His voice was distant, and the image vanished. Now more aware of her stance, frozen in lust, she closed the door with a little more force than intended. "No…um…just. Never mind, what were you saying?" She crossed her arms and spun in his direction, already down the aisle. He slid back a bunk curtain, but given the gleam in his eyes, his curiosity pestered at him to ask. She was in trouble.

"This here will be the only place you have for privacy, outside of the bathroom, of course."

For her size, the bunk appeared spacious, but for the men, like a coffin. "Do you guys really fit in these?"

He laughed and yanked back the curtain to the one she assumed was his, and climbed in. It also happened to be right below hers. “It’s not bad, although we do enjoy the occasional novelty of a hotel bed. You will have to step here on my bunk in order to haul yourself up into yours, I hope that’s okay?”

He dug his phone from his pocket at the sound of a beep and read a message. He rolled his eyes and scooted to the edge. Instinctively, she offered her hand for support. His grasp swallowed hers, but somehow it still fit perfectly. They both stared at their joined hands, speechless.

He tugged her toward the back of the bus. “Come on, only one more room to show you. The guys are here. This is the room we spend most of our time in.”

He opened the last door and strolled in like he’d come to rest at a familiar place. From the large, well-used couch he sprawled out on with a sigh, she figured he had. It was big enough all the guys could relax and stretch out a little.

A big-screen TV hung in the corner with a stand below that held the largest DVD collection she’d ever seen. On the other side of the room was a small table with well-used playing cards thrown about. She’d invaded a man cave.

She scurried in and sat beside him when loud voices rumbled from the other end of the bus. Her heart raced. What would the other guys think of her?

Sitting next to Cole, a somewhat friend in progress, should have eased her nerves. It didn’t. His proximity and the affect he had on her, accelerated him past the friend zone, and right into the fuck me now zone. The picture he’d sent her didn’t capture all of his best features. His sculpted physique, obvious through his snug shirt, was built to embrace a woman. She held her breath, refused to take in the cologne and his natural scent that did wonderful things to her body. If she didn't, the temptation to nuzzle up close wouldn't be satiated until she straddled his lap.

Her heart pounded harder as deep male voices neared the lounge. She jerked her knees up in front of her, and wrapped her arms tight around them. Cole's panic reflected hers, only his stiff posture and the rapid bounce of his knee appeared more out of concern. About her? He placed his arm on the back of the couch, around her shoulders. They both tensed.

"Cole, where are you? Get your lazy ass out here and help with the groceries before—" A bald, tanned, liberally tattooed, and easy-on-the-eyes man stumbled through the door as if he'd been forced to move. He spun to give someone the finger behind him.

"Shit. Sorry Izzy, nice to meet you."

His first impression she'd expected, tattoos and all, but the nipple piercings that poked through his snug T-shirt when he neared—wow.

"I'm Zander Wells, bass guitarist and the talent behind the band." He shook her hand. "Glad you're here. Maybe you can help Cole get the pole out of his ass."

She snapped her attention back to Cole, who glared at Zander.

"And when she does, she can stick it right up your ass. I'm sure you can find some lube in any of the bunks, Izzy, maybe even some cuffs if you search Zander's."

Zander winked. "That *and* more, sweetheart."

Between the sex talk and terms of endearment, her skin warmed and if she predicted right, deepened to a bright shade of red. There was something different about Zander, even more so when he sauntered out of the room. He carried himself with a class that didn't match his appearance.

Caught in a stare, Cole nudged her. She shimmied to get her knees in closer and put her forehead down to hide.

He leaned in close to whisper. "That blush is going to kill me, Izzy. I'm going to go help put the groceries away. There should be a certain box of cookies to hide in my bunk before these losers get their hands on them."

She'd offer to help, but all those men, at once—not a chance. Hell, Zander Wells, by himself, took her breath away.

"Second thoughts already?"

The tender voice calmed her, and drew her from her jitters without a startle. However, not enough to chance the glance up from her hidden position, and check out the source.

"I'm Drew Michaels, Lead guitarist and long-time friend of Cole's."

She grabbed onto the edge of the cushion when the couch sank, and a new male scent joined her. Her eyes widened as she lifted her head, much higher than she had to with Cole, to check him out. Dark-haired, slender, and pale compared to Cole and Zander, but no less attractive. So tall his shoulder towered above her when he sat, he appeared more humble than scary.

"Holy shit, you're tall." She held out her hand and giggled. "Nice to meet you, Drew. No second thoughts.

Just not quite acclimatized to the atmosphere yet, if you know what I mean. Zander is a very unique guy."

Drew's deep laugh could make any woman's panties combust but when he smiled, it was as provocative as his dark hair against his light-colored skin. "Ha. Guys are already acting like two-year olds?"

She put her feet on the floor once again, and folded her hands between her thighs. "Oh, I would give them a little more credit. Maybe more like the five-year olds I teach."

Her body vibrated from his boisterous laugh. She relaxed a little and joined him.

The roar of the engine shocked her from that comfort, and she fixed her gaze out the window. The empty parking lot outside provided nothing, not even a car she could pretend to be interested in. An increase in the commotion outside the lounge drew her attention from the onset of nausea. Cole, Zander, and Brett Young paraded through the door, captivated by something funny enough to make them bump fists.

"We're heading out now, Izzy, sink or swim?" Cole stuffed his hands in his back pockets, focused on her.

She straightened her back and challenged the hesitation in his eye. "I'm pretty sure if I can handle a room full of kindergarten kids, I can handle you guys."

The men laughed and got comfortable in what seemed like claimed seats.

"We're heading out, boys. Try not to scare the little lady, would ya?" Derek appeared in the doorway and offered a father-like smile. "If you need a break, and trust me you will, come on up front, sugar. It won't take too long to get to the venue from here. Relax and get comfortable with the boys." He pierced the men with his gaze. "Stay on the bus for the rest of the night, please. I don't have the energy to hunt ya's down."

The muscles in her legs relaxed enough to sit Indian style. "Thank you, Derek."

Minutes, that's all it took for her to understand why these men could have any woman. They were carefree and uninhibited or so it seemed.

Cole handed her an envelope. "Didn't take Tony long to prove me right."

She accepted the envelope and hit him with it. "I told you I would sign anything."

"Well then." Brett stood up, and shook his hips while he unzipped his pants in front of her. Hoots and hollers filled the common area. Thankful for the documents, she raised the envelope to cover her face.

I have officially met Taryn's match.

Brett zipped his pants up and raised his hands in surrender. He was attractive, young. Lots of tattoos covered what she could see as well as piercings. Although young, his posture was aged and his eyes haunted as if his life's story were incomparable to any other.

A loud smack echoed in the tiny room. She dropped the envelope to see the recipient of the blow.

"Fuck off, man."

Cole's face was serious but Brett still laughed. "Get use to him, Izzy. He always butts his head in when the going gets good."

A little more relaxed with the familiarity of friendly banter, her time to be a wild woman would be now or never. "Too bad, I was really interested in seeing how big a canvas I had to work with." She waved the pen in the air and attempted the naughty grin she'd seen Taryn use many times, while waiting on attractive male customers at the bar.

Brett changed directions, pumped his fist in the air, and headed out of the lounge. "Damn Izzy, this is gonna be a riot. I'm on drinks, someone get a poker game set up."

At the word "poker" all the guys arranged themselves like they'd done it a million times. Cards with her friends could get intense, but these guys would kick her ass.

They carried on with an ease and routine that reminded her of many nights spent with the girls. "Shit."

She scrambled for her phone, the promise to let them know she'd arrived safe struck her a little late. Thankful the guys were busy at the moment, she sent out the first of what would be many mass text messages to the girls.

Sorry, I know, don't get mad. I am here. The bus is just leaving now. The guys are all great. All I can say is, wow.

Send.

She set her phone on vibrate and scooted over to the seat Cole patted.

****

"Now Izzy, the rules of the game are simple. The losers chug their drink."

He leaned in close to whisper the last part in her ear, and she squirmed as if his closeness affected her in a likeable way. Nice. He nudged her and winked, her scent—vanilla—drifted in his direction. He closed his eyes for a brief moment before he glanced around the room and adjusted himself under the table. The brush of his own hand escalated his arousal further, so he searched out the window for a diversion from his lewdness. The usual, a humdrum highway. Crap.

He hadn't experienced a strong gravitation to anyone since Alexis. Their relationship had appeared steamy to onlookers, and was, but also full of drama that ended just in time. Isabelle on the other hand, with her sheltered blue eyes, natural blonde hair, and thin but curvy figure—innocent. That he found attractive.

Fame kept him alert to the possibility women desired the spotlight more than him. Who would believe being known by millions of people could feel so lonely at times? He shook his head to clear the negativity before it creeped in. It would only induce yet another bad mood, and he didn't want her to see that part of him.

The *tssk* of beers opened alerted him back to the room.

"Didn't know what your poison was, Izzy." Brett set a beer down in front of her and smacked the back of Cole's head on his way to his seat.

"This is fine, thank you."

Brett sat down on the other side of him and wiggled in his seat. "Good, 'cause I always get a hard-on when a woman chugs a beer. Ready to lose, sweetheart?"

Laughter echoed in the room along with the smack of many high fives. Cole peeked at her. His knee bounced under the table; this was nothing yet. She held her own better than he'd imagined, but something in her eyes surprised him when she shifted back to the others. Defiance maybe?

"Huh, who knew I'd get to ride in a bus with a bunch of limp dicks, then?"

Cole laughed, raised his hand to her and she hit it. Hers was small compared to his and so chilled he held on while he lowered them under the table. His fingers laced between hers with ease, something he'd been dying to find out since the airport. How much more of her body could use the warmth of his?

From the corner of his eye, he glanced at her. She stared down, stock-still, so he let go and took a long drink from his beer, and emptied it.

Many deals and chugs later, everyone hollered over one another, eager to be the person who took the inappropriate jokes to the next level. Cole raised his eyebrows with his jaw dropped when she gave as good as she got.

"So Izzy, what's on this bucket list anyway?" Zander asked and tossed one of many beer tabs down the front of her tank top.

She dug it out with more forethought about her company than his desperate libido cared for. Her head still down, she scoffed. "Ha, the edited version you read online, or the real one in my back pocket?"

All movement around the table froze when she revealed the silver tab and squeezed her eyes shut tight. "Shit."

She couldn't shield herself in time before Cole tackled her in the seat. Loud whistles pierced the air when the scuffle resulted in the two tumbling to the floor, him on top of her. It took little effort to pin her down.

"No fair. You're bigger." She squirmed so much he lost his grip on one of her hands. She wiggled and shoved it underneath her butt.

"Yes, I am." Cole winked, scooped her wrist in time and slid both up, over her head. The quick motion drew her scent to his nose. He leaned in and inhaled deeper into her neck. A quiet moan escaped her lips.

There wasn't an inch of him that didn't touch her, the bulge in the front of his pants included. If he had to guess, Izzy was just as aroused, and so wet he could slide right into her channel. Her breath caught when he pressed forward, and moaned so low only she could hear. The pulse at her wrist raced in his grip, and when he held them both down tight in one hand, it damn near exploded. He affected her the same way she did him, and now he held the proof.

Cole used his free hand to roam down her arm. Her skin glided under his like silky cream and the urge to bend forward for a lick controlled him. How far will she let this go? He stared into her eyes, waited for her to stop him; she didn't.

"I give up." She panted and relaxed her body beneath him.

He continued downward with his fingertips, along the side of her soft breast and ribcage. Her neckline tugged with it, revealed more of Isabelle's skin. "Me too."

Rather than get caught up on the swell of her breast, Cole drifted his hand underneath her lower back and lifted her into him, but their clothes made it impossible to sink into her heat the way he needed. His head buzzed on alcohol, but Izzy under him like this was a whole new kind of drunk.

His body responded without control, and he thrust his hips for friction. He loved the soft curve of her body, the way she reacted to his silent commands.

He couldn't believe this was happening but wasn't ready to stop it either. It wouldn't be the first time he'd taken a woman in front of the guys. However, she deserved better. He respected her. Guilt now in place, he squeezed his eyes closed and held his breath, avoiding her lush scent.

In one quick motion, he swept his hand under her, and hurried into her back pocket. The wrong pocket. The curve of her cheek warmed his hand. An invitation to stay longer is how he interpreted it, so he gave it a gentle squeeze. He stilled his movements, gave her a chance to reject his advances before he moved in for the other pocket.

Nothing.

Her gaze tested him, as if she not only dared him to go for it, but welcomed him to. When Cole pressed into her in order to extend further for her other pocket, she wrapped her leg around his ass and guided him. He touched his forehead to hers and growled. They both breathed heavily, their faces so close he could feel her breath on his lips and her breasts against his chest.

"Ahem"

The lure of Isabelle's scent intoxicated him beyond comprehension, over and above his ability to abide Drew's subtle caution. Just one taste would do. Her eyes were still closed, so he shifted his body and pressed into her to gain access to the other pocket.

His lips brushed against her neck and the reason for their tumble was lost to him. He inched his tongue out and skimmed her neck for a delicate taste. Her whole body quivered. She was sweet, gave him more satisfaction in that one second than years of hidden cookies in his bunk. She should be in his bunk right now, under the sheets, under him.

His body heat rose, and the trust he had in his own resistance broke. The urge to rip her clothes off overwhelmed him. If he didn't end this now…he'd take her. He swiped the paper out of the other pocket, forced himself up, and collapsed on the couch. The cold seat warmed to his temperature in record time, and his breath came out in pants.

He didn't care to exchange witty comebacks with the guys; the paper and what she held back intrigued him. Curious to know what other hopes he could help her with, he leaned back and read the list before one of the guys could rip it from his hands.

He lowered it in his lap, once again aroused beyond belief, and stared down at the blush that covered her skin. The absence of his heat hadn't hit her yet, or she couldn't make herself forget.

His eyebrow raised at Drew, standing over her with his hand held out, and a grin on his face. "Still need a moment, or can I help you up?"

"Ugh." She threw her arms over and slammed them on the floor beside her squeezed thighs, accepted his help up, and swayed on her feet. Her complexion varied between pale white and green. She covered her mouth, and her eyes widened. Drew let her shove past him to run to the bathroom.

Cole sat there frozen and read the list several times. He couldn't believe this beautiful, innocent woman's desires matched all the scenes that played through his head, only moments ago.

Someone grabbed the paper from him before he could fight back and keep it for his eyes only.

"Share dipshit. The grin on your face tells us there are some very impressive items on the list." Zander laughed while he and Brett sat far enough away they could read the list while Drew held Cole's arms back. The men's eyes opened wide, reflecting Cole's from seconds ago, only their jaws also hung open.

Brett fanned his face with the paper. "Holy fuck, not so goodie, goodie is she?" He contemplated Cole's reaction with a devilish grin. "Do you think she'd let me help her out with number thirteen? You know I have a thing for a hot tight hole."

Cole jumped, cleared the table between them, and grabbed the hat off Brett's head to hit him with. He ripped the paper away. "We all know you like ass, man or woman. Lay a hand on her and I will shove the closest object up yours."

The three men sat back in their seats in silence and gaped anywhere but at him.

Where the fuck did that come from?

****

Isabelle flushed the toilet. A cold sweat along with goose bumps broke out over her skin. She searched the tiny bathroom until she found toothpaste and used her finger to scrub the fuzz from her mouth. With her back against the wall, she slid down until her butt hit the floor and wrapped her arms around her knees. She closed her eyes with a sigh and let her head fall back to the tile wall.

Girl's poker nights did not prepare her for a night with experienced drinkers. In only a matter of hours, she'd second-guessed her bucket list, well, several times. Now they were out there with her most secret desires, the ones that were difficult to share with her friends, who'd known her a hell of a lot longer.

A light tap sounded at the door. She groaned and put her head down on her knees. If she ignored them, they'd get the point.

The tap continued.

"Ugh, clearly they aren't bright as they are talented." She squirmed up off the floor and cringed at her reflection in the mirror. "Not even with a miracle." She whipped the door open to see Cole, and what appeared to be guilt on his face, along with water and acetaminophen in his hands.

"Sorry. I didn't know if it was nerves or the beer. Are you all right?"

She dropped her gaze to his large hands, and chuckled when the tattoos up his arms revealed something other than the gentleness in his palms. "Thank you, Cole, maybe a little of both. I'm such a dork. If you guys don't mind, I am just going to call it a night."

Rather than relinquish the pills, he held them and rested his hand in hers. A current she couldn't describe passed through their contact. She didn't give in to it again, just pried the pills from his fingers and squeezed by him. Every bunk in the aisle mirrored the next. Her stomach fluttered again as she dragged her feet and inspected the curtains, which all displayed the same solid charcoal grey color. She didn't realize he'd followed her until the warm solid body collided into her back when she stopped.

He latched onto her hips with his large masculine hands to prevent another tumble. "Careful, sweetheart. Let me get that for you."

He extended around her with one hand while his

other remained on her hip and wrenched back the curtain to her bunk. She twisted back with a smile, and her breath stalled mid inhale. The proximity of his lips to hers created a surge of attraction she'd ignore, if that were possible. When her gaze lowered to his lips, his noticeable desire nudged her behind, and the memory of their earlier X-rated scuffle rose. Her pulse raced. They leaned into one another like a magnet that found its counterpart, on the verge of a kiss when reality hit. She squirmed out of his hold and climbed into her bunk.

"Thanks again, Cole, you really don't have to take care of me. Please don't let my presence get in the way of what you guys do." With a shaky hand, she closed the curtain, thankful for the barrier that separated her from him, and the attraction that grew stronger with every glance. If one day with these guys unraveled her, she didn't know if she could survive a full week.

She stared at the closed curtain and strained to listen for his retreat. He released a loud exhale of breath, and his footfalls hesitated before they moved away. She too exhaled when she was certain he was out of earshot. With a devious smile, she changed into her Jake Owen concert tee. What would they say if they found out her preferred music?

Her pants vibrated as she folded them. She whipped the pants in every direction, and scrambled for her phone before the ignored text messages resulted in an actual call she'd have to whisper through.

Izzy, we are dying here. Or are you already being ravished? LOL Luv u, Katherine

I know it's only your first day, but do you know where Drew's tattoo leads to yet? Luv Taryn

Send me a picture to gawk at please? Work is boring today. Abby

She tapped the phone with her nail and bit her lip. Should she tease them a little?

Ladies, chill. Drinking, poker, fondling, and puking. I am so out of my element. Passing out now…

They would be drawn to *fondling,* so she loaded the three contact numbers, sent the text, and stuffed the now muted phone in her bag.

Drunken nights with the girls exhausted her, made it quite easy to pass out before her head hit the pillow. A restful night of sleep after all that'd happened with him was beyond possible. Her mind replayed the night like one of her favorite love songs on repeat. The weight and warmth of his body on top of her sparked an addiction she couldn't satisfy.

She rummaged for the journal Abigail insisted on and sat with it in her lap. The tiny space, and all it had to offer, held her attention as she tapped the pen on the hard covered book. She had her own mini TV up in the corner and a light that offered more than enough visibility in the dark. The little bit of anxiety about the trip eased. She could escape the trivial times, or hide, since she was prone to unintentional falters of embarrassment. A family trait inherited well.

****

She closed the book and hesitated. If they found it, would they read it? A lock might be nice, just in case. The men were quiet, only the faint hum of Derek's music from the front of the bus. And a few snores. They must have gone to bed while she wrote, so now should be a good time to sneak out to the bathroom before she slept. She peeled the curtain back slow, every little sound echoed.

She flopped over onto her stomach, and lowered from the bunk with a wiggle of her foot in search of support from Cole's bunk. She didn't want to wake him, so the second her toe touched down she hurried but slipped.

"Eeek!"

Without luck, she grasped at the mattress with one hand and covered her mouth with the other. A large, warm grip caught her thigh, and slid farther up her shirt while she continued to tumble. A deep growl snapped her attention forward, right into his eyes. Only, they weren't on hers. She followed his gaze down to his hand at her waist where it held up her T-shirt, and revealed her lacy red panties.

The image of him using his strength to lure her into his bunk crossed her mind. Within seconds, her panties were wet, and her breathing became shallow. She squeezed her eyes closed and whispered, "I'm fine now, Cole, you can let go."

"Izzy." He panted and rubbed his thumb over her waist. She could sense he held on by a thread. Liked it. He let her drop to the floor and glanced away for a moment, cleared his throat, and then gave her a childlike grin. "Sorry about the slight fondle." He winked. "Well, no, I'm not actually but, really Izzy?"

She raised her eyebrows and followed his pointed finger.

"Don't let the guys catch you wearing that. They will rip it off for reasons other than what's going through my mind right now."

With a seductive sway of her hips and a giggle under her breath, she strolled to the bathroom. "Cole

Davies, I am not sure you men would know what to do with me once you got this shirt off."

He growled again.

She covered her mouth to prevent a full out belly laugh.

"Damn."

She swiveled back to the bunks and inched her way backward to the bathroom. *Drew?*

"Oh, I would know what to do all right."

With a gasp, she opened her mouth under her hand. *Brett?*

"I am sure there is something on your list that can be taken care of, if we get you topless, Izzy." The little lights that glowed along the skirting of the aisle made it possible to see Zander peek out from behind his curtain and wink at her.

She scooted in and closed the door fast, not able to hold in the laugh any longer. Cole laughed too. A nice laugh.

Chapter Five

Dear Diary,
I could feel the heat of his breath...

Utter silence, no hum of music to pass the time and no clit-throbbing masculine voices rumbled when Isabelle braced herself to sit up and opened her eyes. She sighed, thankful for the sleep aid she took while in the bathroom last night. Not a wise idea in light of the amount of alcohol she'd consumed, but this adventure was about taking risks, right? She huffed and flopped back down on her pillow with her hands over her face.

Isabelle Chambers dies at the young age of twenty-nine after a seductive poker game with muscled and tattooed rockers. She succumbed to the use of pills for sleep to avoid fantasies about them that would keep her awake all night in her drunken stupor. Ha. Sounds a lot better than, Isabelle Chambers dies at the age of twenty-nine from a brain tumor. Autopsy reveals lack of fun, unused and untouched female anatomy.

She threw her arms over her head and blew at wisp of hair that'd fallen in her face. Sarcasm often encouraged trouble when she needed it the least. Cole's threat about her T-shirt replayed in her mind. Some fantasies would be more than welcome.

"Anyone here?"

The continued silence assured her now would be a

safe time to get showered and ready for, well, she didn't know what today's plans were. The constant flutter in her stomach made the whole bucket list adventure sound more attractive to drop, rather than follow through with. Sober and focused, she ignored the woman she used to be, she collected her things and headed to the bathroom.

The iPod and speakers she packed made it easy to maintain her routine amateur shower rendition of Carrie Underwood's, *Before He Cheats*.

"Eeek!"

The sudden blast of cold water proved he hadn't been kidding around when he said hot water was short lived on the bus.

She threw the shower door open and jumped out, right into a hard, bare, sweaty chest that smelled so good. Unable to resist, she closed her eyes and inhaled the musky male scent that made a little moisture not from the shower, pool between her thighs.

"Ahem"

Her sexual fog cleared, and the heat of his strong hands alerted her that he supported her upper body by the rib cage. Close enough to touch her outer, naked breasts. She reconsidered the need for a cold shower.

"Are you all right, Izzy? I heard you scream, you scared the shit out of me."

She raised her chin to see the most decadent, cocky, smile. "Cole?" She smoothed her hand up his bare chest, to the dimple beside his lip. The intent to tease, get revenge, never worked for her. It worked *on* her.

He responded with a step closer. "Yes?"

Darn it.

"I'm fine, cold water shocked me and well, I'm naked. Think maybe you could get out?"

Her body heat rose; sure to leave a flush on her wet skin. His gaze dropped from hers, and scanned the length of her body. The flimsy shorts he wore did little to conceal his attraction or his length. She tightened her stance.

Reserved might be a good word to describe her, but shy, not so much. She squirmed away from him, flailed her arm behind her until she found the towel, and wrapped it around herself. She took an assertive step forward, and he retreated with a flare in his eyes that didn't convince her he was nervous in the least.

She couldn't resist one more touch and his cocky posture dared her. She poked at him. "I'm a grown woman who can take care of herself, Cole, don't worry about me."

He smiled and raised his eyebrow. "If you hadn't noticed, my lower half is well aware that you are a grown woman. So much so, I have a proposition for you."

He stepped forward, forced her to retreat until her back was pinned against the wall. She held still when he leaned into her neck and inhaled the scent of her soap. "Let us help you with your list, *all* of it. And when I say that, I mean the unedited one." He swayed his head back and forth, and brushed his lips against her skin, ever so light.

Her knees trembled, and she lifted her hands to his shoulders for support. "Cole. You have no idea what the sound of that offer does to me." She shut her eyes, tight. "I want to say yes, but you have to understand, the items on that paper are my only priority. I'm not here to lead you into the false hope my presence is for anything more than the list. There is no future for me."

She shimmied out from the wall, difficult given the small space. A full breath did little to get her libido under control before she opened the door.

"I appreciate the offer more than you know, but I don't want to distract you from the life you lived before I arrived. Sorry I took all the hot water."

No hoots were chanted as she scurried to her bunk in only a towel. He returned by himself. Her heart fluttered at the possibility that he'd intended to be alone with her.

When she closed her curtain, the bathroom door opened. "The rest of the guys should be in soon. We like to work out in the morning when we aren't too hung over. We have a show tonight if you want to tag along and watch, like a day in the life of? It'll give you some time to think about my offer and by the way, nice voice. I'm gonna have to put some better music on that thing for you."

She gripped the towel around her breasts and stared down at her phone. She didn't have to think about it, but she did have to know what the girls would say.

Morning ladies. So Cole just offered to help me out with my entire list. What do you think?

Send.

She set the phone down in order to master a delicate shuffle into her clothes, without injury from the walls that closed her in. The phone vibrated its way close to the edge of the bed.

Hell yes. Abigail

Lucky Bitch. Did you wax? Taryn

OMG Izzy. Be careful, watch your heart,

and...make sure you stretch. LOL Katherine

****

Cole punched the counter and the vanity mirror rattled on the wall. The door provided no obstacle for him to run out of the bathroom and chase after her, plead her to let him do this. Neither the cold shower, nor his hand, relieved the constant state of arousal he displayed around her.

His desperation, magnified in the mirror, exposed more than surface level emotions. Life couldn't have brought him this wonderful distraction at a better time. Strange moods hit him all the time, and the guys bore the brunt of it.

The tour was fun, always, but something still seemed out of reach. They encountered groupies all the time but nothing like her though. She could care less, and he loved it. Drew's caution ran, no, raced through his mind. *Don't get attached.*

What the hell did she mean by there is no future for her? Is the list the real deal; is she sick? She looks healthy. So healthy he used all of his energy to resist the urge to spread her out on his bed and taste her until she moaned his name, and trembled with release.

Voices from outside the bathroom startled him. He closed his eyes, focused on his breath, and well, anything that would minimize his condition. She didn't need to hear the ribs he'd get if he left the bathroom with a hard-on.

"Did you see her tits bounce while she ran? Man, I'd like to get my face in those."

"Not if I get to them first. She said she'd be at the show tonight. Arm wrestle?"

With a towel wrapped around his waist, Cole

stepped out of the bathroom and bumped knuckles with Brett and Zander. He shook his head with a smile when Drew joined the fun, and dry humped the air in an exaggerated motion.

When Isabelle's feet hit the floor, all four bare-chested men spun around. She stood, wide-eyed and jaw-dropped, in her camouflage Capri's and tank top. Red blotches spread over her skin when she surveyed herself and then them, before she changed directions and raced toward the back lounge.

"Don't stop staring on our account, Izzy. Then again, sway that ass a little more for us and make it worth it."

Cole punched Drew in the arm, didn't like that they ogled her but kind of did at the same time. She didn't close the door, so he could see her perched on the couch, rubbing the skin right off her arms. He stood at his bunk, his hand on the towel and winked when her gaze left the window and landed on him. He could read her mind when she tipped her head to the side and raised her eyebrows, more in challenge than curiosity.

He dropped the towel and chuckled when her eyes widened, and she gawked with her hand over her mouth. Yes, he kept himself in shape and well, he never experienced any complaints about his size. He slid into his boxer briefs and stroked himself through the material while many images and positions, filtered through his mind.

"It won't break you, if that's what you're concerned about, beautiful." The sound of his voice forced her gaze up and he smiled. So, it wasn't just men who objectified.

"Sorry."

A deep blush rose on her face, similar to the one he'd seen cover the entire length of her naked body earlier in the bathroom.

Drew hit him on the back of the head and continued to the lounge. "Cocky son of a bitch, isn't he?"

"Hmph." She grabbed the material thrown at her face, and held it up. A Scandals' T-shirt.

"Do not let me catch you wearing that hillbilly shirt to bed again or else." He slid his phone off the table and twirled it in his hand on his way to the couch.

Cole stood at the door, clothed, and smiled as his best friend grinned at the woman who captured everyone's attention.

She held the shirt up in front of her again with a spark in her eye. "I'll have to think about it. I suffer from commitment issues, and I have committed many years to that Jake Owen T-shirt."

He leaned into her bunk before she could stop him, dragged the offensive T-shirt from under her pillow, and threw it at Brett. "Hide that, and no matter what she says or does, do not give it back until the day she leaves." He blocked the aisle, and made it impossible for her to get through while Brett stuffed the shirt into his own bunk.

He admired her with her hands on her hips and chin held high, but she didn't budge. "Cole Davies, you said my bunk was my private place? You just violated that."

He grasped her hips with a slight squeeze and took a step forward so little room existed between them, kissed her forehead, and whispered. "Stay and I promise I will violate you in all kinds of ways. Your list, remember?"

She shivered.

He could feel their stares. They chuckled behind him when she acknowledged his intention with a subtle nod, out of breath.

He mentioned his desire to help her with her entire list earlier. Being men, they didn't have any argument with his itch to get laid. Their only concern? How many items *they* were going to be a part of. She didn't fawn over them or acknowledge they were famous; it was nice.

Derek climbed on the bus with a whistle. "Boys are running late. Get your asses in there. Stage is set up for sound check. Hello, dear. Hope the boys didn't snore too loud and keep you up last night."

Cole stumbled when she gave him a little shove, and headed to the front of the bus for the well-used passenger seat. He tapped his fist on the bunk and stared as Derek joined her.

"It may have taken a little sleep aid to knock me out, but other than that," she shrugged, "I have no complaints."

"Good to hear. The boys have to do sound check, an interview with a local radio show, and meet and greet, all before the show. Are you going to grace us with your sweet smile, or have these jerks scared you off already?"

She leaned over and placed her hand on his knee. A sentiment beyond his comprehension filled her eyes. Sorrow maybe? He really didn't know much about her.

"I wouldn't miss it. Thank you. I will try not to get in the way."

Cole, Drew, Brett, and Zander stood in the aisle

with their mouths open when he offered her the picture of his wife and daughter. He pointed at them and bestowed information on her even they weren't clear on. He didn't open up to anyone about his family. In one day, she had them all wrapped around her finger; she didn't even know it.

"I know that look Cole, careful."

His chest tightened at Drew's caution but he didn't want to think about it, not now. "Come on guys, let's show Carolina how real men party." He could fake it well, but the unknown reason for her list got under his skin.

Everyone got off the bus, tipped their heads, and waved to the few fans who always showed rain or shine, no matter what time of day. Venues catered to their privacy as much as possible, ensured a place to park behind buildings and away from the streets. Fans gathered at the gates in the distance, some with binoculars and lawn chairs, others with only a camera and an article of clothing to be signed if lucky. He'd try to find the time and make it over to them. He let everyone go ahead and held his arm out for her to go first.

She stood up and placed her hand on Derek's shoulder. "Thank you for sharing that with me. Your wife and daughter sound like they were wonderful women." He eyed the picture with fondness; his smile extended to his eyes.

Seems I may not be the only one who needs her.

****

Isabelle shifted her gaze between his hand and devilish grin, before she stepped ahead. The loud slap and sharp bite of pain on her ass confirmed her suspicion. She raised her hand to retaliate but he stopped her with his grip, and they both exited the bus with a quiet laugh to several camera flashes in the distance. It wasn't until her foot hit the ground and someone yelled "who's the new chick," that she glanced down at their joined hands. She freed herself in casual fashion and put both hands in her pockets. Katherine's text about that little piece of gossip would arrive in no time.

The side of the stage where she stood allowed for a great view while people hustled, monitored their watches, or talked into earpieces. She never could have imagined the size of the crew necessary to organize a concert. Then again, the many country concerts she'd attended before this were much different. There, men paraded around in cowboy boots and hats, with plaid shirts tight enough to reveal their muscles, and hold her attention from anything else.

Her usual view from out in the crowd, in nosebleed seats, didn't compare to *this*. Only an arena, but more like a stadium of empty seats that'd be filled later. It was intimidating, to say the least. She held her hand over her stomach, not sure if the nausea was anxiety for the guys, or the tumor.

Led to believe, by said men, she'd blend in; she clenched her jaw with a smile every time someone greeted her by name. She spun to see if anyone else cared to approach her, before she used her phone to take a picture of the view. The legal document only mentioned no pictures of the band, not the stage. She sent the picture to her friends and titled it *Get a load of this view...*

Incredible...have you seen where the tattoo ends

yet? LOL Taryn

I expect backstage passes soon. Abby

Wow. How u feeling? Katherine

She laughed and responded to Katherine. She could never get away with white lies to her, even in text.

I'm okay. Better than okay. Really. My pain is still a well-hidden secret, but the guys are very good at distraction. She tacked on a smiley face to the end of the message before she sent it.

"Enjoying the view?"

Warm arms wrapped around her from behind. She inhaled Cole's familiar scent until it teased her body into delightful tingles "I am. Thank you."

Things between them veered in a direction she'd planned to avoid and could if she broke the contact in this moment, but it was warm, comfortable.

"And who exactly did you send that picture to?"

She bit her lip, wiggled to face him, but his arm around her waist tightened.

"I'm sorry, I know I'm not allowed to take pictures but my three best friends back home, they are my world. I let them know I am enjoying myself, and I didn't see anyone around to catch me. By the way, how does everyone know my name?"

She couldn't see his face but felt him smile above her.

"Well, I made sure everyone knew. Things can get a little crazy on the road, and I don't want anyone to mistreat you. No worries about the picture. Here, give me your phone." He grabbed it before she could protest, dipped his head beside hers, and held out the phone.

"Send this. Let them know I'm taking care of you. Smile."

She did, not because of the picture though, but because of the lack of space between them. Her body tingled like a giddy teenager. A horny one.

He swiped at her phone like a boyfriend would, with no concern for secrecy. “Which numbers in your contact list?”

She stood on tiptoe to steal it from him, but he was too tall. It’d become too natural, too fast between them. She placed her hands on her hips, and glared at him. “Katherine, Abigail, and Taryn.” She swiped the phone from him when he pressed a button and lowered it within reach. The thread of sent messages to her friends were still visible, and reminded her just how much he could have found out about her. She opened his message, couldn’t resist being nosey. The picture was perfect, but the message attached to it, warmed her chest.

Hello friends of Izzy’s…isn’t she beautiful? I promise you she will have fun—wink wink—and will be safe. Cheers, Cole.

She dragged her attention away from the phone. Her conscience ate at her. He regarded her as if he’d found his own adventure in her.

“Izzy?”

She swallowed hard. “Cole. I need to tell you something.”

Before she could get the words out, a strange man handed Cole a guitar. Zander, Brett and Drew joined them.

“Sorry, we have to do sound check. Will you be okay here?”

“Of course. Go.”

He kissed her cheek, strolled out to center stage

with the guys, and shoved plugs into his ears. She needed to find some time alone with him and explain. The contentment on his face while they sang and played their instruments, over and over as people made corrections, told her now wasn't the right time. They were good though. She took a step closer when Cole pivoted to the opposite side of the stage and shook his head.

"They can hear our directions in their earpieces."

She jumped when the same strange man settled beside her and offered his ear bud. Thank goodness, he didn't take it any further, and try to put it in. Gross.

She leaned in closer and listened to the strange instructions. Cole glanced her way and stuck his tongue out right before a guitar pick hit him in the back of the head. She laughed when a woman's voice bellowed through the earpiece to scold them. The man shrugged and took off as if he feared a lecture as well.

Words couldn't describe Cole's effect on her. The others as well, if she were being honest. They were hot. She fanned her face with exaggerated motion, but dropped her hands at her sides when voices neared.

She needed to get back in control of her hormones. Being around him, she'd become fearless, untamed, lust filled…free from moral restraint. And she enjoyed it. She'd prepared herself for the time of her life but what she neglected to prepare for was a connection with him.

Sound check wrapped up in no time, but was still long enough to get the men sweaty. They bounced off the stage, and peeled off their soaked shirts.

"Hey Izzy, what d'ya think?" Brett put his arm around her while they sauntered back to their designated change room. The halls reflected the image of any arena she'd ever been in—concrete everywhere.

"It was awesome. I can't wait to see the full show tonight. You guys are amazing. Girls must cry out proposals and throw their bras at you every night."

They jabbed one another with eager grins and high-fives. When she glanced back over her shoulder, Cole trailed behind with his hands in his pockets. His gaze was locked to the floor as if he summoned it to swallow him whole. Did he think she'd be bothered by those girls?

****

She sat on the couch in the not so private room, while the guys showered and got ready for their interview at the radio station. People drifted in and out, the band opening for the Scandals included, whom she didn't recognize. Lots of beer was poured as they reminisced with the guys about the last time they opened the show for them.

She stood up and politely shook her head when another man offered her a beer. She dug out a bottle of water from the cooler of ice instead and pinched the bridge of her nose on her way out the door.

"Hey, Iz."

She stepped aside, dug her sunglasses out of her purse, and let the roadie in. Pills. Now. That would teach her to ignore a headache for too long. When a large, tattooed man vacated a stool along the poster-covered hall she sighed and sat down. The cold water hurt her head more, but she swallowed it down with the pills.

She relaxed her head on the wall behind her and closed her eyelids behind the shaded lenses. The rumble of noise around her faded, and her muscles loosened.

Cole's voice in the distance caught her attention.

She rotated her head a little too fast and could have sworn her brain came in contact with her skull. She rubbed her temple and stared in his direction.

He amused some female fans who managed to make it backstage. They weren't shy in the least as they fondled his arms and chest. The overzealous giggles at whatever he said reminded her of what not to do if she ever encountered a celebrity.

Wait? When he put his arm around the brunette and spoke in her ear, Isabelle resumed her position on the stool, scared she would lose the little amount of food her appetite allowed today.

A breeze drifted at her side. "Are you okay? I couldn't find you in the change room."

He stood at her side, unaware his height offered some shade from the horrible florescent lighting.

"Just a headache, nothing to worry about. There are many *people* around to keep you entertained Cole, you don't have to babysit me." She kept her eyes closed, didn't want to see his reaction to her clipped tone.

"I know I don't. Are you sure there isn't anything else bothering you?"

She clutched the top of her head with one hand and whimpered when a sharp pain radiated through her skull.

Before she could protest, he placed his hand gently on top of hers and anchored her head to his chest. "Baby, are you sure you're okay? Can I get you anything?"

His heart raced against her chest and her muscles stiffened with worry, even more so from the angst in his voice. "I get migraines. I already took some medicine.

It will kick in soon."

She sighed and dropped her hand when he smoothed her hair back in the direction of her ponytail. He even loosened the elastic. Her heart swelled and her body relaxed while the pain faded. She didn't know how long they stayed like before a kiss on the top of her head sparked her attention.

She peered up into his eyes; they were beautiful. The butterflies that stormed her stomach earlier while they performed, built once again. He raised his hands to her face, slid off her sunglasses and locked gazes with her.

He hesitated, battled with some unspoken thing, before he leaned forward and kissed her forehead. He eased her pain, and his attempt to do so very clear, but there was more to it. She tilted her chin up to catch sight of him and their gazes locked, the lure of a kiss drew them closer. So close, his breath touched her lips.

"There you are."

They closed their eyes and he leaned his forehead on hers. "What do you want, Zander?" Now his tone was clipped.

"Derek's bringing the car around. We gotta get to the radio station."

With a growl, he laced his fingers with hers and started for the car. She tugged her arm, to yank her hand free, but he refused to let go.

"Cole. I don't want people to get the wrong impression." She whispered so no one else but he could hear.

His pace increased, and he clenched his jaw. "Izzy. I don't give a damn what people think." His whisper was firm.

Chapter Six

Dear Diary,
I held on to keep from falling...

From her seat behind a window, she was intrigued. The Scandals' stage presence astounded her, but wow, what you see is not always what you get. The radio interview proved that. They exuded sexuality to the listeners, needing to maintain their image, but they were different. Yes, raw sexuality added to the package, yet there was so much left unrevealed, so much more to them than they let on.

She startled when the vibration in her pocket signaled a message, long overdue.

The 3 of us are at the Pub, Izzy, drinking to you. Holy shit he is hot. We have all made your picture our new wallpaper on our phones. It would appear you're having fun and we assume from his message, have made an impression. Katherine—momma bear—wants me to tell you a couple things.

1. Be careful, protect your girl parts and your heart. LOL

2. There are some rather interesting pics on the Internet and don't think she wouldn't have known. LOL

Cheers to you, country girl gone wild, Taryn

When she peeked up, she caught him in a fixed stare, at her. He glanced down at his phone, which he hid under the desk as he answered questions at the same time. Her phone vibrated again and she laughed when the picture of the two of them appeared saying, *Hey hot stuff*. She laughed at his sneakiness, even more so when Zander slugged him in the arm after he missed a question. The pretty brunette with headphones, opposite the table from him, didn't register to him as she flipped her hair and asked rather intrusive questions.

Isabelle focused out the window on the way back to the venue while the men talked about the interview. Katherine always snapped her back to reality when she needed it. The inevitable pictures. Maybe she'd check them out when she gets home. It would be too easy to get consumed with how others viewed their time together, and lose sight of her purpose.

The list.

The evening raced by in a blur, but the meet and greet was rather up close and personal. She sat off to the side with Derek while the guys signed autographs and had their pictures taken with fans. More time was required to get ready for the show than she'd anticipated. Rocker clothes, hair gel, and a little makeup took finesse.

That surprised her. Her heart swelled when a woman ignored the other men and groped Cole's ass. He sought her out in panic, raised his hands in the air, and shrugged his shoulders to suggest *I can't help it if they adore me.*

The show blew her away, and yes, bras were thrown. She danced in the same spot from earlier, even sang along to some of the songs. Taryn's influence, of course. She shimmied in a circle and tapped her thigh with her hand, surprised by the amount of flurried activity that continued while they were on stage.

She assumed that would've been the time for everyone to sit back, relax, and enjoy the show. She was wrong. People flew around with guitars, and handed them off to the guys when they passed off ones with broken strings. Frantic talk shifted from person to person about an issue with the lights and a busted peddle? There were many flaws fixed backstage but out in the crowd, it appeared to be nothing more than a perfect performance.

Drew joined Cole at the front of the stage, wrapped his arm around Cole's shoulders, and offered him a guitar pick. They both hurled the tiny pieces of plastic out into the crowd, and the chant from the fans increased beyond a pitch she could tolerate. She rotated away from the noise, to the many relieved smiles from the roadies, and even greater frantic behavior about plans to tear down the stage and move on to the next venue.

She swiveled back in the direction of rowdy footfalls behind her, stiffened with surprise when three of the four men kissed her on the cheek while they paraded by. She placed her hands on her hips and laughed at the guys, but she was confused. The first off stage was always Cole, if she remembered right from their banter during cards last night. Where was he?

She caught him as he lingered at the bottom of the stairs, his gaze locked on her. He stalked toward her. She could see the sweat that dripped down his face like the others, but he didn't wipe it away. His focus on her never wavered.

He wrapped his arms around her waist and lifted her in the air. His sweat-drenched face touched the side of hers and he whispered, “I have a major adrenaline rush right now, and all I can think about is kissing you.”

A rush of air escaped her. “Cole.”

The current between them shifted when she no longer cared to check for onlookers. Her folds dampened at the mental image of him claiming her in front of everyone.

“I will kiss you. Not now, the moment isn’t right, and I am disgustingly sweaty, but it’s going to happen.” He put her down. “We’re gonna get cleaned up and head back to the bus. The after party is just us on the road tonight, no fans.”

Cole strolled away with a very confident swagger. She held up her finger and opened her mouth to argue. Nothing. “Crap…”

“Ahem.”

She glanced over at Derek and offered him a hesitant smile.

“Come on darlin’, let’s go back to the bus.”

“Okay.”

She smoothed her clothes down in front and followed his lead. *Has he been there this whole time?*

Groupies already crowded the barrier outside. After parties were a known occurrence, and the anxiousness in the young women’s eyes told her they’d join in a heartbeat. She stumbled up the stairs of the bus and grabbed onto the handrail, thankful she held no interest for the swarm of fans.

“The seat’s always open if you need to talk.” He smiled at her and sat down. He didn’t pressure her for more and that in and of itself, lured her into the seat. Her muscles relaxed, were more exhausted than she’d expected.

"I don't know specifics, but have you told them yet?"

She whipped her head around with her mouth gaped open and no words composed in defense.

"Their manager did a background check on you, procedure and all. I know this bucket list is the real deal. I see the way Cole looks at you when your back is to him. You seem like a wonderful woman, but I have to caution you to be careful. He's been in a rut up until now. What's happening between you and him seems to be changing that. I don't want to see him get hurt, or you, for that matter."

Cole wasn't kidding when he said Derek was like a father.

"I don't know what to say. Yes, it is the real deal. No, I haven't told any of them." She sighed. "I'd hoped not to, but I know I can't lead them on. After this, I will be heading into surgery. The odds are not in my favor." A tear spilled down her cheek.

"I didn't expect Cole, and I'm trying hard to keep my distance. He could have any woman he wants. I'm sure you don't have to worry."

Hoots and hollers alerted them their heart to heart was over for now. Derek had moved the bus closer to the exit, planned for their departure and what she imagined would be a scene to leave behind for fans to remember. The door opened and the female shrieks deafened her. Heavy footsteps rushed up the stairs.

"Derek, have you seen—"

She swiveled in the seat and the corners of her mouth rose a little. Drew kissed the top of her head as he passed by. "She's in here." He spun, still on his way to the bar, backward. "Cole has been searching everywhere for you. I suggest you hide." Brett winked and Zander air-kissed her, also on their way to the bar.

She glanced at Derek, who stared at her with furrowed brows. He raised his finger and opened his mouth to say something, but dropped his hand and adjusted back to the wheel instead. He was tuned in to everyone's needs, even the ones kept secret. She straightened her back to convince more than just herself she had everything under control.

"There you are."

Her resolve faded when Cole raced up the stairs. He leaned over the seat, held her face in his hands, and kissed her on the lips. Her eyes drifted closed. She forgot about the tear that'd managed to fall until Cole brushed it away with his thumb.

"You okay, babe?"

Yep, she was in deep. She shoved at his hands. "I'm fine." He stepped aside as she bypassed him, and the tear, to join the others. "Whatever you guys are making, I need one, too."

She stood at the bar beside Zander and glanced back at him, while he glared at Derek, pissed. Derek only shrugged, faced the windshield, and started the bus.

It was clear all four men suffered from an adrenaline rush after a show; the provocative banter hit an all-time high. She smiled at a few of their comments, held back her laugh in order to spy on Cole.

"Ever been to Virginia?"

She shook her head at Zander, who handed her a shot of tequila.

"No *virgins* allowed. Are we going to have to take care of that before we get there?"

Her cheeks warmed. He tapped his shot glass to hers and tipped it back. “Pfft.” She followed suit, swallowed the liquid, and slammed the shot glass down on the counter. “I have no cherry to offer you, but I am sure we just left some behind if you would like to go back.”

He flicked his tongue between two fingers and continued to the back lounge. “Nah, the women without cherries are way more fun.”

She followed the three men to the back. Familiar hands seized her at the hips from behind. She twisted in his arms to face him and sighed when he wrapped his arms around her and squeezed.

“Come on, beautiful.”

When he loosened his hold to follow the others, she enveloped him with her arms and held tight. “Not yet.” She inhaled his scent.

He tugged her hand free and coaxed her to the back of the bus. His failure to cave to her pout didn’t appear too difficult. “There’s something I want you to be a part of.”

She perked up. “Well, get going then.” With a light nudge, she urged him to pick up the pace.

“About time.” Brett handed them both a shot of tequila. Awestruck, she ignored the shot in her hand as the four men raised their glasses in unison, and hollered “years behind us, years ahead” before downing the drink. When all eyes were on her, she tipped the liquid back and did a little jig with her eyes closed as it burned its way down. Someone mumbled *hot damn*, but only coy shrugs greeted her when she opened her eyes and glared at the men.

****

Cole sat on the couch after a quick shower, a beer in one hand, and his arm around her. The guys reminisced about the show. Life was perfect or close to it. The fantasy of her underneath him, naked, made it difficult to hide the raging hard-on in his pants. He should just give into it.

When the football Drew lobbed from hand to hand fell to the floor, she stood and bent to pick it up. His groan at the view of her backside wasn't the only one. "I need something sweet to lick now, and it's all her fault. Derek, can we stop at a convenience store?" He slapped Zander and shrugged when she straightened herself and glared at him.

The bus jerked when Derek downshifted to veer off the highway. She stumbled and landed on Cole's lap, straddling him. "Fuck." He held her by the hips and thrust into her once. When one of the guys let out a low whistle, he lowered his hands to the seat beside him. He expected her to run. She didn't. Instead, she rubbed herself on him, and her eyes drifted closed. The guys left the room without a word, left him to battle the tease that now bordered on torture. He couldn't recall the last time it took so much work to get into a woman's pants.

They both startled at the sound of the air breaks.

"I need to go in and get something. You coming in?" He needed to get the blood in his body to flow back to the rest of his extremities. It took every ounce of control to stand up alone and not with her in his arms on their way to *his* bunk for the night.

She followed close behind him on the way to the door. He forced his feet forward, away from the temptation to halt so that she'd collide into him. Give him a reason to touch her again.

"I'm just going to get some air while the guys go inside. Derek, need anything?"

He spoke about directions to someone on the phone and waved them by.

The brisk nighttime weather replaced the heat that consumed him inside the bus. He preferred the heat.

"Aww yeah. Smell that, boys?"

They paused, raised their chins, and inhaled deep after Brett's cue. The smell of burning wood in the distance slowed their stride and brought back memories of nights back home for all of them.

He hurried in and out of the store, but halted, halfway back to her. Her casual beauty glowed in the moonlight, and the smell of the campfire made it easy to place her back home, around a fire with his dad and brothers.

She stood with her shoulder against the bus at the rest stop, gazing in the other direction, at the stars. The light of the moon highlighted her hair like an angel. He stepped up behind her and slid his arms around her waist. She inhaled and let her head fall back to his chest.

"Did you enjoy the show?"

She offered a silent nod, at ease in his arms.

He kissed the top of her head and flexed his muscles around her. To some extent due to the chill that'd touched his back, but also to cling to her and this perfect moment. "I haven't pried since it's none of my business, but I can't help but wonder." He exhaled. "Is there a need for the bucket list? You seem quite healthy for someone with one."

She tensed, not able to avoid it or prepare. "Cole."

Her hesitation was silent, but screamed loud

enough to make his pulse race.

"Yes, the list is real. I have a brain tumor. I will be going into surgery when my list is complete. I might not come out of the OR the same as I went in."

She struggled to face him with her chin raised. The contented haze in her eyes he'd imagined when her back was to him now revealed misery. "My chances for survival aren't good given the size and location. The headache earlier was minor. It's usually worse, and I can't keep much food down. That is why the alcohol hit me so hard the other night. I hadn't eaten much."

She fixed her gaze on his chest when she spoke, but tears glistened in her eyes.

Fuck.

She fit so well in his arms; he wasn't ready for that. It was possible, her being sick, but he refused to let her unspoken truth affect him. When she gave her attention to him, shared her sorrow, his world fell apart. He took a step forward and braced her back against the bus, his willingness to continue with their teasing game gone.

He cupped her face in his hands and stroked her cheek with his thumb. Her eyes didn't give him any indication she wouldn't be okay with his surrender to their attraction. He leaned in close, his lips only an inch from hers. If they did this, things would change.

From the desperation in her eyes, she battled that too, but didn't resist when he closed the gap and kissed the side of her mouth. She still didn't reject him, and he couldn't hold out any longer. He crushed his lips to hers, not gentle or tender, just demanded. The last twenty-four hours of attraction to one another created a tidal wave he couldn't stop.

When she smoothed her hands up his chest, he

accepted the invitation and curved his body into her heat. Her lips parted with a moan. He took a chance she thirsted for more; *he* did. He slid his tongue inside her mouth and all but came in his pants, her taste an instant addiction.

She clutched his shirt with her fists to bring him closer, deepen the kiss in a way that would cause pain if they were stopped before they were both satisfied. The bell on the convenience store door rang in the distance, and he remembered where they were. He stepped back and placed his forehead to hers. It wasn't long, but they were out of breath. He'd go for more, if he hadn't gone too far already.

"Cole." With her hands on his chest, she controlled the space between them. "We can't do this. I will probably die on the operating table, and I won't cause you heartache when I can prevent it. Besides, look at me." Her voice lowered. "I am far from your type, and I don't want pity. You don't know me."

****

"What'd he do?"

She barreled onto the bus, past Derek. She rushed to the bathroom, slammed the door, and fell to the toilet heaving. When the episode faded, she braced her way to the counter and stared at the tears she could no longer hold back.

The guys hadn't come back on the bus, but there was no time, or sense, in repair. Not even the prettiest of women could make the aftereffects of what just happened attractive. She brushed her teeth but her hopes for a few extra minutes didn't come true; she could hear them. Another quick glance in the mirror confirmed her suspicion; it was time for bed. They would notice her pale face.

With her head down, she left the bathroom and headed straight for her bunk. “Gonna call it a night guys, thanks.”

She donned the Scandals T-shirt Drew gave her; it smelled like cologne. What is it about the scent of a man that can weaken an adult woman into an overdramatic teenager again? She sent a quick text message to the girls saying she attended her first Scandals show today and enjoyed it, but failed to mention the kiss that left her weak in the knees. They’d demand details she wasn’t prepared to admit, so she shut her phone off, stuffed it under the pillow, and got out the journal.

****

He stood at the bar and glared down at her empty shot glass. Why did he ask? The large gulp of Jack Daniels in his mouth burned. He deserved it. “What happened?”

He held up his index finger, closed his eyes, and swallowed. “Nothing. Just reality sinking in.”

Drew shook his head. “She’s upset. It’s real, isn’t it?”

Nothing was private on tour. “Yep.” On his way to the back of the bus, he let his fingertips trace the edge of her bed. “Deal a game, would ya? Let me grab some beers. I’ll meet ya back there.”

They understood each other well, which also meant knowing when to back off.

Chapter Seven

Dear Diary,
My senses came alive, the vibration exquisite…

Charleston, West Virginia. Finally, a day off. With his forearm over his eyes, he sighed. He hadn't told her yet, and come to think of it, she should be up by now trying to beat him to the shower. She liked to hog *his* hot water. He didn't intend to let the secret out; he'd give her anything. He held his wrist up enough to squint at his watch. *Eleven a.m.* The guys would be asleep for a while, since the poker game dragged on forever last night, which also included the drinking. He focused on the ceiling, on her bunk.

She has a tumor, what the hell?

He scrubbed the fog away from his head and slammed his arms down on the bed. What next? He rolled out of his bunk—okay, he crawled and groaned through the pounding hangover. The bathroom and lounge were empty.

He stood at her bunk with the curtain in his fingertips, and his lip bitten so hard between his teeth it'd leave a mark. Point taken, they don't know each other. He eased back the curtain, not wanting to startle her and the image knocked him back a step. She lay in the fetal position, hands on her head and tears streaming down her face.

Scaring her no longer a concern, he yanked the curtain the rest of the way and placed his hand over hers. “Hey, baby?”

She opened her eyes part way. They were rimmed with a pain he couldn’t bear to see. He scanned her frail body; a pale, clammy shell replaced her usual beauty. Although, to him she still stole the show.

“Hey,” she whispered and closed her eyes.

“You don’t look well. Can I take you to the doctor?” He closed his eyes and swallowed hard before he focused on her again.

“No, no doctor. In my bag.” She pointed, so weak she struggled to raise her arm. “Pain pills, Gravol.”

He rushed for the pills, threw the contents of her bag everywhere, and handed them to her with a bottle of water.

She braced herself upright, only high enough to take the pills. “It will pass, always does. I am going to just stay in bed for the afternoon if it’s no trouble. I should be good to go this evening. Please don’t tell the guys.”

“Uh. Yeah. Sure.” He uncoiled from his concerned posture, trying to convince her tough men with ink like him, could handle anything. As he fixed her pillow, he imagined laying there with her, and *his* body was all the support she needed. But they weren’t there yet.

He kept his voice calm, experienced after many hangovers, present one included and kissed her forehead. “No problem, babe. We have the day off, and I’m sure the guys would like to do something a little more casual today. We’ll leave you alone, but I will come back to check on you later, okay? You have my number, call if you need anything.”

"I'll be okay."

She wiped the tears from her face, and rolled over. He hated to leave her, but what choice did he have? She wasn't his.

****

She took a deep breath, opened her eyes, and sat up slow. No pain, no nausea, still alive but mortified. A smile relaxed her while she piled up the clothes Cole upended from her bag but faded when the pill bottles tapped together. She picked them up and stared at the labels. No refills. She wouldn't need them. The guys would be back soon and she didn't want the train wreck that was sure to be her current condition to cloud their fun. She threw the bottles back in her bag. Able to handle more noise, she switched on her iPod and stumbled when the music blared, Scandals.

That little…ugh.

Impressed to be catching onto the lyrics, she tried her best to sing along with him while she enjoyed the hot water.

Without wariness, she opened the door and strolled toward her bunk to get dressed. Whatever they've planned for tonight better involve fun. The gasps from behind gave her an instant chill, and no mirror was necessary to confirm that the color had drained from her skin. No headache to blame this time.

Eyes closed tight, she twirled around. The whistles of appreciation made it easier to open her eyes again. Drew, Zander, Brett, and Cole stood there gawking like teenage boys who'd stumbled across their first porn flick.

"I am sure you boys have seen a lot more than what's revealed around this towel. Girls throw themselves at you all the time, prettier girls I'm sure." She spun away, refastened the already snug towel but didn't budge any further. One by one, they passed her to go to the back of the bus, although they lacked discretion.

Brett kissed her on the cheek. "You're hot, Izzy."

Zander smacked her on the ass and she jumped. "I'd do ya."

"You're giving me a hard-on, Isabelle."

Drew's words shocked her the most. Her skin tingled everywhere when he leaned in and kissed her neck. What surprised her most—she tilted her head toward him.

She froze and attempted to act as if the last few seconds never happened. Drew's kiss lingered on her skin, so without delay, she rubbed it off. Only she was pretty sure she more like caressed it. Cole still lingered behind, and her heart beat so hard her body vibrated with it.

He didn't say anything, just strode past her, and closed the door to the back room, causing the others to laugh and holler obscenities. She closed her legs a little tighter when he spun back to her with heat in his gaze. He stalked her with an expression she couldn't read. She raised her hands to grip the towel above her breasts.

"Hands down."

Her throat tightened at the command. Before she could process his intention, her lips parted, just enough to let out the breath she'd held. She lowered her arms, now covered with goose bumps, and complied with his dominance.

"How are you feeling?" He strolled toward her.

"I'm fine Cole, one-hundred-percent better," she squeaked. "A-about Drew."

He put his hands on her waist and guided her back. She twitched when her warm skin touched a cold surface of the slim amount of wall separating the rows of bunks. Before she could explain his mouth covered hers, possessed her with strength she couldn't fight. She didn't want to.

He lightened the kiss a little and teased her with his tongue. Her breath caught when he slanted his lower body into her. He was hard. What started strong morphed into a deep exploration. His tongue touched every part of her mouth, and she played the game just as well.

He tasted like a mint after a long swallow of beer. When she nipped his lip, he growled and repositioned his hand. He slid it into the slit of towel that hung open. His fingertips dug into her bare skin, and he roamed from her lips, down to her jaw, her neck, that sensitive spot just below the ear. He massaged his hand to the base of her bare butt and squeezed, molded their bodies together to support her weakened knees.

Her body tingled. She fancied the idea of wrapping her leg around him and grinding against his shaft for release.

"Did you like it when Drew kissed you here?" His lips touched where Drew's were not long ago.

"Cole," she panted. "A-about that." Her body trembled when his right hand drifted from her ass to her front, and brushed the tender skin inside her thigh. He still didn't touch her where she needed to be touched, dammit.

"I want to get to know you, every inch."

She shivered as he traced lines on her neck with his tongue. The ability to form words became so difficult. "I need to explain."

She pictured his cocky smile.

"No you don't. He gave me the finger behind your back, forced me to make a decision. It's what we do."

"You have to back off a little, and let me focus." She leaned back, just enough to see his wicked grin. Her hands clenched into fists at her sides, still down as he'd directed, but also distracted from slapping him. "Since I can't seem to say no to you, yes, I want everything you have to offer. We need to keep clear heads though, that's my only rule. No attachments. I can't stand the idea of another person left behind to mourn."

Setting the boundaries in place interrupted the eagerness to bond that brewed in his eyes. Instead, he withdrew his hand from under the towel and hugged her tight, resting his chin on her head. "I told the guys the list is real, no details. I want to do this for you, we all do. We were in an arena full of bikini-clad women sprawled out on hot rods today, yet the topic of conversation always reverted back to you. I didn't sleep well last night 'cause maybe I'd asked too much of them, but Drew is a jackass sometimes and forces me to follow my dreams. Right now, that's you."

She leaned her forehead into his chest. How could she be mad at that? They offered so much, and they didn't even know her.

"I understand why you told them. It's okay. We're okay."

He put distance between them and straightened her towel with a satisfied grin. Cold air hit her, created a need for his warm hands to touch her again. Brand her.

"Good. Now get dressed, casual. We start tonight." He whistled while he strolled to the back of the bus with his hands in his pockets. "And grab some food out of the fridge. Something tells me you're going to need to tolerate liquid courage tonight."

A beep signaled a voicemail on her phone.

When did the damn thing ring?

She rubbed her face, to clear some of the fog Cole created, and dug for her phone. Without checking who the message was from, since privacy only lasted minutes on the bus, she played it.

"Hello Isabelle, this is Dr. Peterson. I'm just inquiring about how you are feeling, and if you're ready to book your surgery? I don't want to nag, but it really should be done soon. Please call me."

Before he could finish repeating his private phone number, she hit the end button and stuffed the phone back under her pillow.

****

"Where are we going? This is so not fair. I don't like surprises, guys."

They laughed. Many experiments took place on the bus before they were confident she couldn't see through her blindfold. She sat still, calmed her breathing, and listened for clues; certain Cole sat to her left, a close left. The dead giveaway, his leg bounced hard enough to cause her body to vibrate. It was cute, though not something she would say out loud—okay, well maybe just not in front of his friends.

She tapped her fingers on the seat. He controlled her, and although she didn't know how to respond without the possibility of embarrassment, she liked it.

Each time she managed to calm her breathing, he massaged her hand with his and excited her once again. Without sight, she could interpret the contact to be more erotic than he might've intended. Maybe that was his plan?

She didn't need to see his face to note his resistance to flipping her palm over and lacing their fingers. If he conceded to his desire, she'd like it as much as him.

Instinct told her Drew sat to her right. She fought a grin that would only result in uncomfortable questions she didn't want to answer. Being teased, blindfolded between two gorgeous men—totally something she should have added to the list.

Her eyes drifted shut behind the cloth when Cole leaned into her side and tucked her hair back to whisper in her ear. The slight touch of his hand on her neck gave her goose bumps.

"Is there a problem? Your skin is a little flushed. Feeling okay?" The way he said it was not out of concern for her illness. He enjoyed this.

"Payback's a bitch, Cole."

The brush up against her other shoulder and similar smell to the Scandals T-shirt she wore to bed last night let her know Drew itched to get involved. "Is there a problem you need *my* help with?"

She couldn't take it anymore. The proximity of testosterone unraveled parts of her not touched in a really long time. "Ugh. Are we there, yet?"

Even Derek joined in on the laugh at her expense. "We're here sunshine, enjoy. Low key tonight, boys. Everything's been arranged, so call me when you're ready."

She held Cole's hand and stepped out of the car, into the cool night air. It offered relief from the heat that coated her skin in the car, but only the visible areas. Others still demanded attention. She waited for direction. Someone jerked the knot at the back of her head and the blindfold floated to the ground, revealing a flashing sign.

"Karaoke."

She took a step back, slammed into Cole's solid chest and a rush of air escaped her, whether from the impact or something more, she didn't know.

He wrapped his strong arms around her waist and sighed, followed by the most exotic hum of contentment.

His arms anchored her. She held on to him and transferred her gaze from the sign to Drew. He focused on Cole, and from the sight of his furrowed brows and the slight shake of his head, she missed something unsaid. It didn't have to be. Cole stepped back, and a cold breeze replaced the warmth on her back.

Drew stepped forward, to lead the way with his arm around her shoulders. He glanced back at Cole. "Come on sweetheart, we are *dying* to see you put on a show for *us*."

It took a second for her eyes to adjust to the darkened atmosphere. Subtle glows of gold and blue, the state's colors, highlighted the popular areas of use—the bar, and the stage. The walls had donned a symbolic motif or autographed portraits of people of significance. Quite a bit of it was tacky, but well-placed to offer a modern style. The light crowd danced and mingled to the vibration of music, however they did pause to stare when she and the men entered the roped off area. Fame did elicit special treatment *and* attention. Zander left for the bar while everyone took their seat in the booth, her in the center with Cole's arm draped around her like it were any casual day. She stared down at her twined fingers; it didn't take much focus to feel the spotlight.

"I'll get the first round."

"Make mine a double." The music ended just in time to make her voice echo. Cole tightened his embrace around her shoulders and chuckled. She giggled too.

Zander returned with empty hands and a killer grin on his face. Yes, they loved their lives. Three beautiful blondes followed him with trays of beer, a bottle of tequila, and many shot glasses ready to be used and abused.

She extracted the first glass from the woman's hand before she could set it down and drank without coming up for air.

"You boys need anything, and I mean *anything*, let us know okay?" The well-endowed blonde bent over the table, low enough to display her rack for Cole, and slid him a drink.

Isabelle coughed a fit mid chug at the innuendo.

Tramp.

Brett banged on her back with a firm hand. "No need to choke. If you're anything on stage like you are in the shower, you will have men making you offers too, hot stuff."

His wink and smile could melt the panties off any woman.

No wonder.

She sat back as women approached their table,

some for autographs and pictures, but most to flirt. The men laughed and joined in, teasing; it didn't faze them. Within an hour Brett, Zander, and Drew held women on their laps, very comfortable. She stared into her drink whenever one approached Cole. He flirted back and appeared interested in every ridiculous thing they said, but his hand, the one no one could see under the table, stayed twined with hers every time. What was that about? So caught up in the mystery of him, she didn't notice the man in front of her.

"Hello."

A beer cap hit her in the chest.

"Damn it, Zander." She snapped her head in his direction. He tipped his chin up in the other direction and she followed his gaze.

"Hello."

"Hi." She smiled wide and leaned forward to shake the attractive man's hand. The combination of painkillers and alcohol relaxed her. The label told her not to mix the two, but hello, Karaoke.

When she sat back, Cole placed his arm around her, and glared daggers at the man. He stood confident, not bothered by Cole's *back the fuck off* vibe. "Save a dance for me?"

His dimples were beautiful. "Sure."

"The stage is open, folks. Let's see who can make a scene."

She snapped her attention back to the stage.

Hoots and hollers sounded and people made their way up front to pick a song they were sure to butcher. The attractive gentleman got the hint and shuffled away when the four men harassed her and ignored his presence. Cole dropped his arm to the table, picked up his beer, and drank all of the amber-colored liquid in one swallow.

"Come on. Get that hot, young ass up there."

He leaned in to kiss the side of her head. Compliments from Drew, well, from any of them, often resulted in a tender touch and a smile filled with pride. She took a deep breath; her heart raced. "I'll go last. I want to ensure everyone's too drunk to notice me." She straightened her back and practiced the bullheaded glare she'd seen from Cole moments ago, on all of them.

"I'll always notice you."

His words in her ear were beyond exciting. Her breath hitched when he tucked his hand under the table, and squeezed her knee before he slid it up her thigh. The denim skirt and tank she changed into before they left allowed for easy access, skin-to-skin contact. He held her legs apart when she clenched her muscles to close them. Heat scorched the path he grazed with his fingers as he continued along her bare skin.

Everyone's attention was averted to the many novices who took the stage; she sat back and closed her eyes. His seductive ways overwhelmed every one of her senses. Never had she been so uninhibited in public, driven by erotic fantasy. She spread her legs further apart. He teased, traced tiny circles up both of her inner thighs. The wild woman she intended to be would've taken charge, directed his hand, and demanded that he please her. A moan escaped her lips just before he hit her sweet spot. She lowered her hand to the hem he'd hiked up, anticipated that he'd drift in another direction once again. Not this time.

"Your turn, Izzy," Brett hollered over the loud

pounding, and the music.

She had vaguely heard the many horrific renditions, but he kept her afloat a cloud of pleasure she didn't want to come down from.

"Nooo," she whispered, close to a whine.

Cole chuckled. He smoothed his hand back over the path he forged until it cleared her skirt, and gave her leg a quick tap. "You're up, darlin'."

Four pairs of eyes stared when she crashed back down to earth, and Drew's wink said it all. "Well now, Izzy, a little frustrated over there? Should make for one hell of a show, although the one we just caught was pretty damn hot."

She jostled out of her seat, a lot easier to do with alcohol in her blood and the sexual frustration that tormented her body. "You guys are asses."

They laughed and tipped their beers back. She stormed away.

****

Cole sat up, elbows on the table, and waited while she talked to the DJ. She took his breath away. The women who hit on him tonight and in front of her no less—none compared. He played along, needed to for the band's sake, but no one could hold a candle to the fiery need that washed over him when he caressed her thigh. He neared the point of no return when it came to her, and it scared him.

She can't die.

His gaze traveled down her body to her knees as she rubbed them together, uncomfortable. The corner of his mouth rose with curiosity. Did her cooling body crave more of his hand, other parts of him, perhaps? When a brief moment of sadness crossed her face, the urge to shove everyone out of the way to get to her pained him.

Laughter from the guys brought his attention back to the table and the drinks that vibrated along with his knee.

"Hey Cole, man, chill. Got it bad, don't ya?" Before Drew could finish his inquisition, the music started and all four men froze, their attention stolen by her tenacity. She belted out the words to Nickelback's *If Today Was Your Last Day*.

The crowd joined in with the lyrics but the men only mumbled curses. Brett, Zander, and Drew shoved the groupies off their laps, their grumbles at the rejection not even on the men's radar. Cole glanced at his friends while they stared at the stage and if he presumed right, somewhat in awe of her strength, but also concerned.

He rubbed his thighs, forced himself from the seat, and before it hit him, stood in front of the stage. Her confidence fooled the crowd and maybe that's what she needed right now, but he didn't buy it. The dance floor thinned out when her song finished, and the DJ announced last call, but they continued to stare at one another.

A slow song calmed the room around them, set the pace for a dramatic night's end. He extended his arms, grabbed hold of her waist, and lowered her to the floor in front of him. Her body grazed his on the way down and ignited more friction between them than their clothes alone could produce. "Dance with me?"

He didn't wait for an answer, just seized her beautiful torso and swayed with his chin on top of her head. "You could have picked a song a little more…*uplifting*."

She leaned back and peered up at him. "Would you have preferred, *Live Like You Were Dying* by Tim McGraw?"

He clenched his jaw and narrowed his eyes at her. If their roles were reversed, he'd act the same way, but they weren't, and that was too far.

"Cole," she sighed. "I'm trying to cope with the worst news of my entire life for the second time. Cut me some slack." With her head held high, her gaze lowered to his chest. "Please."

He'd absorb her pain if that were possible, lessen the agony in her eyes. He'd store it with his own, wear the burden for her. He touched her chin with his hand and their gazes met before resting his forehead to hers.

"Please."

She didn't need to plead with him for help to forget. He held her face in his palms, crushed his lips down on hers, and forced his tongue inside. It wasn't a moment to be gentle; desperation to be in an entranced state of mind overpowered him. He needed to touch her, all of her, but didn't feel she was ready to delve *that* deep into her list. She could stop him at any time, and he'd be fine with that, but until then, he'd test her limits. He lowered his hands from her face and down her front, over the swells of her soft breasts. She moaned as he brushed his thumbs over her peaked nipples and continued down to her hips. He urged her backward, to a secluded area. When her back hit the wall he cupped her ass and molded his body to hers, but it wasn't enough. He broke away from the sweet taste of her mouth and kissed down her jaw, her neck, her collarbone. She ran her fingers through his hair and fisted the untamed locks. If she urged him down, he'd oblige her every demand.

"Cole." The last frayed thread of restraint within him broke at the sound of his name on her lips. He slid his hands down, below the hem of her skirt and massaged up again, raising the material with them. Her legs trembled. "You have to stop me," he panted. "'Cause I won't stop until I'm balls deep inside you, and this isn't the place for that to happen."

"Damn right, it isn't." Drew tapped him on the shoulder and yanked him back. "Derek's on his way with the car. How about you take it somewhere there *aren't* cellphone cameras. We've already promised tickets to tomorrow night's show in order to get people to delete pictures. It's a sold-out show."

Cole smiled at her when she panicked, scrambling to fix her skirt but couldn't do a damn thing about the flush of her skin. "Oh my God, I'm so sorry. I will pay for the tickets."

Drew tossed a cocky glance at him before turning back to her. "Relax sweetheart. It isn't the first bribe for pictures."

He elbowed Drew. "Did you at least send them to my phone before you deleted them?"

She smacked him. He held his shoulder and pretended to be in pain but couldn't maintain the charade without a glint of amusement.

"Cole Davies." Her shriek only incited howls and fist bumps. Drew tugged her from the wall by the hand, toward the exit. "You'll have to take that up with Zander, buddy. I am pretty sure they're on his phone though. We're gonna have to get his number changed—again." He leaned down to kiss her cheek and winked before he flashed a grin over his shoulder. “Make sure to send me a copy if you get your hands on them. It gave *me* a hard-on watching.”

Cole held the door open and composed himself into the perfect gentleman, albeit an overdramatic one.

“Pfft.” She elbowed him on the way by.

She stared out the window of the car, very quiet. Did he go too far? He didn’t regret it. He was falling for her, hard. He let his head tip back to the seat and sighed when he laced their fingers, and she didn’t stop him.

The cool night air didn’t fix a thing, he was still hard enough to pound nails, and her scent lingered on his skin.

The guys climbed the stairs of the bus first, and he’d followed their lead, until she squeezed his hand to hold him back. “Cole, we need to talk.”

“Yes Isabelle, we do. You said something at the bar, about getting news for a second time. What did you mean?” He raised her hand up to his mouth for a kiss, but this time she rejected him.

When he took a step forward, she held her hand up between them. “Well, the news of my diagnosis was terrible. It changed my life.”

He nodded and fisted his hands. It hurt to see her glance anywhere but at him. He’d tell her she could trust him with anything, but more experienced than most, trust didn’t always come easy.

“I’m married.”

Now he stepped back.

She held her hands in the air. “David Chambers is my husband, or, *was* my husband. Not so long ago a police officer, and family friend, showed up at my door.” She lowered her rigid arms to her sides, hands also fisted. "David was killed in a motor vehicle accident. We were only married for two years."

A single tear rolled down her cheek. He stepped to her with his hand raised, not quite sure if wiping the moisture from her face would do any good. Could any act of empathy erase that kind of loss? Before he could try, she shoved him away, but this time it hit him more like a punch to the heart.

"I need to fulfill this list before I get on the operating table. Never in a million years did I imagine this—" She pointed from him to her. "—would happen. I want to continue, but without all these feelings. I refuse to leave behind more loved ones than I have to." She darted onto the bus before he could respond.

Did she just imply that she could love me?

Chapter Eight

Dear Diary,
With the depth of his gaze, the weight of his words, how could I not?

Cole rubbed the back of his neck as he trod the stairs of the bus. *Could this get any more complicated?*

Derek mumbled, but he ignored it, plucked a beer from the fridge, and continued to the back of the bus. If space was what she required, he'd give her some, but the grief in her eyes damn near killed him. His suspicion she'd built a familiar barrier between them was confirmed when he stood in the doorway. Only the guys were there.

"She went to bed." Drew held out another drink after he downed the first in one long swallow. "You okay?" He didn't let go even though Cole now gripped it too. Temptation to go after her nagged at him, the anchor helped. "No."

Drew let go and nudged his head toward the lounge.

When he glanced at her bunk, the pale light glowed behind the curtain and he could hear the faint turn of a page. He closed his eyes and pinched the bridge of his nose as he stepped in to join the guys, and closed the door behind him.

****

The bus slowed to a stop, and the driver who'd taken over so Derek could get some sleep yawned. Ohio. He didn't check the time when they crashed, but it couldn't have been long ago. The hum of the road didn't drown out the many text message alerts from her phone, and it took all his willpower not to slide the curtain back and demand *he* be the one she talked to. She consumed him now, much like last night, and he didn't know how to stop the free fall. His father's words kept coming back to him.

If you find her Cole, fight like hell to keep her.

His father regretted he hadn't done that for his mother, but how could he fight for someone who didn't belong to him, wasn't guaranteed long term?

"I may not be able to fight *for* her, but I will fight *with* her." A rush of adrenaline hit him when the idea of her failing to complete the list made his own life feel incomplete. He glanced down at himself, shook his head, and rushed out of the bus with his phone. Arrangements for her list, with his resources, could be fast-tracked.

****

Cole skipped up the stairs a little lighter on his feet, until his gaze fell on Drew propped against her bunk, rubbing her back. His heart raced. With all she'd confessed so far, any number of things could be wrong. He ran to her in a fog much like the slow motion of a horror movie. The bottle of water and acetaminophen came into view, so he lightened his steps and winced. "Another headache?"

He glared at Drew's smugness, a little too amused, seeing his best friend fall apart over a girl.

"Hangover."

He ran his fingers through his hair, and over exaggerated his exhale. "Izzy dear, you are aging me. I have a rock star image to maintain. That won't be easy with a cane." He smoothed her hair back so he could see her beautiful eyes and leaned forward, to place a light kiss on her forehead. She groaned. He chuckled so deep, his entire upper torso shook with it.

"Ugh, not so loud. How the hell do you guys do it? Do you have the tolerance of elephants?"

When she let her eyes drift closed at his touch, a piece of the wall he built around himself for years crumbled. Drew patted his shoulder and edged away. She opened her eyes again, with a glint of something he couldn't define. Need, maybe? Being on the road for years with a group of men didn't offer much opportunity to take care of someone, to feel needed. The real kind of needed.

He bit his bottom lip. What happened last night still lay heavily on his mind but he didn't want to provoke her into giving him all he longed for, to know everything about her. He'd been so focused on a label for his attraction to her he neglected to consider what type of baggage she brought with her. To know she had baggage, much like the rest of them, only made the desire to know her stronger. He kissed her forehead once more. His plans for tonight might offer them the opportunity to discover more, in many ways.

"I have a surprise for you."

"Oh really, and what would that be?" She put her hands over her eyes and sighed. "Please tell me I won't need liquid courage, my liver needs a break."

He placed his hands over hers and guided them until they were held in place, above her head. The motion stilled her distress, but lifted her shirt. Her black panties, sheer enough to see through, didn't distract him from her pulse racing against his hand. He ignored his body's involuntary advance in her direction and covered her with the blanket. He couldn't form words while imagining climbing on top of her.

She giggled as if she understood his silent behavior.

"Better. Now, the venue we are playing at tonight is a hotel/casino. What that means is we get a night off this bus." He raised his eyebrows. "We get a private room. With a large bed. You know, to sleep in or whatever. There may even be a bucket list item I could help you with, if you'll stay with me?"

With his hands gripped on the edge of her bed, he backed away and dropped his gaze to the floor, whispering the last few words. He acted like a teenager again, asking a girl out on their first date. Only more concerned about the nightcap rather than the date.

"Cole?"

"Yes?"

"Are you sure you will be up for it after the show?"

His laugh echoed. "Uh yeah." He stuffed his clammy hands in his pockets and bounced on his toes. "My hand could use the break."

Chuckles murmured from the back of the bus. Yeah, privacy would be nice for a night.

****

"I see the way you watch her." Drew spoke under his breath so the other guys didn't hear. Not that they would anyway over the pompous banter that always ensued during a game of hoops in their typical concealed location at the venue. Passing time. Maybe he could convince Tony to arrange for a private, high-rollers room in the casino. It'd been a while since he'd seen Brett dump a fortune.

"Cole?"

"Drop it, man." He threw the ball up and missed.

"She's a beautiful woman Cole, who doesn't even know it. That alone makes her desirable, much more than what we see every day out on the road. You didn't ever look at Alexis the way you do her. This is different. It kills me too, ya know, that she has this list. I don't want to pry, but what is wrong with her? You said the list is real, but never said any more."

He lowered his gaze and scuffed his shoes on the pavement. The ball hit him in the chest. He picked it up and lobbed it to Zander. The game continued, but he veered for the curb. Drew followed.

"Look." He sat down and scrubbed his face, not sure how much information to give. He'd promised. "The list, it's real. I gave her my word and with her, that needs to mean something. The hopelessness in her eyes when she told me was—"

He made sure no one else stood in earshot, but he could trust Drew. "After the list is done, she's having surgery. The odds aren't good, and it's killing me. You're right, she has me tied up in knots, and I don't know what to do about it. Don't bust my balls about it. Please."

"Shit. I don't know what to say, man. She's so young, and beautiful. I'm a little jealous I didn't get to her tweet first."

He leaned his shoulder into Cole and they swayed. "I'm not going to say my usual don't get attached. I think you already are. What I will say is, whatever happens we're here for you, and that will never change. Let me know if you need my help making plans." He elbowed him in the ribs and chuckled. "Or, if you need a break, I could take over an item or two."

The game, like always, morphed into a full-out contact sport in front of them. "Something about that woman makes me want to give her the world. So let's get one thing straight, I want her, for as long as I can have her. If that means I get crushed in the end, so be it. I won't have her going into surgery feeling incomplete." His gaze dropped to the ground. "I know that feeling all too well. It sucks."

He stood up, and tilted his head from side to side. He needed to get his head back in the game. "I'll let you know when I need your help, and I'm sure I will. I can't thank you guys enough for this, and don't think I am oblivious to her impact on everyone. I see it."

He held out his hand and Zander passed him the ball. Swish. Back in the game.

****

The day raced by. It wouldn't have been the end of the world if it'd dragged a little. Her stomach was in knots about which bucket-list item he had planned. With little on the agenda and lots of down time, sound check along with fan greets ended before she could blink. And already, she stood off to the side with the best view. The opening act finished their set and introduced the Scandals. She couldn't imagine being out in this crowd, the heart of the beast. She smiled, totally a groupie.

The guys paced, fiddled with drumsticks or guitar picks, and in general, appeared skittish. "Do you guys get nervous before a show, after all these years?"

“Yes,” they answered in unison.

She laughed so hard tears formed in her eyes. She loved these guys. Her back stiffened. She glimpsed at their expressions to find out if that had come out of her mouth. The girls used that word a lot last night while texting. Must be that.

“Get walking, guys.”

She jumped and glared at the man who yelled right behind her.

Brett, Zander, and Drew climbed the stairs first. Her eyes widened and her mouth formed a silent O when the three men kissed her on the cheek as they passed, like some kind of good luck charm. The wall of ice she’d worked so hard to build the night before melted a little. She spun on her toes with a smile, knowing who would be next and lost the ability to talk.

Engulfed in his heated embrace, he ignored the second cue to get his ass out on stage and kissed her as if tomorrow would never come. She’d have fallen into a puddle of lust if he hadn’t held on so tight. His body was firm against hers but his lips were soft, warm. He broke away, but still held on and displayed the most adorable dimples.

“Well, this is a first for me.”

She stared at him until he nudged his very hardened length into her.

“Usually the hard-on doesn’t come until after the show.” He tore himself away and winked on his way to the stairs. With his fist in the air, he ran on stage as if he’d just won over more than the fans. Her heart beat in rhythm with their chants because he had.

She replaced his arms with hers and stared in adoration. The group of men she’d come to care for motivated people and had created boisterous commotion in a room quiet only hours ago. Never in her life had she imagined standing backstage, with a lanyard around her neck that named her as a special part of the band. And also with bragging rights from experience, able to say she preferred the *real* men behind those instruments.

They played the crowd with a skill that convinced every woman and man they were doing a private performance just for them. It worked just as well on her. He sang rough, and with an edge. But when he started their newest single "Dazed," the slower melody of his voice would melt the panties off any woman. Her eyes widened, but her smile faded as he extended his arm, and caught a large red bra before it hit him in the face. He held it up to the crowd and their excitement increased. She tightened her arms around herself, and leaned up on tiptoe to see around the speaker. The owner of said bra beamed at him. Her fists clenched and an instant hair-pulling altercation entered her mind.

She stalked over to the wall, out of view, and dug out her phone. She needed to get her head on straight.

Ok Ladies, am I doing the right thing? He wants me to spend the night with him at the hotel after tonight's show to work on.... the list. Plus, some blonde well-endowed woman, by a talented surgeon nonetheless, just whipped her bra on stage at him and well...should I really be feeling the need drag her off by her hair?

Send.

She tapped her phone on her thigh and huffed. The usual commotion backstage held her attention. The girls were mindful of keeping their phones close while she was away, but it didn't compare to having them there with her. Her phone vibrated in her hand, ring tones being useless when the guys were loud enough to make the floor pulse beneath her.

I am dying to know what he is like in the sack so if you don't give me details after, I may take you out by your hair. It's just a performance for the crowd. Taryn

If what I've heard is true.... I'm jealous of you. You have spent a lot of time with them. Feelings will come with that sweetie. Don't read too much into it or you won't enjoy yourself. Katherine

If you can manage Kindergarten kids, you can handle groupies. Immature, needy, have a lot to learn.... ring a bell? Abigail

She put her phone back in her pocket and the tightness in her chest eased; the girls were right. She inhaled deep to avoid tears, not wanting to be too hypersensitive about the loss of time with them while she pursued her list.

She paced. When the encore ended, she stopped with her back to the stage. The crowd went wild and more bras were sure to be thrown. The first hard smack on her ass startled her. Unlike the sweet kisses she reveled in pre-show, she now imagined herself with a reddened behind as each man landed a blow and laughed on their way by.

"Your backside must be a very pretty shade of red. I'll take it easy on you, for now," he murmured from behind and held her hips while he pressed his sweaty body against her back, still hard everywhere. She trembled.

"You're shaking. Are you okay? Do you need a doctor?" He spun her around; concern filled his eyes.

Up on tiptoe, and only a breath away from his lips, she whispered back. “Cole. I’m really nervous about later, that’s all. Although, if you are a good boy, I’ll let you play doctor and examine me to make sure.”

His hands, still at her waist, tightened. He inched them up and her top rose as well. A low groan passed his lips. He stroked her soft, bare flesh and leaned into her lips but still didn’t follow through. “You’re killing me, sweetheart.”

The heat of his breath hit hers and she fisted his sweaty T-shirt. Her gaze scanned his and all sorts of images that excited her, entered her mind. Cole on his knees in front of her, licking her swollen nub. On his back in bed while she rode him, touching herself and driving him insane. Better yet, his strong hand down the front of her pants right now, stroking *that* spot.

His laugh wrenched her from a fantasy unfinished. “Why Isabelle, do tell what wicked little dreams you’re having right now?” The bulge in the front of his pants touched her abdomen.

“Not little at all.” Before she had time to think or talk herself out of it, she smoothed her hands up his chest and laced them behind his neck. She closed the slight gap between them and licked his lip with the tip of her tongue. The salty taste of him added to her hunger, to have him in ways she’d never had anyone.

It didn’t cross her mind people might have been nearby. She needed him. Every time he deepened the contact, she wiggled away, set the pace. It wasn’t difficult to figure out he usually got his own way sexually, that he dominated his prey. Not this time.

His eyes drifted closed and he gripped her while she kissed him, with only enough pressure to feel her lips, but not satisfy. When she broke their contact, they both panted, fought the urge to go further. He traced a line along her jaw with his finger and stared into her eyes.

For the first time since meeting him, his experience with intimacy sparked her curiosity. What was his life like before her? The corner of her mouth rose. Did he fight dirty or was he always a charmer? She brushed her thighs together, imagined an argument with him, which she'd win. Would he apologize to her, up against a wall?

"Damn. There's an after party in Brett's room that I was going to ask you to, but I don't know if I can even make it to the shower without ripping your clothes off."

A sound. If she had to guess, Drew coughed in the distance. She giggled, "I would love to go to the party. Go take a *cold* shower." She unlaced her fingers, dropped them to his ass, and yanked him in tight. The bold action stirred his arousal. "You don't dare take care of that in the shower. That is mine."

He squeezed his eyes shut tight and muttered something a lot like *Lord, help me.*

****

He jabbed at the button for the elevator to descend, now, and counted in his head with the numbers as they reversed.

"This VIP fan stuff is nothing you haven't seen already. It'd bore you. Really, you won't miss anything. We're just gonna shower, get it over with, and come find ya. Feel free to get the party started for us." He slowed his nervous ramble and stuffed his hands into his back pockets, as if he wasn't trying to get rid of her, even though, he was. The elevator he nudged her into closed, and he let his stressed shoulders drop.

He distracted her from certain parts of their life; didn't know if what they had could stand the test. The other guys would invite ladies of choice back to the room with them, and the fans they were on their way to meet…well, played along with it. He didn't want to expose her to the kind of behavior he now believed was immature, that they exhibited in order to maintain their image.

Maybe the reason for the mood swings before her? He loved to sing rock music, but the image grew tiresome and this VIP experience, no different than the others. Women fondled him, and he smiled for pictures. He adored his fans; even the ones without restraint were a little entertaining. But she waited for him, and no amount of cleavage or grabby hands sparked his desire or attention. He could only imagine what the pictures the fans took were going to turn out like.

****

He hit the elevator button that would take them to the top floor and to her. The number increased overhead and he stuffed his hands in his pockets. Female giggles from behind drew his gaze to the reflections on the walls. The men held beautiful women, one in each arm, except him. He shook his head and chuckled. That would have been his reflection not long ago, and it now seemed like a thing of the past, which didn't bother him in the least.

He punched the button again. Drew scoffed at him in the mirrored walls, so he raised his hand over his shoulder, and gave him the finger with a glare he couldn't maintain. When the elevator stopped, the doors opened, and he rushed out. The people who came and went from Brett's room forced his stride to lengthen, more so when several attractive, *normal* men paraded in.

"Great selection in there tonight, boss man." After quick handshakes with backslapping hugs, he passed the bodyguards and drilled his way through the crowd in Brett's room. As usual, obscenities were hollered by the crew and several other people. There was never a shortage of praise for the Scandals.

He punched his fist to his palm when he couldn't find her. The beautiful blonde who stared out the window while every man in the room ogled her, twirled around and smiled. She lowered her gaze to the floor. He let his arms drop to his sides.

Wow.

Someone tugged at his shoulder from behind. "I totally dug the schoolteacher getup, but damn. She can rock me anytime." Zander bumped into his side and passed him. He slapped the idiot on the back of the head, but he didn't flinch, just rubbed his head and laughed.

Every little inch of fabric on her, *just* covered the parts he hadn't seen yet. He pursued her with slow determined steps. She stood tall in heels, wearing a ripped denim mini skirt that showed off her long, creamy-white legs. What caught his attention the most was the black halter tied around her neck and lower back. The closer he got, the more his heart pounded. Two perky little peaks appeared, hard, and there was only one reason for such a great view—no bra. He raised his eyebrows and adjusted the front of his pants a few steps away, letting her know she affected him in ways he would show her soon. A pink hue formed on her pale, white cheeks. "Isabelle."

"Cole."

"Can I get you a drink? A sweater, perhaps?"

Her gaze lowered to the silky black material before returning to him, with a twinkle in her eye.

"I changed, I hope you don't mind. I would love a drink, and I can assure you, I'm not cold."

He threw his head back and laughed at the innocence in her eyes, accompanied by a confidence he hadn't seen before. He mumbled and strolled away, a little more uncomfortable in his swagger to get her a drink. Yeah, this was going to be a fun night.

****

Glued to her side, he checked his watch often. Men showered her with attention, and it drove him nuts. The laser-beam glares he gave them didn't sway their decision to approach her.

"Relax buddy, she's going back to your room tonight." Brett put his arm around her. With his gaze on Cole's scowl, he snuggled her in closer and grinned. The three he could trust with her didn't bother him; the other barbarians in the room were a different story.

He crossed his arms, and huffed with annoyance when she strolled away under Brett's arm, composed with that same wicked grin. He came on strong, yes, but couldn't stop it in time. Did she need space from him?

He spun to face the floor to ceiling windows and leaned his forehead against the cold glass. His warm breath fogged the city lights outside. When he circled back to the crowded room, she stood still at the bedroom door, her jaw dropped in the cutest form of shock. It didn't take much to imagine what took place in that room; it could make a dead person's heart race.

He sauntered over to the bar, and without delay, received a shot of Jack Daniels. The pretty bartender hired for the evening had, on past occasions, made for a rather interesting evening, but not tonight. He leaned back with his elbows on the bar and surveyed the room.

Pride swelled in him when Drew shook his head with a smile at a man who held out an object and swayed off balance. They had a pact about drugs—do them and you're out.

Drew didn't make a scene out of it, just passed the man and made his way over to the bedroom. He hugged Isabelle from behind. She touched his arm with her hand and leaned into his words. Her gaze dropped to the floor and a blush covered her skin when he whispered in her ear. He didn't linger, or pressure her, just chuckled and moseyed into the room.

The sudden temptation to make the rose-colored hue that Drew started, deepen, overwhelmed him. He shoved away from the bar. Her need for distance drove her away earlier, but he decided she'd had enough.

He strode to the bedroom and the same man as before held out a vial; he shook his head. While he continued forward, he signaled to one of the guards with the slight raise of his chin in the man's direction. The problem would be taken care of with little commotion, so he focused on her.

His gaze traveled from the heels on her feet, up the length of her body, over each beautiful curve. His heart raced. She touched the side of her face with one hand, and the doorjamb with the other. The soft satin of her back was on display, along with the flush that tempted him to trace its path with his fingers. He longed to explore the exact locations where the sweet, yet spicy vanilla scent lingered. He wrapped his arms around her, the silk top so delicate and thin his skin warmed from her body heat. They admired the woman and two men, in the throes of extreme ecstasy.

He leaned into her ear. “Adding to your list?”

“I don’t think so, but I can’t seem to stop myself from watching.”

He nipped her earlobe and smiled. “Good. I don’t want to share you. Are your panties wet?”

With a large inhale of breath, her chest expanded under his embrace before she nodded and rotated in his arms, ever so slowly, to face him. He stepped forward and forced her back against the door. It banged into the wall.

She slid her hands under his shirt, and latched onto his sides for support. Since the day they met, his dreams involved her touch, and now that he had it, the contact created more pleasure than he’d imagined. Every gaze in the room might be focused on them, but his remained on her. The most beautiful blue eyes, parted lips waiting to be ravished, and just as he liked, the pulse at her neck raced. He placed his hands up on the door to cage her in. Her lips shined with a sweet gloss that drew him in. He stared at them as long as he could in his slow decent to claim her. The first taste on his tongue overpowered him, and he lost all control.

She moaned into his mouth and massaged her hands up his body. Her warm, soft touch became a demand when she scratched her nails through the hair at the back of his scalp. She used the tangled grip to pull him in deeper. A growl escaped him.

When she arched into him, he lowered his hands from the door and slid them over the silk that covered her stomach, to the soft, bare skin behind. He caressed his way up to the sides of her breasts. The thin material floated away from her skin and invited him in. He inched his thumbs inside, and stroked her bare nipples until they hardened to stiff points.

Her body trembled against him. He broke the kiss, needed to see the beautiful, undiluted pleasure on her face. Would she come from the stimulation alone?

She dropped her hands to her sides and her eyes drifted closed, fell back to the door, and surrendered to his touch. He slid the thin fabric of her top aside with his thumb, until her rose-colored peak was bared to him. He brushed his fingertip over it and lowered his head, to take it into his mouth.

"Fuck"

He fixed her top with caution not to startle her and glared over his shoulder.

"Every time Drew. Every time."

He shook his head at Drew, who stroked himself through his jeans. "Buzz off, man." He squared his attention on her, now aware of her current state, and lowered his forehead to hers. "As much as I want to beat him right now for stopping us, again, how 'bout we go back to our room? The idea of claiming you right here, right now, makes me hard as steel."

He angled into her midsection, letting her know he spoke nothing but the truth. "I want you alone, first. Not in front of these goons."

She bit her lip as though she endured the same urgency and temptation to give in to the moment.

"Okay."

He clasped his hand with hers and yanked, steered her from the room when a cushion hit him in head.

"Go easy on the woman."

Drew laughed but Cole was confident his best friend would soon find a woman interested in blowing out the spark he and Isabelle lit.

****

He touched her every inch of the way, which made the distance to the elevator a challenge. He stopped every few steps in the hallway and kissed her into complete oblivion. A great video if he could get his hands on the security footage.

He'd asked for their room to be far away from the others, on another floor. No drunken fools were going to find them and ruin what he planned. She broke their connection and pressed the button for the elevator. Cold air filled the small amount space between them. When she stepped in close once again, the lust in her eyes grew wild, sure to reflect his own. She stood on tiptoe and laced her hands around his neck. Not being one to pass up an opportunity, he smoothed his hands down her back, placed them on her ass, and squeezed to lift her. "Let me help you, darlin'."

With her legs wrapped around his waist, he stared into her eyes, and his shoulders relaxed. They fit, perfectly. The elevator doors opened and he ushered them in, hit the button, and pinned her body to the wall. She grabbed the back of his head and kissed him with a force that drove him mad.

A faint ding sang out when they arrived at their floor, but she didn't stop, nor did he want her to. He adjusted her skirt to cover her, and resisted, for now, the urge to slide his hands up underneath and feel how wet she was. Thank God, the room wasn't far.

She startled at the sound of the door behind them,

and showcased beautiful, swollen lips. The haze of lust in her eyes captured him. He kissed the tip of her nose and smiled.

"Well, Mr. Davies. You have some talent. Without much of a view, other than me, you managed to get us here rather quickly. The ability to multi-task is one of my favorite qualities in a person." She wiggled, forcing his hands to loosen so she could right herself on the floor.

He took a step forward. "Oh, honey, you will soon find out just how skilled I am at multi-tasking."

She retreated at his advance and put her hands up. He stuffed his fisted hands in his front pockets.

"Cole. It's been a while. I would be lying if I said I wasn't a little nervous. Can we slow this down?"

That's fair. He let his shoulders drop and released his fisted hands from the confines of his tight jeans. When he stepped toward her again, she stiffened but didn't signal him to stop. "We can take this slow, very slow. I want to savor every moment."

He held out his hand, smiled when she placed hers in it. With a small tug, he guided her into him and wrapped his arms around her. Things were moving fast. He kissed the top of her head and swayed with her in his arms; let her make the next move. Her honesty, strength to share all she had so far, attested to how special she was. He'd treat her that way, even if the vulnerability of it hurt him. Again.

She shoved her hands up between them, gave herself the distance she needed to drop her attention to the floor and close herself off.

"Isabelle? What is it?"

She didn't budge, just traced the pattern on the

carpet with her toe. "Cole. Forget it. I don't want to spoil things." She spun on her toes and traipsed about the room as if she pondered a burden that nagged at her.

He let her. It didn't take a genius to tell something weighed her down.

He lowered his gaze and wandered back to the door to lock it. His hand trembled as he raised it to the deadbolt. With slow, even breaths, he waited until the twitch faded, didn't want her to misinterpret it as apprehension.

She stared out the window when he returned. He didn't want any secrets between them. "Izzy? You can tell me anything, I won't get angry. We barely know each other, and the things you want, well, they will be more enjoyable if you can trust me."

At the noticeable, safe distance, she faced him and a tear ran down her cheek. "Cole." She held her hand up to stop him before he could even try this time.

He stood stiff, his toes curled into the floor and he pounded his outer thighs with fisted hands. He'd take a step back from the hurt in her eyes, but moments ago, their combined touch eased all discomfort. They could get that back.

"David, my husband, he was a good man."

"I gather that. I see it in your eyes when you speak of him." Lucky bastard. Ugh, he couldn't be threatened by a man who no longer lived.

"Things were good with him, but I wanted more and even asked for it. What I seem to have with you. He died, maybe feeling like he wasn't enough for me. He was."

Her guilt, an unfortunate outcome of being true to herself and not able to predict the future, struck him from where he stood. Relief washed over him when she crossed her arms and let her shoulders drop. A way to let him close again but still not close enough.

He continued forward and sat on the edge of the bed. She inched in front of him but still didn't give him the clarity he searched for in her red-rimmed eyes.

"I guess what I am saying is, I'm scared of what I'll be leaving behind. I don't want these experiences to make me angrier about—"

He put his hands on her waist, urged her closer. "I think you are the strongest person I have ever met in my entire life." Water pooled in his eyes but he blinked to hold it back. "No man would ever feel inadequate with you, he'd feel lucky. There is something about you that just makes us naturally strive to give you more, without reservation.

"I have no doubt if David were still alive, your friends would tease you without restraint about never spending time with them because you and David would have found something too damn enjoyable to leave home, even for a moment." He smiled up at her. After tonight, he too, would have a hard time letting go. He brushed his hand along her jaw and wiped the tear from her cheek with his thumb.

She mirrored his smile and let her arms, crossed in front, fall to her sides and relax. "You certainly know how to say the right thing. Thank you."

Chapter Nine

Dear Diary,
I wouldn't take it back, but it scared me…

The calluses on his hands scratched over her silk top. He massaged the hem of the delicate material between his thumbs and forefingers, and lifted it to expose her flat yet soft midsection. She stared into his eyes, could see the desperation sure to be a reflection of her own, and nodded when he stilled. She needed this.

He slid forward on the bed, held her gaze until no longer possible and kissed her just above the navel. She secured her palms to his shoulders, her head fell back, and she moaned.

His words comforted her, allowed a connection of trust that until now, was only a fantasy. He didn't even flinch at David's name, and yet here she was, jealous over groupies throwing their underwear at him on stage.

She closed her eyes and focused more on him. His lips on her belly were warm as they roamed. The trail of moisture left in their path cooled and made goose bumps form on her skin. He sustained just the right amount of pressure in order to make her crave more. With his lips a breath away from her skin, he hovered as though he'd continue the torturous path, but he didn't. Her body ached for him to get on with it. She let go of his shoulders and grasped his hair, understood his test of her readiness, but my God…

He chuckled and kissed her in the same spot once more, before he strayed over to her hip. His hands shook as he sought out the waistband of her skirt in order to tug it down, and continue lower. She shivered.

Encompassed in his arms, he held the rear clasp and paused to seek out her approval. She nodded with slow seduction, her lip caught hard between her teeth to refrain from mimicking an excited bobble head. He closed his eyes for a moment and sighed. Their gaze held while he lowered the zipper on her skirt, at a pace that made his hand pause after every tooth gave way. He wasn't kidding when he said they'd go slow. Her anticipation built to an extreme high, his every touch teased her.

When the skirt loosened, it fell lower on her hips and showed off her lacy, black panties. She ran her fingers through his hair and he dropped his forehead to her waist with an exhale of breath. This was it, the loss of control she'd fantasized about.

The skirt fell to the floor with a slight shake of her hips, a way to tease him back. She fidgeted behind her waist, then neck, and let the delicate material float to the floor. He gripped the bed and admired her through half-lidded eyes as she stood there in front of him, sans bra.

His Adam's apple bobbed with a deep swallow before he traced a line with his finger from her belly button down to her smoothly waxed mound. "God, you're beautiful. The smell of your arousal is making my mouth water. I'm dying to taste your cum."

Her body quivered, and she stared at him to see if he detected her contentedness with his wild nature.

Never had anyone spoken with such blatant sexuality to her; she loved it. She squeezed her legs together. Her body wound so tight in response, it wouldn't take much for the long overdue release.

"Let me take care of you, baby." He stood up, placed his hands on her bare hips, and directed her back onto the bed. "Lean back, hands or elbows on the bed, whichever is more comfortable. Spread your legs for me." The smile on his face when she did so, without hesitation, spoke volumes. He loved the slight edge of control.

Something in his voice shook her to the core. The way he held her gaze, used his hands to help her lie back before he stood tall and grabbed the hem of his shirt to lift it over his head—wow. It shouldn't have surprised her he would tend to her first. He'd been doing it for days. The dimple in his cheek when he smiled said Boy Scout, but she doubted he collected any badges.

Her eyes dried as she stared to take in every inch of his muscled, tattooed body. She didn't want to miss a detail. From her angle, his dirty-blond hair and blue eyes magnified his godlike body. What would the scruff along his jaw feel like scouring her? And, until now, men with pierced ears wouldn't grab her attention. For him, it worked.

Dampness swelled between her thighs while she imagined using her teeth to tug at the silver studs. He smoothed his hands up her thighs, brought her back to the moment, and held her legs open so he could stare at her. He lowered to his knees.

Right now, she needed him inside her but, oh God, the other parts of her body he could flirt with too. His smile exuded all kinds of sin. She may never recover from this night. He blew the slightest breath over her swollen nub. Even when she tried, she couldn't stop the shudders that raced with her pulse.

"Cole."

He smiled and traced his finger around her opening, never with quite the amount of pressure she needed.

She squirmed. "Damn you Cole, I will haunt you."

He chuckled and continued the same torturous path with his tongue. Her juices flowed with every scratch of his stubble, the friction more sensual than she'd imagined. His moan of pleasure overwhelmed her. She let her head fall back and eyes close.

"Look at me, baby. I want to see you when you come."

She lifted her head and glared at him. "Then you better hurry, or I make no promises about using my teeth on you."

He shook his head and laughed at her. "Feisty. I like it. Hang on tight."

She scowled at him when he lowered to lick her once again with a teasing smile on his face. This time he inserted his fingers inside her, palm up, and drew her clit into his mouth to suck on it, hard.

A tidal wave flowed through her unlike anything she'd experienced before. It tingled, developed into wave after wave of pleasure. He took in her reactions, responded to them in all the right ways. When he curled his fingers up with just the right amount of pressure, she grappled for the sheets and arched her back.

"Oh God, I can't stop it." The muscles in her body clenched and she struggled to keep her eyes open. His touch created a sensation beyond ecstasy, and she could no longer control its urgency. Her toes curled when he rubbed that spot, oh that spot, and all ability to hold back gave way. A rush of excitement burst inside her and she came, erupted like a firework that'd shot into the air with an anticipated whistle, and exploded. She rubbed against his face without resistance, until warmth flooded her. She latched onto his hair with sweaty palms and grinded against his tongue to draw out her release.

When the tremors subsided, he licked the last bit of pleasure to gush from her body, but she forced him away, the sensitivity too much.

He drew his fingers out, put them in his mouth, and moaned. "Mmm, tastes better than I imagined. Hope you're not too spent. We're just getting started, sweetheart."

She collapsed back onto the bed. Never had she come like that and yes, she'd heard about "the spot," but didn't really think of herself as having one. Sex with David was great, even in its routine, but this was so much more.

"Wow. Wow."

He laughed. "So I'm guessing you've never had a G-spot orgasm before?" He leaned back onto his heels with his eyebrows raised. His smile glistened with her climax. "I gotta tell ya Isabelle, you taste incredible. Not ever have I needed to work so hard to keep up with a woman. I could eat you all night."

He winked at her with a devilish grin. "But I hope you don't think I am done with you yet." He stood and unzipped his pants.

She leaned up on her elbows again, studied him

while he hooked his thumbs in his pants and lowered them to the floor. "No, I haven`t. I thought a woman's G-spot was a myth made up by men, to, you know, get more sex."

She tilted her head to the side. "Commando hey?"

He kicked his pants aside and stroked himself with a gleam in his eyes that stirred her excitement once again. "Underwear is overrated." He climbed on the bed, placing gentle kisses up her body. She reclined with him while he crawled over her. His hard length captured her entire view and she swallowed hard.

"Like what you see?" He kissed the tip of her nose.

"I don't think that will fit."

His laugh relaxed her. Exposure to his lifestyle made it easy to dwell on why he chose to be here with her. She shook her head to clear the doubt that would only get in the way of satisfying many things, along with the list.

"Yes, it will fit, if we go slow. Think you can do that, go slow?"

She nodded. The ability to form actual words more absent than usual.

"And stop thinking negative things while you're agreeing to my every wish." His tone grew serious. "I'm right where I want to be. Believe it or not, I need you, more than you know." He leaned down and kissed her with tender passion.

A tirade of emotions shortened her breath, so she placed her hands on his chest to counteract the lightheadedness he often created. "I don't know how you could tell what I was thinking but yes, I have a hard time believing a man as gorgeous as you would be the slightest bit interested in me. That is my problem to overcome, not yours. I need to remind you, no attachments. Can you do that, for me?"

****

He fisted the sheets on either side of her head, didn't like the doubt she had about her beauty. Not get attached? Too late. The image of her leaving killed him. If he didn't find a way to accept her as is, she'd go elsewhere to fulfill her list, and he wasn't cool with that. He could do this. After all, he could put on a convincing show.

He stilled himself and focused on her lips, refused to show her the weakness in his eyes. "How many lucky bastards get to have sex with women, no strings attached? You're every man's fantasy." That sucked.

She smiled when he leaned down and rubbed his nose on hers and stole another kiss. He monitored her gaze for any indication his little white lie hadn't succeeded. He swallowed hard and his arms shook, unaware until now how much he needed her.

"It's okay."

She laced her fingers behind his neck and guided him down on top of her. Their bodies trembled together and he kissed her with every ounce of the desperation that overwhelmed him. He skimmed his hand down her outer thigh to the back of her knee, directed her leg around him. She moaned into his mouth when he used his hard length to rub her swollen nub as the movement opened her to him. She was so wet the silky friction would undo them both.

As he thrust through her folds, he let go of her leg and roamed up her body with his hand. Goose bumps formed on her skin while he massaged his way to her breast. With light, feather touches, he outlined her breast with his fingertip, worked his way to the center and rolled her nipple between his thumb and forefinger. Her eyes glazed over with the small amount of pain.

He closed the distance between their bodies, placed more pressure on all the points he stimulated and licked her neck, just below the earlobe. She rocked her hips, sought out her own satisfaction, and coated him with her pleasure in the process. He loved it.

"Cole."

He smiled into her neck, loved the desperation in her voice. He needed to see how far he could take her, what heights she was capable of. He kissed down her neck and collarbone, latched onto her nipple, and sucked, hard.

"Oh yes."

Cream flowed from her body and she rotated her hips enough that the crown of his hardened length slipped inside. He froze, overwhelmed by the desire to thrust forward, into her heat.

"Isabelle." He closed his eyes and felt the heat of his own breath on her breast. "Now would be a good time to push me away. God, you feel like heaven. The idea of claiming you bareback makes me hard as steel."

She smoothed her hands down his back, shifted her hips, and forced him in deeper.

"Uh, I have a condom in my pants pocket. Several, actually." He rested his forehead on her breast, a little embarrassed but still determined to use each and every one of them.

She stroked her fingers through his hair. "Cole. David was my only and we were tested. I'm clean, *with* an IUD. The doctor wouldn't let me leave his office without protection. I couldn't risk getting pregnant before surgery." She writhed beneath him. "Unless you pull out, I'm not stopping you. I want you."

Her tight passage stretched as she used her legs to urge him in. He put his hands on either side of her head and held her in place while he kissed her through another inch. They both moaned.

An unexplainable sense of emotion washed over him; the offer was so desirable. "I've *never* taken a woman without protection, ever. I get tested regularly just for my own peace of mind. I'm clean."

He slid free from her body and she growled. He drove back into her, a little deeper than before. "Are you sure?" He needed to hear her say it.

"I'm sure. I want you. I want to feel you, feel alive. Just promise me one thing?" She closed her eyes and her breath paused beneath him.

"Anything. I think we've already established that I will do *anything* for you."

Her smile touched her eyes before they opened. "After I get used to your—" She half coughed, half laughed. "*Size.* I don't want you to hold back. Don't be gentle with me, okay?"

A gush of moisture coated him. The added lubricant made it easier for him to drive into her passage, and moan in sheer ecstasy. "I promise you. I have never experienced anything more amazing in my life. I don't think I'll be able to hold back. I want to fuck you so hard. When I'm deep inside you, I'll only want to be deeper."

A quiet gasp escaped her, but the lust in her eyes spurred him on. He kissed her hard, overwhelmed with a need so strong his body ached to touch her. She wrapped both legs around his waist and flexed to force him forward, balls deep inside her.

He broke the kiss first and leaned his forehead against hers. “Vixen.”

She massaged around his muscled body and scratched her nails up his back. He closed his eyes and let the feel of her heat swallow him at a slow pace.

“I won’t break. You fill me more than I have ever been filled. Make me scream. I want to feel you explode inside me.”

“Fuck.”

He knelt between her spread legs and slid his hands under her ass to lift her. The spot that would make her see stars was in perfect alignment. He pumped into her slowly and swirled his hips, until her body informed him he’d hit the right spot.

“Oh yes. Right there.”

Her half-lidded eyes and her body gave her away. No need for words, her walls swelled around him, and squeezed him out. The cream that flowed from her body with each stroke enabled him to demand his way back in. He buried himself so far into her his body tingled at the brink of release.

From the gleam in her eyes, and grasps at his sweaty skin to hold him in place, the sensation was too much and she held back. He leaned into her ear and whispered, “I don’t think so,” as he maneuvered his hand down between them. Her nub was so swollen with need that the second he touched it, her hands loosened. She threw them over her head and gripped the edge of the mattress. Let him have his way.

The spotted blush that surfaced on her skin after her surrender, told him she needed to let go. He played with her nub with the determined precision he stroked a guitar string and pumped into her hard.

"Oh. Cole. Don't stop."

Her deep, fixed gaze compelled him beyond the boundary of her rules. No other experience would ever compare.

His gaze roamed to where their bodies joined, mesmerized by her spilled juices with every back and forth motion. The sight alone aroused him, the need for relief unbearable. Before she could come back down from her high, he flipped her over. "Hands and knees beautiful, this one's for me."

Only just into position, he captured her by the hips and slammed into her from behind, hard. He kept an eye on her for any indication he'd hurt her. Nothing. In fact, she anchored herself with the bedding and propelled back on him, thrust for thrust.

"One more beautiful, give me one more, now."

"Asking a bit much, don't ya think?"

She laughed but he caught her off guard, used his thumb to gather her cream and circled her puckered, virgin hole.

"Ohhh."

"Mmm, like that do you? I can't wait to fill every inch of you, even here."

The second he eased his thumb inside, she rocked back for more. "Touch yourself."

She followed his direction and the added stimulation relaxed her tight hole. He slid his thumb in a little farther. She writhed as if she had no say over her body's actions, a complete loss of control. He swelled to an unbearable size; he couldn't tease it out any longer.

With his arm out to brace himself, he fell over her

back and plunged into both of her holes. Her body shook along with his while he erupted deep inside her. Marked her. When his orgasm subsided he closed his eyes and held himself still, buried to her core and with no intention of leaving.

Ever.

She collapsed onto the bed and he on top of her, too weak to hold himself up. Sweat covered their bodies, and their breaths panted in rhythm to one another.

"Cole?"

"Hmm?"

"Can't. Breathe."

He lifted his upper body to rest on his elbows. "Sorry, honey."

She giggled face down into the mattress.

Did he *really* want to know? "May I ask *why* you're laughing after sex? That's not quite what a man wants to hear."

She twisted, extended her arm behind in search of his face, but he bit her fingertip.

"I laughed because I had a brief flashback to all the wicked and dirty ways you touched me, and still, you call me, honey. I am lost for words. No one has ever made me feel more alive than you have in the last, oh hell, how long have we been in here?"

He could only think of more perverted things to corrupt her with, but yes, she was still precious. He bit her shoulder and she yelped. "Would you rather I call you minx? Sex fiend? Insatiable? I am pretty sure half the floor heard you scream, so maybe rock groupie?"

They both laughed, and he pulled out of her body.

She winced.

"Sorry, baby."

She buried her face into the bed again and her body vibrated. He swatted her ass and her muffled laugh altered into what sounded like, a moan. He glared down at her with raised eyebrows. "Interesting. New bucket list item?"

She flipped onto her back and opened her mouth, with some smartass comment in mind from the cocky tilt of her head. He stepped back to give her room, tripped over his pants and tumbled to the floor. They both curled up in hysterics. She stood before he could regain his composure, with that spark of challenge in her eyes. The defiant one he'd seen every morning for days now, before she'd shove him aside and beat him to the bathroom.

"Fuck. That's the hottest thing I've ever seen."

She followed his gaze and shook her head with a smile. His cum dripped down her inner thighs. The sight of it held him in a trance as he imagined all kinds of territorial innuendos. *Mine.*

"Knowing *you* put it there, is even hotter," she whispered.

His gaze met hers, and he bit his lip. The words of commitment he held in could very well ruin the moment. Something about the way she spoke with such enchantment in her eyes, made every heartache along the way worthwhile. He'd found *her*, in the end.

She broke eye contact and held her hand over her heart. Panic replaced the enthusiasm he'd acquired an instant addiction to. She rushed for her bag and sprinted to the bathroom. Did she regret what she said, what they just did?

He lay back on the floor naked supported by his

elbows and stared at the spot she vacated, caught in a whirlwind of emotions he never expected. The evidence of his claim on her opened something in him that would never close. How was he going to pretend to be okay with letting her go?

He wasn't.

Chapter Ten

Dear Diary,
There was no net to catch my fall…

Isabelle knelt in front of the toilet with one hand on the seat and the other clutched around her hair. She closed her eyes and swallowed several times. A distant buzz rang in her ears, and a cold sweat beaded on her skin. Tears streamed down her face while her muscles contracted with each retch, to the point of pain.

Her name echoed faintly in the distance before he rushed to her side and brushed her hand away, so he could hold her hair back. When the last of the heaves subsided, she folded her arms on the toilet seat and put her head down. He shuffled around the room but she didn't raise her head. The hair at the nape of her neck was swept aside and a cold cloth placed to her skin.

"I never wanted you to see that."

He chuckled and rubbed his warm hand down her back. "You're on tour with a bunch of rockers. Do you think I haven't seen anyone hurl before?"

She lifted her head up, intended to smile but the florescent light in her eyes stung her head. She winced, snagged the wet cloth from his hand, and scooted back to sit against the wall. "I'm sorry. Nothing like a little brain tumor to get in the way of an otherwise *perfect* night." She dabbed at her face and sighed.

He rummaged through her bag while she spoke and that word—perfect—apparently put a little bounce in his concerned steps. Turns out even when not on the bus with the Scandals, there was no privacy. The smugness on his face deepened to worry, the longer his search progressed.

She bent her knees up and put her forehead down. The amount of time and his lack of coordination riffling through her bag made it impossible to hold her head up and watch without a snicker. His movements and huffs of breath sounded panicked, as if he'd never tended to anyone other than himself before her. It was cute. She didn't want to laugh at his expense when he tried so hard.

She lifted her head when he tapped her arm. He crouched with pills and water held out to her. She caved and glanced up to his proud smile.

"Perfect, hey?"

She allowed the corners of her mouth to lift a little, and plucked the pills from his hand. The second the water filled her mouth, she closed her eyes and swirled it to rinse away her embarrassment at the same time the pills washed down. "Yes, perfect. You, without a doubt, know your way around a woman's body." Her smile grew and her grip on the glass tightened in jealousy, about the practice he'd had before her. "I'm just going to brush my teeth and get my pajamas on. I'll meet you in bed?"

He shook his head, stood up, and offered her his warm hand. His strength guided her up in seconds, but still gently to not to jostle her.

"No pajamas." He held up two fingers like a Boy Scout, but nothing about this man screamed Boy Scout.

His voice softened and he tucked her hair back over her shoulder. “I promise to restrain myself from molesting you the rest of the night, so you can rest.”

She closed her eyes and reveled in the compassionate stroke of his delicate fingertips along her collarbone.

“I want to feel you next to me. Besides—”

Her pulsed raced again and she opened her eyes in time to see him wink.

“I like to sleep nude when I’m not on the bus.”

A shiver traveled from her head down to her curled toes.

“Don’t worry, baby. I give off enough heat, you won’t even need blankets.”

She laughed and steadied herself with the sink to brush her teeth. The urge to peek at him in the mirror ate at her, but she ignored it. And him. When she tossed her brush back in her shambled bag, she stole a glance at him and hugged her Scandals T-shirt in front of her.

He leaned against the door and shook his head. She didn’t know whether to be amused or troubled by the fact he hadn’t left her side. She’d never considered how the truth of her illness would worry him. *Well thought out, Isabelle*.

When she held the shirt out to fold it, he snagged it from her and threw it over his shoulder. She stood firm with her hands on her hips, but he scooped her up into his arms.

“What are you doing?” She laughed and the heat of embarrassment surfaced on her face.

“You’re still weak, I can see it.” He flicked the lights off and carried her out of the bathroom.

She was weak, too weak to fight with him, so she

conceded and leaned her head on his shoulder. He tore back the covers with one hand and knelt on the bed, to place her with gentle care in the middle. It took a few seconds, and a couple of tries, for him to get the covers tucked just so around her.

"I'll be right back. Just gonna go get cleaned up a little. My little sex fiend had me doing all kinds of dirty things tonight. I loved it." He kissed the tip of her nose and strutted to the bathroom.

Serenity washed over her at the sound of the rainfall from the shower, tempted her to dim the lights and go to sleep. The pain subsided with the softness of the bed he'd cocooned her in, but she couldn't relax yet, not without a text to the girls. She snatched her phone off the nightstand.

Have multiple orgasms during sex…check. OMG, I didn't think it was possible. I'll give you details when I get home. Not feeling very well right now so I'm going to bed. Sweet dreams, I know I will.

Send.

She startled when the bed dipped behind her as she set the phone down again.

"Bragging to the girls about the big three already?" He folded his arms behind his head, so sure of himself.

"As a matter of fact, yes." When she faced him, she froze.

"What's wrong? Are you going to be sick?" He scrambled for the covers, but she placed her hand on his arm.

"No. I was just a little star struck for a moment. You do things to me." Her words faded to a whisper.

He waved his arm around until he hit the switch on the lamp. Her body vibrated with his chuckle. "You have the same effect on me. I know you think little of your beauty, but I promise you, it's not just me who's attracted to you. You're gorgeous. I'm a little nervous about bringing you back on the bus tomorrow after the outfit you wore tonight. I think all the guys were stiff around you."

Relief washed over her when the room shaded with darkness. Her muscles relaxed and she sighed.

"The dark make it hurt a little less, baby?"

He enveloped her with his arms and the smell of his just showered body stirred her desire once again. Not being able to act on it sucked. She rested her head on his chest instead and put her hand on his abdomen, loving the feel of him. "Yes it does, thank you."

He kissed her forehead, and the last tense muscle in her back let go. She melted into his side. In such a short amount of time, they'd found easy ways to comfort each other before she could stop it.

"I know those meds are going to make you tired. I read the warning label."

She smiled.

"Do you mind if we just talk? Get to know each other a little better, until you get sleepy? I promise, I won't bug you for sex." He placed his hand over hers, on his chest, and urged it down. "However, I can't promise to calm this down. I seem to be in a constant state of arousal since I first laid eyes on you. I *think* I can control it."

Her giggle made it twitch. "Yes, the pills do make me sleepy, so talk fast. I want to know more about you."

He raised her hand up to his mouth and kissed it with a tenderness she could no longer fight, and situated it back on his stomach. "How about you go first? That way if you fall asleep while I talk, well, let's just say you wouldn't be the first."

Both of their bodies relaxed when their tangled limbs found cozy angles to rest, snuggled close. He comforted her, enough to tell him everything. Some things not even Katherine was aware of. She told him about her father dying and being raised by her strong-willed mother. She told him about the kids she taught. Darkness blinded their vision, but he squeezed her in a delighted way when her smile widened against his chest. She loved them.

****

He rubbed her back, loved the softness of her skin. The image of her belly swollen with his child and pressed against him played in his mind.

Whoa. Where the hell did that come from?

She spoke of her girlfriends and the drunken night she created the list. He didn't think she would but, she even broached the subject of David. A tear hit his chest, but he didn't want her to stop, so he ignored it.

She talked about the night she asked David to experiment more in their sex life. Pride swelled in him. If she were his wife, she'd spend her time trying to come up with *new* kinky ideas. He shifted a little when her hand smoothed down his abdomen, so close to the hard-on that wouldn't go away.

He pictured a future with her in his bed, but the image faded when she described the day she met with the doctor, the tests he ordered. The results. He stared up at the ceiling, thankful for the dark. Water pooled in his eyes and he didn't know if he could hold them back.

She stopped talking to offer him a chance to speak,

but he needed another moment. He was the weak one compared to her. The lump in his throat eased and he began from the start. Explained the early childhood he could remember, his mom walking out and leaving his dad to raise four boys. The many fights that took place in a house full of testosterone. He told her about his friendship with Drew and the days he spent using Drew's house as an escape. Before he could stop himself, he admitted his mom's abandonment left him fearful to love a woman.

She stiffened in his arms. She too would leave him, but not by choice. He continued, didn't want his admission to cause her any regret.

He talked about school and how he got involved with the band. The whole, wild girlfriend in university topic, he condensed. The tour hadn't hit New York yet and she didn't need the added stress. When he paused for a moment, her breath had evened out and she lay heavier on him than earlier. She was asleep. He let out a contented sigh, and his eyes drifted closed.

****

The vibration of his phone alarm so soon, pissed him off. He growled. Never could he imagine himself as a morning person. He squirmed to get it and laughed when he opened a picture the guys texted him last night. Zander wearing a strap on, cowboy boots and a hat with Brett bent over in front of him. Yes, this was his band.

He shifted back to her side of the bed to find it empty. Now wide-awake, he bolted upright. A quick scan of the room revealed her purse and the odd items she brought with her. He slouched, not so concerned but still none the wiser about her absence.

Her low mumble, now noticeable, came from the direction of the bathroom. He tilted closer but still couldn't make out her words. The bedsheet slid down as he stretched enough to expose more of him that probed for attention. He smiled and glanced at the clock. Still time. He stumbled to the bathroom door, scrubbed the sleep from his face, and raised a hand to knock. Her mumble cleared and he froze.

"I know your concern, Dr. Peterson. You have made it clear it would be in my best interest to have the surgery now, but I feel different."

Is her condition worse than she let on?

"I will call you as soon as I am home, so you can make all the arrangements. A little more time, that's all I ask. A little more time to experience life the way I denied myself until now. Please understand, Dr. Peterson."

He'd barrel in and wrap his arms around her when she sobbed, but that would mean admitting he eavesdropped. That wouldn't go over well, so he ran back to the bed and pretended to still be asleep instead.

God, I am such a loser.

The water ran for a few moments before the door opened. She scurried at a measured, delicate pace, to be quiet and sneak back into bed. With the sheets gripped tight in his hands, he snarled when a loud bang at the door started, and didn't stop. "Get your asses up. Bus leaves in an hour."

He grumbled, made a good show of being rudely awakened before he shuffled to the door and whipped it open. "Go bang your fucking drums and leave my damn door alone."

Brett brushed past him and entered the room

without a care. She sat up, and yanked the sheet with her. Her red-rimmed eyes didn't spark Brett's concern, but it did his.

Brett winked and sat in the chair beside the bed. "Don't be shy, gorgeous. You're hot, flaunt it." He reclined in his seat and raised his eyebrows at Cole. "Guess you worked on the bucket list last night." He smiled and shifted his gaze back and forth between the two of them. "Which item are we checking off today, and, is there anything you need my help with?"

Cole picked up the nearest shoe and threw it at him while trying to get his pants on at the same time.

"We will be ready and at the bus probably before you, party boy. Don't think I didn't see the picture. Now, get the fuck out of here."

He rose with a grin and sauntered toward the door. Though, not without a nosey touch or peek at anything in his path. "Just offering, old man. Thought maybe my *youthful* stamina would better suit some of Izzy's wishes."

He spun around with his finger in the air, just a hair outside of the door. Cole waved him off and slammed the door. His pulse raced when he returned to her, on her way to pack her bag.

"Sorry about that. Boundaries aren't something we practice, obviously." He chuckled. "We still have a little time to relax if you want?"

She stopped rifling with her things and smiled at him, but he wasn't fooled. The phone call lingered on her mind, and he couldn't do anything about it without letting her know he intruded on the little privacy she has these days.

"I am, of course, a little less sheltered with you

guys. There's no need to worry. Please continue to live your tour out the way you always would. I don't want my life's wishes to cause you regrets."

She yanked the sheet free from the bed as she cloaked herself with it, and headed to the bathroom. "I'm just going to take a quick shower. The restaurant in the hotel smelled good when we arrived last night. Maybe while I'm in the shower you can order some food for us to take back to the bus?"

She didn't wait for an answer before she closed the door.

****

He was right. The hotel restaurant took what seemed like forever to get their food ready and they still beat everyone back to the bus. They took a cab, something he hadn't done in a long time. She insisted it would do him good to do some *less* rock star like stuff, such as not always relying on a driver. He held his phone out to her on their way up the stairs, to show her the text messages the guys sent him after he let them know they were cabbing it.

"I'll find us some plates. I think your eyes are bigger than your stomach, that's a lot of food." She furrowed her brows and shifted her confused glare from him to the cupboards. "If any plates exist on this bus, where would they be?"

His laugh stalled and he contemplated the cupboards with the same puzzled expression as she did. They worked out hard to keep in shape, and the statue of perfection displayed before her last night proved it, but they ate like pigs and ignored certain details, like plates.

"Good question. Maybe, in the top cupboard?"

She shook her head and spun to the cupboard he pointed at. A territorial buzz filled her at the lack of female attention to the bus, before her. He unpacked the bags as if he'd starved for days. With her hands splayed firm on the counter for support, she lifted herself on top, still a little weak from last night's episode. It would take a while to recover, but she forced herself to keep up anyway.

She wasn't as tall as the rest of the men and got the sense he might die of laughter if she asked for a stepstool. The height didn't bother her in the least as she gripped every edge possible, and opened the top cupboard door. A pile of junk fell out on her. It didn't take a genius to see the cupboards that held the alcohol were used much more than this one.

She sifted through the junk, found some unique knick-knacks. Some she couldn't explain and others she wasn't sure if she'd enjoy the story behind them. She found a shape that resembled plates far in the back.

On tiptoe, she stretched for them and the shuffling of bags in the distance stopped. He enjoyed the view, and was obvious about it with his whistle. She stood straight again with the plates in hand, and a strong wave of nausea hit hard. A cold sweat broke out over her skin.

"I don't know what you're talking about. This may not be enough food."

She blinked away the dark spots from her vision, but his voice faded in the distance. It was too late. She swayed and lost her grip on the plates and the cupboard.

"Isabelle."

A faint, familiar voice along with a warm touch on her face brought her to. "Please, baby, you're scaring me. Wake up, honey."

She opened her eyes but they fluttered with weight. "C-Cole?"

He kissed her all over, eyelids, mouth, cheek, and forehead. "Thank God, baby. You scared the shit out of me. Are you okay? Should I take you to the hospital?"

Still weak, she cupped the sides of his face with her hands. His cheeks warmed her clammy touch. "No, no doctor's please. I'm okay, really. This isn't the first time I've passed out." She raised her eyebrow and winced. "It's not that bad."

The memory of moments ago, the food, crossed her mind. She braced her hands on the bed and sat up but he wasn't having any of it. He helped her back down. "You're still very pale."

She chuckled. "So are you."

The line of his jaw tensed. "Yes, I am. I almost didn't get to you in time. It could have been much worse. You fell in my arms, unconscious."

A warm tear slipped down her cheek at his description, his desperation. He used his thumb to wipe her face dry and replaced it with a kiss.

Noise from the front of the bus alerted them to the rest of the guys' late arrival.

"Stay here, baby. I better go get your food before the vultures help themselves."

"Let them have it. I don't think I could stomach it right now, anyway. I'm just going to get in my own bunk and rest a while. You go eat with them. You must be hungry."

He shook his head. "Scoot over."

When she didn't budge, he tapped her arm and waited with an annoyed glare.

"I'm fine. Really." She slid back in the tiny bunk when he didn't give in. Stubborn man.

"I am not letting you out of my sight until I know you're okay. Besides, we need to talk." He laid down close and gathered her into the crook of his arm. The comfort of his arms didn't ease her stress as fast as it had last night. His tone gave her the fight or flight warning in the pit of her stomach.

"Hey Cole, Izzy, you guys see all this food?" Zander's muffled words made it known he already spoke around a mouthful.

"Ugh." He yanked the curtain closed. "Help yourself guys, but leave us alone."

"Come on man, just give me a number already, I'm dying here."

Brett, like all the guys, managed a similar thought pattern, sex, food, and music. The pattern could shuffle but never did a day pass where any, if not all of the three took place.

She leaned over him to slide the curtain back a little.

"Don't give candy to the baby, Izzy."

She raised her eyebrow in challenge and smiled. "Twelve."

Three very loud groans echoed from the lounge. "Now you did it. You're in trouble now, baby."

"Can I help out with number fifteen?" Brett shouted.

"I'll take thirteen." Zander laughed, followed by the sound of hands smacking together.

"I'm in for fourteen." Drew added.

She covered her mouth. "Have you all memorized the damn list?"

He tilted his head at her as if to say "duh." She poked at him with her elbow and closed the curtain. He made being serious more work than being happy. He clutched onto her hips and guided her on top of him, did it with such ease. Her giggle changed to a moan when his shaft grew hard under her. Their bodies fit together, as if they were molded for one another.

"I thought we were going to rest?" Her tone remained serious, until her body moistened to his advance and she bit her lip to keep quiet.

"Oh, baby, we are. I just need to examine you a little more. Make sure you're okay." He slid his hands up either side of her body to cup her face. The seductive way he used his thumb to tug her lip free, gave her the second wind she needed.

"Kiss me."

He smiled and a sparkle in his eye replaced the concern from moments ago. Thank goodness. If he handled her with too much care, out of anxiety for her condition, she wouldn't achieve the purpose of this trip.

"You don't have to ask me twice." He closed the distance between them and teased her lips with licks and nips, without the intensity from the night before.

"I said kiss me," She whispered close to his lips.

The combination of his subtle chuckle, held tight behind closed lips and the bus full of men made it impossible to scream at him, "I want to come."

He didn't flinch at her demand. "Need I remind you, you're a screamer?"

She buried her face in his neck and inhaled his fresh-washed scent. It didn't help the very evident pulse between her thighs, which yearned to make him dirty again. The focused intent in his gaze made it clear his mind was elsewhere. He shifted her once again, so she lay alongside him. She slipped her hand up his shirt and scratched her nails down his chest; he tensed.

"Izzy, dear."

Mimicking his controlled amusement from seconds ago, she stilled her hand.

"Like I was saying, we need to talk."

She righted his shirt and patted it in place with her hand, a little overdramatic. "Why do I get the feeling I am not going to like this?"

The patience on his face faded and his body froze under her hand. "I heard you on the phone with your doctor," he blurted out.

She shoved up onto her elbow and gave him her most Katherine-like glare. "You eavesdropped on my phone call?" She moved farther away but he held her waist, not that she could escape since her back already touched the wall.

"When I woke up you were gone. I heard noise from the bathroom and rushed to the door, in case you weren't feeling well again. Also, because I missed you. You sounded upset. I froze. I'm sorry, for listening when I had no right but—" He averted his concerned gaze to the curtain, but not in time to hide the pain in his eyes.

"But?"

When he cast a wavering smile back at her, the usual guard she'd come to know didn't exist and showed no signs of returning.

"I'm sorry. I shouldn't have listened. It won't happen again. Just promise me—"

His effort to keep some semblance of a boundary between them broke her heart. They were in deep, more than she'd ever planned, and the ability to hold firm dwindled. She'd rescue him with assurance, words that'd comfort his helplessness, but she couldn't.

"—you will let me know if there is anything you need?"

The air in the bunk stifled her mood. "Of course."

"I mean it, anything. This business is busy, chaotic, and at times full of rumors that could crush one's spirit if they aren't prepared. I don't want to hurt you in any way but you *will* see your picture in tabloids, with assumptions about my past, our present, our—future."

The desperation in his eyes made it difficult to breathe. His large intake of breath confirmed he, too, struggled with time, or the lack of it. There was no future written in her cards, or theirs. He would make a good provider some day for a lucky woman, just not her.

"Actually there is something I need, if you don't mind?"

The anticipation on his face was priceless but she needed distance, and there was only one way he'd let her have it. She lay back in his arms and stared at the closed curtain but couldn't hold back the chance to lighten the mood.

"I need a nap. Your stamina last night was beyond my personal best. You're easy on the eyes, have an amazing voice and your—" She massaged her hand up his shirt once again. His abs tightened but he resisted, as if he was tempted to sway her from her nap, just not convinced of her boldness. "Oh so talented hands. Not to mention impressive—" She closed her eyes and shifted her legs a little. He laughed at her and ran his fingers through her hair, down her arm. "Anyway, I'm exhausted." She stopped her advance and slumped.

Laughter filled the air, but it wasn't theirs.

"Ha. Spend a night with me, and I'll put you into a coma. It's been known to happen," Brett called out from the back lounge. A ruckus of slaps and hoots ensued.

She couldn't be more thankful she didn't embarrass easy.

"I told you not to tempt him." He squeezed her close and kissed the top of her head.

She melted into his side with the familiarity of an experienced lover.

"I could use a nap too, baby."

She threw her leg over his, and scooted for the curtain when his large hand halted her. "Where do you think you're going?"

She held her breath and offered a fake smile, not sure a coy diversion from his seriousness would work to her advantage. "To my bunk?"

A swift attempt to maneuver past him only made his grip tighten. "I wasn't kidding when I said I wasn't letting you out of my sight. You're sleeping here, with me, so get comfortable."

She raised her eyebrows, exaggerated her uncertainty about how they were going to do that.

"Just think of me as your own personal body pillow." He winked. "However, I can't promise *lumps* won't form in this pillow."

In order to get even, she beat her pillow a few times. He held his arm around her tight, as if he feared she'd reject him or leave. She wasn't going anywhere, not yet. She eased her leg over both of his, caged him in, and let him know she'd stay—for now.

He sighed and tipped her chin up with his fingers, placed a gentle kiss to her lips. “Sweet dreams.”

She closed her eyes and the need for sleep consumed everything except her worry his lust and affection went beyond the surface, deeper than the shallow kind she intended.

****

Within seconds, the tension in Izzy’s body faded with her quiet slumber. Cole stared at the top of the bunk, where most of the guys taped family pictures, kept grounded in their roots. But his? Bare. That would only make him miss it, or remind him every day of his mother’s choice to not be a part of it. He could however, stare at Isabelle forever.

Every moment of concentration on her outweighed the need for sleep. Her long, silky blonde hair draped over his arm, and he longed to comb his fingers through it, comfort them both. He smiled, studied the length of her beautiful pale skin. For someone from Florida, you’d think she’d have a tan, but she didn’t. She would be average in most people’s eyes but to him, a priceless gem.

The bus jerked when Derek pressed on the brakes. She stirred in his arms. The hum of the road that always lulled him to sleep, kept him rested for sold out shows like tonight, no longer calmed him. Her phone call replayed in his mind, several times.

We need to get more serious about this list.

Chapter Eleven

Dear Diary,
My body was his to command...

Two hundred thirty one bumps in the road in three hours. Cole bounced with every one, counted them. The bus stopped in Portland, Michigan a half hour ago, yet he still lay there wide-awake and even more exhausted. He didn't want to miss it, the sounds.

She talked in her sleep. The only explanation for missing it the night before, a crash much like sleeping pills, chased with a bottle of whiskey. Heated, ravenous sex as they'd had would do that. He clung to the edge of sexual frustration and her moans held him there. He contemplated finding his own relief but he'd experienced it, the real thing, her.

It would never be the same again. The rest of the guys made their way to their bunks a while ago, naps all around. They weren't the only ones who benefited from the use of the hotel to all hours of the night. The details he listened to, of their *Scandal-less* behavior along with her moans drove him to the edge of sexual insanity.

He squeezed his eyes closed and raised his arm over her. He didn't want to touch her beautiful curves too much, didn't think his libido could handle the torture, but he needed her. With the tips of his fingers, he tickled her back.

Please let her be feeling better.

He didn't have to move too far; she stirred so much in her sleep she darn near laid on top of him now. Not helping matters.

She bolted upright, well, until she hit her head on the top of the bunk. "Ouch."

****

"Oh shit. Sorry honey."

She scowled at him and rubbed the back of her head. "This better be good."

He squinted as though he could feel her pain, but his smile gave away his lack of regret. They stared into each other's eyes for what seemed like an eternity. Her painful haze cleared the second he gripped her tight and rolled with her, until she lay beneath him.

His warmth blanketed her, much like his luring scent. Her panties soaked with desire when she closed her eyes and inhaled. His male aroma filled the tiny space and she didn't think another night of sleep above him was an option.

He held her face in his hands, and paused as if he fought his own resistance. He leaned in slowly, kissed her forehead, eyelids, cheeks, and with light pressure, her lips. She smiled at the desperation in his kisses.

"Sorry baby, pleeeasse let me make it up to you."

His tender kisses continued to the side of her mouth, down her neck, lower. She moaned. The tender touch of his lips on her collarbone, combined with the feel of his hand as it roamed to the hem of her shirt and lifted, stirred the wantonness in her that only his touch produced. A spontaneity that he accepted, 'cause he craved it too. His plea struck her heart, and she'd drain herself of all sensibility to sate him.

She arched her back, allowed him to get her shirt loose and slide his hands up to the clasp of her bra. Alert now, she opened her eyes to his and the same desperation to be lost in one another's devotion.

"I need you, now."

"Then take me."

She stretched for the hem of his shirt and lifted it up. He raised his weight off her. With one hand braced on the mattress, he freed the other hand from under her shirt long enough to grab behind his head and tug his shirt. It slipped over his head with ease and messed his hair in the process. He threw it aside and stilled above her with temptation in his eyes, to seduce her beyond the list. He didn't have to fight it, not in this moment.

She bit her lip and admired his upper body, still not able to fathom his interest in her. The way he'd confided in her the night before only heightened her desire for him. For a moment possession flooded her emotions, hope that only she held a special place with the real, Cole Davies.

She couldn't recall a need for something so bad, the way she needed him now. Images of last night flashed through her mind and the way he smiled at her, anticipation had hit him too. He crushed his lips to hers as if it was the last time he'd ever get to touch a woman. It excited her.

She forced him up with a shove of her hands, lacked patience, needed to feel his skin on hers. She scrambled for the hem of her shirt and yanked it up. When she arched, extended her hands above her head with her shirt and bra, his pupils dilated. He used one hand to stop the clothing at her wrists, firm. On his elbow, to balance himself without crushing her, he looped the shirt and bra around her wrists. It wasn't too tight, but it held.

She gasped. The slight power he held over her excited her. She peered into his lust-filled gaze and relaxed into his dominance. She was safe to let him have his way with her.

He stared into her eyes and the corner of his mouth rose. "I figured your list was all the permission I needed."

With a wicked smile, he urged her on with a slow thrust against her lower half. She let her eyes drift closed and took long, slow breaths, to regain control. When she focused on him again, everything else around them had faded. He traced down the side of her body with a feather touch of his fingertip and followed the path with his intense gaze. He lingered at the button on her pants. She shivered.

"Cold?"

She glared at him. The seductive tone in his voice forced her patience, "If you don't get inside me soon, I might—"

The rashness of his kiss cut her off. Their teeth knocked but it only spurred her on. He used the distraction to his advantage, undid her pants and slipped his hand down the front. He smiled, enjoyed how wet he made her. He traced around her opening with his finger, dipped into her heat with the tip but it wasn't enough. She shifted her hips, to get his finger where she needed it.

"Patience, my love."

The heat of his words sent tingles through her, like a tidal wave determined to make every tiny hair on her body respond. It did. The way he handled her made the impact of climax too intense to seek out. She pressed her butt into the mattress and away from his hand, but he pinned her tied wrists and kissed her into a trance before shoving two fingers deep inside her.

"Cole."

Her body contracted as he kissed his way down her neck to just below her collarbone. She could feel his smile on her upper breast.

"I'm gonna come. It's too much."

At that moment, he latched on and sucked, hard. The combination of this, while his fingers curled to stroke her G-spot, made all her senses soar. Her body followed his command; she no longer controlled it. Her muscles vibrated as she fought off release, bound and at his mercy to please.

It built too strong, too fast. Her skin gave into the suction of his lips and the high of being marked by him intoxicated her. He let go and kissed up her neck. "My mark on you is beautiful," he whispered in her ear and stroked her with more pressure.

She could no longer fight it, tease herself with pleasure. The power he used over her, in her, gave her no choice but to let go. The warmth of release exploded in her passage. She needed to move, ride out the wave his hand created, but she couldn't. He held her in place and used his fingers to compel her to come so hard her body trembled beneath him. She closed her eyes and bit down on his shoulder to muffle her scream.

"God. Isabelle, you're flooding my hand."

Before she could come down from the most delightful high, he lifted off her as much as the space allowed and tugged her pants free from her body, followed by his own. She gathered her senses enough to open her eyes. He stared at her like a feral beast desperate to take its prey.

"Yes. Whatever it is you need, yes." She relaxed and surrendered to him.

He spread her thighs with his knee, put his elbows down on either side of her head, and fastened his grip to her bound hands. The spasms of her climax still lingered while he moved his feet for leverage. He kissed the side of her neck and whispered. "Hold tight, baby. This isn't going to last long."

She spread her fingers enough so he could lace his through hers and squeeze. With one forceful thrust, he embedded himself in her, deep. Not given a moment to come down from the first orgasm, she startled when her body responded again, not as intense but enough to make her scream.

He pounded into her, hard. His feet braced at the end of the bed powered a force sure to leave her sore but she could see it in his eyes, he needed to be deep, needed all of her.

She threw her bound hands over his head and drew him in for a kiss. "I want to feel you explode inside me," she whispered in his ear. Sweat beaded on his skin and his thrusts filled her at a desperate pace.

He drove in hard one last time, pulled at her stiffened arms to force his shaft in deeper yet. It was as if he wouldn't be satisfied until his seed touched her core. He dropped his face into the crook of her neck, and panted while his body jerked with the last of his release.

"Isabelle. Mine."

He didn't scream. His words were soft and the intensity of them touched a depth in her she didn't know existed.

He collapsed on top of her. Butterflies fluttered in her stomach as he twitched inside of her, still affected by her even though the height of their passion had ended.

"Cole?"

"Hmm?" Her skin vibrated under his muffled, deep voice.

She giggled. "C-can't breathe, again."

Happiness washed over her when he rose up on his elbows, disheveled, satisfied. He tugged at her shirt and bra and relieved the tension in her wrists with the massage of his warm hands. "That was—"

She opened her mouth, intended to finish his sentence when the bite mark on his shoulder caught her attention. "Oh my God." She touched it with her fingertip.

He raised his eyebrows. "Well, I do think I'm pretty damn good, but God?"

She smacked him on the bite mark and he flinched.

"Sorry." She gasped and covered her mouth with her hands.

"Believe me. You biting me only made me come harder." He brushed hair back out of her face and kissed the tip of her nose. "I don't think I have *ever* come that hard, or that much." With a light touch of his finger, he traced her lips. "You may be dripping me for days."

He eased himself from her body, renewed with excitement at his words, but she still winced.

"Sorry for being so rough, baby. Are you okay?"

An admission she'd held back surfaced to her mind, and no physical gesture alone could express it, only words. "Cole?" Her voice was quiet, close to a whisper.

"Yes?"

"With you, everything's perfect."

They stared at each other, lost for words.

Her pulse increased and her legs were restless with his weight. She snagged the first shirt within her reach, which happened to be his, and threw it on. "I'm going to go get cleaned up."

Before he could respond, she opened the curtain and stumbled in her escape. When she stood up, Drew lay in his bunk at eye level, the curtain wide and a smile on his face. "Didn't peg you as a screamer."

****

Deep red blotches covered her dewy skin while she scurried to the bathroom. He glared at his best friend, but shrugged with a smile when the bathroom door closed.

"Fuck that was hot." Zander shouted.

Brett laughed. "My hand and I get the bathroom next."

He fell onto his back with a sigh, still buzzed from lust. He'd been there, alone and listening to one of the other guys get laid, so he was well aware of the effect it had. After all, they were human and men.

Drew laughed and closed his curtain, blocking the view of his best friend. He didn't have to see his face to know what troubled him.

"Cole, my love, you have some 'splainin' to do." His laughter trailed off into a quiet mumble. "Gonna get your heart broke, man." Drew's words hit him, hard.

He covered his eyes with his forearm. "I know."

****

Isabelle stared at her reflection in the mirror, flushed, red, wild. She tugged the collar of his shirt down and covered her mouth with her free hand. A deep-red spot marked her. It seemed rather childish but at the same time, wonderful. Even when fully clothed, he'd be with her.

She touched the spot and something in her changed. No more need to analyze, just pure unadulterated fun. She'd be leaving friends behind, that was a given, but thinking of him as another friend, not too unbearable.

They would say goodbye either way. She considered herself somewhat lucky, thankful to have notice of death when others didn't.

The shirt draped her body, the neck wide, showed his possession. She shrugged and opened the door with a liberated breath, lighter on her toes than she'd been in months.

She held out her hand and skimmed everything she could with the breeze of her fingertips. She was meant to be here. With her toes on the edge of his bunk, she hoisted herself up when he grabbed her ankle.

"Eeeek!"

He laughed. She could hear the sadness in it, but at least he tried.

"Where do you think you're going? I haven't changed my mind."

She needed to get back to their light-hearted relationship. The phrase, "life is too short" couldn't be truer. Time didn't allow for deep-seeded connections, love. All of which she could see with him.

She practiced her smile, and then titled her head so she could see his face. "If I may have your permission, sir, I'd like to get a couple things before I return."

"Wench."

Deep male laughter filled the air. She rolled her eyes and gathered her phone and journal in one hand. When she crouched down to climb over him, a little revenge simmered in her veins. She smiled.

Let's see how the smartass likes this.

A bout of clumsiness hit her while she kneed and elbowed her way in. "Oops. Sorry. Oops." Not quite satisfied yet, she placed her hand over his face for leverage and climbed the rest of the way in. "I am sooo sorry. I don't have a clue where this clumsiness is coming from, it is so unlike me." For the first time, she could make light of her situation and the weight of the injustice she'd lugged with bitterness, lifted. "Must be the tumor?"

She stared at him, needed to know if she'd gone too far, if he could handle her way of coping. When he raised his eyebrows and smiled, she slouched and returned his beautiful expression.

"Then we must get you home now." He arched his upper body out of the bunk. "Straight to the airport, Derek."

She swung at him with a closed fist, but he caught her by the wrist. "Now, now, you know I can render you helpless."

He glanced down at the items she entered his bunk with and raised one eyebrow up further. "Hmm, not my idea of sex toys, but we can always experiment."

She picked up the journal and swatted him. The bus might appear large on the outside, but the male hoots that bellowed when the hard-covered book came in contact with his bare skin, made it seem like a tiny closet.

“Abigail’s idea. I have strict orders to write about my experiences, as well as text.” Her gaze fell to the items in her hands and a solemn stare stole her smile. “I wish they were here. I wish I could multiply myself, be with everyone.”

He twisted to the wall behind him, and lifted a crinkled piece of paper taped in place. For many years, by its appearance. She covered her mouth to muffle the gasp when he produced, with a grin, a box of cookies from the hole hidden by the paper.

“Cole.”

He held up a warning finger before he whispered. “I will share with you, but if any of the gluttons find out, I will know who told them.” His smile fell. “Sometimes we all need comfort.” He over exaggerated his movements to do just that, get comfortable. “And a way to replenish our energy after a round of hot, steamy sex.”

She smiled and accepted the treat. Never in a million years would she have pegged Cole Davies as anything other than rugged, but the sheer joy on his face as he bit into the cookie was priceless. “You’re cute.”

He laughed and sat up, leaned into her for a light kiss. He tasted sweet, like vanilla cream. “Don’t forget it, baby. But, maybe think of something a little more rough around the edges when others are around?”

He winked and her stomach fluttered like a teenager all over again. There was something pure and genuine about him. He didn’t just care about the list; he cared about everything he set his mind to, even her.

He kissed the tip of her nose and stepped out of the

bunk, hiked on his pants like he were on a mission. "You know, image and all. I'll give you some privacy. I need to make some arrangements anyway."

She bent forward while he strutted away with a gloat, sans shirt. His muscles flexed with every step and when she closed her eyes, she could still feel them use her body for pleasure. When she opened her eyes, Drew trapped her in his sight, but his face said worry, not joy. She plucked the edge of the curtain and closed it.

The tap of her pen to her book echoed in the confined space, but her gaze continued to drift to the curtain, in the direction where Drew lay. From the thump on the floor after she closed him out, he chased after Cole. She took another cookie from the hidden spot, their spot, and opened her journal. She needed to get things out of her head and if she were being honest, which she could on paper, she'd scared herself with that last blackout.

With the last of her messages to the girls sent, she slid the curtain back and climbed out. Cole, Drew, and Brett stood at the front of the bus with Derek, all on cell phones.

I wonder what's up?

Her stomach chose that moment to growl. The four men jerked in her direction with raised eyebrows and smiles. She shrugged; she would never make a good ninja. He glared and pointed to the fridge, still on his phone.

Point taken.

There wasn't much in it since the men ate like pigs. A bowl of cereal was the only decent option, unless she chanced the mysterious take out containers.

She jumped when Cole wrapped his arms around

her waist. He laughed in her ear and kissed her neck. "Sorry, didn't mean to startle you. Is that all that's left?"

She cocked her head at him as if to say, does that surprise you? He chuckled and nuzzled her neck. "We'll send one of the roadies out for groceries later. We have a video to shoot today, interested? It's going be more fun for us than it will be for you though, so I understand if you'd rather not."

The milk she'd drained from the container spilled over the edges of her bowl when she spun too fast. "Duh. Of course I want to watch."

She offered him bites from her spoon, and he accepted them with a smile, caressed her body with his hands while he did. He lifted the T-shirt she wore, his T-shirt, so he could feel her bare skin, and give the others a perfect view of her naked body. Her heart raced. The shared bowl of cereal not only made the start to her day perfect, but something about it combined with the erotic interaction in front of the guys, sparked her uninhibited desires.

****

She sat in the car and observed what she could only describe as organized chaos. With a subtle prod, the guys gave her privacy and entered the large warehouse without her. The last message she sent to the girls suggested an increase in symptoms, so if she didn't let them know she was fine, they'd panic. More than anything, she should let her mom know she was okay. She'd avoided this call and the chance it would break her heart and make her regret her choice. Before she changed her mind, she sat back and held the phone to her ear. The ring on the other end didn't last long.

"Isabelle Maureen Chambers, if it weren't for the beautiful and caring women you have as friends, I would be calling the police to look for you."

She winced. "Mom, I'm sorry. Katherine assured me she would keep you updated. I should have called sooner, I just—" She squeezed her eyes shut and pinched the bridge of her nose. She regretted nothing about the choice she made, but it took time away from her mom, which didn't make it any easier.

"Isabelle, I get it. A mother wants nothing more than to see her child happy. If this is what makes you happy—"

The quiet sob through the phone was what she avoided until now. A knot formed in her throat, made it difficult to speak from the heart without the onset of tears. "Mom." The one she held back slid down her face. "I wish I could be everywhere, with everyone. Yes, I am having the time of my life, I won't deny that, but I miss you and the girls."

"I hear there is a handsome, tattooed man wooing my daughter?"

Crap. I'm going to make Katherine pay for this.

"Mom. Wooing. Really?" The sound of her mother's giggle confirmed what she needed to know; she was doing the right thing. Her mother's voice, her acceptance, motivated her to move forward. She sized the warehouse with her gaze, the next direction she now itched to experience.

"Mom. Thank you. I love you so much, and will see you soon."

She caught sight of a tall, familiar man at the side of the building and leaned into the window in time to see him scurry inside. Cole. The glances he gave her when convinced distractions held her attention were easy to read. Concern. Nothing came to mind about how to ease that for him. She'd have to give it more consideration later.

She stuffed her phone into her purse and rushed into the warehouse. Their success made sense now, and tired her out. How do they do it? City to city, one way or another, they performed. Concerts, public appearances, video shoots, and recording studios, wherever and whenever they were told.

Their manager must have one hell of a sequential brain to map this out. In five days, she'd traveled to four cities, with very little time to enjoy the amenities of their surroundings. But, they loved it. From where she stood in the open doorway, the commotion resembled the format of one of their performances. The set up for the video, so detailed you wouldn't be able to distinguish between real and make believe, drew her attention away from the vacant areas off to the sides. Lights of all colors flooded the place and people scurried around to complete what was already, to her, finished. Instruments and speakers filled the stage while beams of light scanned what would've been the crowd, groupies nowhere to be seen. She smiled.

"Pretty spectacular isn't it?" Zander wrapped his arm around her shoulder and squeezed.

She swayed in admiration with him. Being friends with such a unique group of men wouldn't be possible in her everyday life. She crooked her head up at him, his face covered in perfectly applied make-up. Impossible to contain, she burst out in a howl and held her stomach without shame.

He winked, used his thumb to wipe away the

dampness on her face she forgot about from earlier. "Way to bruise a man's ego, hot stuff." He slapped her ass hard enough to make it sting.

She rubbed her behind but still needed a moment before she could control herself enough to talk. "I'm so sorry. The make-up—" She covered her mouth with her hand, muffled her giggle as she righted herself.

Warm arms wrapped around her, not Cole's. She took a deep breath, Drew. She liked knowing them so well. It wasn't just Cole and Drew, whether by voice or scent, she could identify any of the men without laying on eyes them.

"Behave, little girl. Your turn is coming."

With another smack on the opposite cheek, Drew and Zander strode away. Their superb backsides she'd expected, but their cockiness, didn't match its usual form.

What does he mean by that?

****

Five hours later, Cole's attention shifted to her, up from her chair again to pace.

Every so often their gazes met, and he'd mouth the words "you okay?" while they paused to change the background or before singing the song for the millionth time. When the director on set said, "I think we've got enough." She sighed, but it didn't faze them.

If anything, they could have continued, but he needed to get to her. That was the longest he'd gone without being close to her in days and he could feel his mood shift with the distance. The smile on her face made it difficult to focus; her beauty compelled his attention. Flashes of their pseudo private time together on the bus kept his libido at a low simmer. He could feel her, taste her. Her desire had drenched his fingers when he latched on and marked her. His leather pants, already too snug, became painful and didn't accommodate the erection he still couldn't control in her presence.

When they were cut loose, he strode to her with long even strides. Not easy in restrictive material. As he neared her, her hands twisted in her lap. "Bored?" He waited for his sham of an annoyed tone to make her jump. It did.

"Not at all. You guys are amazing. I can't take my eyes off you."

Something about her genuine admiration made the day's hard work and distance from her a little more bearable. He leaned down and kissed her, but not hard; he was covered in sweat and make up. He didn't want to get her messy—with make up anyway.

"I have a surprise for you."

She shifted in her seat and bit her lip. His pulse sped with the direction of her mind. He'd be more than happy to fulfill any of her sexual needs.

"You'll find out soon. We have to go wash up first. Do you mind?"

She shook her head and lifted her thighs one at a time, to place her hands on the chair underneath. The demands of his lifestyle didn't faze her, not at all like the other women he'd seen fall apart over it. The rest of his life…he could do this, her, for the rest of his life. He took a step back and shoved his hands in his pockets, with his gaze at the concrete floor.

Where did that come from?

The guys shoved him aside to kiss her cheek, one at a time before they scooted off to the change room.

The ritual developed on its own, all of them showed her affection. He smiled when the last loud smack landed. He leaned in for his own, held out his hand, and tugged when she placed hers in it. They strolled along with their fingers laced and swayed, their unbreakable hold between them.

He couldn't get enough of her; his days centered on her. She chose to sit on a chair in the hall and wait, which helped. He needed to get his head on straight, and being close to her made it impossible. He rushed through his shower and threw on a black T-shirt and faded jeans. The lust in her eyes whenever his tats were exposed amused him. He smoothed his still damp hair back, put his ball cap on backward and smiled as he rushed to the door.

"Cole." He spun around at the sound of Drew's voice.

"What?"

Drew took a step back with his hands up. He squeezed his eyes shut. "Sorry, didn't mean to snap.
What's up?"

"You've planned things to happen pretty fast from here on out. Is there something more we should be aware of?"

Drew stared at the floor, hands in his pockets and voice uncertain. The sight damn near killed him. He was falling for her, hard, but he hadn't considered the impact of her presence on the rest of them.

"I think it's worse than she's letting on, but I'm not a doctor, so unless she admits it, we won't know. What I do know is she *will* finish her list."

He blew out of the room with his palm on the top of his head, and mood a little deflated until he spotted, her. Gabrielle. What he'd planned could go wrong so many ways, inviting a woman you've slept with back into your life with your current girlfriend.

He smiled, and his heart raced. Girlfriend. Gabrielle was dressed to kill with long legs that wrapped around a man's waist just fine. That's what lured him in the first time. And the second, if he was being honest. But this time, nothing.

"Gabby, thank you for coming." He held out his hand, but she leaped in for a hug.

"Hey, handsome."

He rolled his eyes and squirmed out of her embrace. A quick glance in Isabelle's direction revealed what he'd expected, given Gabby's ability to draw attention to herself with enthusiasm. Isabelle's gaze was fixed toward them.

"It's been a long time, Cole Davies. I was surprised to hear from you."

She clung onto him, but he ignored it and waved at Isabelle to join them. "Gabby. You are here for a favor for my girlfriend, not the usual. It will *never* be that again, sorry. My heart belongs to her."

As Isabelle neared, the pieces of the puzzle had connected together from the fake smile on her face. The temper behind it scared him, and he would have to fix things quick if she were going to enjoy what he'd planned next.

"Isabelle, I would like you to meet Gabrielle." He stepped beside Isabelle and put his arm around her shoulders, gave her a little hip check. "Gabrielle, this is my girlfriend, Isabelle Chambers."

The tension in her shoulders deflated and she smoothed her hand around his lower back, to pinch his side until it pained him. He used his free hand to lift her chin and kiss her before he addressed Gabrielle.

The smile Isabelle tried hard to maintain softened when she stepped forward and shook hands with her. "Hello Gabrielle, it's a pleasure to meet you."

The unease was written all over her face; it was adorable. She was jealous, had a right to be. His reputation, his past, wasn't spotless. He forced her hand out of its curled up fist and laced his fingers with hers. Linked tight, he raised their joined hands up to his mouth and kissed the back of hers, hoping to calm her. "Gabrielle is your surprise, sweetheart." Yes, he laid it on thick. "She's here to teach us how to tango."

The deer in the headlights expression on her face couldn't have been mimicked even if she tried. And for sure, he would have fun with the wicked things he could do to make it happen.

"T-tango? N-now?" she sputtered.

When the sound of laughter erupted behind her, she whipped around to see Zander, Drew, and Brett with grins like they'd just gotten away with something sneaky. She whirled around so fast she lost her balance and grasped his hand when he offered it. "Wait. Us?"

He leaned into her ear and nipped at it. Her instant tilt into him, with her eyes closed, aroused him so much that a slight breeze would make him come in his pants. He checked his watch and winced. Excusing themselves to another room wasn't an option.

"The guys have this crazy idea it may help them with the, ladies." He winked, gripped the hem of her shirt with his fingers, and tugged her into his chest, to face him.

"And you?"

"Well..." He kissed her and the scent, her mixed with spicy vanilla, stirred his addiction for her. How could he let her know he wanted her forever without too much pressure? Life never seemed so calm until she entered the picture. He could balance the rock star image and still have a relationship based on trust and love. Not experience more chaos and hurt, like the past with Alexis.

He didn't want to think about Alexis while he kissed the woman he was falling in love with. Although, he'd have to tell her soon if they had a chance at something more committed. He deepened the kiss, explored every inch of her, and enveloped her in an intimate embrace so loyal it'd leave no doubt in her mind that he was here for her alone.

"Ahem. Cole, we should *really* get started."

He broke away first. He didn't like to ignore the sting of disappointment in Gabby's voice, but his past was behind him.

"Sure thing, Gabrielle."

****

The entire stage vanished, dismantled by experts in no time. A few lights and one lone tripod stood untouched. Did they forget it? Now, it resembled the warehouse she'd expected when she entered. The men ribbed each other about dancing, called each other "twinkle toes." They surrounded her with their bodies while Gabrielle set up her music. Huh. Whether they shielded her on purpose or by unconscious effort, their natural vigilance to protect their own was a lot like home. She missed the girls. Some of the backup dancers hung around, and strolled over to join as partners for the other guys. She giggled at Brett, who'd already hit on the young girl beside him.

When everyone stood with a partner, he guided her over to the other side of the temporary dance floor. Did Gabrielle affect him that much?

"Why are we moving?"

He shrugged. "The lighting is better over here. I love looking at you."

The sensual music played and Gabrielle jumped right in with their first instruction. She delivered the lesson tough, critiqued their form, and made it obvious she had a successful career in dance. Isabelle scanned the group, in awe of the tattooed rockers gone ballroom style. She leaned back and laughed as the girls screamed the occasional "ouch." when the guys stepped on their toes.

As seriously as Gabrielle took her job, the group before her didn't. Everyone poked fun at her instructions with exaggerated motions, and made fun of Gabrielle, to her back. Being a nice person most of time did get tiresome, so Isabelle found herself in the midst of the not so hushed banter as an active participant.

The petty behavior eased the slight sting of anger over her suspicion Gabrielle and Cole once hooked up. There were only a few people who straggled in and out while they laughed and danced. She glanced over to the man beside the camera. He fixed something on it. She searched the group of them, to ensure no one bumped into it while they fooled around. Synchronizing this group of amateurs would take a lot more than one lesson. They were all over the place, beyond help.

The sexual nature of the dance drove Cole insane and she loved it, took advantage of it. She rubbed her body against his with a devilish grin, again. He broke form, wrapped his arms around her waist, and hauled her in for a kiss, tender and soft. The world around them slowed and melted away as their lips continued to dance. She massaged her hands up his hard and defined chest. A mold of perfection.

"Ahem, Cole?"

His muscles tensed around her, not pleased. He solidified his annoyance, and loyalty, when he broke the kiss. The slight distance he allowed between them was only enough to speak. He stared at her with seduction in his eyes, as if they were alone. "Yes?" His gaze didn't wander, not once.

"I am all done with the lesson. My purse is in the other room if you want to come with me, we can figure out payment?"

Even though he made it obvious he was not in the least bit interested, it troubled her to think he gave up things in his life he found joy in before her. She squirmed to get space, but he wouldn't let her.

"Gabrielle, Derek has your money. You should be able to find him on your way out. Thank you for the favor. We appreciate it."

She melted a little at the sound of that word, we. Gabrielle huffed and stomped away on her ridiculous high heels.

She smiled. "Thank you. I will never forget this. So, what's next on the agenda? Are we due back at the bus?"

The smug grin on his face, displayed his self-satisfaction. "Actually, our tour manager was able to knock back a couple of our public appearances."

She bent her back over his arms, still wrapped around her. His eyes gleamed with anticipation.

"We now have a few days off."

He laughed when Drew appeared beside her and put his arm around her shoulders. "I am sure we can think of a few things to keep us busy for three days, don't you think?" Her body heat surfaced, sure to make blotches cover her skin. He slapped her on the ass and joined the, "still amused with their new moves" men, with a pompous sway. They were all so damn confident.

He whispered in her ear. "Will you go on a date with me, Isabelle Chambers?"

She couldn't understand the nervousness in his voice. *I'm sure he dates all the time.* She squirmed out of his embrace, put her hands on her hips, and raised an eyebrow but he only smiled like a teenager asking a girl out.

"Fine. I'll say it. I haven't gone on a real date in years." He scooped up her hand and yanked her back to him. "There's never time on the road for more than, well, anyway. Then we're in the studio to record during our off time."

He shrugged his shoulders when she raised her other eyebrow. She didn't like how his life sounded so limited; it wasn't what she expected. He asked for something that sounded like a rare occurrence, to be done with her—how could she say no?

She stood on tiptoe and scrunched her nose, still not able to get close enough. With the help of his collar, she jerked him forward, smacked a kiss on his lips, and sighed. "Yes."

Chapter Twelve

Dear Diary,
Not all sweet things appeal to me, but candy apple red is delicious...

The bustle of the airport tried her nerves and the fact it was six a.m, didn't help. Coffee called to her, a lifeline since she met these men. It didn't bother them; they were calm, used to it. They sat in the chairs, cracked jokes, and people watched. The occasional person greeted them in their casual disguises, but they were discreet about it.

She was impressed, thankful. The headache that ruined their evening the night before subsided. She'd gone to bed early, gave him some much needed alone time with the guys, and eased her guilt about his sole focus being her. They didn't leave the bus when Derek had announced they were parked at the airport for the night. The commotion and hollers from the back lounge made it obvious they enjoyed their time anywhere.

He put it all out there, held nothing back, not even in public. He sat in the chair beside her with his arm relaxed around her shoulders and his free hand rubbed up and down her arm. It was as if he couldn't get close enough, and nor did he care to be discreet.

"You okay, baby? You're a little more quiet than usual. Do you need more medicine?"

She closed her eyes, rested her head on his shoulder, and exhaled. "No, I'm okay. When you asked me on a date, I didn't picture flying to Beverly Hills. I feel like Julia Roberts in Pretty Woman."

He'd explained while they waited in the uncomfortable airport chairs. She didn't know Zander's family lived there, why would she? His parents are the rich, snobby, Ivy League School type people. Zander tried his hardest not to be anything like them, but his sister is pretty cool, was Cole's description.

Until this moment, she couldn't place Zander's perfect posture, opposite of his sex on legs appearance, and personality. It made sense now.

The group of men before her, covered in striking tattoos and piercings, had such good-natured souls. They gave her goose bumps. It wasn't just Cole who cared about her list, about her. They were *all* going along for the trip. She giggled when Brett flicked Cole's ear, and he just ignored it, resting his head back on the wall. *They really don't get sick of each other*.

Brett and Zander talked about their scheduled visit with Zander's family. Drew didn't mention much about plans, other than copious hours of sleep in the hotel and maybe a pretty lady in the bar who would entertain him for the night.

Their boarding call sounded over the speaker and Brett, Zander, and Drew gathered her and Cole's bags, so they could stay together, hand in hand. Her heart swelled. She extended her hand to her bag anyway, but the men shooed her away.

The diverse travelers aboard the flight were entertaining, but she still managed to fall asleep, a side effect of being medicated the night before. He held her hand the entire time and during the moments she resurfaced, could feel his stare. She shifted in her seat. Her body tingled as the dream of how far things could have gone in the karaoke bar, in front of everyone, pleased her. She was so close—

"Isabelle?"

"Hmm?"

She jumped when her seat wrenched back in someone's grip. The warm kiss to her cheek and musky scent that followed lured her body into it. Zander.

"Wake up, gorgeous. I hope you feel rested, you're going to need it."

He kissed the top of her head and sat back down. She opened her eyes in time to see the flight attendant's hands on her hips. She peeked at Zander between the seats. He winked at the attendant while he buckled back in. When she righted herself in her seat, she covered her mouth at the pretty blonde's blush, the scowl from seconds ago now a fan girl smile.

Cole ignored it all as he glared at her with an unspoken question in his gaze. The dampness in her panties, from the dream, caught her attention. Shit. She spun to the window, they'd already landed. "Sorry I fell asleep."

She stretched with her arms over her head, cold air hit her midriff. When she twisted around, his eyes were glued to her exposed skin, so she shoved him in the shoulder.

Drew hit him on the back of the head. "Let's go."

The baggage claim posed somewhat of a delay for everyone. The Scandals were popular in California. Girl's screeched and formed lines for autographs and pictures.

"I'm going to find a bathroom and change into something a little cooler."

He managed a nod before being groped by girls and stolen away from her. He gave her the *help me* plea with his hands grasping out to her, but he enjoyed every second of it. And, she wasn't bothered by the groupies anymore.

When she staggered out of the bathroom with her bag, a security guard stood at the door and faced her head on. "Are you Isabelle Chambers?"

"Uh…yes." She crossed her arms in front of her chest.

He spoke into the microphone at his shoulder. "On my way with Ms. Chambers." He took her by the arm and guided her, offered the occasional point with his finger to show her the way. "Things were getting a little out of hand with the ladies, ma'am. I'll take you to the group. They are guarded as well." He led her through a roped-off area that said STAFF ONLY.

The guys were talking and laughing with a young blonde when she neared them. Cole separated himself from the group, met her halfway, and wrapped her in a tight embrace. When he stepped back, his gaze lowered and he bit his lip.

She followed his gape, down at her bright-yellow sundress. He smoothed his fingers over the faded hickey and by the admiration in his eyes, and lack of words, he contained his pride. "More comfortable?"

She couldn't stop her curious glance at the young woman in the distance. "Yes, thank you."

He laced their fingers. The kiss to the back of her hand teased her with the memories of Gabrielle, a little too déjà vu. He tugged her in the direction of the woman of interest. *Dear Lord, please let her not be another conquest of Cole's.*

"Isabelle Chambers, I'd like you to meet Amanda Wells, my baby sister." Zander put his arm around the beautiful young woman in a protective, brotherly fashion.

Isabelle smiled, the resemblance hit her, and she sighed. "It's very nice to meet you, Amanda."

She held out her hand, only to be tackled by an overzealous hug. "I am so excited. I love shopping, Isabelle."

She pleaded with the guys over the ecstatic woman's shoulder. Zander placed his hand on Amanda's arm, and she stepped back with a wide grin "She gets that from our mother."

Cole folded his arms around her from behind, and rested his chin on her head. "Amanda is going to take you shopping on Rodeo Drive to get you ready for our date this evening."

Everyone stared at her with excitement, like her list gave them something special in return. When she spun to check out his expression, he beamed with yet another secret revealed.

He kissed her on the tip of her nose; it was sweet. "My treat, have fun."

She couldn't hold back the girly squeal as she jumped into his arms. "Are you for real?"

The grin on his face confirmed it for her—all he offered, even himself, was a gift impossible of repayment.

"This is just the beginning, gorgeous. We're only here until noon tomorrow, though, so make the most of it."

She twirled to make plans with Amanda.

Smack. She jumped when the bite of his hand landed on her ass. She rubbed the sore spot, lifted the thin material in the process, and gave him a view that would leave him tortured until their next encounter.

"You'll have to kiss it better later." The act of seduction backfired on her. She was now wet and ached for attention.

He raised his eyebrows and adjusted the front of his pants as he followed her with a predatory grin.

"Down boy." Brett slapped him on the shoulder.

"She doesn't even realize how amazing she is, does she?"

She accompanied Amanda to the exit, though it wasn't easy to maintain the younger woman's eager stride. The chaos of the airport made it difficult to listen to the men as they trailed behind. Brett's question surprised her but her heart raced with curiosity to see Cole's face, the truth in his response. She did hear the slap, followed by his exaggerated "nope," while the security detail led them out to the busy streets of California.

As each of the men exited the building, they covered their eyes with dark sunglasses for shade and discretion. She followed suit, only because of the sun, and strode to the parked limo. He snagged her arm before she could open the door. "No sweetheart, this one is ours." He pointed to the approaching white limousine. "That one is yours, for the day anyway."

He kissed her cheek. "The driver already knows which hotel we're at, so just let him know when you are ready to come back to me. We have dinner reservations at six, don't be late." He exhaled as he engulfed her in his arms and held on tight.

She didn't want to let go either, but Drew gripped his shirt from behind and yanked him away. "I'd tell ya to get a room, but you already have. Use it." He glanced back over his shoulder. "You can scream as loud as you want, honey."

Cole elbowed him.

She sat in the back of the limo, while he talked to her driver at the front of the car. The driver nodded at whatever he said and she could see his Adam's apple bounce with a hard swallow before they parted ways.

"Amanda? I don't mean to be rude but would you mind if I text a few friends back home on the way?"

Amanda shook her head. "Not at all."

She placed her hand on Amanda's knee, caught her attention before she occupied herself with the bustle of the vibrant city out the window. "Please, my friends call me Izzy."

OMG. You are never going to guess where I am headed? Rodeo Drive. Eeeek. I really wish you ladies were here with me, I miss you.

Send.

Wow. You know my sizes. LOL Taryn

Go crazy girl…you deserve it. I have to tell your mom. Katherine

I've been once. You are going to have a blast. Abigail

She stuffed her phone back into her pocket and adored the beautiful, modern buildings, bright patches of green grass and palm trees situated anywhere space allowed. She couldn't believe she cruised along the streets of Beverly Hills. People strolled the sidewalks as if it were any other day, but to her, so much more. She braced her hands on the seat when the driver stopped the car and opened the door. A much larger breath escaped her compared to the shallow ones she managed during the drive, so enthralled by the beauty around her. Let the fun begin.

"Thanks, James." Amanda hopped out, eager to get started.

When she stepped out, she squinted up at James, her sunglasses not quite dark enough to eclipse the bright California sun. He handed her a credit card. "Mr. Davies asked me to give this to you and his strict orders are for you use it, generously."

Her pulse raced when she held out her hand and James placed a shiny gold card in it. Her savings wouldn't afford the trip Cole expected. She stared at the card a moment before she slipped it into her back pocket. She needed to think about it.

****

She talked James' ear off as she nipped through the hotel lobby. That's what she did when she was nervous, and the amount of bags he carried for her—impossible to hide. He smiled and ushered her into the elevator, hung on her every word while she told him all about her extravagant day with Amanda. She spared no detail, about the handbags, dresses, lingerie, and makeup. Not to mention, the very attentive sales ladies when she handed them Cole's credit card. He laughed at all the right moments and appeared interested; she liked him.

At the room, he put the bags down and opened the door for her. "I will be taking Miss Wells home now. If you need anything, you can call the front desk."

She paced around the room, peeked around corners and in the bathroom.

"He isn't here yet. He wanted to give you time to get ready but will be here at five-thirty to pick you up." He placed all the bags on the bed and stared in her direction, but not really at her. She caught a hint of sadness in his face, his tone. Did he know?

"I am glad you had such a wonderful day, Ms. Chambers." Before she could once again scold him for not calling her Izzy, he left.

****

The woman in the mirror was someone else, not her. Yes, a bout of nausea washed over her in the shower, and her skin clammed up, but this, this wasn't her typical reflection. The makeup artist Amanda convinced her to sit for showed her in great detail how to transform her appearance. It worked. You would never be able to tell she suffered. Tears pooled in her eyes at her beauty. It wasn't just the makeup.

The knee-length, red-satin halter dress shaped her perfectly. It also disguised the flaws, and kept her from the usual ditch and take cover in bed. Her hair was swept up with little wisps left falling at the side, elegant yet easy to let loose. She bit her glossed lip. Amanda's tutorial in the limo on how to make this hairstyle work, and how to let fall before being ravished, replayed in her mind many times. As a result, the night now dragged before it even began. How would he look at her? Would he like it? Would she still be here now if she had a sibling of her own, to offer such advice sooner? Her mother managed life well, always strong, never neglected a precious moment. How did she do it?

A knock at the door startled her from delving too deep into her childhood. She glanced at herself in the mirror one last time. "Don't ruin it, Izzy." She took a deep breath and opened the door to the rather plush bathroom, in the swanky hotel frequented by celebrities, and now her. Goose bumps covered her skin. She used the peephole, just to make sure.

There he stood, as nervous as her. *Boy aren't we a pair?* She smoothed her hands down her dress one last time and opened the door. Her jaw dropped. He was a god. His hair was gelled, every strand in its perfect place. Stubble framed his face, gave him a rough, bad boy appearance. He wore slacks sure to showcase a drool-worthy ass, and his crisp, white shirt rolled up to his elbows showed a few of the tattoos she'd lick, again, if he'd let her. She'd be amendable to the date starting off in bed, in the shower, or on the floor. Whatever, it all suited her just fine.

"Hi"

"Hello yourself, beautiful." He stalked toward her, paused to kick to door closed behind him, and continued toward her without a hitch in his determined glare. She stepped back with his advance, but in one swift motion, he grabbed her by the waist and forced her back to the cold wall. She stared into his heated gaze and swallowed.

He leaned down and brushed his lips against hers. "I'll try not to mess up the masterpiece, but I gotta taste you. Better now than laying you out on the table at the restaurant in front of everyone. You are the most beautiful woman I have ever seen."

She shivered at his words. He brushed his lips down her neck, hit the sweet spot that always made her wet. And it did just that, like clockwork.

"Cole" His name sounded more like a moan; she couldn't help it. "We better go, or else we won't get out of here at all." Her knees were weak, along with her resolve to make this date venture anywhere but the bedroom.

"Keeping me on edge the entire evening may not bode well for you later, Ms. Chambers." He tore himself away but kept her hand in his, lifted it to his mouth for a light lick. "I take it your shopping trip was fun?" His gaze drifted from hers, down. "You are exquisite."

Heat surfaced to her face. She admired him like a seductress, had never pictured herself as *ogle* material, until the way he gawked at her now. "It was one for the books. Thank you so much. Zander's sister is fun."

His eyes widened. "Fun isn't exactly the word I would use to describe her, erratic maybe."

She laughed and sidestepped out from the wall, distanced herself from the enchantment of his scent. She swayed with confidence, intended to tease him, but the movement evoked sensual friction to her swollen folds, and teased her as well. She ignored it and slowed her pace to the table, for her new clutch. It was soft and silky compared to the pleather, scuffed-up bag she always carried. "I'm ready when you are. Cole?"

His gaze, the one on her ass, roamed up again. "Yes, baby?"

She smacked his ass and passed him to open the door.

"The dress isn't the only new thing I'm trying tonight."

****

She closed her eyes and tipped her chin up to soak in the warm California sun. She missed Tampa. Many things about being with the Scandals reminded her of home. If the circumstances were different, she'd bring him there.

"Miss the Tampa heat?" He held her waist from behind and kissed her forehead when she tilted it back far enough.

"Mmmm, yes I do, but this is nice. Are we waiting for the limo?" When she opened her eyes, she caught sight of a flash from across the street. She jolted and placed her hand on his chest.

"Don't worry, baby. I like being seen with you in my arms. I will forever have keepsakes of you online, in the tabloids, the paper, and whatever else they use to gossip these days. Unless it bothers you?"

She shook her head at the same time the purr of an engine and male hoots sounded behind her. Curiosity about the smile on his face nagged at her. She spun around to see Drew and Brett drive up in a candy-apple red Lamborghini.

"Cole." She jumped into his arms, and he plunged one foot back to brace the impact.

He chuckled and held her tight. She could feel his arousal.

"Careful sweetheart, I have a lot planned. We don't need any injuries getting in our way." He wiggled his eyebrows with a devilish grin.

She peered up into his eyes; he was always honest about what he wanted.

"Cole, this car rocks." Brett jumped out of the passenger seat, a splayed grin and wild gaze fixed on the car, while he forced his steps away. He inched back to it every few paces as if he couldn't let it go.

Drew climbed out of the low to the ground car with as much finesse as a tall man could. "Seriously Izzy, your list kicks ass."

"Hope you guys didn't leave any drool marks." He patted Brett's back and pranced with a cocky stride to hold the door open for her. "If you're good, I may let you drive later, but right now, it's my turn. Besides, I'd kinda like to keep my man card in front of the guys. Drew is right baby, your list kicks ass."

"Yes, it does. I regret to inform you though, with a strut like that, you won't lose your man card. You'll just give it away."

His grin and lack of rebuttal caused her to follow his gaze, to the wide-eyed, speechless men.

"Hands off boys, *she's* all mine too."

Heat rushed to her face, sure to be noticeable.

Before she crouched in, she locked gazes with him, held back tears. "How am I ever going to repay you for all of this? I still don't understand why someone like you would do so much for someone—" She let her gaze fall to her body. "—like me?"

He guided her chin with his fingertips, back up to him again. "The guys are right. You don't realize how beautiful you are."

He helped her into the car. As he rounded to the driver's side, he gestured something to Drew with a slight nod of his head. *Hmm. I wonder what that was all about.*

The sight of him beside her in the very fine sports car was hot, but the ridiculous smile on his face, priceless. "You sure are happy."

He smoothed his hands around the steering wheel, still focused on the road ahead. "Driving a car like this is a first for me too."

"I would have guessed, given your success, you

would own something like this. Aren't cars like toys for grown boys?"

He smiled and reached for her hand, lifted it up to his mouth for a kiss. His lips were warm, soft. "I own it now, thanks to you."

She bit her lip and placed her free hand on her stomach.

"I may look wild on the outside in order to maintain a certain appearance, but my priorities have always grounded me, kept me from the temptations of our success. I told you about my dad raising me and my brothers?"

"Yes. Of course."

Still fixated on the traffic, he tilted his head in her direction when she answered. Every moment since day one, he let her know, somehow, he was with her.

"My dad sacrificed a lot, trying to keep a roof over our heads. You see what it's like to keep *us* four grown men fed on the bus. My brothers and I were no different. Dad did everything for us, even if it meant he went without. He worked so many jobs to help us grow into the men we are. We are all very successful, in our own ways."

His interpretation of his upbringing inspired her, reminded her of her own childhood. Even as an adult, she modeled her mother's selflessness, made sure everyone else was happy long before herself. She'd give her lunch away at school to the student who didn't have one, until she smartened up and made a little pantry in her classroom.

"Anyway. I support my dad now and give anonymous donations to a fair amount of charities back home." He shrugged his shoulders. "It's the least I can do. Drew often gives me shit for not splurging on myself. Guess he'll have you to thank. Enough of the heavy, here we are."

She didn't want to leave the confines of the beautiful car, didn't want the purr to fade. He placed his hand on her bare knee when she put her hand on the door. "Please, allow me." He hurried out of the car, handed the keys to the valet, and opened her door. He ushered her in, with his hand on her lower back. The slight touch took her breath away.

The restaurant gleamed with elegance. She inspected the dining area while the hostess ushered them to the back. The tables glowed with the soft light of golden-colored candles arranged on top of white table clothes, each spaced far enough from the next to allow for privacy. The dark-brown chairs and floor were distinct, and captivating next to the cream-colored walls. She placed her hand to her stomach when they entered their own room. A table similar to the others sat in the center, and flames from a fireplace off to the side offered subtle light. It smelled of baked bread.

"Mr. Davies, it's a pleasure. Your evening has been planned out to your specifications. Please don't hesitate to alter anything, at any time." The young woman bowed and left them alone.

"Your specifications?" She raised her brows at him and sat in the chair he held out for her.

"Yes, darling. I took the liberty to arrange things ahead of time. This night should be perfect, like you."

She laughed, really laughed. He sat back in his chair and gave her his most annoyed smile.

"I'm sorry. I just find it hard to think of you not dating." She waved her hands around the room. "Look at this? You could have any woman."

The waitress chose that moment to serve their champagne and hors d'oeuvre. By the relief on his face, he held something back. He took a deep breath, accepted the champagne bottle, and poured a glass for her.

She placed her hand over his, to stop him, and glanced at the door to make sure the waitress was gone. "I can't."

He set the bottle in the ice bucket. With concern in his eyes, he cradled her hand in both of his and waited for her to continue.

The current of his worry traveled through their embrace. "I was feeling rough earlier and took some medication. I should avoid alcohol for now anyway." She slouched in her chair and sighed. "I really want to drive the car."

He laughed, let go of the unnecessary tension and relaxed back in his seat. He pointed to the food placed in front of them and smiled. "Then I guess we'd better eat."

"Is that what I think it is?"

"Uh-huh. Caviar."

A slight shuffle from under the table caught her attention. His leg. "Believe it or not, a lot of this I have never done before, either." He inspected the serving platter and scrunched his nose. An image of him flashed before her, with meat and potatoes, not fine cuisine. Either way, he was perfect for her.

"One, two, three?" She shrugged her shoulders when he shook his head and laughed at her. "Hey, I teach kindergarteners."

They stretched, with hesitation, for what appeared

to be toasted baguettes covered in something her students would describe as turds.

"One," they raised their delicacies together.

"Two," touched as if to cheers one another.

"Three," and breathed deep before taking a bite.

They chewed, and stared at one another, quiet. The moment lingered and all she could think of were discreet ways to get this offensive-tasting crap out of her mouth. She didn't want to spit it out, how awkward would that be? She was close to projectile vomiting, which would be worse. He smiled while he chewed, as if he enjoyed it. She could too. Maybe.

Be strong.

She caved, peeled the napkin from her lap, and spit it out. "Oh my God, that is awful."

Cole followed her lead, all but gagging. "OK, I take it back, sweetie. Your list isn't *all* great. How do people like that shit?"

They both wiped their tongues off with the napkins when the waitress entered the room again at just the right moment. Neither was very skilled at covers ups, as they composed themselves and knocked dinnerware over in the process.

"Is everything all right, Mr. Davies?" She also queried in Isabelle's direction. "Mrs. Davies?"

She sat back speechless, fixed the napkin on her lap, and laced her hands together in a white knuckled grip.

"My apologies if we were too loud. My girlfriend and I are just experiencing some firsts." He pointed to the caviar. "It is apparent neither of our palates finds this as appetizing as we'd been led to believe. Would you mind taking it away for us? Please charge the full amount. I am sure those who desire it find it wonderfully appetizing."

"As you wish. I will put a rush on your entrées."

The waitress exited with a bright blush on her pale skin. She waited until the frosted French doors closed. "Girlfriend?" She swung back to him. It wasn't the first time, but the past one was about redemption. Did he believe it to be true?

"Well, I am not opposed to referring to you as my wife, but I figured girlfriend might be a better start. After all, I do happen to think of you as a friend, and given the things I've enjoyed doing to you, I know you are all woman."

He scooted back in his seat and tilted his head, patient for her reaction. Waited for her to argue? Not tonight. He'd gone to a lot of trouble, and well, what he said made sense. She waved her hand in the air and told him about her shopping trip on Rodeo Drive. Long term didn't need to be spoken about; it wasn't an option.

The entrées were to die for. The combination of mouth-watering goodness and the anticipation of the car didn't bode well for lady-like manners. She inhaled every bite. "I take it you like pasta?" He held his fork half way to his mouth and stared at her with satisfaction in his gaze.

"A—" Chew. "—maz—" Chew. "—zing." She covered her mouth with the napkin. "I'm a little excited about driving the car."

He set his fork down and removed the napkin from his lap and placed it on the table. "I hate to break it to you, honey, but if you keep that up I may be the one driving again, to the hospital."

She shrugged her shoulders as if to say it will be

worth it.

"Well, my beautiful lady. This meal has gone by faster than I planned for, and we now have some time to kill. Whatever can we do with it?" He used his foot under the table to stroke up her leg.

"Duh." She held out her hand. "Keys please?"

While he handled the bill, she waited as patiently as possible behind the solid engine. Her butt vibrated with its purr. She glared at Cole through the window when he wandered to the car, hands in his pockets, and a sing-song whistle from his lips.

You'll pay.

He sat in the passenger seat in a calm fashion, took his time with the seat belt. She shrugged, braced her hands on the wheel, and peeled out from between the white lines. She giggled at him, fallen over in his seat. "That'll teach ya."

His seatbelt clicked and in her peripheral vision, he scrambled for the door handle and forced his back into the seat.

"Isabelle?"

He gripped the armrest between them, sure to have a frightened, wide-eyed glare as well. It was priceless. "Yes Cole, problem?"

He threw his hand to the dashboard when she swerved into the other lane. At least she signaled.

"Please slow down, honey. Death by hysterically happy girlfriend isn't the description I want for my obituary."

That got her to slow down, the car anyway. Her heart raced much faster. *Girlfriend? I can't. I want to, but I can't.*

She didn't know if her anxiety showed, but it must

have since the hum of the engine was all that filled the car on the way to the beach. He set the GPS, but even with its help, dusk had fallen by the time they arrived. They sat in a lot that overlooked the water, silent, taken over by the serene picture before them. The sunset glowed over the water, all the way to the beach, and the sand sparkled as if mixed with crystals. "Wow." She let her hands fall from the wheel.

Beaches were nothing out of the ordinary for her, but this was different. Was his presence what made the difference?

"I'd say."

He stared at her, so intensely, like he was aware of the things she refused to even admit to herself. The devotion in his gaze compelled her over the seat. She straddled his lap, a cool breeze drifted up her dress. They focused on one another, and the world, along with all of their worries, melted away. Their desperate inhales of breath echoed over the crash of the waves outside.

He placed his hands on her knees, and slid them up her thighs. He closed his eyes and moaned, clutched onto the garters Amanda swore drove men insane. "Oh, Isabelle."

She smiled. Amanda was right. She placed her hands on the sides of his face, guided him in for a passionate kiss, and rubbed her swollen nub against his hard shaft. They had too many clothes on. "I need you."

He broke the kiss long enough to inspect the dusk around them. "It's not quite dark yet, are you sure?"

She clasped her hand to his, and forced him under her dress. "Does that convince you?"

His eyes widened. She was bare, hot, wet. "No

panties. Are you trying to kill me?"

He growled, freed his hand, and used his thighs to hoist her up so he could undo his zipper. His rush to get inside her, and struggle to get his pants down low enough to do so, amused her.

She leaned forward to kiss his stubble when he seized her hips, lowered her to the right height, and glided his bare shaft through her folds. The tender kiss she'd intended ended up a moan, with her forehead dropped to his cheek. He twisted his hands in her hair and tugged her head back for a kiss; her body moved in frantic need without his help. Her juices covered him with each stroke, and her legs trembled. She squeezed her thighs together, held back the fast approach of her climax.

"Oh no you don't. I want it. Now." He let go of her hair, grasped her waist, and lifted, guided her down to sheath him. Urgency to be embedded in her body flashed across his gaze while he stretched her, with care not to hurt her. Every vein of his girth massaged her passage throughout the slow decent. The buildup to climax lost, not necessary. Her body tightened in spasms by the time he filled her.

"Oh God, yes."

She remained still, with him buried deep, and calmed herself down to make it last.

He tipped her chin toward his lips, kissed her as gently as he entered her. "Take what you need, baby. I'll give you the world." He stared at her as if his life in that moment changed for the better. Hers did.

She couldn't hold back. Every moment with him exposed the woman inside her whom she'd searched for. His serene face glowed in the moonlight and his hands trembled at her sides. His blue eyes sparkled with passion, locked with hers and determined to go with her to the place that'd become their own.

She held on to his muscled shoulders, rose and lowered without a sound. His fingertips dug into her hips, controlled their unhurried pace. Their breath became heavy. Every movement remained precise. The friction stimulated her beyond restraint. Her tightened muscles gave, set her free. "I'm coming," she whispered.

"Me too, baby. Me too." He thrust his hips upward, and drew her down onto him at the same time, sealed their bodies together. He convulsed as he emptied his seed deep into her core, but he still held her gaze.

She lowered her dewy forehead to his while they descended from their high, it was too much. The moment would have been perfect to scream *I love you,* if they could.

Chapter Thirteen

Dear Diary,
Sometimes it isn't what's visible…

They sat there with their foreheads together. A trickle of sweat traveled down the side of his face, moisture coated hers. The car was silent, except for the erratic inhale and exhale of breaths.

She leaned back for distance but the air was as warm as her body. "Well that's one way to break in a new car."

Movement out the corner of their eyes forced their attention out the window. A young man stopped and eyed the gorgeous car. When he'd scoured the length of the vehicle with manlike appreciation and landed on the window, he stared. Within seconds, the woman at his side yanked his arm in their intended direction, yelling at him.

He eased out of her snug heat, tried not to make too much of a mess, but his laugh at the poor bastard sure *not* to get laid tonight made it difficult. "We better get out of here before we're arrested for indecent exposure."

She climbed back over to the driver's seat, "Aren't all rock stars supposed to get arrested for that at some point in their careers?"

He smacked her backside before she sat. "Ha, ha

smartass. Are you sure you are okay to drive?"

She glared at him and smoothed her hands around the wheel. "Pffft. Try not to act like a scared little girl, like you did on our way out here."

He shook his head and zipped up his pants, mumbled a few derogatory terms. "You will pay for that."

She turned the key and the purr of the engine hummed, much like the strong pulse that still beat between her legs. She shifted in her seat, squeezed her thighs together and enjoyed the lingering sensation of him inside her, and because she didn't want to ruin her dress. First stop, ladies room.

His phone beeped with an incoming text. He glanced at the screen, typed out a quick reply, and put the phone back in his pocket. An uncomfortable shiver traveled up her spine in reaction to his posture in the seat—relaxed, yet cryptic. She straightened her back and pressed her foot on the gas pedal with a little more clout, resisting the urge to ask.

"Drew. Asked how our date is going. We're a little late. He and the guys are waiting back at the hotel for us, and the next part of this evening."

With her eyebrow raised, she glared at him, but he just shrugged his shoulders and let his sly gaze drift toward the oncoming traffic. Surprises she loved, being teased about them beforehand, not so much. She huffed and returned her focus back to the road. Not to appear too desperate, she casually pressed the button to lower the window an inch. God, it was hot.

****

A cool blast of air hit them the second the door swooshed open at the hotel. She squeezed his hand to stop his march, and exhaled. The heat created in the car not long ago lingered on their skin.

"The guys are up in Drew's room. We better go get them or we will never make it in time. Do you need anything from our room?"

She used her finger to trace lines up and down his arm and smiled up at him. "Not if Drew doesn't mind my using his bathroom to freshen up. What exactly are we late for?"

He shook his head and chuckled, tucked his arm around her back and gave her a gentle shove ahead of him. He didn't want to cave. Gorgeous women had that effect on him. "He won't mind, and, I'm not telling."

She sauntered in front of him, exaggerating the motion of her hips like a seductress; he liked it. The curves of her body showed through the thin satin material and for a second he fisted his hands, maybe they could forego the planned evening and stay in bed. "You know I plan to fuck you again, Ms. Chambers, so this display will only seal the deal, not sway me."

She spun so fast on one heel to scan the room for anyone who may have heard his brash words she staggered. A blush formed on her skin and embarrassment rose in her eyes. He fell for her even more. She hit the button to call the elevator several times and glared at him over her shoulder.

He stalked toward her slowly, hands in his pockets with a devilish grin. "I don't care who knows I've fucked you or that I'll do it again, many times."

When the doors opened, she rushed in and took out her embarrassment on the button again. He held out his hand, halted the door, and stepped in. The ding sounded and both of them swayed when it accelerated to the next floor. The motion sent her off balance; she lost the fight to maintain her pointed, angered stance.

She growled and extended her hand to the wall beside her for support. He continued toward her and she retreated, as far as the tiny space allowed. He placed his hands to the wall on either side of her head, caged her in, and consumed her with his possessive stare. She shifted her legs. The tension in her gaze weakened, unable to hide the fact their combined arousals dripped from her body.

“Can you still feel me? Is my cum dripping down your leg?”

She closed her eyes and forced an inhaled breath.

“Cole. Your words embarrass me and turn me on at the same time. It’s a rush that’s new to me.” Her gaze fell to his chest. “Yes, I can still feel you, and if I don’t clean up soon I will have to change my dress.”

He kissed her forehead, squeezed her hand, and ushered her out of the elevator. For the first time, he understood why his dad told him to do whatever it takes to hold onto the woman you love.

Male cheers echoed from Drew’s room as they neared. A tall blonde strolled out with a blush, and a not so innocent spark in her eye. He tightened his grip on Isabelle’s hand, and nodded with polite acknowledgement as the young woman passed. Her reaction, to glance back over her shoulder and threaten the woman’s backside with a glare, impressed him.

He squeezed her hand to get her attention, assured her with a silent shake of his head that she was the only woman in his eyes. The one woman they’d all like to stay, not leave.

He held his hand out, suggested she go first

through the wide open door. As her stiff hand unwound from its vulnerable grip, Drew strolled out of the bathroom naked. He dried his chest with a towel, wandered over to the bed, and got dressed without a second glance. Like her presence was no different from Brett and Zander, who lounged in the chairs on the other side of the bed.

"Holy shit." She let go of his hand and closed the distance between her and Drew. "May I?"

Drew looked back over his shoulder, gave his most self-assured nod and mouthed the words, oh yeah.

He laughed and gave him the finger.

"Help yourself, darlin'." Drew purred.

She leaned down to get a better view of his tattoo, a dragon. Common knowledge since he would sometimes perform with his shirt off. What the fans didn't see was how far down, and where, on his body it molded. It started up at his left shoulder, curved along his lower back to the front of his hip and all the way around his upper right thigh. Cole remembered the several appointments and many hours it took to finish all the vibrant detail.

She kept her distance. Cole leaned his shoulder against the wall. What would her comfort level be? When she crouched down even more and traced its path with her fingertip, he crossed his arms in front of his chest and bit the inside of his cheek. He could trust them, but this brought back memories he buried a long time ago.

She read the script along the end of the dragons' tail. "The will to live will always outweigh the ability to die. That's beautiful."

Drew glance his way, shrugged. "You can tell her

later, not now."

He dipped his head with compassion, understood the time wasn't right. She raised her gaze at both men but didn't ask.

"The bathroom is free now." He couldn't help the bite in his words; *she* hadn't done anything wrong. She hurried to close the door behind her without a word. He stared at the door and dropped his head back to the wall with a thud, forced his muscles and his once-broken heart to chill the fuck out.

"She's not Alexis, Cole. Nor am I a jackass."

He left the room to wait out in the hall.

****

The limo ride to the venue flew by, thank God. He double-checked his watch many times and used the phone to call up to the driver, insisted he find a faster route. They were very late. She'd mentioned how quiet the floor was back at the hotel, and reminded him he hadn't given the guys the necessary lecture to keep it a secret. He glared at them before they could respond, and they all strolled away confused, but quiet. He'd booked the entire floor and the amount of money this trip cost would make her uncomfortable, so he didn't want her to know.

The car stopped and the privacy window slid down an inch. "We're here, Mr. Davies."

"Thank you, James. I apologize for being an ass."

The middle-aged man smiled in the rear view mirror. "Not a problem, sir. Have a fun evening. I will be parked around back when you're ready to leave. Let me get the door."

In his peripheral vision, she demanded answers from the men with her gaze, but no one spoke. James extended his hand to help her out of the car, followed by him, eager to provide a tip of reasonable compensation for his moodiness.

Security stood at the door, waiting as he'd asked. The night was improving. Every detail caught her attention. A line-up to gain access to tonight's entertainment stretched a mile long down the city street. Her pace slowed with each step, until she paused with her hands on her hips. "Grand Performances. What is this place?"

He glanced back at Zander, who took the backpack from James. "Thanks, man."

"No problem."

With furrowed brows, she accepted his hand when he extended it to her. "Well. Sometimes it's nice to sit back and watch others perform for a change. Zander's buddies are playing here tonight, they're pretty good."

He tipped her chin up with his hand and kissed her lips. The gloss she wore tasted like strawberries. His mind raced with ideas, flavors he could use on her body that would go well with strawberries.

Zander hurried ahead of them, shook hands, and gave a backslapping hug to the large man at the door. They were ushered inside. People roamed the modern bar and there were many open tables for them to relax, but they wouldn't. The best was yet to come. They continued forward, through another set of doors and outside once again. Her face lit up when what seemed like a typical bar transformed into a small, outdoor concert venue. His heart swelled at the sight of her enchanted gaze. Tall buildings closed the area in, created a space with its own unique presence, and privacy. Not that they'd need much of the latter tonight.

****

She squeezed his hand and stopped just outside the door. The excitement of the incredible site before her and the intensity of the loud music pumped through her veins. People were everywhere; but the clouded night sky dimmed the energetic atmosphere so you couldn't tell what kind of trouble was taking place, unless you really focused.

They stood on a veranda that circled the lower half, overlooking the stage. Hundreds of people crowded the band, as close as the space allowed, just like one of the Scandals shows. The upper tier held a fair amount of people but the roped-off section they were brought to could have accommodated ten times their group.

A stocked mini bar along the wall allowed them to make themselves at home, and not have to fight through mobs while they enjoyed the show. She scanned the area and never would have envisioned from the exterior of the building this exquisite ambiance existed behind it. An illuminated canal of water separated the stage from the crowd. The band played on an open concrete platform with vertical, meshed, metal towers that held spotlights. Their meticulous placement allowed only the band to glow. Very few pyroglyphics, smoke or beams of light commonly used to enhance the energy of the crowd filled the empty spaces, not necessary anyway given the boisterous crowd's ability to make the smaller rock group appear well known and large. She paced her steps, took her time up to the railing, not able to focus on any one thing. She held on to the cold metal, absorbed the vibrations from the guests below. People danced to the music and simply enjoyed life.

A warm chest brushed up to her back and the scent

with it, spectacular. Cole.

"Like what you see?"

"It's incredible." She smiled, still occupied with the hundreds of people who laughed and socialized like they'd spent many nights there before.

"I planned for us to be here for the opening act." He wrapped his body around hers and placed his hands on top of hers; they were warm. He rubbed his erection into the hollow of her butt and she let her head drop back to his chest with her eyes closed.

Without sight, every other sense heightened her awareness. The loud music, the vibrating bass, his scent, him. "But, the detour this evening will never be regretted, or forgotten."

She hummed with delight as a similar desire built once again. She blocked out their current whereabouts, could still recall the waves that crashed outside on the beach. The ones that hit her while inside the car.

"Here darlin', you're going to need this." She opened her eyes at the sound of Drew's voice. He held a shot glass with amber liquid up to her lips.

She opened her mouth and let him tip the liquor in. It burned, but also warmed every tissue in her chest as it traveled its course. Cole took his hand off hers for a brief moment while he downed the two shots Drew brought for him as well. He didn't linger, just returned to the group of men, and girls by the sound of the giggles that blended into the background.

"Mmm" She swayed to the music; he followed suit, still in contact with as much of her body as possible. "They're good. I had no idea places like this existed." She twisted her head to the side and caught his gaze fixed on her.

Her presence appeared to be the only thing in existence for him, and even though it thrilled her, it scared the shit out of her. He leaned in and kissed her, forced his tongue inside her mouth and massaged every inch. Her stomach fluttered at their public display. He drew away slowly, left them both in a desperate pant for more.

"Oh, baby, I would love to show you the world. There are so many places I would…" He hugged her tight and leaned into her ear. "Take you." She could feel the smile in his whispered words.

Zander stepped up beside them and held out another shot. "Last one sweetie." He wiggled his eyebrows. "I'm sure you won't need anymore."

She raised her eyebrows but didn't ask. Like Drew, he too held out the drink, and waited for her to let him feed it to her. It seemed awkward, all this attention. She caught sight of Cole's headshake, refusing his shots.

She admired the crowd and the band, found it hard not to join in and get all fan girlish, and dance like an idiot. She shivered. The temperature dropped a little; she should've gone back to the room for a sweater. Goose bumps broke out over her skin, not from the chill alone, but also her memories of the hotel room filled with inked men.

"I'll be right back."

He didn't wait for her to respond, just left. A cold breeze replaced his absence. She wrapped her arms around herself and ignored the nightlife to peek behind her. Drew, Zander, and Brett stood in front of the bar, each held a pretty woman and a beer, but still paid more attention to the band than the girls.

The smile on her face withered as she considered

the excitement in the strange women's eyes. Did they want more out of life than just the one night? But her own lack of adventure was what started this rollercoaster, so who was she to judge.

Cole tugged a large, dark blanket out of the backpack Zander carried in and brought it back to her with a smile that made the bumps on her arms multiply.

He draped the blanket behind his back first. When he threw his arms around her, still holding the blanket, he enclosed them and huddled close. She repositioned herself back toward the stage and held the blanket closed around her shoulders. His fresh, earthy scent surrounded her.

He leaned forward, used his chin to clear the hair from her neck and kissed below her ear. "Warm now?" He nuzzled her ear with his nose and continued to kiss and lick her neck.

She shuddered. Without hesitation, she rubbed the cleft of her backside over his hardened length. She meant to relieve the ache that developed between her thighs, but it only fueled the sensation more.

Anticipation clawed at her the second his hands roamed from her sides. She swayed with weak knees.

"Hold the blanket with one hand, baby, and hang onto the railing. Spread your legs."

As she followed his direction, her pulse sped and she scoured the crowd with wide eyes.

"Don't worry, no one can see us," he whispered in her ear and the music faded like background noise to her beating heart. "I want to make you come."

She closed her eyes and let her head fall back on his chest. He smoothed his hand over her butt and lowered to the hem of her dress. He eased the material up in slow motion. She bit her lip. Her arousal heightened with the unhurried glide of the soft fabric up her thighs, and her knees weakened further. He clutched her hip with his free hand to steady her and continued to explore under her dress. He touched her mound and she moaned.

"Scream all you want baby, you'll just blend in. When my dick is deep inside you, you'll have no choice."

She wanted to. God did she ever. His words added fuel to the fire that burned in her. When he touched her swollen lips, she came undone.

"Fuck. Isabelle. You're so wet. I wish I could taste you right now."

The heat of his breath in her ear and his roaming hands snapped all the restraint she'd maintained. She angled her head to meet his lips for a kiss, bit his bottom lip with her teeth. He growled and used his fingertip to trace around her opening, teased her swollen nub with light flicks. She broke away but kept her eyes closed. "I want to come. Please."

She pictured his satisfied smile at her bold request. He inched the hand at her hip up to her breast and pinched her sensitive peak through the thin material, dipping his finger into her heat at the same time. "Come on my hand, and then I'm going to fill you. If you have any doubts about this, speak now. I want you right here, in front of everyone."

She opened her eyes. With her body still to the stage, she glanced back to meet his gaze. "I'm not stopping you. Fuck me."

He dropped his forehead to her temple with a pant. "No Isabelle. I want to make love to you."

The warmth in his words hit her in the chest.

He smiled, used her own sleekness to tease her. “Come for me, baby,” He took his time, studied her body, and lingered on every inch when she whimpered in response to his touch. He tormented her, traced feather-light patterns around her swollen nub, dipped inside her only enough to gather more juices and continue.

She seized the railing with a rigid arm, and opened her mouth to yell at him when he flicked it. He played her with both hands, much like the strings of a guitar. One pinched and flicked her nipple while the other strummed her bud to the beat of the music. When a loud guitar solo screamed, he shoved two fingers inside her, curled them, and stroked her sensitive spot. Her juices flowed with the firm pressure, over his hand, and down her inner thigh.

“Oh God. I’m gonna come.”

He brushed his tongue along her earlobe, kissed beneath it and whispered, “Ride my hand, baby. Get yourself there. Let me see you fly.”

She tightened her singlehanded grasp on the blanket and pumped her hips, rode his hand. Within seconds, all noise faded and she struggled to keep her half-lidded eyes open. Every muscle in her core contracted as the blood in her body raced for that delicious spot. The tension wound so tight, she feared its release and fought against it. She couldn’t. Warmth exploded within her. His hand slid in and out with ease and she drenched him with her arousal.

“Oh God. I’m coming.”

“Yes, you are. Holy fuck.”

He didn’t let her ride it out long before he raised

his wet hand up between her grip on the blanket and her chest. "Lick yourself. I want to taste you when I kiss you." She dipped her chin and took his two fingers in her mouth, sucked her juices clean from his hand.

He closed his eyes. "You're perfect for me."

He tugged his hand away and scrambled behind her for his zipper. She giggled.

"Laugh now, beautiful woman, but I'll have you screaming louder than the music soon."

She stopped the second he raised her dress in the back and smoothed his length between her spread legs, rubbed his large crown through her folds.

"Oh. Holy of all—" She couldn't grip the railing strong enough.

"Oh yes, baby. Watch the stage, I'll hold the blanket. It's gonna take all of my strength not to bend you over this rail. Let me get a rhythm going with the music."

Thankful for the slower song, she fixed her attention to the band, though not with the same intent as she had when they arrived. He clutched the blanket in one fist, still hidden and placed the other on her bare hip to help guide him.

When he crouched a little behind her, for a fleeting second, she closed her eyes and thanked Taryn for the heels. Her legs shook as he nudged her entrance, still swollen from her release.

"Mmm, I love a challenge." He dug his fingertips into her hip and coerced his way inside with the swirl of his hips.

She clenched her hands around the cold steel, aware of the struggle with resistance he spoke of earlier. Without his spoken admission of frayed resistance, she might've bent over the rail, and when he bit her shoulder, she damn near did.

Once her body caved to his demand, he slid in and out of her with an unhurried speed. Her pulse raced; she lacked the patience required to keep their movements discreet. His shaft massaged her puckered hole at the angle he entered her, and drove her to madness. There could have been an earthquake around them, she wouldn't have known.

She relaxed her muscles and focused on his thrusts with the beat of the music. Her body built again with anticipation of another orgasm. So much heat radiated under the blanket she'd rip it off if it weren't for the hundreds of people who surrounded them. Her toes curled in her high heels.

He leaned into her ear, positioned himself closer, and slid his free hand around her front. "I'm close, baby. Let me in more. I want my cum deep inside you."

She couldn't speak. His words were so erotic she floated with lust and fell in a way she didn't want to put words to. She touched the side of her face to his and they kept their visual attention on the spectacular show in front of them. He smoothed his hand over her soft mound and down, used his fingertip to circle her swollen, aching clit. He tightened his grasp on the blanket and forced her body onto him with the other, rooted himself and held still. A low whimper escaped her as he trembled, spilled his seed inside her.

The feel of his warmth around her, in her, sent her over the edge with him. "AHHH."

The chorus of the song belted out but she could have sworn he whispered *I love you*, even over her scream and the sexual high that buzzed in her ears.

The last chord of the song extended, faded into dead air. The crowd quieted along with it. He couldn't have timed it better. She wouldn't have been able to hold back if they ended before her orgasm. The band exited the stage, a break before the encore. She scanned the crowd, let go of the railing and put her hands under the blanket. Her grip closed them in tighter. He stirred inside her while the crowd of people roamed for drinks. The sexual high faded and her body stiffened. "People are going to see us."

"Sweetie. people are far too drunk to see, or care." He withdrew from her body and righted himself. Before he tugged the blanket off of them, he smoothed his hands down the back of her dress, made sure she was covered.

She faced him, leaned her lower back against the cool steel, and grabbed onto his shirt for support. She could feel her skin flush from his wicked smile, so damn proud of himself. The slight ounce of regret faded.

He put his forehead against hers and whispered, "I love your list. I love—"

"If you two are done getting the rest of us hot and horny, Tweedledee and Tweedledum would like to take their ladies back to the hotel and get a little too."

They jumped when Drew slapped him on the back. His interruption was indeed perfect this time. She didn't want him to finish that sentence. "Wait. You knew what we were doing?" She forced him back a little so she could see Drew.

Drew picked the blanket up off the ground and stuffed it into the backpack. "Sweetheart. It may not have been obvious from the front, but we could see him fucking you from behind. It was hot, and besides, your screams weren't well timed to the music." He kissed her forehead and returned to the other guys with a cocky swagger.

All the heat in her body rose to her face.

Cole put his arm over her shoulder and guided her to the door. "He was wrong about one thing, you know."

Not able to respond to his statement until the small crowd cleared, along with her head, she ignored him. He led the way, which was nice, because she held his waist for support. Her legs wobbled like limp noodles.

When the others proceeded through the door ahead of them, he closed it and pinned her back to the cold glass. He held her face in his hands and kissed her for all to see. She surrendered to his demand, fisted his shirt in her hands as if her world would fall out from under her if she didn't. To some extent, it would. Hoots and hollers sounded from outside as well as from the inside. People stared now.

He broke away first. "*Fucking* isn't how I would describe what just happened between us."

The heat of his words drifted across her lips. Left her without a comeback.

Chapter Fourteen

Dear Diary,
Nothing could extinguish the fire that consumed me…

Cole sat on the edge of the bed and his knee bounced. The mirror he stared at on the wall reflected the closed door that kept her from him. The sound of water as it filled the tub calmed him somewhat. She deserved the alone time after all they'd done tonight, but the closer they got to the end of her list, the closer he got to losing her.

He rubbed his chest. The quiet room and the feelings held inside suffocated him. He scribbled a quick note and placed it on the table, in case she wasn't long in the tub. Drew crashed in the room next door, and never rejected an opportunity to set him straight.

He banged on Drew's door.

Drew whipped it open and shook his head. "You have a beautiful woman next door and you're here with me? You have issues, man." He trudged back to the bed, sprawled out, and switched off the TV. He lay against the propped-up pillow and crossed his arms over his chest, waiting.

Cole dragged a chair up to the bed and sat. His knees vibrated with a similar turbulence to his heart, so he stretched his legs out on top of the bed, crossed at the ankles.

Drew laughed when his foot twitched instead. "Give it up man, it's a lost cause."

He scrubbed his face and sighed. "I'm screwed."

Drew chuckled and raised his eyebrows. "Well I hope so, that's what you brought her here for, isn't it?"

He planted his feet on the floor. He didn't need this. "Fuck you. Thanks a lot, man." Bent forward, tempted to leave, he slumped with his elbows on his knees and stared at the diamond pattern in the carpet.

"Ahem." He lifted his head to Drew, who held his hands up in surrender. "I'll stop. Sorry."

He put his feet back up where he could control his nerves, but his throat tightened. He couldn't control everything.

"I love her."

"I know."

He stared down at his hands while he cracked his knuckles. The slight sting was a welcome distraction from all of the pleasure he'd experienced in the last several days. Never did he think he would be overwhelmed with it or need a break. He scrubbed his hands through his hair, broke loose the stiff strands. "It's only been six days—"

"Love doesn't come with a manual. You can't explain or predict it." Drew got up and made his way to the fridge and like on all the other difficult days, chose the hard stuff. It was a quick fix, disguised the problem much like a Band-Aid. He poured the tiny bottles of Jack in glasses and handed one over on his way back to the bed. They held their glasses out but didn't say anything, just tipped their heads back and swallowed.

"Thanks." He swirled the empty glass around and swallowed again, hard. "I'm gonna lose her."

"Yes, you are." Drew set his glass down on the nightstand beside him. "It's not easy losing someone you have a strong connection with. I can't change this, make it what you want. I can tell you, you are blessed to have this opportunity with her. Don't take it for granted."

He shifted his gaze to the window, at the darkened sky that offered nothing more than a blank slate for troubled minds.

Cole sighed, put his feet on the ground, and leaned forward with his elbows to his knees. Held them down. He had considered the fact that her focus on Drew's tattoo earlier would bring up the past. "I won't. Sorry, man. I know this must be stirring up all kinds of shit for you. I wasn't thinking. Thank you for the support. It has meant the world to me. Finding the missing piece in your life—" He scrubbed his face again with his hand, but couldn't finish.

"We're flying in to St. Louis tomorrow and meeting Derek at the bus. Flight's earlier than you wanted, ten a.m. We fly out again the morning after, Cole, for New York. Have you told her yet?"

He shook his head. He'd offered to make her dreams come true, not throw his own baggage at her. "Not tonight. I better get back to her. She's probably out of the tub by now." He set his empty glass down on the dresser and left without confirming the possible heartache his best friend drowned in once again. Drew would want him to go for it while he could. It's what friends did.

He dragged his feet on the carpet; the retreat back to the room was quiet, as it should be. They were rich rock stars who could afford to book an entire hotel floor, and life on the outside portrayed perfection; only a select few had insight to the real troubles they carried within them.

He stood at the door. The green light flashed, but he couldn't remove the key let alone open the door to what he'd just admitted to Drew, and himself. He should tell her, but maybe he didn't have to. There were only five items left on her list, nothing he couldn't manage in twenty-four hours. Then, she'd leave him. Why add stress she didn't need? It's not like he and Alexis were together, not the *couple* people read about.

He opened the door to silence. The bathroom door remained closed, and his gaze dropped to the light that shined out the bottom. He placed his hand on his stomach, but his feet wouldn't budge. "You okay, baby?" Her shuffle, now loud enough to hear, calmed him. Somewhat.

She opened the door and ambled about the bathroom with renewed energy. Moisture from the steam coated her skin, exposed around the towel tucked snug at her breasts. She'd washed away her makeup. Even natural, she was beautiful.

"Four in one day Cole, I don't think I can fly a plane tonight. I don't want my list to endanger others." With a contented smile, she wrapped him in a hug.

He lowered his chin to her head and closed his eyes. From her tightened embrace, she could sense something weighed him down. When did it get this way? Not that he cared to complain, but really, how could two people be so right for each other that confessions weren't necessary.

He forced a laugh and steered her toward the king-sized bed with his arm around her shoulders and of course, leaned in to get a glimpse down her towel. She slapped him in the stomach. He stuck his bottom lip out and rubbed the sting away. “No planes tonight, baby.” He drew the blankets back. “Get comfortable while I go shower. TV, booze, room service, whatever your little heart desires.”

****

He didn’t pin her to the mattress and peel her towel off with his teeth. Granted, they’d had an eventful day and when she lowered into the tub, she was sore, the best kind of sore. She sat on the bed where he directed. The towel squeezed around her but he didn’t respond, just fixed the sheets and covered her legs, kissed her forehead, and left.

She traced the fold in the towel above her breast with her fingertips. Her gaze in the mirror followed its path. She scanned her body but the image before her, at some point, changed. The woman in the mirror displayed confidence, experience, passion.

Grief still lingered under the surface but it no longer hurt. Fate brought her Cole. A man, who gave her his all and did it with a natural charm, didn’t change who he was for her. Time with him changed her in ways she hadn’t imagined. She sat up on her knees, tugged at the towel and held it out to the side, dropped it.

Her reflection in the mirror had altered. The parts of her body she once cringed at now appeared beautiful, as if she were gazing through his eyes. She admired herself and sighed with more contentment than she’d ever allowed herself to experience. The soft mattress hugged her curves as she laid back and relaxed with her newfound freedom, without covers.

The lamp on his side of the bed gave off a subtle yellow glow while she lay there, fixated on the ceiling. Her life and her body had come alive the last several days with the Scandals. Each detail so engrained in her memory, just thinking about it brought every sensation to the surface.

She startled when the light clicked off and the bed dipped beside her. When did he come out of the bathroom? His fresh-showered scent on the other hand, that stole her attention. She inhaled deep. She loved his soap, how the scent of it changed when they got all sweaty. Like hard work and him.

"It's late. We have to head out in the morning." He settled in beside her and she curled up into the crook of his arm. "I hoped we could explore a little before leaving but the only flight we could get leaves at ten a.m."

She snuggled in closer, leaned her bare hip into him, and twined her legs with his.

"Isabelle? What's on your mind?"

"What did Drew mean earlier, that you could tell me?"

He squeezed her and a tidal wave of sorrow crashed in on her with his embrace. "It's important this stay with us, important to him. Only people close to Drew know, and he wants to keep it that way."

"Okay." That kind of privacy she could relate to.

"Drew is a twin."

"Huh?"

He chuckled and kissed her forehead. "Yep. Had a twin sister."

She traced her palm down his arm until she found his hand to grab onto. His sympathetic grip eased the instant distress. *Had?*

"She died at birth. He was born first, loud and wailing. She was stillborn."

"Oh that's terrible."

"Yes, it is. His parents have come to terms with it, had more children. He—" He took a deep breath. "Has always felt the loss, like a part of him died with her. He's missing someone he never had the pleasure to know. He says he feels some type of twin vibe that's out of reach, if that makes any sense. He has a picture in his wallet, carries it everywhere. Him and his sister in Kate's arms, that's his mom. They look like they are sleeping, peaceful. Only, he is the one truly asleep."

A tear slid down her cheek, onto his chest. She hurt as if she'd been smacked in the face. She cursed God, or whoever, that she wasn't going to get to live a full life and Drew's sister didn't get the chance to live a single day. "My heart breaks for him."

"He's okay, honey, just gets down from time to time. His birthday is the toughest, but we do what we can to help him through it." Her head bounced on his chest when he laughed. "He's gotten used to our extreme ways of distraction. You know, strip joints, drunken stupors, sex clubs—" He squeezed her again. "Bungee jumping. He's okay, really."

She put her arm over his abdomen and hugged, tight. "Thank you for telling me."

He squeezed her back and kissed the top of her head. "You're welcome. Now get some sleep. It's quite late and we have to get up early."

****

The red numbers glowed 6:00. She lay on her side and stared at the clock as they changed. A bout of nausea woke her an hour ago, and her body rebelled against the quiet slumber the medicine most often induced. His contented breath and spectacular chest, at rest, soothed the anger that would've consumed her on another day.

Her gaze roamed the length of his body, and many times, she neared his skin with her hand, but made a fist and retreated. The sheet just covered the large bulge below his waist. A glow from the early sunrise shined through the edges of the curtains. It illuminated the room enough to make his tattoos and well-cut muscles drool worthy. She bit her lip and scanned the room several times. She could write in her journal but temptation consumed her.

She lifted the sheet and stared at his face, he didn't stir. Without too much of a jostle, she slid underneath, down to his impressive erection. She grinned. Was this *the* typical male morning thing, or was she in his dreams?

She leaned over his body, braced her hands on the bed at his sides and lowered her mouth over him, swallowed him in deep. Her cheeks indented as she sucked him hard on the way up, his taste an instant addiction.

"Oh God. Isabelle."

A cool breeze hit her when he whipped the sheet off. She grabbed his shaft in her hand and stroked in sync with her mouth.

"Fuck."

The bed sheets tightened under her when he gripped them. The corners of her mouth rose around him and she grazed his skin with her teeth. She followed the path of his well-cut body with her gaze and moaned around his girth when the V at his waist caught her attention.

With her eyes closed, she lowered down his length until her lips brushed against her hand, tightened around his base. His engorged crown touched the back of her throat. He smoothed his hands over her hair and gave a gentle thrust with his hips. She swallowed.

"Fuck. I'm not going to last. If you don't want my cum down your throat—"

She got up on her knees between his legs and grabbed his wrists, pinned them to the bed beside his hips. She sucked deep, hard, indulged them both.

"Holy fuck. Ahhh."

His legs stiffened and he balled his hands into fists, swelled further in her mouth. Every vein slid through her lips and warm jets of cum spurted down her throat. She continued to suck, was the ceaseless force that drove his waves to the shore of her mouth. The same as he'd done for her many times. She swallowed to take in all he had to give and a sudden awareness hit her. She did want *all* of him.

As the tightness in his body faded with every last drop gone, she let go of the suction with a pop. She freed his arms and sat back on her heels. His lax body glistened with sweat. "You taste wonderful."

He opened his eyes, still filled with lust, and yanked her down on top of him.

"Eeek!"

"Really? Show me."

He clung to the sides of her face with firm hands and smashed his lips to hers, forced his tongue inside to explore with a hum of delight. She placed her hands to the bed on either side of him and got up. He rose with her, didn't allow the connection to break.

"I need to use the bathroom." she mumbled around his lips and he smiled in return.

"Okay, okay."

She scooted off the bed and was halfway to the bathroom when a pillow hit her in the back. She spun around to see him propped up on his elbows, exposed. "You were right darlin'. I do taste pretty damn sweet in your mouth."

****

Cole flopped down on the bed when the door clicked shut. He loved her. It didn't take a spectacular blowjob to confirm that for him but it sure was an added bonus. He stared at the ceiling and scrubbed his face. How could he keep her alive? Were there better doctors his money could buy?

A light tap on the patio door drew him out of what tortured him, losing her. He sat up and threw his legs over the side of the bed, glared at the repeated noise but still not able to put his query aside. The mental battle over options weighted him down.

With his toes, he picked up his pants, shuffled into them, and left the button undone. He tiptoed over to the glass door and lifted the curtain back an inch. Dark clouds swept across the sky and drops of rain hit the windowpane. Since when did it rain in California?

He traced the droplet's path with his finger and tipped his head back with his eyes closed. The big guy answered his prayer. He'd never been the religious type, but the last few days he prayed often, every word to do with her. He repositioned the curtain tightly and rushed over to the nightstand for his phone, entered his password, and scrolled through the lengthy playlist. His fingers worked faster than his phone. He paced. When the right song appeared, he propped the phone up on the table, hit play, and increased the volume. He stood with his hands twisted behind his back. Rascal Flatts sang out the words to *My Wish.* Would it make her cry? That would destroy him.

The door opened.

"Shit." He mumbled. Too late to find something else.

She inched around the corner, in a pale-pink, cotton sundress and the cutest confused smile on her face. Without hesitation, she placed her hand in his when he extended his palm out to her. He brought it to his mouth and kissed it. "I have another surprise, not planned but the timing couldn't be better."

The curious sparkle in her crystal-blue eyes wasn't, at all, like anything he'd ever seen before.

"Really? I'm intrigued."

He brushed her long blonde hair back over her shoulders and smoothed his hands down her bare arms. He could feel goose bumps form on her skin and loved that he affected her so much. "Trust me?"

Her eyes were certain to mirror his, how could she not? A bond, trust, they had it all. "Yes, of course."

He lifted his hand to the edge of the curtain and peeled it open, impressed with himself. She raised her eyebrows at the window and back at him like she didn't understand. In that moment, she was now here for *him*. Her list didn't register and for some reason, it meant the world.

He smiled and slid the door open, the headiness of her list lifted from his shoulders as he stepped out. Still facing away from her, he held his hands out and tipped his chin up. He spun around slow and extended his hand to her. "Dance with me?"

Now she understood. She followed his lead, and placed her hand in his. The rain was a little cold, but perfect for the heat that generated through their every touch. With each step toward him, her chin rose to hold his gaze. She blinked many times to clear her vision as the rain hit her in the face.

"Are you for real? Have I died already?"

Her tone reflected his inability to make sense of this. How could they accept the idea that this *isn't* a forever kind of thing?

He leaned down a little, touched his cheek to hers, and whispered, "If this is heaven, I am in love." Not quite *I love you,* but close enough, for now. Before his words derailed their perfect morning, he wrapped his arm around her waist and twirled her around to the music. It did feel like heaven.

She snuggled in and swayed with him, but avoided his statement. They didn't speak, just danced. He leaned back a little and his hand guided her chin up. He used his thumbs to wipe her cheeks, tears she couldn't claim as rain.

The desperate need in her eyes lured him in. He kissed her with the tenderness she deserved. His lips touched each side of her mouth, teased them both before he dove for what they craved. The connection. When he broke away, they were both short of breath.

"Isabelle?" He couldn't stop himself. He scanned his gaze down her body and clenched his jaw.

"Yes."

"The rain has made your dress completely see through. I also see you are not wearing a bra or panties." He squeezed her butt and rubbed his erection into her front. The material of her dress cooled from the rain, but he could feel her heat. "If I don't get inside you soon, I may be joining you in the hospital with the worst case of blue balls they have ever seen."

She flung her arms around his neck, leaned her forehead on his chest, and laughed. He rested his chin on the top of her head and took a deep breath to calm more than just the belly-aching laugh.

She forced distance between them, hadn't done that in a while. His pulse raced wild with worry.

"Cole?"

He didn't speak, just raised his eyebrows.

"Take me inside?"

That was all he needed. He kissed her hard, touched every inch of her as he braced his hands onto her waist and lifted until her legs folded around him. Instant regret hit him about the pants he put on. He would only have to lower her to be embedded in her body. He stepped forward, refused to break their connection, and made his way to the bed. He didn't close the door. The sound of the rain and now thunder, only added to the moment.

He crawled up to the head of the bed with her in his arms, and placed her down in the middle. He kissed and nipped at her until his lips brushed across the strap of her dress. It needed to come off. She wiggled for him as he peeled the cool wet fabric up her body. He threw it to the floor and lowered himself to her, to lick the dampness from her shoulder. She shivered.

His gaze roamed to the spot above her breast where he once left his mark. Temptation called to him. He drew her damp skin between his lips and sucked.

Nothing in life would ever be the same again without the taste of her on his lips.

"Cole," she moaned.

He tore himself away and admired his art, his mark. "Perfect." He stroked the spot with his nose and kissed it before he moved down. The way she rolled her hips into him told him she needed to come. He'd get there, but not yet. There was so much of her he couldn't leave untouched. He kissed her breast, traced the tip of his tongue around her rose-colored nipple.

"Cole?"

"Hmm?"

"I want my lips on you, too."

He chuckled. "Honey, if your lips go anywhere near my dick, it will be over. I want to come inside you." He kissed his way over to her other breast and the corner of his lip rose when she wiggled under him.

"Then get it in me already."

He ignored her demand and continued his assault. She shivered when he placed soft kisses around her navel and stared at her beautiful, pale skin. She'd be cute pregnant. Images of him with a little pink bundle hit him hard.

"In good time, sassy woman. I'm not done with you."

Before hope overwhelmed him, he scooted down the bed and used his hands to spread her legs farther apart. Her juices already trickled from her opening. He loved the fact she couldn't hide her desire; it wouldn't take much to make her come. Her eyes were half-lidded with lust when he crouched down to swipe her sweet dew with his tongue.

"I will take care of myself if you don't—"

He pressed two fingers into her.

"Ahhh."

Her cream drenched his fingers, and her walls spasmed. She refused to wait for him, swirled her hips and rode his fingers. He kissed her inner thigh and withdrew his fingers.

"Nooo."

He smiled with anticipation. He could take her to new heights she, until now, only wished for. He'd give her that wish and many more.

****

She'd slap him. He would fulfill every need for sure, but to hold back her release like that—torture. Her gaze traveled down his body and up again, on every tattoo and muscle. He was too beautiful to slap.

He traced his finger, already lubricated with her juices, in a circular motion around her nub. When her admiration landed on the tattoo on his bicep, a house restricted in a chain, he eased his way back to her virgin hole. She thrust her hips forward and closed her eyes; the sensation combined with her sexual frustration excited her every nerve ending, and would only be satisfied if he touched her everywhere.

"Cole." She moaned his name, not able to direct him with words. Pretty sure she didn't need to.

He laid over her and braced his weight with his elbow. He kept her on edge with every kiss, and swayed above her body as if he was already inside her. His free hand teased her with every motion, dipped inside and then back out again. When he used her cream to roam back around her puckered hole, the erotic sensation overwhelmed her. She grasped at his body to let him know she needed it.

"Okay, baby." he whispered.

The next time he thrust forward with his body, he entered her with his finger. It burned. The kind of burn that tempted her to tear away, yet demanded to go back for more at the same time. The world around them faded, except for the heat of his touch that radiated through her, branded her.

"Does that feel good, baby?"

"Take me there."

He eased his finger out, and lifted off her to sit back on his heels. His body trembled. "A-are you sure?"

She got up on her knees in front of him, placed her hands on either side of his face, and didn't let her attention roam anywhere but into his eyes. "You. Only you. Ever."

He smoothed one arm around her back and lowered her to the bed with a passionate kiss. They parted but his breath skimmed her lips. "Hands and knees, beautiful."

She maneuvered into position without hesitation and peeked over her shoulder.

He scrambled through his bag, yanked out a tiny bottle and shuffled back to the bed, kicking his pants off. When he glanced up from the bottle, he wobbled from the pants leg that wouldn't free him, and stopped. "You're stunning."

His words aroused her to the point where, if he didn't satisfy her now, she'd do it on her own. He climbed on the bed and brushed his hand down the center of her back and over her crevice. She held her breath when the bottle cracked open. Whether from the position or nerves she didn't know, but her body shook.

"Cole?"

"Mmhmm?"

"I'm nervous."

He stroked his engorged length, coated it with lube, and threw the bottle on the bed. He cradled her around the waist, hoisted her up so they were on their knees, her back to his chest. She peered back over her shoulder and their gazes locked together.

His soft kiss calmed her. "I won't hurt you, baby. Say the word and I'll stop, no hard feelings." He continued to caress her skin with his lips. Her muscles relaxed, and her body craved more. At this point, he could do anything.

He caressed his left hand up her side and around her front, to roll her nipple between his fingertips. She wished there was a mirror in front of them; the erotic image they must portray kept her on edge—a constant state she'd experienced since day one from being near him.

He fell forward with her in slow motion. She stopped when in the position he'd asked, but he used his weight to lower her further.

"No, baby. Change of plans. On your stomach. I want to be close to you. The kind of close where my body, my breath, becomes yours."

With the light touch of his fingertips, he urged her tailbone down until her stomach touched the cold sheets. He lay on top of her, but supported his weight with his elbows on either side of her shoulders.

The warmth of his body and touch of his lips down her spine relaxed her, their bodies melted together. He rubbed the crease of her butt with his lubed cock and she moaned. Within moments, she pressed back into him, in quest of the exotic friction. He massaged down her body with one hand and teased her opening.

“Oh, yes. I need you. There.”

She envisioned his smile on the heated skin between her shoulder blades.

“I need you, too, baby.”

She inched back and the lube made it easy for his finger to slide in deeper. It burned but she wanted more. How could she possibly want more? She did. He stretched her with his finger, more when he inserted a second.

“You okay, baby?”

It hurt, but she couldn’t to tell him to stop. Didn’t want to. Her body had a mind of its own as she lifted her hips. “More, Cole.”

He chuckled and withdrew his fingers. He leaned down on his elbows again and his chest brushed against her back. He kissed her neck, and slid his hard shaft up and down the hollow of her butt. Filled with lust, she thrust in tune with him, aligned their bodies so he could ease into her.

“Ahhh.”

The now very swollen head of his cock slipped inside and she froze. He held still inside her. “I’m not going to push anymore, baby. You do the work now. Give yourself a moment to let your muscles relax, and press back on me when you’re ready.”

The strain in his voice was evident, being stimulated so intimately and not being able to lose control. She didn’t want this just for her; but for him too, the connection.

When he kissed the back of her neck, her muscles relaxed and she let him in deeper. His hands gripped at the sheets. She slid her hands up beside his and he laced his fingers over hers. Every part of their bodies meshed as if their intimate desires were familiar, unable to live without the other. They were in this together.

He filled her, so much she couldn't stretch anymore or she would split in half but the pain was soon replaced with something else, a pleasure that craved to be stroked.

She dug her toes into the bed and eased forward. Without hesitation, she thrust back to be filled again when he'd come close to leaving her body. Every time she did this, she ached for more, and forced him deeper.

His hands clamped onto hers tight. "I'm in, baby."

The sound of satisfaction in his voice spurred her on, made giving him anything in the world seem possible. She couldn't take it anymore. "Now, please, I don't need gentle anymore."

He dropped his forehead to her shoulder blade and growled. He drove so deep into her, their bodies joined as one. Their fingers balled until white-knuckled and he slid out, to the tip before lunging in, with more force each time.

"Fuck. I'm not going to last, you're so tight. You need to come, baby. I want you with me."

He loosened his grip and guided her hand down with his. She lifted her stomach when she figured out where his hand intended to take hers, only he didn't let go. He massaged his hand over hers and down her front until they skimmed her nub together.

It was so swollen the second he placed her finger to it, and thrust his hard shaft into her at the same time, she hit a climax like no other. He buried himself so deep inside her, the magnitude of their connection radiated out in waves around them.

Her cream flowed at the pressure of their fingers, together, in a circular motion on her nub. He came, hard, and didn't stop. Her name was a whisper out of his lips, and just when she didn't think her heart could beat any faster it did, as she imagined the love in his eyes.

When they both floated down from their extreme high, he eased out of her; she winced.

"Sorry, honey. I'm just going to go get a cloth to clean us up. I'll be right back. Stay there."

She didn't need to see him to know he smiled with his stern words. He learned fast that she enjoyed challenging others' demands. She complied, didn't like it, but she did. The water ran strong, and in no time, he sat beside her, but she didn't even have the energy to hold her eyes open, so she let them drift closed.

The warm cloth smoothed over her skin and she relaxed, except for the slight awkwardness that it was he who cleaned her. She took a peek when he wiped himself down and threw the cloth away. He lay down beside her.

"You okay?"

"Mmhmm." She smiled, didn't want to worry him.

"Have I told you how amazing you make me feel? And I don't just mean when I'm inside you."

She let out a short snicker before she contained herself and squeezed her lips together, still not able to hold back her smile.

He smacked her ass.

"Ouch. You make me feel it, too." She opened her eyes but wasn't prepared for when his awe-struck mouth gaped open. He held something back, *it* maybe.

She couldn't let him go there; she'd already accepted more than she planned for. "Mind if I go relax in a tub?"

He held out his hand to help her. "Of course not. There's a jar of salts on the counter. Put some in the water, it will help with any soreness."

The corner of her mouth rose and she stared at him. She didn't want to ask. He brushed his thumb over her cheek but didn't say anything while he held her gaze. She bit her bottom lip, thankful her public request online resulted in him and not some creepy psychopath. She giggled as she shoved off the bed to grab her bag, and pranced to the bathroom, knowing he'd catch on.

"Seriously. When my woman laughs after having earth-shattering sex, not cool."

She halted her steps and composed herself. "I'm sorry, it's not you at all, I promise. I just had this random concern about how lucky I am it wasn't some psychopath who answered my request."

He threw a pillow in her direction and wiggled his eyebrows at her. "How do you know I'm not?" She chuckled with him as she closed the door. She needed her journal, and her phone.

Chapter Fifteen

Dear Diary,
He's in, deep. Should I?

The valet brought a rental car around for them. They leaned against the side, people watched while they waited for everyone to arrive. The early morning charm of Beverly Hills masked any forlorn dilemmas. She now understood it benefitted no one to conceal your troubles and go about life in disguise.

It was time to head back to the airport. Drew strolled out of the lobby doors and threw his bag in the trunk. She tapped her toe on the hard pavement, wiggled away from Cole, and threw her arms around Drew when he neared.

His chest vibrated, amused at her overzealous compassion.

"So, I guess he told you?"

She broke away before the tears could spill and slid her sunglasses over her eyes to cover the sorrow she couldn't hide as he did.

He tossed his arm around her shoulder and squeezed. "I'm okay, beautiful. Don't let it bother you."

A taxi drove up and she breathed a sigh of relief. Brett and Zander got out of the car with their typical childlike eagerness.

"Damn. Did she add another item to the list?" Brett

wiggled his eyebrows at Drew before Zander hit him on the back of the head. "Ouch. What was that for?"

Drew opened the passenger door for her. "Classy Brett, real classy."

Everyone slouched in their seats, quiet on the drive to the airport.

Guess everyone had a late night.

"Cole?"

He let go of the wheel with one hand and rubbed up and down her thigh. "Yeah, baby?"

She shivered. "What about the Lamborghini?"

The back of her seat jerked when Zander snagged the sides of it to get closer to her. "It's at my parents already. Sweet ride." He hit Cole on the shoulder. "Don't worry. My folks are going to see to it for now."

Cole glanced back at Zander in the rear view mirror, self-satisfied, before he faced her with a wink. "I owe your entire family a round of thanks, Zander."

She dropped her jaw and spun to the window in time to hide the heat that rose to her face.

****

With her elbows on her knees and her face in her hands, she took deep breaths. She blamed her nausea and the pressure in her head on the altitude of the plane. He massaged her back and the uncontrollable bounce of his knee knocked over the ginger ale on the tray in front of him. He didn`t have to see her face. Every inch of her skin appeared pale, clammy. *Please, please, please, hurry up plane.*

Her symptoms were getting worse. She acted as if she didn't think he understood the severity of her situation, but he did. "Is there anything else I can do?"

She shook her head and then groaned. He squinted

in pain at Drew, Brett, and Zander; their gaze on her reflected his own. Her medicine didn't seem to work as well these days.

Tears streamed down her face under her sunglasses while they made their way through the airport. Security insisted she take them off to go through the metal detector, and the officer glared at him. As the last question was answered by Zander, he tore the paperwork from her hands, passed it back to Drew and bent to lift her. He cradled her all the way to the limo outside. She didn't fight him. Not a good sign.

He held her in his arms while she slept. She passed out before they even made it to the car. He was relieved; sleep always helped.

"I-is she going to be okay, man? Brett and I are kind of out of the loop here." Concern echoed in Zander's voice.

How did he answer that? He inspected her lifeless form and swallowed. With a light brush of his fingertips, he smoothed the hair back out of her face. "It isn't good. She's having surgery when she returns home, not favorable odds." He was caught in the middle. He didn't want to betray her trust, but didn't want to lie to the friends who had his back for years. Hers now, too.

"Surgery?"

He glanced up to Brett's waiting stare. If he told them right now, she'd never know, but he'd have to form words in order to make that happen. As he scanned her limp body, he couldn't. The rest of the drive was quiet and he didn't know if they just let her sleep or because there were no words.

The limo arrived at the bus and he could feel the

breath of his best friends' stop, like his, when she stirred and opened her eyes. "Hi."

He brushed back her hair again. "Hey yourself, beautiful. How are you feeling?"

She tipped her head from side to side. "Much better, thank you. What are the plans for the rest of the day?"

He helped her from the car, and shielded her with a blanket from the chilly St. Louis air. He'd never encountered a time when Derek arrived for them, unprepared. Drew put her bag on her bunk in passing; they were all quiet. She paused at her bunk but he tugged her hand toward the lounge. "Come sit down. I want to make you a proposition."

She didn't ask, just followed suit like part of the family. She sat on the couch where he pointed, careful not to jostle too much. He joined her. Within moments, everyone sat with their eyes on him.

"We fly out again tomorrow morning. We have a show in…" He made note of their joined hands and inhaled deep. "New York."

"Oh that sounds fun."

By the excitement on her face, she'd never been and if he got his way, she wouldn't now either. "We're only there for one night and know from experience, Friday night shows in New York are so chaotic it's not as much fun as you'd think. I'm sure you're a little homesick, maybe even a lot. Why don't you stay back? Have your friends fly in to see you. There will be lots of empty space on the bus."

He glared around the tiny lounge, made direct eye contact with the three men to shut them up before he focused on her again. "Besides, you want to get a tattoo. Isn't it kind of ritualistic for groups of girls to do that together, a drunken bonding experience?"

He couldn't read her blank expression as she surveyed the group. When she smiled wide, he let out the breath he'd held. She bit her lip as though she stopped herself from speaking.

"That sounds wonderful." She scanned the room; Derek now joined them. "Are you sure it isn't too much? Us taking over the bus?"

He held up his hand when Derek perked up, to say something he shouldn't. "Not at all, right?" He remained firm with his unspoken words to the guys, who all shrugged their shoulders, tight-lipped.

"I'll take care of the cost. You take care of the arrangements. I'm afraid it will only be for one night though. When we get back, we will be off again, in the bus."

"Believe me. We can do a bang up job in twenty-four hours." She laughed and brightened up from her earlier spell, but tension still radiated from the men around him.

"But no to the cost. We will pay our way. You have already done so much. Too much." She let her gaze fall to her lap, picked a piece of nonexistent lint. A tear slid down her cheek and he could tell she avoided eye contact to prevent a waterworks display. "Thanks, guys."

"Ahem. Boss man wants you in the other bus for a meeting."

Derek raised his eyebrow but Cole glanced out the window instead of going head to head with him. *Fuck.* He kissed her and followed the rest of the guys off the bus. "We might be a while. If you have any problems with the arrangements just shoot me a text, and I'll help out anyway I can."

"There shouldn't be any problems, but I'll let you know if I need you."

Her furrowed brows were a clear indicator, she suspected something was up.

****

"Hello?"

"Hi Katherine."

"Oh my God. It is about damn time you called, I've missed you."

She laughed and wiped the tears now falling, at will, down her face. "I've missed you too. I have a surprise."

The sigh on the other end said it all. Katherine stressed. "I could handle a surprise right about now."

She used the back of her hand to wipe her face and took a breath, on the verge of an outright sob. "The guys are leaving by plane tomorrow morning for a show. Think you, Abigail and Taryn could manage to get away? Come spend a night here, on the bus? I think we are due for a girls' night."

The break down began, but not from her. Katherine, who most often held the group of them together. She was the strong one. "Yes. God, yes. Are you sure the guys are okay with a group of women taking over their *domain*? Scrap that. They would, in all likelihood, want pictures or something." She could still hear the pain behind her best friend's laugh.

"I'm not fooling anyone here, Katherine. In some ways, these guys are our carbon copies, with penises, piercings, and tattoos of course." She closed her eyes, pressed her back into the cushion, and curled her legs up to her side, savoring the memory of last night. “That reminds me. Cole had a brilliant idea. You ladies need to be a part of my list too. So, while you’re here, we’re going for my tattoo.”

Silence fell on the other end of the phone. It wasn’t like Katherine to be quiet.

“I’m in, all the way. Whatever you get, I’m getting it too. Please don’t leave me marked for life with something ridiculous.”

She laughed but Isabelle could picture the tears on her face.

“I will talk to the girls, book our flights. Wait. Where are we flying?”

She placed her hand over her stomach. Katherine’s episode passed, but to hear her say she’d get a tattoo, the same tattoo, offered a memory she could leave them with. Cherish.

“Well,” she sniffled. “I expected to return from Beverly Hills to Michigan, but we’re in St. Louis. They must have an upcoming show here and Derek drove the bus while we were away.” Sniffle.

“Izzy?”

“Yes?” Sniffle.

“We will be on the first flight out in the morning. I am going to let you go now before you make me start to cry again.”

She smiled. Katherine didn’t do tears. “OK. Text me to let me know what time you land so I can meet you?”

“Will do. I can’t wait to hear all the juicy details.”

The dead air roused her sob, so much so, she glanced down the aisle to make sure they were still gone. If she had to explain, it would only make it worse.

When her tears cleared enough to see and move without injury, she hurried to the bathroom and splashed cold water on her face, something she'd seen her mother do many times when she was a little girl. She now understood why. Single parenthood wasn't the piece of cake her mom led her to believe.

She wandered around the bus a little heavy footed. The side effects of the medication lingered. She peeled back the curtain and crawled in his bunk. The cookies were right where expected. She took a bite and dialed.

"Hello, baby girl."

She scrunched her nose. "Really, Mom?"

Carol laughed. "Hey, you are my only child so by rights, will always be my baby. How are you, honey?"

She peered into the near to consumed box and grabbed another. She made a mental note to stop at the store while out tomorrow. "If you're referring to my list, I only have three items left and am having the time of my life. If you are referring to the tumor…" She couldn't lie to her mom, never could. "The symptoms are a little more intense. It's probably a good thing Cole has made so much happen for me in such a short amount of time."

"Dr. Peterson called me."

She dropped the cookie and closed her eyes. *Oh boy, she isn't going to like this.* "He's called me, too, Mom."

Silence. Not good.

"Isabelle. I want you home safe. Don't push it too much, okay. Leave Dr. Peterson to me."

"Okaaay." She let her hand fall to her lap. The surprises were endless today.

"Katherine has been doing a great job with updates about your trip. So, Cole's his name?" Her mom laughed and it was the best sound in the world. If things were different and she was the one with a daughter, would she be as strong?

"Yes, Mom." She laughed and placed the cookies back in their concealed spot. "Cole is his name. He is the lead singer of the band. They're all fabulous." She didn't want to make too much of it, since she still wasn't sure what to make of it herself.

"I want details when you get home sweetie, even the juicy ones."

She covered her mouth to prevent cookie crumbs from flying when she laughed. "Mom." *Then again, why not?* "Okay. If you are sure you can handle them?"

"I think I have proven I can handle a lot, hmm?"

She leaned out the bunk and checked down the aisle. "Yes Mom, you are the strongest person I know. I will tell you everything. I should get going though, just needed to hear your voice." She squeezed her eyes closed. Things were too damn emotional today.

"Okay, sweetie. Let me know when to expect you back home. Talk to you soon."

Click

****

Isabelle's voice trembled. Crouched in the stairway and behind the cupboards, Cole listened. Eavesdropping on her needed to stop, but how else would he find out? If she'd let him, he'd hold her, make it all better. She was worse, just like he'd suspected.

He fisted his hands. To force her admission would damage what they'd built. His mood sucked. Getting reamed out by the guys about these last-minute plans of his to avoid the truth…well, it sucked. They were all in this together. They made that clear, again.

She'd sought out his bunk though. His. The significance in that hit hard; she found comfort in his space. He coughed, stood up, and climbed the stairs with his hands in his pockets. When she peeked out of the bunk, he wasn't fooled; her smile was fake, much like his.

"Hey, you."

Brett, Zander, Drew, and Derek climbed the stairs behind him. They continued the obscene jokes that had launched without boundaries on the other bus—after the lecture of course.

"In the back?" Drew asked, but made his way to the lounge without a glance behind for confirmation.

"Yeah."

He held his hand out to her, and she accepted it without hesitation. Their comfort with each other filled a void that had consumed him for so long; the possibility of an end to it choked him up. He kissed her on the forehead and leaned into her ear. "Enjoy the cookies?"

She jerked her head toward him, her mouth hung open.

He winked. "It's okay," he squeezed her hand and tugged her arm to lead her to the back lounge.

Everyone sat in their usual spots; even she possessed one now.

"What's going on?"

He relaxed his muscles at the sight of her nervous fidget with her arms. They were more than right for each other. He put the DVD in the machine and joined her with his arm draped, carefree, around her shoulder.

"We—" He surveyed the group and shook his head. The three men sat still, waited with their hands tied in knots on their laps. "Have a surprise for you."

He held the remote up and hit play. Everyone sat to face the television with a grin. He glanced to catch her surprise but she stared at the screen, blank faced, nervous.

The music played through the speakers first, *God Gave Me You* by Blake Shelton. Then there they were, all of them, dancing like idiots. A slideshow of edited clips slid across the screen in time with the music, as they learned to tango.

The excitement of the day hit him, remembering the man she believed stood by fixing the camera, but really recording them. The guys pointed at the screen to make fun of one another.

She tensed in his arms when the close up of her and him filled the screen; it was powerful. He didn't know until seeing it with his own eyes, how he tended to her, like she were the love of his life.

She shoved him away and stumbled off the bus. The video continued but everyone scolded him with their glares before they returned to the screen once again. He ran after her.

****

The tears made it difficult to see, but she was pretty sure she stood behind the bus. With her arms tight around her waist, she sobbed, too loud to hear him creep up behind her. She stepped out of his embrace when he wrapped his arms around her. The heightened emotions created by the video, sent her instinct to flee into overdrive.

"I thought you would like it."

She faced him, could feel the puffiness in her eyes. "I can't even tell you how much the video means to me. No one has *ever* done anything so thoughtful for me."

He tucked a stray hair behind her ear and the heat of his hand on her skin made goose bumps travel the length of her body. Again, she stepped back. He rubbed his face with his hands and she could no longer see his true emotion.

"Is that why you're crying?" His voice was quiet, cautious.

"I'm scared of the feelings I have for you. This can't go any further. If I die—"

He kissed her with a fierce need and guided her with a desperation he didn't care to hide, until her back came in contact with the bus. It didn't matter how hard he anchored her with his hands, he couldn't get deep enough to satisfy. He broke the kiss and lowered his forehead to hers, panted so hard his breath warmed her face. "Here or on the bus?"

She tipped her head in confusion.

"I need you. Now."

He touched his lips to hers but his arms shook, on edge and ready to lose control. "Here or on the bus? Either place is fine with me as long as I'm inside you. I don't care who watches."

Her body tingled at his blunt, erotic words. She'd give him the world if he continued to speak with such desperation in his voice. "Bus," she whispered.

Still focused on the excitement of his words, she struggled to put one foot in front of the other while he yanked her arm in haste. His need to be lost in one another, again, traveled through their contact. He slammed through the doors of the bus. When she'd admitted there was more between them than just the list, it altered him.

His determined stride, either to validate that he felt it, too, or tend to an awakened arousal, made it difficult to keep up. A few feet into the aisle, he spun and she braced her feet to the floor to avoid the impact, since she'd followed so close behind. He grabbed the sides of her waist and pinned her back into the counter, his gaze fixed on her lips.

"Everyone out." He hollered, but didn't wait for a reply. He ravished her with his tongue, much like the expertise she'd already experienced, lower. She squeezed her legs together.

The guys complied with the odd slap of approval on his back as they shifted passed.

"Guess she liked the video," Derek mumbled on his way by.

"Strip."

The door wasn't even closed before the order left his mouth. Groans echoed. She didn't hesitate. He tore his clothes off at the same time and kicked them out of the way. She stood in front of him, naked, nothing between them but the spark that never died. He stared at her; his mark from the night before was a deep purple.

The intensity in his eyes made the world around them fade. It was just them. He smoothed one hand over her collarbone, to the back of her neck, and wrenched her body into him for a kiss more intense than any other. Her knees weakened. She threw her arms around his neck for support and like always, he responded. His large, warm hand scooped up the back of her knee and raised it around his waist. Her feet rose off the floor as he continued to hoist her onto the counter.

“Cole,” she moaned into his mouth. “Fuck me, please.”

He bit her lip and then brushed the sting away with his tongue. “I will, baby.” He stepped back and used his hands to spread her knees, his attention drifted to where he intended to go next. “I want to taste you first.”

Her pulse raced at the erotic sight of him, dropped to his knees in front of her. His gaze on her body was like he’d finally found a part of life he couldn’t live without. As he neared her sex with his mouth, she placed her hands back to the counter for support.

She’d need it. His tongue was the most pleasurable form of torture. Every light tickle with its tip created greed in her only he sparked. She let her eyes drift closed and rolled her hips into his assault. Her legs shook and her body moved with a mind of its own, demanding he take care of her.

He growled when she braced one hand on the counter and weaved her fingers through his hair with the other, grabbed hold, and scratched his scalp in the process. She rubbed herself against his mouth. She didn’t have to hold back with him, and didn’t have to ask. Her muscles clenched to prepare for the release she now demanded. He placed his hands over hers and loosened her grip so he could stand. Satisfaction covered his face at the temptress he could compel from within her. He gripped her butt, lifted her to the edge of the counter, and thrust into her, hard.

“Ahhh.”

Their reaction was identical.

She latched her arms around his neck and her legs around his waist as he pumped into her. Very little room existed between them. They held on to each other with fierce need. His muscles flexed under her grip.

"This isn't going to last long. Ahhh. I can feel you squeeze me baby, are you close?"

"I'm with you," she whispered.

He tipped his head up and mouthed the words "thank God." She giggled. He buried his face into her neck and impaled her with himself. His body trembled with a release more than just physical.

Her channel swelled with desire to give back to him, and accept the claim he'd staked with his cum deep inside her core. She came with him. "Oh God. Yes."

Through her scream he whispered, *I love you.* Every sense awakened from those words, she came harder.

The bus was quiet except for the sound of their satisfied pants. He stayed inside her. Every few seconds, he'd give a gentle thrust, wouldn't allow the moment to end. *What should I say?* The words, the same ones he used, were frozen inside.

"So. What are we doing today?" She tried, but casual still sounded ridiculous after that.

He chuckled, his face still buried in her neck. "Well, I planned to book the bungee jump but after your episode this morning on the plane, which I am sure is still there somewhere under the surface, I've changed my mind."

She relaxed her muscles and placed her hands on the counter behind her. The lust in his gaze from moments ago was now replaced with concern. She didn't know what to make of his ability to read her so well in such a short time. "Probably a good idea." *Don't make it go any faster than it has already.* “What do you have in mind, instead?”

He kissed her on the forehead. “Stay the night with me again? In a hotel, just the two of us?”

She nodded at the same time the doors to the bus opened and the guys climbed the stairs.

“Shit sorry. The screaming stopped, assumed you were done.” Zander halted his movement forward and Brett, Drew, and Derek slammed into his back like dominos. They stood there, jaws hung, and speechless,

He laughed and picked her up with her legs still curled around him, his semi erect cock still inside her. He carried her to the bathroom with a grin. “Eyes off my woman.”

He closed the door behind them, and they could hear the hoots from the guys. He freed himself from her body and set her down on the floor. She covered her mouth to laugh but he just shook his head as if their antics were part of a regular day on the job.

She touched his arm with tenderness as he raised it to the shower door. “Just the two of us sounds wonderful.”

He opened the door and waited for her to step in first. She jumped when he smacked her bare ass. “You’ll pay for that, Cole.”

“I hope so.”

****

She let him take the lead with their bags on purpose. His drool-worthy form became an important, every day object to admire.

He opened the hotel suite and stood to the side. “Get a good look, darlin’?”

She strolled with a sway of her hips into the

enormous suite loaded with amenities, most they'd never use. "Thank you, handsome. I sure did."

A large, flat screen hung on the wall, overtop a stone fireplace. Tan leather sectionals spread throughout the living area for people they wouldn't be inviting to join them tonight. The window that extended the full length of the far wall stole her attention, and the view of the beautiful St. Louis skyline took her breath away. Her imagination raced as she strolled over to the king size bed and smoothed her hand over it. The soft, white material cooled her hand. For some reason, this night had to be one he would remember while they were apart.

Several beeps blared from her phone. "Ugh."

She scrambled for the sound and sat down. A wide smile crossed her face when she read who the messages were from.

Can't wait to see you. Too bad the hunkies won't be there too. I'm in for the tattoo. Taryn

Your timing is perfect. Miss you sweetie. Pick a tattoo that will look nice on me too. Abigail

Tears pooled in her eyes before she could get to Katherine's message.

Everything's set. Plane lands at 11:30 a.m. Can't wait to see you. Katherine

Squatted down in front of her, he wiped her tears with his thumbs. "What is it, beautiful?"

She dropped her hand with the phone, and raised her gaze to his tear-blurred face. "The girls. They get in at eleven-thirty tomorrow morning and want to get a tattoo as well, to match mine."

He smiled, and wiped the tears that didn't seem to stop. "You have pretty amazing friends."

She nodded, couldn't stop the waterworks. "The best. I love them so much."

His smile fell, along with his attentiveness before he stood up and retrieved the box of tissues on the table. He held his hand on the box, but kept his back to her. "I can see how much you love them."

His back heaved with a noticeable breath before he returned to her, the box in one hand, his other in his pocket. Fisted?

"They're the lucky ones in my eyes." He didn't linger when she accepted the tissues, just excused himself to the bathroom.

She didn't know what to make of his sadness, and choked-up cough as he plodded away.

It didn't take much to understand what bothered him. The L word. She said it, and not about him. She could feel it though, the love. If she refrained from the use of the word, she prevented hurt, or so she'd convinced herself.

His face on the other hand, couldn't have been clearer; he already hurt. She didn't want to ruin this night, needed to fix it before he left tomorrow. She used a tissue to wipe her face dry, and took a deep breath.

He roamed out of the bathroom with his smile back in place, but his pain still showed behind the mask. "So. What would you like to do?"

She tapped her hand on her thigh and scanned the room for anything that would offer a distraction. "Cole?" His chest expanded at the sound of his name on her lips.

"Yeah?"

She crossed her arms over her chest and straightened her back, but his attractive fake smile even melted her. "You have spent more than enough time making our days about me. What do you want to do? For you. Not me, for a change."

He strolled forward, tucked her hand in his with a grin on his face, and guided her toward the bed. She smacked his arm. That could wait a bit.

"One track mind these days, huh?" He wiggled his eyebrows at her.

She never had seen his smile so wide.

"You *really* don't want to know what I want."

The suspense killed her, more than the tumor and it sounded kinky. Although a little sore from the night before, she focused on the bed, and couldn't think of anything they left undone. "Okay, I can't take it. Tell me now."

He nudged her down on the bed. "I would really love to get under the covers with you—"

He grabbed the hem of his shirt and her pulse shifted into overdrive. She put her hands down on the soft bed and scooted back further. A strip tease by Cole Davies was sure to be worthy of millions. The sound of his zipper filled the air.

He lowered his jeans, kicked them off to the side, and crawled toward her on the bed. The mattress bounced when he plopped down beside her. "—and watch a movie. It has been so long since I have done something so simple."

With her mouth hung open, she filtered through her assumptions to get out a response for his absurdity, but he tackled her. She rolled around to avoid his tickles, but he overpowered her and pinned her beneath him.

She stared up at the childlike glow in his eyes. This could backfire, but she had to. "My head." She squeezed her eyes shut.

He fell for it. She'd never seen him move so fast. He rolled off her and placed his hands on either side of her face. "What's wrong, baby? Do you need a doctor?"

She shoved him back down on the bed, beneath her. "Got ya."

"That was too far, Isabelle Chambers. Not fair."

His face boiled an angry shade of red but she leaned down, gave him a loud kiss, and jumped off the bed. "If I have learned anything, it's that nothing in life is fair." She laughed and rushed to the door. "I'll be right back."

****

He practiced patience, not one of his better qualities. When she returned, it appeared as though a vending machine exploded in her arms, and she rushed to spill it on the bed as if she'd just scored the biggest jackpot. He did, with her.

"I didn't know what you liked, so I bought one of everything." She shrugged her shoulders. "You can't watch a movie without snacks."

She dumped the assortment of candies and chips on the bed and climbed under the covers with him. The mountain of sugar held her attention while he scrolled through their options on the TV. He glanced at her every few seconds. He loved her, and the next perfect moment with her, he'd shout it out loud. No more whispers.

A movie, with her, was priceless. He laughed, hard, every time she yelled in an animated voice at the TV whenever a female character crossed right into the path of the killer in the horror flick he selected.

She threw a chip at the screen. "This is the reason

us blondes get a bad rep. Run in the other direction, stupid." She threw her hands in the air, and sunk back into the pillows with him. "I give up. They never learn."

He smiled and kissed her forehead. "It's just a movie, baby."

When the credits and music played, he held the remote up and paused. *One of our songs would sound cool at the end of a horror movie*. He made a mental note to run the idea by Tony, and shut the TV off.

She nestled into his arms and lay there, quiet. After a long silence, he assumed she'd drifted to sleep, so he eased the cover up over her, but she snuggled in closer.

"Thank you, for everything."

When she stretched, uneaten junk food trickled to the floor. They giggled. He needed to say something to her. It was getting to heavy to keep it in.

"Isabelle?"

"Mmhmm?"

"I'm scared, too, you know, of my feelings for you. You should know…" He placed the forearm that didn't hold the woman of his dreams, over his eyes and closed them. The dark couldn't hide enough. "Everything I have said to you, I've meant."

He didn't know whether his earlier words, I love you, were loud enough for her to take in. In case they were, he needed her to know he'd intended to say it. It wasn't something thrown out in the heat of passion.

She sighed, but the dark room kept him from her beautiful face, he couldn't tell what it signified.

"I didn't count on this experience leading me to you and the guys. I care about you all. If things were different." She laughed. "The guys would have a blast getting to know the girls. I have a feeling my group of friends would mesh with yours and create a lifelong bond of friendship and love."

She trailed off at the end, as if the words pained her. He didn't know what to make of it. He veered his gaze in the darkened room, to her journal on the nightstand. She said the word love but it didn't sound like a declaration.

"Speaking of. The girls want to get matching tattoos tomorrow. What can we get?"

It didn't take long to brainstorm ideas; he had experience. She yawned, a lot. He fixed the blanket over them, and even though their topic of conversation reminded him they would say good-bye soon, she needed her rest.

"I just want to memorize what it's like to have you in my arms, if that's all I'll ever have." It sounded pathetic, his voice low, choked up. They laid in silence for a long time. Sleep seemed impossible. He evened out his breath and closed his eyes, didn't want her to stay awake because he couldn't relax.

"I love you," she whispered.

He fell asleep with a smile.

Chapter Sixteen

Dear Diary,
With pain came beauty, for all of us…

"What time does their flight come in?" Cole climbed the stairs with caution while he lugged the bags of groceries she insisted they stop for on the way back to the bus.

"Eleven-thirty. Yippee. I'm so excited."

He laughed. "I couldn't tell."

He'd gotten used to whatever the roadies managed to pick up for groceries. They had their requests, but he forgot how many good things they lived each day without. It was nice doing normal things, with her.

"That's perfect. Our flight takes off at eleven. Derek and one of the security guys will hang out with you until they come in." He glanced back over his shoulder, and winked as he put boxes of cereal in the cupboard.

"Did you see the pictures of the beautiful woman plastered on my arm in the trash rags at the checkout counter? You will probably need a little more security from now on."

She threw the bag of M&M's at his head.

He caught it and did a little happy dance. "I'm really pissed we aren't going to be here."

With her hands on her hips, she tipped her head to

the side. "Why?"

He gave her the *duh* expression he was so used to from her. "Hello? Four gorgeous women, probably drunk judging by all the booze we bought, in our bunks without us?" He held his hand over his chest. "Tragic."

He glanced down the aisle. The sound of snores let him know they were alone, so he yanked her into his chest and planted a kiss on her lips. His heart still pounded hungry to hear her words from last night, *the* words, again. She didn't know what brought on their early morning sexapades, and he wouldn't explain it to her either. He couldn't risk her taking it back. Put her guard up, as she always did.

With a loud smack, he ended the kiss that could get out of control without any trouble. "I think it's time we wake these ingrates. Breakfast to go for everyone was brilliant by the way." He slapped her on the ass and scurried to the stairs. "'Cause we don't love you enough already. You have to win us over with food."

The smell of the hotel's restaurant buffet tortured both of them while they checked out. Her solution satisfied not only him, but would his best friends too. Her selflessness captivated him, much like her humble self-confidence, sassy seductive ways, and willingness to explore.

A slight nag of shame stuttered in her voice when she asked if it would be okay. He didn't know why. Her last interaction with the guys ended a little awkwardly, but was nothing compared to what they'd put each other through over the years. He stumbled back up the stairs with a large box of food, and a piece of bacon already clutched between his teeth. She shook her head.

"Food." Brett called out with a desperate tone.

Several curtains opened to reveal hung over men in need of grease. They were quite the sight. Moans and groans filled the air, until satisfied hums replaced them.

They all scratched or rubbed their tired eyes, and shoveled food into their mouths. "Did we miss a party?"

"Hell yes."

Everyone laughed when Zander spoke, and spit food all over the place. He shrugged his shoulders as if to say I'm a man, I can't help it.

"So, have you guys played in New York before?"

Brett, Zander, Drew, and Cole all froze mid-chew. "Hell yeah. New York is a regular reunion, isn't it Cole?" Derek winked at Cole, not as affected by her question, and more interested in the last piece of bacon. Cole kicked him under the table.

"Ouch."

Fuck.

He had to change the topic fast. A quick glance around the table resulted in worthless shrugs, so he huffed and dropped his plastic fork in his plate. The guys made it clear they were more interested in their food than any attempt to bail him out.

"You guys packed, because we have to get going." He stood up, threw the food on his paper plate in the trash, and headed back to his bunk. He stopped just past her, paused, and then took a step back to kiss the top of her head on the way by. "We usually play there once a year. It's no big deal. Thank you for the breakfast, babe."

****

Every sound echoed on the way to the airport. She sat in the middle of the large tour van, stared down at their joined hands, concerned. Many sights she would, on other days, be hypnotized by, passed without a peek. She didn't want him to leave, not upset. "You okay?"

Too late for an answer; they'd arrived. He opened the door and leaned back to suggest she go ahead of him. A slap, followed by a mumbled, *asshat,* sounded behind her. She peeked in time to see Derek rub the back of his head.

The swarm of fans in the waiting area made the issues left unspoken, impossible to address. She let it go. He never left her side. In fact, as much as it was allowed, he held her. He shook hands and autographed with his arm around her waist. This also meant she appeared with him, in many pictures. He seemed happy about that.

"Who's the chick?" One fan yelled, followed by many others curious glimpses.

"Our good luck charm." Derek called out from the side of the crowd. He offered a kind nod to Derek that she didn't understand, but his grip on her hand relaxed.

She needed the next half hour to go by fast, missed the power of girl talk. Their boarding call blared over the intercom. She let out a somewhat relieved breath. Drew, Brett, and Zander kissed her cheek as they passed, and all of them said, "Have fun with the girls." A rush of warmth spread through her.

"I could use a little luck."

She jumped when the fan piped in, forgetting they were surrounded. He spun her to face him and wrapped his arms around her waist. He made it known her eyes were the only ones that mattered to him. "Find your own good luck charm, buddy, mine is one of a kind." He kissed her with a passion she could only label as love. A mixture of whistles and negative comments echoed.

It didn't feel right. She shouldn't let him put himself on display like this. It wasn't a forever kind of thing. She tucked her arm up between them and guided him back with a smile, to be discreet. "You should go. Don't want to miss your flight. Have fun in New York."

He stiffened. "One night, baby, I'm coming back to *you.*"

What's so wrong with New York, and why did that sound strange? She stared as he handed the lady his pass and continued, with his head down.

A large man stepped up beside her. "Hi Ms. Chambers, I'm Kevin. Cole assigned you to my security detail while he's away. You've been seen in public a lot. He doesn't want you going anywhere without me while he's gone."

"Hello, Kevin." It would have happened sooner or later.

She sat down in the row of chairs and tapped her foot. Kevin's presence was new, uncomfortable. It would take some getting used to. Until then, she needed a distraction. The girls' phones would be off, so she couldn't text. She searched her bag, got out her journal, and set it open in her lap. It'd been handier than she imagined. Whispers from the crowd around her faded while she wrote. The night before, the words, would take more than a journal entry to process but she had the time.

"Well isn't this a heartfelt hello. We were under the impression that you missed us?"

The sound of Katherine's voice was heaven to her ears. She shoved her diary in her bag and ran to them.

They screeched with joy and jumped up and down while they hugged. The anxious flutter in her stomach vanished and she closed her eyes. Calm.

"Let the hot mess festivities begin. Whatever we do, Izzy, I want details, all of them." Taryn captured her in another hug. "Missed you." They all linked arms and left the nosey onlookers behind.

Placed at the end of their chain, she used her free hand to fan her face. "Oh yes. Details."

The giggles continued, all the way back to the bus. She raised her hand, to show them around, when a piece of paper with her name on it caught her eye. She picked it up, opened it.

Hey Baby,

Have a fun day, well, not too much fun. I'm sure Kevin has already introduced himself. You are not to go anywhere without him. Derek will drive you everywhere. I mean it. In order to ensure you and the girls have a stress-free day I have taken the liberty of making a few arrangements for you. At 3 o'clock Derek will take you to your appointments at a local, award-winning, tattoo parlor. Be brave, baby. I can't wait to see it. You should have time to come back to the bus and get ready afterward, for your 7 o'clock dinner reservations at Zander's favorite place in St. Louis. Let me know what you think? Your names are all on a VIP list at the most popular club in the city. If you have taken meds, no drinking. Miss you already…

Love, Cole

Also, Katherine, Abigail, and Taryn,

Welcome. I am sorry I haven't had the chance to meet the ladies who have encouraged this beautiful woman to become a part of my life. I will be forever in your debt. Take care of her for me and please, make it a good one.

Cheers, Cole

"Aw."

All three girls cooed in unison.

They hugged her from behind as she wiped a tear from her cheek. She squirmed out of their embrace. "The bar is stocked, Taryn. Drinks."

She made the tour quick, to avoid their curious stares. They would be able to read the desperation in her eyes. She was in over her head, just a little. Taryn got to work on the drinks, no different from any other girls' night at home, and they sat in the lounge at the back of the bus. The guys weren't there but she still sat in *her* spot.

The door of the bus opened. "I'm just going to hang out in the other bus, honey. If you need anything, you know where to find me."

"Okay, Derek, thanks."

Abigail smiled with her head cocked to the side. "Have them all wrapped around your finger, don't you?"

Everyone covered their silent laughs to avoid a sweet liquid shower. She shrugged her shoulders and took a rather large sip of her drink. "Mmm. Oh, Taryn, I have missed your skills."

"Spill, Izzy."

She smiled. *Just like home.* "Spill what, Abigail?" Bluffs never worked well for her. She choked on her drink in the process. "Okay, okay. The only things left on my list are a tattoo, fly a plane, and bungee jump. We would have done the jump yesterday but I wasn't feeling well. Anyway, what do you want to know?" If she rambled fast, maybe they'd overlook questions about her health.

"If you don't give us the sex details, we may combust from anticipation."

Katherine, the ever so clever one, helped avoid the topic, too. She swayed toward her and mouthed the words, thank you, before she scanned the group of eager women.

"Mmm, the sex." She closed her eyes. Thinking about it made heat rise to her skin. "It's amazing, hot, wild and…" She lowered her attention to the drink in her hand and played with the tiny pink umbrella. One from the pretty package he'd scowled at her about making him carry this morning at the store, but her hands were full. "Uninhibited."

"OK, all I want to know is how many of them have you seen naked? Scratch that. I may want to know more, no promises." Taryn laughed.

"Cole of course, and…Drew." She peeked up, needed to see their faces. Just what she expected, jaws were dropped, speechless. For the first time ever, the envy in their eyes was directed at her.

"I think I'm going to faint. Seriously?" Abigail waved her hand over her face.

Her gaze roamed about the group of women she found to be her extended self until him. Each of them held a place in the world but as a group, they were one, a bond. His presence in her life though, completed it.

"Oh. My. God. The tattoo. I take it you've had the pleasure every woman's dreamed about? Katherine grabbed onto the closest hand for support. Taryn's. They stared.

"Yes. It is uh-ma-zing." She fanned her face. "The

dragon wraps around his waist and down his," With her eyes closed, she fell back into the cushions. "Tight. Thigh. Beautiful." She left out the part about the scripture, his twin sister. It wasn't her story to tell.

"Wow." The room quieted and everyone nodded in silent agreement.

"Time to head out, sweetheart." Derek's call for the girls was not at all the intensity he used for the guys.

"Let's go. Or have you changed your minds?" She widened her gaze and stood with her hands on her hips.

"*Love* from Cole, *honey* and *sweetheart* from Derek?"

"Be right out," she shouted toward the door and then cocked her head to glare at the girls.

Katherine's eyebrows rose, but the concern behind her smile, evident. She shook her head and held up her hand. "Don't. They are a bunch of charmers, that's all." The girls followed her off the bus, sure to stare at her back and each other.

On the way to the tattoo parlor she described the idea she and Cole spoke about last night, a heart overlapped with an infinity symbol, on her shoulder blade. They loved it. Through thick and thin, they were there, friendships that would stand the test of time. Water formed in their eyes, so she shifted her attention out the window. If they kept this up, the night would become a blubbering mess rather than the wild one she needed.

****

"Say sexy bitches."

They stood side by side, held their shirts in front of them and peeked back over their bare shoulders, at the camera. They did it. She needed another drink, several really. The emotions that welled up in that moment got to her. The wonderful and talented artist handed her phone back with the picture displayed for her to see. The girls bumped shoulders, and stared at it with hushed appreciation.

"We are sexy bitches. Send a copy of that to all of our phones will you please?" Abigail tugged her shirt back in place.

"Send it to Cole." Taryn laughed and followed suit.

Good idea.

She and Katherine rushed to get dressed. Her fingers tapped at the keyboard on her phone with jittery anticipation, until the picture uploaded to the message that was sure to leave him restless.

Hey handsome. Do any of the groupies compare?

Send.

It was still early, but he should have his phone on him. She checked her watch. *Maybe in sound check?* Her phone beeped. Taryn, Abigail, and Katherine crowded her to see his reply, a picture of him, Drew, Zander, and Brett with their jaws wide open.

Holy fuck, that's hot. Hope you don't mind if I use that later. Glad you're having fun with the girls. I miss you...lots.

She smiled.

"Okay, okay, let's get going. I am sure the plans for the rest of the evening are going to be as fabulous as this tattoo parlor, so let's live it up." She ensured Taryn still showed enthusiasm for the night's plans. She did. Her day-to-day life involved the bar scene, yet the idea of it didn't appear to grow tiresome for her.

They bounced to the counter to pay, not able to

withhold an occasional peek at each other's tattoo, but were waved off. Instead, the young woman behind the counter handed her a familiar piece of paper with her name on it. The heat of female bodies crowded her.

Hello Beautiful,

You did it. I am so proud of you. Okay, so part of me can't wait to see it as I pound into you from behind...hey, I am a guy.

She cringed at the female shrieks but she continued reading.

I feel pride knowing I helped mark you in a way that won't fade...like my others.

She smiled when the girls gasped behind her.

"You are wild." She tilted her head toward Katherine's hand, which squeezed her shoulder from behind.

I am sure it is as stunning on you as all the wild women probably surrounding you right now.

The noise in the parlor silenced except the echo of the girls' laughter.

Please continue to have a great night and know I am the lucky one, to have met you. I have taken care of the bill, enjoy.

Love, Cole

"Wow."

She couldn't come up with any other words. She didn't want to have any regrets but she did, not telling him. She'd taken the coward's way out and whispered it to him while he slept. She stared at the letter. The weight of her phone caught her attention. She had an idea; it would be a start. After she stuffed the letter in her purse, she held her phone up in front of her.

You are quite the brash talker Mr. Davies...and

charmer. Thank you, from all of us lucky ladies. I miss you too.

Love, Isabelle

That would have to somehow translate into what she intended to say. She bounced back to her friends. "Let's get this party started."

****

Of course, like women who haven't seen each other in a long time, preparation for the evening took a little longer than anticipated. They were late for their reservations. She hated to be late.

"Come on." She shoved her arm through Katherine's and increased their stride through the restaurant door. In Tampa she would have been nervous to show up an hour late for reservations; in St. Louis however, nothing but approachable smiles and "don't worry about its" were expressed. The restaurant was filled with very richly dressed individuals, not a place she could see a group of tattooed, pierced men dining at. What brought Zander here? The hostess showed them to their private, large, circle booth in the back.

"Wow. This place is amazing." She grinned with appreciation at Abigail. Her job involved a lot of travel and fine dining, therefore any compliment from her said something.

Before they could raise their menus, a beautiful server stood at their table. She offered each of them a flute filled with fizzy pink liquid and purple umbrellas out the top. Isabelle's glance fell to the recognizable piece of paper on her tray. "I'm Julia. I will be taking care of you ladies while you're with us. Please let me know if there is anything you need." She handed the paper over and passed around the drinks. "I will be back in a moment to take your orders." She glanced at her with a curious sparkle in her eye. "Enjoy your evening."

The paper tapped loud against the tabletop, while she waited for the waitress to get far enough away from their table. This was getting a little weird. No one touched their drinks, just waited. She opened the piece of paper.

Hello my love,

Her heart pounded hard, she could hear his voice along with the words.

I hope everyone is treating you well. This restaurant has come highly recommended by Zander. His family has vacationed in St. Louis over the years and he was very excited to have you come here. He is fond of the food. Although, I am sure it probably has something to do with the pretty women. This round of drinks was his idea too. I always thought he was a little girly. Don't tell him, please.

I hope your shoulder isn't too sore, and heals fast. I can't wait to touch you, I mean, it. I have been ordered to tell you the Head Rush dessert is a must, so save room.

Katherine, Abigail, and Taryn

Please hold her steady…are you? The server has my information. Please enjoy any and all extravagant delights…on me.

She opened her mouth to protest when Abigail did what he asked, and placed her hand on Isabelle's shoulder. "Honey, why not? He cares for you, obviously a lot. That's what people do for each other. Just go with it and enjoy, please?"

She took a deep breath and rolled her eyes. She

couldn't win with everyone ganging up on her.

I know, I know. Just go with it, sweetie, for me? I have a pouty face on right now, in case you were wondering. I am sure I am sweating my ass off right now on stage and I don't want to be distracted wondering if you are enjoying yourself. There. How was that for a guilt trip?

See you soon. Not soon enough...

Love, Cole

XOXO

She folded the paper, placed it on the bench seat beside her, and took another deep breath. She lifted her head to the excited gazes of true friendship, the kind you were lucky to experience once in a lifetime. There was no way she could contend with them all, so she raised her hands and rubbed them together. "Let's see what's yummy."

The service was impeccable. Julia catered to their every need, and Zander couldn't have been more accurate, the *Head Rush*, well, just that.

Derek drove the limo, without a doubt, aware of Cole's plans. She scanned the car, beyond the women in the seats, to the story of fulfillment behind it all. If she folded her arms around herself she'd hold in the emotions that filled her, not rub them away for a change. Everyone talked with smiles a mile wide. There wasn't anything left undone, she could just sit back and enjoy her time with the people who helped make her the woman she was.

Taryn gave them all a wild update about the most recent public catastrophe that took place at the bar. The vibration in her pocket distracted her, and since everyone else was with her, it was him.

We're on our way out for the encore. Don't be mad at me...remember how my dad raised me?

Cole.

She didn't respond, just tucked the phone back in her purse, and stepped out of the limo when it slowed to a stop at the curb. A long line up blocked the door to the modern, two-story club, but no, they didn't have to wait. Thanks to his VIP treatment, they were able to go right in, to another reserved table. Of course, a note sat right in the center of the table. She picked it up, and squirmed with uncomfortable delight when the girls made jokes about his devotion.

To the prettiest woman in the place,

Okay. Okay. I'll stop. From here on, you're on your own babe. I don't know whether you have noticed but Kevin should still be somewhere in the background. If any of these fools try to hurt you, he's your go-to person. Have fun.

Love you, <— Deal with it.

Cole

She read the last part over again, a few times. *I love you too, Cole.* She couldn't wait to tell him, to his face.

Taryn ensured, as always, nothing but the most delicious drinks were delivered to their table. Isabelle beamed with undiluted happiness. Sure, a lot of it to do with the alcohol and friends but, she was in love again. They gave quite the show for the nosey spectators as they shimmied around the dark, speckled with black lights, dance floor. He was right. She spotted Kevin not long after the note, hadn't at all until that point. She tipped her head back with her eyes closed, and swayed to the music. Sweat beaded her skin. The familiar scenario calmed her. Home. The occasional camera flashed throughout the night, right before Kevin yanked it away from the meddler. He had arranged for this night to be hers, and hers alone.

"I need another drink," She hollered over the music and shuffled through the crowd to their table, at the side of the dance floor. Their private server, of course, arrived with drinks before they were all seated.

"So, where are the Scandals tonight?" Abigail yelled.

The music grew louder as the night progressed. "New York." Her voice scratched, not very audible. The smile on Katherine's face fell as she turned to the dance floor. Isabelle leaned over, close enough to speak into her best friends' ear. "What's up?" She shook her head, but still didn't make eye contact. "Katherine?"

With her attention still averted to the crowd, she swayed closer to Isabelle. "I follow gossip for a living."

Isabelle shrugged her shoulders. "Yeah, so?"

A chill hit her when Katherine downed her drink and slammed the glass on the table. "Cole has an *ex-girlfriend*. Pictures have been taken of the two of them together every year he's in New York."

She sat back in her chair, stunned. The congested dance floor that held Katherine's attention seconds ago, now held hers. Nothing could have prepared her for that. Yes, he mentioned a girlfriend while he was in school, but nothing about still being involved with her. Tears filled her eyes. "What's her name?" She rummaged through her purse.

"Alexis."

She glanced up at Katherine's eyes, filled with sadness, regret even. She raised her chin high, held the phone tight, and avoided the person who could change her mind. She would not cry over a man that wasn't hers to begin with. He lived life well before her, yes, but she still felt a little betrayed. She glared down at her phone and took a deep breath.

Thank you for everything. You shouldn't have, really. Hope your visit with Alexis is as memorable as last year and the many before that. Izzy

She shoved the phone back in her purse and stiffened when three sets of concerned eyes locked on her. "I'm ready to call it a night, ladies."

Chapter Seventeen

Dear Diary,
Through my tears, honor filled the horizon…

The phone crashed to the floor, back cover skidding one way, battery and phone another. Cole's hands shook and the sweat he'd just finished washing off, coated his skin once again. His heart fell with the phone and his breath stopped the second he read her message. He scrambled for the nearest chair, and sat with a towel wrapped around his waist. His knee bounced harder than ever.

"Holy shit. What's up with you, man? You're white as a ghost."

He raised his head to see Drew, who'd just slammed into the larger than usual wardrobe room with a laugh, in time to catch sight of the tear that slipped down his face. He wiped it fast with the back of his hand. "She knows about Alexis, just texted me to *have fun* with her." He put his elbows to his knees, head down, when the room spun.

"Fuck man. I'm sorry."

Flashes of dinner earlier with Alexis ran through his mind. He told her about Isabelle, that he loved her. The smile plastered on her face since meeting him at the airport vanished the second the words left his lips. They talked about their past together, her bipolar disorder, now medicated and under control, that only he and the guys had knowledge of.

He shook his head and stared at the concrete floor.

He'd stormed out on her, after going back to his dorm and finding her on her knees for his roommate. Yet, he held her hand in psych wards and maintained a friendship until now. He avoided comments to the paparazzi for years about her. Their need to dig would only hurt her, so he protected her. With Isabelle, he came up short, should have protected her from himself. He stared at Drew; there would already be pictures online somewhere of him and Alexis. "How do I fix this?"

Drew picked up the pieces of his phone, put it back together, and handed it to him. "You'll find a way, man."

He stared at the phone. "You guys were pissed seeing Alexis. I know you were. I put you in this mess. I'm sorry."

Drew huffed on his way to the door, opened it, and appeared to try his best not to be mad before he glared back. "Yes, you fucked up and dragged us down with you. Do something about it."

His gaze held on the closed door. A silent scream obstructed his breath, and his phone weighted his hand like a tempted object to throw—a temper tantrum. Rock stars could get away with shit like that, right? Instead, he gripped his lifeline and took a deep breath. He'd found the strength to forgive Alexis, although determined he would never invest his heart again, but he had. And now, he may have broken it without any fault but his own.

He dialed her number and held the phone to his ear

but her voice message played, no ring. She'd shut off her phone. He left a brief message, "call me please," and stood up and paced with reluctance to the bathroom counter. He stared at regret in the mirror. Tomorrow's flight couldn't come fast enough.

****

A pin dropped would have produced more noise than what took place in the car. The girls shuffled in their seats as if unspoken words haunted them, but none dared to surface.

Derek and Kevin helped the girls onto the bus.

"You ladies are going to have quite the hangovers tomorrow." Due to Derek's fatherly tone, the tears she'd held back slid down her cheek.

She twisted in his grasp. "Did you know about New York, too?" Her words were slurred, sad.

His averted gaze said it all. She let go of him and used the wall for support the rest of the way to the bathroom. The door, left open, allowed her to hear Katherine and Derek's words.

"My fault. Should have kept my big mouth shut."

Isabelle shook her head, placed her toothbrush on the counter, and spit in the sink. What is it about drunkenness that influences the ugly cries? Katherine's sniffles were loud.

"No honey. He should have told her. It isn't your fault. Drink this water and get some sleep."

"Still—"

She didn't want to hear anymore. She slammed the light switch, barged down the aisle and climbed into her bunk, not his. Her eyes were sore, and the tears wouldn't stop. Her mind screamed over the sound of the girls as they stumbled about, and got settled into bed.

He said he loved me. One of many lies, maybe?

Anger consumed her, wouldn't let go of its grip until she yanked out her phone and booked a flight home the next day with the girls. She buried her phone under her pillow and lay on top of it, thankful for the consumption of alcohol or sleep wouldn't have come otherwise.

****

She drifted not long before the buzz sounded. Not so much from her head, anymore, but the alarm she'd set. She'd endure her last moments on the bus alone; pack before the girls could talk her out of it. She tiptoed around the bus to collect her things, astounded how fast she'd settled in. She took a deep breath and wiped another tear just as several alarm clocks sounded, followed by unhappy groans.

She sat at the table that now brought heartache instead of happiness, waited with her guard in place. One by one, they climbed out of the bunks, cursing. She laughed, a little. The image before her couldn`t be more similar to the men who most days occupied the narrow beds.

As expected Katherine, Abigail, and Taryn stood frozen with confused stares. Her suitcase sat on the floor at her side. "Well, get a move on, girls. Our flight leaves in two hours." She put on her most collected smile but she wasn't an award-winning actress by any means.

"No." Katherine's authoritative voice always made them jump.

"Yes. I only have two items left on my list. I can manage back in Tampa. I have taken up enough of the

Scandals time and money. Besides, my flight is already booked, non-refundable. I will always be thankful for the kindness and friendship Cole has offered me." She threw her hands up in the air. "I am just some woman he met on the Internet, a charity case."

Taryn grabbed Katherine's arm when she raised it to rebuttal. "No. If she wants to come home, let her. She's right. There isn't anything left undone she needs the Scandals for that we can't help her with." Her voice dropped to a whisper. "We need her, too."

She locked gazes with Taryn and mouthed, thank you. Taryn's reasons did not match her own but she was okay with that, as long as she could get on the plane and not face the man who'd broken her heart. She glanced down at her phone on the table, considered the messages she assumed were on it, but tucked it into her purse.

"I'll be in the car with Derek. Don't be long." She raised the handle on her suitcase and stalked away with it trailing behind on wheels. The swift stride of her departure didn't distract her from the heavyhearted stares at her back.

Derek opened the door to the van. He didn't ask any questions late last night when she sent him a text to ask for a ride to the airport. His wife and daughter, for the short time he had them, must have taught him well about a woman's limits, breaking points.

"Isabelle?" He closed her door and got in behind the wheel. Much liked she'd witnessed many times, he checked the rear-view mirror. Only this time his hesitant smile was for her. "Are you sure?"

She drew her sunglasses off her head and covered her puffy, watery eyes. "Yes, I am. There were pictures online last night. It would appear he enjoyed his night. I'm happy for him, really."

She smiled and rubbed her arms. "Thank you, for everything. You're an amazing man. Just what the Scandals need. Oh, wait." She picked her bag up off the floor at her feet and retrieved a box, held it out to him over the seat, and scooted to the edge of her own so she could see. "Here, please accept this, as a thank you."

He opened the box to reveal a black velvet bag. He tipped it in his hand and a silver compass fell out. The inside lid of the compass held a copy of the picture he took with him everywhere, his wife and daughter. The inscription read *you never know when you will find what you were never looking for in the first place*.

He closed his hand around it and raised his head with his eyes closed. When he opened them again and smiled back at her, his eyes were red. "Isabelle," he swallowed. "I have no idea how you managed this but from the bottom of my heart, thank you. You have no idea what this means to me."

She sat back against her seat and fixed her anguish out the window. "I'm pretty sure I do."

He climbed out of the car to help the girls with their bags, and mumbled, "Cole is in deep shit."

The ride to the airport couldn't have been quicker, and now she paced. Kevin stood at his post, a discreet distance away. The guys' flight was scheduled to come in just as theirs left. She didn't want to see him; he'd change her mind. Their flight was called over the intercom. She forced her breath in and out as they made their way aboard. Today's headache could be the result of many reasons. The window seat, which she always loved, now displayed what she could only assume was his plane, and he wouldn't be happy about missing her. She reclined in her seat and relaxed, well, kind of.

Katherine nudged her and handed over some pills with a bottle of water. "For the headache."

She glanced down at the familiar pills and back up again.

"I haven't forgotten what they look like."

"Thank you." She took the pills, swallowed, and then lowered the back of her seat. The darkness from her closed eyes simulated the day's end. Splendid.

****

"Where is she?" he yelled at Derek as he ran through the terminal, bumping shoulders on his way.

Derek pointed to the plane taking off on the tarmac.

"Fuck."

He'd blow up at Derek for not stopping her, but it wouldn't be right; it wasn't his fault. He dropped his bag and fell into a chair. He'd been an ass all morning trying to rush everyone, and he still missed her.

"I'll be right back." He jumped from his seat. Everyone else sat down and rested with their eyes closed.

****

She shifted in her seat several times. Weeks ago, she would've cursed the side effects of her medication but now she craved them. She couldn't sleep.

"Ugh."

"Ms. Chambers?"

She jerked to the nice woman and covered her mouth. "I'm so sorry, I'll be quiet." Without him at her side, being the center of attention didn't feel the same. Her gaze roamed from the cordial attendant to the many passengers who paused to cast their glance her way. She rubbed her arms but it didn't produce the same level of comfort, they weren't his arms. No blanket they'd bring her would smell like him.

The attendant laughed. "No, that's okay. Would you mind coming with me for a minute?"

"Sure." She braced her hands on the armrests and stood up. Her pulse, that'd calmed not long ago, raced once again. A quick glance at her friends confirmed they also had no clue. She followed behind the nice woman at a snail's pace toward the front of the plane, through the attendants' quarters.

A brunette with the nametag reading *Sylvia* greeted her. "Nice to meet you, Ms. Chambers." *Shit. What'd I do wrong?*

When the flight attendant who retrieved her from her seat waved, all eyes stared at her, unable to force another step. She scurried ahead out of embarrassment, in front of a white door beside the lady while she knocked. A very handsome man opened it. He held his hand out to her as if he'd expected her, so she shook it, still confused.

"Hello, Ms. Chambers. It is a pleasure to meet you."

"I, uh, I, hello?" She narrowed her eyes when he laughed. *How dare he? Men suck.*

"My name is Daniel. I'm the co-pilot of this aircraft today." He pointed behind him. "This is Jared, the pilot."

She smiled at them both with her eyebrows raised. *If they are smart enough to fly a damn plane, why can't they see I have no fucking clue what's going on?*

"It has come to our attention you have a wish to

learn how to fly."

She closed her eyes; it all made sense. "Cole." When she opened her eyes, they nodded, and offered her a seat in the co-pilot chair.

"Yes ma'am. Cole Davies is a very generous and stubborn man. His only concern seems to be you, and by the sincerity on your face, the feeling is mutual."

She wiped at the warm tears that slipped down her cheeks. Apparently, she still had a few to spare. She sat in the chair and glared at all of the controls in front of her. "I'm sorry for the inconvenience. We don't have to do this. I can just go back to my seat." She rose from the seat, but was stopped by Daniel's gentle hand on her shoulder. Jared's interest in her suggested some uncertainty, too. She obliged at their gracious smiles and sat, distracted by the soft appearance of the clouds ahead. How much of her story did they know?

"It is not an inconvenience at all. Sit back and relax, I'll explain a few things before we get to the good stuff. Okay?"

What else was she supposed to do? It wasn't as easy as one would expect. Cole demanded her attention, even when not there. *How did he manage this? What is he doing? Does he miss me? Is he with her?*

"Are you ready?" Jared chuckled. "There is a lot more to it than I can show you in a few minutes, but with your hands on the yoke and the flip of a button, we will be at your mercy."

She snapped her attention back at him. "Yoke?"

He laughed and pointed in front of her. "Steering wheel."

"Oh. Sorry." She held onto the wheel tight, her knuckles whitened and her heart raced.

"Are you ready?"

She checked behind her to make sure Daniel stayed close by—always good to have backup. She took her hand off the wheel for one quick second to make sure the tears were good and gone. "Sorry for the tears. This is all a little overwhelming. The view is beautiful." She took a deep breath. "Ready."

She gripped the wheel, soared with a front seat view. Flew a plane.

Daniel stood over her shoulder and gave clear instructions on what to do next. His calm directions were easy to follow. She was on top of the world. Only a few minutes passed but her nerves were making her stomach do flip flops, not the good ones. "I think that's enough flying for me, guys. You can take over now." She glanced at Jared and then back out the window, as if she could run into something if she weren't attentive. "Please."

When he told her she was good to let go, she stood and changed spots with Daniel. There were too many buttons and in all likelihood she'd hit one and not the right one either. "Thank you. You have no idea what this means to me. I have a great respect for the job you do and all the people you take responsibility for."

Something in Jared's mindful nature warmed her, genuine compassion, not the sympathy she expected. "Are you going to be okay, Isabelle?"

She smiled, leaned over, and kissed his cheek. "No, but I've accepted that."

In unison, they glanced at one another and then back at her with more questions in their eyes. She didn't know whether to be nervous because neither straightened to look ahead but she figured it probably wasn't as necessary as driving a car.

"It's our pleasure. We only have one request?"

She shrugged her shoulders. Why not?

"Don't tell anyone." They spoke at once and laughed, punched each other in the arm as if they'd been friends for years.

She wandered back to her seat, speechless. Three sets of curious eyes glared at her when she buckled in. "When the time is right, ladies, I'll tell you."

****

She stood on her front porch and waved. Their reaction to her short-lived pilot career would be forever engrained in her mind. She opened the door, wandered in and twirled in slow motion, taking in the room that hadn't changed since she left. It was a different person who came home.

She placed her luggage on her bed and dragged her feet to the kitchen to make tea. Okay, so some things were still the same. With the warm mug on the table in front of her, she tapped her finger on her phone. It glared at her.

She switched it on and sat back in her chair. Ring tones alerted her to the inevitable. Three voice messages and two text messages, all from him. She raised the phone to her ear and rolled her eyes toward the ceiling, to hold in the tears that pooled faster than she cared for.

"Call me, please."

Delete.

"Isabelle, please don't leave. I'm sorry I didn't tell you. I'm such an ass. Yes, I met with Alexis, as I do every year. It's not what you think. Please give me the chance to explain. She is only a friend and doesn't even have to be that if you're not cool with it. Ugh." Click.

Delete.

"Isabelle. There is a long story you need to hear, please." Silence "I love you." Click.

She wiped her tears and read the text messages.

Please forgive me…I love you

My life isn't complete without you. I'm sorry…

She placed the phone down in front of her. The urge to throw it was intense and wouldn't take much effort. What she needed to do would come with a cost—her heart. She picked up the phone and hit reply.

Best flight ever. I didn't kill anyone. Words cannot express what the last several days have meant to me. You will be blessed with one more angel watching out for you. Take care of yourself. Love, Isabelle

She hit the send button before she could chicken out and within seconds, her phone rang. Cole. She hit ignore but another beep signaled a text and his determination to get her attention.

My love, I am pretty sure I have mentioned this before…I would do anything for you, I mean it. I know I screwed up. Second chance? Love always, Cole

Although the mug warmed her hands, the chill in the rest of her body craved the burn of another distraction.

"I need something a lot stronger than this."

She trudged to the counter with her shoulders slumped and dropped her mug in the sink, cringed when it shattered. A peek in the fridge didn't reveal much of anything, let alone alcohol. "And food." She leaned against the counter and the hard surface dug into her back. It only brought back memories of her last time in that position.

"First things first." She nabbed the phone and dialed before the courage, or maybe the anger that fueled it, faded.

"Hello, Dr. Peterson's office, may I help you?"

She curled her free hand into a ball, so tight her nails dug in. "Yes, this is Isabelle Chambers. Can you please let Dr. Peterson know he can go ahead and book my surgery?"

Silence.

"Dr. Peterson will be very happy to hear you've called. I will give him the go ahead. The second we hear from the surgeon, I will call you back with the surgery date and time. Is there anything else you wish for me to pass on to the doctor?"

She sneered at the broken porcelain in the sink. This secretary was unforgettable, the grumpy one. Only she oozed pleasantness, not a good sign. "No, thanks." She hung up.

What is it about pending doom that makes people change their ways?

Her stomach grumbled and she placed her hand over it. "Patience. One more." She scrolled through her messages from him. Now it was her turn. It would hurt him but she didn't see any other solution.

No second chances necessary. It was just a tour, remember? Please say good-bye to the guys for me. I have a lot of things to take care of, so I need to end it here. Enjoy the rest of your tour. You really have built a wonderful life; cherish it. Love Isabelle.

Send.

The distance between them helped the anger simmer rather than boil, but the taste of guilt in her mouth was sour. After all he'd done, her cold treatment didn't sit well.

"Wine should take care of that." She wrenched her purse and keys from the entryway table, locked the door behind her, and strode to the car. This time, she didn't care to observe the life around her.

Her phone rang but she adjusted the radio instead. Thankful for being behind the wheel, she kept her eyes on the road and let it go to voicemail.

She circled the parking lot many times before a spot opened. "Come on." She gripped the wheel. The elderly person, who backed out of the spot she waited for, tried her nerves. She counted to ten before she maneuvered into the spot, with a little more patience, and no accident. She picked up her phone from the empty passenger seat she'd tossed it on and dialed her voicemail. The possibility that her mother may have received word she flew home and hadn't called yet would make the day that much worse.

Her purse spilled onto the floor. "Ugh." She put her phone down on the seat, placed it on speaker, and picked up the mess.

"Hello Isabelle, this is Dr. Peterson." Her hand froze, no longer interested in the tube of Chap Stick that rolled out of reach. "I'm very happy to hear from you. I have spoken to the surgeon himself and we were able to schedule your surgery for two weeks from today. I'm guessing this is sooner than you expected, but when you have time, please call my secretary back and she can give you all of the pre-op instructions." Silence "I am glad you made it home safe. I hope you were successful in your endeavors." Click

"Ha."

Chapter Eighteen

Dear Diary,
I'm awake and surrounded by love, but not his...

"Fuck."

Cole threw his phone in his bunk and stared at the empty space. He'd done all he could think of, and still failed her. One item on her list, that's all that remained. Her text message couldn't have been clearer; she was done with him.

"Cole?"

With stiff arms braced on her bunk, he closed his eyes and lowered his head. Derek always surfaced when someone fell apart, his gift. He let out a deep breath and sat down, hunched over. He scrubbed at his face, not able to resign himself to the fact that she would never share his bed again.

"Yeah? Are we heading out soon?" The thin mattress dipped when he sat down beside him. He wouldn't let plans get derailed. They were booked solid, night after night of shows, and he needed to get his head on straight.

"Yep, but that's not what I want to talk about."

Here it comes.

"Isabelle."

Cole sighed. Her name alone made his chest hurt.

"I know this is messing you up. She was perfect, is

perfect. What you have with her reminds me a lot of what I had, once. Look?"

It didn`t take much to notice the beautiful compass in his hand. Cole read the inscription. He clenched his jaw and water formed in his eyes. Anger consumed him and not because he hurt her. Oh that was still there, but this, this was about how unfair life is.

"I need her."

"We have two weeks of shows. Get your head on straight enough to get through them. You have a couple weeks off after that. Go get her then."

Cole huffed and nodded. "Two weeks of hell."

Derek smiled, patted him on the back, and strolled to the front. And, like usual, picked up things the guys left lying about. "You were a moody bastard before she came along. We can handle a couple of weeks."

Derek was right, as always, but two weeks seemed like forever. Getting in to see a doctor required time. She hadn't even been scheduled yet, so it wouldn't be possible to get her in that quick, right?

He needed to know she arrived home okay and not being able to see this in person tortured him. He stood up quick and banged his head on the bunk that still smelled like vanilla. He rubbed the back of his head. *Not even here and she's making herself known.*

He snagged his phone from his pocket and raced down the stairs of the bus. Much like her group, they too had an inquisitive one. Zander was a man of many talents, even online.

Katherine.

****

"Mom, I'm home."

The trip to the grocery store resulted in nothing

more than wine. After that message, how could anyone eat, or even look at food. She stopped at the bottom of the stairs, and braced herself on the banister when her vision grew murky, unfocused. *That's a new one.*

"You didn't let me know you were coming home." Carol ran down the stairs with her arms out.

When her mother wrapped her in her arms, it seemed like an eternity since she'd cherished the familiar embrace. But then again, she was a different woman now. Would her mother notice?

Carol shook, still discreet with her sobs. She could relate. The strong woman who let her go, gave up limited time so she could pursue her goals, needed a moment to crumble. She held on tight, let her. She'd never seen her mother cry, not that she could recall.

Carol forced her back in a gentle manner and scooted past her, to the table in the entryway. She plucked a tissue from the box and cleaned herself up. "I'm so sorry, honey. I have no idea where that came from."

"Mom, crying doesn't make you weak. God knows I've done enough of that in the last couple days." She wandered to the kitchen. As expected, her mother followed close behind.

"I'll make some tea."

She sat at the table, and her mother dawdled about with familiar grace. For the first time since she arrived home, she relaxed her shoulders and let go of the tension, the stress. She slouched back into her chair and reflected on the many familiar items around the kitchen, a room with so many wonderful memories. She took the flower-patterned mug from her mom and held it in front of her face to smell. Chamomile and lemon.

"Thank you, Mom."

She took a sip, and the warm citrus blend coated her mouth and tasted wonderful. They sat across from each other, quiet. Uncomfortable silence worked for her mother, and for as long as she could remember, it roused the confessions out of her.

"Mom." She leaned forward, searched her mother for any reaction but didn't get one. Carol demonstrated the patience she longed for. "Where do I start?"

Carol placed her hand over hers. "Let's take our tea out on the back porch. I put in a new swing. I've spent a lot of time out there, thinking."

She shivered. She left her mom here, to worry. The dark circles under her eyes showed more than usual. *What have I done to her?*

Carol grabbed her hand, held onto it until they were in the beautiful backyard, which had seen a lot of attention since she left. Bright-colored flowers, stone paths, and even a pond filled the space she remembered being flat and green.

"Oh, Mom, it's beautiful back here. You did all this?"

Her mom shrugged, pointed to the swing, adorned with thick cushions and large enough to hold two people. "The girls dropped by every now and then to help. You have wonderful friends."

Her tattoo came back to her memory. "I know. I'm glad they kept you company while I was away. It made it a little easier, knowing you weren't alone."

She scooched sideways in her seat, bent her leg so she could lean against the back of the swing with her shoulder and see her mother's face. "Thank you, Mom, for everything. I wouldn't be who I am today without you."

Carol rested her hand on her leg and squeezed. "You made it easy on me, honey, a little too easy. Will you tell me about your trip?"

She peered down in her mug; the Merlot in her car might make this easier. "Sure." She sighed; she could do this. "The Scandals are amazing." She smiled wide, just thinking about the guys. "I can now say I have a thing for rock music, go figure. I have a lot of things on my bucket list, Mom, things I haven't shared with you."

Carol adjusted herself to match her.

"First, all but one item is complete on the list I showed you." She closed her eyes, tipped her head to the side, and rested it on the cushion behind her. "Cole is a very resourceful man." She swallowed hard and gripped the mug tighter. Saying his name out loud was tough. "He made my every wish come true, and then some."

"You fell in love."

She raised her head to her mother and the truth. "I did." A tear slid down her cheek, she left it. Never did she have to hide them from her mother, her best friend. "I didn't plan it. I couldn't stop it, as much as I tried."

She breathed in through her nose, to ease the sob that crept up her throat. "The things on my list—" She slipped the list, the real one, out of her back pocket and handed it to her mom. She couldn't say the words but somehow, allowing her to read them would be all she needed. "Only made falling for him easier, I guess. He is a very caring and passionate man. Ugh. The way he looked at me. Me."

Her mother's eyebrows rose as she read through the list. With unhurried movements, she folded the paper neat again. "Isabelle." She laughed. "I am a little lost for words, so bear with me."

She passed the list back and tapped her fingernails on the empty mug in her lap. "You never could see the beautiful woman you are. The things on your list would require trust. If you trust him that much, it's only natural to fall in love. I only have one question."

Isabelle closed her eyes, not sure if she could face this one question.

"How was it?"

They laughed at the same time and she fanned her face. Warmth flushed over her entire body.

"Mom?"

"Yes, darling?"

Her mother still giggled and she didn't want to stop the beautiful sound she missed so much, but Carol deserved to know.

"Two weeks from today," she whispered, and goose bumps rose on her mother's skin.

"Okay," she whispered back.

"Mom?"

"Yes?"

Her voice sounded strained, words difficult to form. "Can I come home?" A tear dropped from the corner of her eye and landed on her hand. She missed her mom, more than she'd let herself believe. Two weeks wasn't enough.

"Go back to your place and pack, honey. I'll get your room ready."

****

He paced. The crowd hollered, demanded their encore. His cell phone never left his side in case she called. She didn't.

Zander'd worked his magic. He now had Katherine's cell number programmed into his phone but he couldn't do more than scroll through the contacts and stare at it.

"Get your head on straight, buddy."

Brett hit him on the shoulder, but the moody Cole they, even he expected, didn't make a grand reappearance. Instead, he often found himself quiet, being snapped back into conversations. The nightly drinking binges that used to make for an entertaining evening now only resulted in an early escape to bed with tears in his eyes. He could still smell her on the pillow and often buried his face in her scent to mask his sniffles. Drew tried all of the distractions he could think of that once mended bad days, everything he'd known him to enjoy, it didn't work.

They were lost, too. Her presence changed them all. Whenever someone passed through the aisle on the bus, they tapped *her* bunk, the one no used now. He didn't know whether it was out of hope she'd return, or the same loss that consumed him.

"Get your asses out there, now."

The three men wandered about backstage, and ignored the shriek in their earbuds as much as he did. It wasn't just he who was out of sorts. He checked his watch again, but she was a few hours behind him. The same voice yelled in his ear again, louder. He touched his phone through the front of his pants, and then ran out on stage.

****

Two weeks would fly by, but the arrangements she rushed through today took forever. A quick glance in the rear view mirror offered no more safety than if she were blind. The mountain of things she packed obstructed her view. She didn't need that much, but she did it anyway.

Tears hit her hard as she wandered through the house to collect personal possessions she held dear to her heart, said good-bye to others. Pictures of her and David still covered the walls and while she held one in front of her, an unobtainable moment flashed before her. A day she'd pack them away, to put up new ones.

Cole.

He'd managed to finagle his way into every scene of her life these days, not allowing her mind to be quiet.

What is he doing? Where is he? Is he okay?

Even if they had the opportunity to be together, she'd still wonder the same things, with him out on the road. She scanned the busy road ahead and brushed the spot above her breast with her fingertip, the mark that now faded. His mark.

She stopped at the bank, lawyer, and funeral home, the last being the toughest. She didn't want to leave any loose ends for her mom to deal with, and it really hadn't been *that* long since she'd been there. They still greeted her with familiarity, which gave her a chill she couldn't shake. It was surreal, to plan for death at her age.

The motions of the day were that of a sad movie, in slow motion and not able to speed up. Not far from her mother's home, she steered the car onto the side of the road and parked. Her head hurt. Her stomach churned from all of the sympathetic nods she encountered today.

She rushed to the passenger side of the car, shielded herself from anyone else`s sympathy, and vomited. When the heaves subsided, she snagged a piece of gum from her pocket, got in the car, and drove off, all too accustomed to ill-effects.

She bustled through the door with a couple bags; the rest could wait. “Mom, I’m home.” Silence “What is it with the damn silence.”

She dropped her bags in the doorway to the living room, organized with its usual furnishings only hours ago, but now cleared out. Air mattresses, blankets, and pillows scattered the floor.

She pivoted, glared at everything else kept in its usual place. Yep, she was in the right house. “Mom?”

“Out back, honey.”

Her errands had taken a lot longer than expected and night already darkened the sky. She tiptoed through the French doors and stood on the porch. A small fire blazed in the middle of the yard, with four female silhouettes huddled close to it. Her mother, Taryn, Katherine, and Abigail came into view as she neared, with roasted marshmallows, and wine in their hands. The image couldn’t be more perfect.

She smiled when the smell of the burned wood drifted her way. “What’s going on?”

Katherine handed her a glass of wine. “Slumber party. Carol’s brilliant idea.”

She smiled with appreciation at her mom and mouthed the words “thank you.” She did that a lot these days with the people she loved.

Carol nodded and dropped her attention to the orange flames.

She fixed her gaze on her wine glass, now aware that her mother may have missed out on things while she made life perfect for her. No challenge dismayed her mom, troubles just disappeared.

The fire cast the only glow of light around them.

She studied the area around her that offered so many memories, not able to stop the tears as her gaze landed on the people who meant the most to her. With her free hand, she placed it to her heart. It still ached with need, for him.

"Hey, did you show Carol your tattoo?" Taryn smiled.

She brushed her tears away and glanced over at Taryn with wide eyes. "Not yet, thank you. Maybe we should take this party inside, where we can all show her." She tipped her head to the side. That reveal included them as well. Thanks to him.

They changed into their pajamas with tank tops that displayed their tattoos. Carol got out the camera and took pictures, all night. Even the girls snapped some with their phones. She smiled for all of them, but a knot in her throat made it difficult to talk at times. She could guess why this night took place; they'd remember it.

The girls, Carol included, laid on the air mattresses and photo albums littered the room. She slammed a few books closed and hid them under her pillow. The ones from college she'd forgotten existed and her mother had never seen before.

Carol gave her the look. She huffed and handed them over. She stared at her mother's grin while she explored the past, nothing she did was wrong in her mother's eyes tonight.

She held up her hand and shook her head to stop Abigail when she passed her the album of her and David. Katherine shuffled over to sit beside her, made everyone laugh each time she faltered as her feet sunk into the mattress. Her focus was on the wine and book in her hands, which she saved from unwanted release with each unsteady step. She didn't recognize the book. She folded her hands, and stared down at the lime-green album Katherine propped in her lap.

Katherine nudged her in the shoulder. "Please open it, sweetie. I made it for you."

She sighed, set her wine down, and picked up the book. With her hand on the cover, she shook her head at the many anticipatory smiles, even her mom's. Hesitation controlled her pace as she drew the cover open. Her gaze fell to the picture before her, the Scandals, her included. The pages were full of the pictures she texted while on tour with the band, their girls night out, and even the ones from the trash rags, as he put it.

The last picture in the album filled the page, the day he kissed her at the airport for everyone to see. Goose bumps formed on her skin when she touched the picture and closed her eyes, felt again his lips on hers.

****

Katherine took a long swallow from her wine while her best friend remembered, was reminded about a love unlike any other. When Isabelle closed her eyes, she could only imagine what Carol battled, to witness her only child suffer so much loss. Her glance up to the ceiling to hold back tears and a hasty retreat to the bathroom to hide, confirmed just how hard it was. Carol never hid.

Katherine's gaze snapped from the hallway to the familiar ring that sounded from her purse over in the corner. She stumbled to race for her phone, didn't want Isabelle to be distracted from the memories she needed to process. Not find any reasons for regrets.

She could recall many of her own with little effort. She stared at the display screen with her eyebrows scrunched together, glanced up to the clock and then down to her phone again. It was late and she didn't recognize the number. With her thumb over the button, she peeked at the girls, now with their attention on her. Typically, she'd ignore it, but the urge to know who needed her would keep her awake tonight.

She waved everyone off when they caught sight of her hesitation. "Hello?"

"Katherine?"

"Yep, who's this?" She shrugged at the room of curious women.

"It's Cole Davies." His voice had a sadness in it similar to Isabelle's.

She held the phone away from her ear, covered it with her hand, and pointed to the door. "Work. I'm going to take this outside."

They chattered once again, pointed with fondness at the pictures, and sipped their wine. She closed the door and glanced through the window to make sure no one followed. "Hi Cole."

"How is she?"

She took a breath and leaned against the rail. Her best friend's trust was not something she'd ever betray, but she wouldn't let someone important slip away either. "Hang on a second. I'm going to send you a picture. Call me back when you get it? You can see for yourself."

She hung up and searched through the pictures she took out at the fire. Izzy didn't think anyone caught her, but she did. The flame lit her face perfectly, showed the tears she hid with the quick tilt of her head. She captured it though, Isabelle in a weak moment. Her innocence created such beauty, but she couldn't fathom it when others spoke of it. Revenge nagged at her to cause him pain, similar to what haunted her best friends' eyes. She sent the picture and waited.

Her phone rang again. "Well?"

"She's beautiful. Why is she crying? I can't stand to be so far away from her, not hold her."

"She has decided to move back home with her mother. We are all here for a slumber party, of all things." She laughed. "She's torn. Her surgery is scheduled for two weeks from today and part of her still has a broken heart."

She wasn't going to take it easy on him; he didn't deserve that.

He sighed. "She doesn't know the story behind my relationship with Alexis. How she found out—" silence "I should have been the one to tell her."

She gripped the post beside her. If someone called her an ass right now, they'd be right. "I'm the one who told her. I don't think you'd be surprised that a reporter for a tabloid would've heard gossip over the years." She sat down on the step, the weight of that drunken night with her once again.

"I understand you protected a friend whom you care about. What you and all other reporters don't know is the truth. I haven't rebutted the stories on purpose to shield Alexis from the pain I know too well, because of the tabloids. I don't want to be disrespectful to you. I have read your work and you are good at your job. But, it's your job that has given many males in my lifestyle challenges when it comes to trust, all because of the *wrong* camera angle."

Very true, how could she fault him for that? She placed her hand to her stomach. "I'm sorry. You are very right. I fight my boss daily about those stories, even refuse to write them. It's a business I am not always proud of."

"You have nothing to apologize for. If I tell you something, will it be in tomorrow's cover story?"

Gah. She sprung off the steps and paced the yard. The tone of his voice broke her heart. She had a gut instinct he'd done nothing wrong, and the way she'd led Izzy on hurt them both. "I have given you no reason to trust me, but you can. I would never do anything to intentionally hurt Izzy."

He was quiet.

"Alexis and I dated in university. It was a relationship full of wild rides and turmoil. She was the type of young, untamed, and immature woman men fantasized about. I'd reached my limit the second time she attempted to kill herself, or so I'd concluded, but I guess not. When I found her giving my roommate a very enthusiastic blowjob it damn near killed me. I didn't know what to expect from day to day, high or low? When me and the guys hit it big, it was a blessing, I got to leave. Our first show back in New York, she was there to explain. Bipolar disorder. She still struggles but is in therapy. We are friends, nothing more."

Well isn't that just peachy. For years, he wears a bad reputation, all to protect a woman. He is *perfect.*

"I had no idea. I'm sorry I misrepresented you. You kept that secret very well. She needs to know."

"I know. We have nonstop shows for about a week and a half. I plan to come to her after, to make it right. I just hope she will forgive me."

She chewed on her nail, a habit broken a long time ago. "She's booked her surgery, two weeks from today."

A thud, as if he'd hit a wall, echoed through the phone. "I'll make it. I have to. Thank you. If anything changes, please call me, day or night. I don't sleep much anyway." His voice faded, as if he'd lost the strength to talk.

She faced the house and spied on the girls. They talked, laughed even, but her heart hurt for him. "Okay. I have to get back inside. Take care. Same goes for you, day or night."

She hung up and stood, admiring the stars that shone bright on such a gloomy night. Anger unlike any other bubbled inside her, that this perfect man hadn't come to her best friend sooner.

She took a deep breath and rejoined the group of women as if nothing happened. But it had. Her best friend might die, and no amount of handholding would have the same effect as a man who loved her.

"That took forever. What juicy story was that about?" Taryn grinned and rubbed her hands together.

She scolded her with a glare and trampled over the bedding to the wine bottle with her empty glass. "As I have said a million times, Taryn, wait and see."

****

She peered at Katherine, who filled her glass, and then downed it. Something bothered her. What were best friends for? They notice things, like the nail biting and pacing out the window.

Everyone settled into bed and said their good nights, but as the fast approach of another headache would determine for her, it wouldn't be a good night at all. When peaceful, even breaths sounded, she crept over to the armchair in the corner of the living room and curled up under a blanket. The window view showed the calm glow of embers still ablaze in the backyard.

She startled to a bang from the kitchen, still in the chair. It wasn't much sleep, but she'd take it. The smell of bacon was always the best part of waking up in her mother's home. Carol believed a successful day started with a full stomach. The girls smelled it too, hummed delightful noises of hunger, much different from the hungover moans on the bus.

She sunk in her chair, lifted the blanket up to her chin, and waited for her best friends to come to life. She didn't sleep well herself, but the fact they had comforted her.

"Time to get up, ladies. Even though it's the weekend, I know some of you have to work today. Breakfast first. Buffet style at the dining room table. Help yourselves."

The delicious aromas were a clear indication her mother outdid herself. They made their way, slowly, to a feast worthy of men. A pain, much like the stab of a knife, struck her head. The pressure she applied to it with her hand dulled it, a little. The chairs that scraped on the floor didn't help but the sight of all the delicious food distracted her. It reminded her of the breakfast that had created such pride in his eyes. Guess there was more of her mother in her than she figured. She grinned. That must be what drummed up the pain.

She sat back in her chair and held her stomach, didn't want to break it to her mother that her appetite wasn't as agreeable as it used to be. Her body gave her the, "are you kidding me warning signs," but she ignored it and stretched for the dish of bacon.

Many groans from the overindulged women filled the room while they sat back and enjoyed the coffee that would start their day off right. Carol relaxed in her chair at the end of the table, sipped her coffee, and stared at the women around her. It was as if she needed to brand it on her memory. She did love all the girls in her home, said often that she viewed them as daughters.

She shook her head. A strange weak sensation traveled through her body, one she wasn't familiar with. Her stomach churned. That she did recognize well. With her plate in her hand, she stood, but the room hazed in her sight.

"Thank you so much, Mom. Have I told you lately I love you?" She shoved the chair with the backs of her knees and strode out of the room, fast.

When she entered the kitchen, she opened her jaw wide, to pop her ears. She wasn't too far from everyone, but they sounded so distant. She stood beside the kitchen island, rested her hip to the counter, but was no longer able to shift her feet.

"What the…"

****

A loud crash of dishes came from the kitchen. Carol, Katherine, Abigail, and Taryn flung their chairs back. Some fell over as they shoved to the kitchen, to the noise.

"Call 911!" Carol yelled as she rounded into the kitchen first.

Taryn ran for the phone but Katherine and Abigail stood there as Carol knelt on the floor, with Isabelle's head in her hands. Her body convulsed. Seized.

Carol jerked her head up, only long enough to make brief eye contact. "Abigail, go unlock the front door so the paramedics can get in. Katherine, go find a pillow for her head. We c-can't do anything other than insure she doesn't h-hurt herself."

She shouted out orders, ignored the warm tears that streamed down her face. She had to keep them busy; they shouldn't see her this way, and she needed time to gather herself. Her throat tightened with each swallow as her daughter's pale body bounced in her hand.

Please God. Not yet.

She could fall apart with ease, scream. If it were just her and Isabelle, she would, but she needed to be strong.

Taryn ran in with the phone and knelt down beside her with the dispatch through the speaker. "911, what's your emergency?"

Taryn`s hand shook. "Taryn, please hold her head for me, j-just like this." With slow motions, she showed Taryn what to do. "D-don't let her head hit anything. Can you do that for me?"

"Okay." Taryn wiped the tears from her face, handed over the phone and got into position.

Carol shut off the speaker and held the phone to her ear. "My daughter is having a seizure. She has an atypical meningioma, a brain tumor. We need an ambulance."

She gave the address but never averted her eyes from Isabelle. The trembles that shook her daughter's body subsided, but she hadn't regained consciousness either.

She held the phone between her shoulder and ear,

and placed her into the recovery position as directed by dispatch, just in time for her to vomit.

She took the pillow from Katherine and set it under Isabelle's head. Abigail ran out into the hallway and returned with a towel. She didn't clean it away, just covered the vomit the best she could with nervous hands much like Taryn's. It was the least of their worries right now. She mouthed a thank you, to Abby.

She and Taryn stayed on the floor, stimulated Isabelle with touch, and checked her pulse while Abigail and Katherine paced. The paramedics couldn't get there fast enough. They all cried.

"Where is the damn ambulance?" Katherine yelled through her tears.

No one responded; there was no point. They were all with her on that one. Just then, the sirens approached, fast.

It wasn't easy to stand back, let them take her. The women stood there, helpless. She answered questions but other than that, there was nothing they could do. Abigail held her own stomach as Isabelle's lifeless body was wheeled away on the stretcher, secured in straps, and taken down the driveway, out to the ambulance. Taryn and Katherine squeezed each other's hand for support. Not even her children, but she paid attention, always.

"Girls?" She made eye contact with each of them. "I'm going in the ambulance with her. Get yourselves dressed and drive carefully to the hospital. Bring my purse, please. It's on the floor beside my bed. If there is anything you think she may need, gather that too. Like I said, drive safe." She climbed in the back of the ambulance, didn't wait for the girls to respond. The short distance to the hospital didn't offer much time to breakdown.

****

Just as the paramedic tapped twice on the back of the closed ambulance door, Abigail hurried for the bushes, and heaved. Taryn sprinted into the house, not in any better shape.

Katherine snagged her phone from her pocket. Why she kept it close by after her conversation with Cole last night was no longer a mystery; she would need it. She dialed his number and held the phone up to her ear. His life would never be the same.

"Katherine, what's wrong?"

His voice sounded rough, sleepy. "C-Cole, she collapsed. The a-ambulance just took her away. It doesn't look good."

"I'm leaving now. I'll be there as soon as I can. Which hospital?"

Now his voice grew strong, awake, and full of fear. After she gave him the information he needed, she hung up and closed her eyes to say a silent prayer.

Please Izzy, not yet.

Chapter Nineteen

Dear Diary,

He held the scribbled paper in one hand and his chest with the other. His feet crashed into every sharp corner while he stumbled out of his bunk to the back lounge; he couldn't breathe. The room spun, and faint voices trailed behind him.

"Breathe, Cole."

A firm hand on his back encouraged him to sit on the edge of the couch and lean forward, head between his knees. "If you don't get a breath in, you're gonna pass out, and I'll let you fall on your face. There is no way in hell I'll be able to hold your dead weight on my own."

Drew. It was Drew's voice. He fisted his hands over his face, and took a deep breath. His body vibrated from head to toe. Water hit his fingers, the spasms throughout him a result of his sobs. "I have to get to her."

Drew dislodged the paper from his fisted hand, but didn't leave. "Brett, Zander. Get your asses in here."

Thumps from their feet as they dropped to the floor drew him out of his breakdown. He still couldn't bring himself to glance up at their concerned faces.

"We need to get there, now."

Paper crumpled in the distance. He took another breath in through his nose and out through his mouth. His senses returned to normal, but pain still radiated through his chest.

"Tell Tony to cancel whatever shit he has planned for us indefinitely, until he hears otherwise. Get us on the first flight to Tampa, that hospital."

He sat back in the seat and used the hem of his booze-stained shirt to wipe his face. Through blurred eyes, he scanned the lounge. He sat in her seat, empty since the day she left. When he tore his attention from anguish strong enough to consume him at any moment, he raised his chin up to Drew, who stood helpless, with a tear tracking down his face.

He spun around, wiped it away with the back of his hand, and kept his back turned. "Is she okay?" he whispered.

"No. She just collapsed and was rushed away by ambulance." He slammed his hand down on the pillow beside him and threw it. It knocked over empty beer cans on the table, shot glasses, and a pair of bright red panties floated to the floor. He shook his head. "I don't know if I'll make it there in time. The jet?"

Drew huffed and sat beside him. "First of all, you aren't going alone, we love her, too. The jet? Shit. It's still in for repairs, man."

He stood up, weaved his fingers through his hair, and squeezed his hands, along with his hair, into fists. The sting didn't replace the absolute worst pain in his heart. He stormed out of the room, stopped in the aisle, and braced himself on the nearest bunk. Brett and Zander were already packing. He took in Drew's sympathetic smile over his shoulder.

"I told ya dipshit, get packed."

****

"Shit. Did you not hear Carol when she said drive carefully?" Taryn yelled, and latched onto the armrest beside her when the car they'd just cut off blared its horn.

"Yeah well, too bad." Katherine gripped the wheel tighter. Taryn had a point, but if the idiot she pissed off had ever experienced this helplessness, he'd understand. She glanced up in the rear view mirror at Abigail, now with her attention out the window. Tears streamed down from under her sunglasses.

The three women sighed when a close parking spot was vacated as they drove into the lot. She didn't care. It would have been worth the tow to park right in front of the emergency room doors. They ran for the door. Only minutes had passed, but it seemed like hours.

The doors swooshed open and cold air hit her in the face. Each woman halted in shock. Busy hustle swirled around them. Loud beeps and cries of pain came from all directions. Katherine scrambled for Taryn's hand and didn't need to actually see it, to confirm that Taryn had done the same with Abigail. They stood, frozen, searching the room using only movement from their eyes. Sweat formed between her and Taryn's palms.

"Over here, girls." Carol waved them over to the counter and then resumed the paperwork in her hand.

"Where is she?" Katherine asked, out of breath.

"They took her up for a CT scan. She still hasn't regained consciousness. They need to know what they're dealing with." She handed the nurse back the forms and pointed toward the elevator. The girls followed.

The elevator doors closed. Abigail stared at the buttons, motionless. “Two.” Carol placed her hand on Abigail’s shoulder and offered all of the girls a motherly glance that didn’t reveal much.

Katherine took a breath, couldn’t read Carol’s expression, but it wasn’t one she’d seen before.

“They’ll take her into emergency surgery once they have a better understanding of her condition. They don’t get the sense her scan will show good news, that’s for certain. There’s a lounge where we can wait. The doctor will update us as much as he can.” She faced the corner and raised her hands up to cover her face, her body shook.

Katherine and the girls surrounded her, held her up.

Dr. Peterson was pacing the hallway when the elevator dinged and the door opened. He held his hand out in the direction of the waiting room. His dress shoes tapped the floor behind them, a sound she would never forget.

“Ladies, please.” He held the door open.

Once inside, he closed the door. Carol took a deep, anticipatory breath, and waited for the doctor with unshed tears in her eyes, a state she’d never seen Carol in before. Ever.

“Carol.” He hugged her and then stood back. “The scan shows the tumor is placing pressure on her brain, more than it can handle. It hasn’t grown too much in size, which is good. Dr. Harris will perform the surgery, he’s the best.” The breath he took next was a clear indication it wasn’t good. “I must be honest. I am sure she filled you in with the odds?”

The women all nodded at once and fastened their

hands together.

"That hasn't changed."

Katherine tilted her head and glared at the doctor. "Dr. Peterson, I get the impression you're attempting to lighten the blow. Stop it and just tell us, please."

The doctor shoved his hands in his pockets. "Okay. The surgery is typically done with the patient awake. This allows the surgical team time to do tests throughout, for any signs of impairment. She hasn't regained consciousness. We are forced to go in blind."

She ignored the doctor, and let her gaze follow Carol as she plodded with cautious steps to the row of uncomfortable blue chairs and sat. Her skin drained of color, as pale as Isabelle's had been on many occasions.

"Yes, get comfortable." He raised his eyebrows to the rest of them as if to say you, too. "Dr. Harris has estimated a ten-hour surgery. I've cancelled my office appointments today and will observe. I'll come out and update you as much as possible, but like I said, with Isabelle not able to show signs of deterioration, we won't know much until after the surgery if—"

When the doctor swallowed rather forcefully, Katherine sat beside Carol.

"She regains consciousness. I'm sorry Carol, girls. I'll be back when I know more."

Everyone sat in the chairs and stared at the closed door. She scrambled through her purse when her phone rang. It'd be him. "Hi Cole."

Everyone glared at her, but smiled when she shrugged without regret. He needed to be there.

"We're at the airport. I won't be able to get there for at least three hours. Damn it."

In the background, the guys ordered him to calm

down. “That’s okay. She’s going into surgery now and the doctor estimates at least ten hours. You aren’t going to miss anything other than us wearing out the floor.”

His breath hiccupped. “Katherine?”

She closed her eyes, expected the next question. “Yes.” Abigail sat down in the empty chair beside her and laced their fingers. Tears warmed her face.

“Is she going to make it?”

Taryn squatted in front of her, with the same tear-smeared face. “It doesn’t look good, but there’s no way to tell. I’ll explain more when you get here. Be safe.” She hung up. The torture in his voice only fueled her tears.

“It was him who called last night, wasn’t it?” Abigail asked with a low voice.

She couldn’t form words, just squeezed Abby’s hand and closed her eyes, tight. This horrible nightmare needed to end.

****

“Come on.” He flipped up the empty tray in front of him; a tiny piece of hard plastic broke free and flew into the aisle.

His patience had worn thin on the tarmac, cooped up tight and at the mercy of another plane that disembarked before theirs. His jaw clenched, he surveyed the guys, also on the edge of their seats.

“This is bullshit.” Zander’s anger wasn’t any better.

Drew scrubbed his face and huffed. “A public spectacle isn’t going to make our exit out of here any faster, assholes.”

His self-control had drained throughout the long flight and the many fake smiles for fans who requested pictures. Everyday life now cornered him in his own sense of hell. The plane finally steered into place, but he wasn't interested in the attendants' instructions for everyone to wait their turn. He led as they shoved their way to the exit door, toward the angered flight attendant. Brett marched beside him and flipped her off when she mumbled behind them. Tony would probably hear about it, but he didn't care.

Their smiles got them through security fast. No effort at disguise produced a crowd in record time and the employees worked double time. Each of the guys passed through, put on their sunglasses and hats, kept their heads down, and proceeded as Derek had trained them to for years—prudently. Drew took the time to explain they needed a quick exit and why.

He stood with his hands in his pockets. A security guard rushed in their direction to usher them to a door away from the crowd. Someone explained to the mob of disappointed fans that they were sorry, but due to an emergency, they were unable to hang around.

He knotted his hands in his lap and his knee bounced on the short cab ride from the airport. The guys were in rough shape, too, unable to remain still or speak.

The car slowed in front of the emergency room door and Drew threw a wad of money at the driver. "Keep it."

They rushed out of the car but needed to slow down. The least helpful thing would be to get kicked out of the hospital. He texted Katherine just as they entered the lobby. He startled and swore under his breath when someone screamed.

Hey, we're here. Where are you?

Send.

Oh good. Second floor, turn right off elevators. OR Waiting Room #1.

He kept his voice calm as he spoke to Brett and Zander. "Second floor, Waiting room one. I'm sure the girls could use some coffee and snacks by now. Can you take care of that?"

The guys spun around until a sign for Starbucks caught their attention.

Brett hit Zander in the shoulder. "Score. No cafeteria sludge for us."

Drew yanked on his arm. When the elevator doors closed, he jabbed two and then punched the wall. "Fuck."

Drew slapped him on the shoulder. "There's a roomful of women who don't need to see that shit, man. Get it together. She'll be okay." His gaze fell to his feet. "She has to be."

The hallway was quiet when they stepped out of the elevator, their destination only a short distance away. He and Drew stood outside the door, stared at it as if they would receive an electrical shock on impact. He took a deep breath. "Please God, give her back to me."

He opened the door and placed his hand over his stomach, where his heart landed. Four women sat there, silent, blank stares on their faces.

A young, attractive woman with brown, curly hair jumped from her chair and ran to him, hugged him. "Thank God you're here."

He smiled and hugged her back. A chuckle escaped him. "Bartender, reporter, or workaholic?"

The beautiful redhead stood up and glared. "I'm

not a workaholic."

Laughter filled the room. Each beautiful woman's shoulders relaxed and smiles formed. If there were nothing else he and the guys could offer, it would be that.

"Yes, you are." Another attractive woman stood and hugged the cynical redhead before making her way over to him and held out her hand.

He pried his arm out of the brunette's embrace and shook it.

"Nice to finally meet you, Cole, I'm Katherine." She pointed to the woman who still clung to him and laughed again. "That would be the bartender and fan, Taryn." She pointed at the redhead. "Abigail, the workaholic. It seems Izzy has given you a rather accurate description of the people who love her."

"Cole?" An older woman with many similarities to Isabelle shuffled up to him with puffy, red eyes. The same likeliness he imagined she had the day she left him. "I'm Carol, Isabelle's mother." She held out her hand, but he separated himself from Taryn and wrapped his arms around her.

****

The tattoos and rough appearance screamed rocker, but he was gentle. She now understood what Isabelle explained to her yesterday. She relaxed and hugged him back; the smell of his cologne reminded her how long it'd been since she'd been held by a man.

He leaned into her ear. "Thank you for giving me the most extraordinary woman. I love her more than anything in the world, even vanilla cookies." He chuckled. "I'll let her explain."

She took a step back and the passion in his eyes for

her daughter took her breath away. "Let's hope," she whispered back.

He pointed over his shoulder to the tall, thin, but well-built man behind him. "This is Drew. Any news, yet?"

She held onto his warm, large hand and shook her head.

The door opened and two more attractive, tattooed men rolled in a cart littered with coffee and snacks galore. "We didn't know what everyone liked, so we bought at least one, um maybe more, of everything they had."

The younger one maneuvered the cart in and raised his hand to the door to close it but it resisted. The doctor jostled his way into the room. She smiled, and covered her mouth when the doctor's eyes widened as he scanned the room. It didn't faze the men whatsoever.

Katherine stepped forward. "Dr. Peterson. This is Cole Davies, Drew Michaels, Zander Mills, and Brett Young." She pointed to each of them as she spoke their names. "Also known as the rock group Scandals, and close friends of Izzy's."

They stared at her with the same wide eyes as the doctor. She shrugged and smiled at Katherine, in awe of her protective nature. She would never have let Izzy leave with strangers. She probably had more information about them than they would want her to have.

"Well then." She appreciated the doctor's dumbfounded stare.

"Ahem."

She liked Cole already.

The doctor slid the pale-blue cap from his head and

held it in a tight fist at his side. "She's still in surgery, of course. There isn't much to say. Dr. Harris is doing the best he can, given the circumstances. There's been a little more blood than he'd hoped, but he will manage it.

"After the surgery, they'll give her medicine that will place her in a coma. There will be swelling to monitor, which is normal to a certain extent, and then the rest will be up to her."

He stared down at his feet on his way to the door, offered everyone a solemn smile over his shoulder with his hand floundering in search of the knob. "I will let you know if there is any further information."

Silence filled the air, the only sound the door as it closed. There were no words, nothing to make it better.

"I need some air." What Carol really meant was I need to break down.

Cole put his arm around her shoulders. "I'll come with you."

His attention to her every movement told her he didn't want to leave her side, as if his connection to her daughter would help the two of them through this. A nice idea to hold onto. He was the man who'd completed her daughter; how could she ever repay him for that?

They made their way in silence outside to the gazebo and sat on the bench. She covered her face and her body shook while sobs, sure to leave her a mess, consumed her.

He tucked her into his side, even kissed the top of her head. "She'll be okay. She has to be."

She wiped her face with the back of her hand and admired his handsome, caring eyes. Her daughter always did have a good head on her shoulders and wisdom in the choices she made.

"Oh, I have something for you."

From the shock on his face when she dug out the book, he'd seen it before. The journal.

She handed it to him. "I'm somewhat sure she would be okay with you reading this. I have no clue what's in it. But if I were to guess by the memories written all over your face, you have a pretty good idea." She smiled at him and sat with her hands folded in her lap.

He took the journal, stared at it. A single tear fell from underneath his sunglasses. She placed a hand on his arm and squeezed. Before she was tempted to join him in his torment, break down too, she sat back and delighted in the world around them. The ambiance of Tampa could revive anyone.

Sunday, a day of rest, would never be the same for her again.

"If we're lucky, she will wake up and hate me for letting you read it. I can live with that."

She didn't want to peer over his shoulder, quicken his pace as he battled with his emotions. Just as the rest of them, though, the urge to help happened to be too difficult to ignore. She placed a supportive hand on his leg.

He sat there for a long moment, just gawking at it. He sighed and opened the cover, would now find out what he meant to her daughter. The desperation on his face when he entered the waiting room told her he needed to know.

He took his time. She could imagine that in his head *her* voice spoke the words as he read. When he finished, he closed the book and held it to his chest. The sun streaked his face through the gazebo slats above as he tipped his chin up. His eyes closed tight behind his glasses.

"Well?"

He wiped his face and sat up straight, but his knee bounced. "I can't thank you enough. I am only sorry her time with me took her away from you." He nudged her shoulder. "She talked very highly of you, a lot."

She smiled, hadn't expected that. "I'm not sorry. There were moments yesterday when I was sure she thought about you. The longing in her eyes…" She rubbed her arms and he laughed, hard. She shook her head. "She does it too, hey?"

"She was happy with David."

"Yes, I know. I'm glad."

"But with you, she's become the woman she has held back from being, and for that, I give you my love and acceptance. I only wish—"

"Don't" He put his hand on her knee. "*When* she makes it through this, I want her as my wife. I know it is extremely fast and maybe to others, a bit premature, but I want her to be the one I come home to from a long stint on the road. I want to call her, probably drunk, after a show and tell her she is the only one who matters to me. I want to see her sneak into my private stash of cookies and hear her hum around her mouthful as she rubs her belly, pregnant. Sorry. Too much information?"

She hiccupped, wiped away more tears, and shook her head. "No, that's very sweet. She said you were a passionate man." She giggled. "I want that for her, too. Let's go see if there is any news."

Cole laced his hand with Carol's and led her into the hospital with a little more hope in his stride.

She checked the clock by the door to the waiting room. Only six hours, but more like six days.

When they entered the room, the sight before her hit her as strange, yet it comforted her. Each one of the tattooed and pierced men held a woman in their arms. Everyone lay back in their chairs, eyes closed. "Seems it's been a long day for everyone," she whispered.

He smiled. "It has."

****

The doctor offered support once more, but didn't have anything further to add than before. At eleven hours, a man in scrubs entered the room. "Carol?" Everyone sat up, alert to the unfamiliar voice.

She stood with Cole at her side. Then they all stood. "Yes. Dr. Harris, I presume?"

He nodded, made his way over to a chair, and sat. His head fell back to the wall for a moment of silence as he scrubbed his face to regain composure. "It was touch and go for a while. Her vital signs declined once, but she came back to us. There was a lot of bleeding, which made it difficult to keep the area visible to retract the tumor. We managed to get it all."

Everyone cheered and she placed her hand over her heart.

He held up his hand and stopped them. "That was the easy part. Now the hard part is up to her. She's in recovery right now but will be taken to the ICU, where she will stay for the duration of her coma. I have no idea yet how long she will need to remain that way.

"Swelling of the brain can be life threatening. We will monitor her closely, but it is up to her to fight now.

When she is in the clear, we will reverse the meds and hope, I stress hope, for her to wake up. The next forty-eight hours will be critical. "Hospital policy states only family can visit in ICU." He offered everyone in the room a hesitant smile. "I'm sorry."

Cole stepped forward. She joined him, linked her arm with his, and squeezed. "Dr. Harris, I'd like to introduce you to Cole Davies." She raised her chin at Cole and smiled. "Isabelle's fiancé. Surely there won't be a problem with him seeing her, right?"

The doctor shook his head. "No, that's fine. Everyone should go home and get some rest. There is nothing more to do but wait, and that's easier to do when you aren't exhausted." The doctor squinted from her to Cole. "You may have a few minutes with her when they get her settled into the ICU." He shook their hands and surveyed everyone in the room with curiosity in his eyes. A low chuckle escaped him, but he shrugged and left the room.

"Fiancé?" six voices said in unison the second the door closed.

She and Cole laughed together, but refused to explain.

****

He stood behind Carol to tie her mask. She smoothed down her paper gown and then checked his. Laughed. Ridiculous would be an accurate description of him, covered from head to toe in the pale blue get up, but it had to be done. He glared at her as he would Derek.

The nurse buzzed the door open when they rang the call button. He squeezed her hand between his underarm and ribs when she slid her arm through for support. They followed the nurse.

"It isn't as quiet in here as you'd expect." The nurse laughed. "There will be lots of beeps and noisy machines. They monitor her vitals. She's comfortable. Feel free to talk to her and hold her hand. She won't be able to wake, but I do believe the voices of loved ones can work miracles." She took a quick glance at the machine and jotted down some notes on her chart before she left.

Carol squeezed his arm tight. He couldn't imagine what it must be like to see your only child hooked up to machines with a bandage secured around their head. It was nice to know the medications kept her from pain, but it didn't make the sight before them any easier.

"I'll give you a moment alone." She held up her hand, panic filled her eyes. But he shook his head, could feel the color drain from his face. "I need a moment."

He noted her cautious movements while she dragged a chair up to the bed as close as the machines would allow. She sat, focused on Isabelle's frail hand. Tape covered the IV tube. Goose bumps rose on Carol's arms. He stepped back with his arms around his midsection, but he didn't go far. The bed on the other side of her curtain was vacant, so he hid there.

"Hey baby, you did well. The doctor got the whole tumor, now it's up to you. Cole is here. Actually, there is a roomful of tattooed and pierced men waiting to see your pretty eyes. They're *slightly* intimidating. I see the appeal, baby, he's pretty cute. He's lost without you, so am I. You have time to heal, so do it, momma's orders. Then, come back to us."

He relaxed his shoulders when she spoke so gently,

but held back a laugh when she, too, said that word "cute." He was going to have to work on his image with these ladies. He tapped his toe on the floor and his hand shook in the air, not quite on the curtain.

After a deep breath, he eased it back and inched up beside Carol. He placed his nervous hand on her shoulder. "She's beautiful."

She stood, scooted aside, and pointed for him to have a seat. "I'm just going to go ask the nurses some questions."

He waited for her to go before he adjusted in his seat toward Isabelle. Guilt shook him, bad. No one else could see her, be reassured, and they'd known her much longer. He made sure the nurses were all busy and took out his phone. As discreetly as possible, he snapped a few pictures of her. It was difficult to capture her in a way that showed few tubes; there were a lot.

The nurse said they were routine, but his uneasy stomach refused to be swayed. He tucked the phone back in his pocket. With his hand palm up on the bed, and ever so gently, he slid his hand under hers and laced their fingers. He didn't want to disturb the IV taped to the top of her hand—her still warm hand.

"Hey beautiful, you scared me. The guys are all here. It seems you haven't just affected me. We were lost without you. Your mom, the girls, they're all fantastic. I'm not going anywhere. I will get the chance to explain, to make it right. I love you. Did you hear me? Only you. I'll be here until I see your eyes again, your smile. The stage isn't going anywhere, it can wait."

"Cole?"

Carol stepped alongside the bed and straightened

the blanket with a hesitant tug. His chest weighted with an unfamiliar envy he couldn't describe.

"We should get going, she needs to rest. We can come back first thing tomorrow."

He leaned up on his toes from the chair and whispered in her ear. "I'm going to marry you." He stood up and squashed his toes into the floor so he wouldn't climb into bed with her. She wasn't cleared for that yet.

****

Going back into the waiting room wasn't as dreadful now. Although, what about everyone else? They didn't get the same reassurance, or see her heart still beat.

"How is she?" many voices asked.

He smiled. "She's beautiful, see." He held up his phone for everyone to see.

Carol stood back and shook her head, but smiled. They gathered around the phone and stared, speechless. She'd just been through major surgery and her pale, lifeless body showed that. But she was still there, alive.

"The girls crashed at my house last night for a slumber party. If you guys stop at the hardware store and pick up some more air mattresses, you are more than welcome to crash in my basement. It's not fancy, but it's close, and I hear the lady of the house is a pretty good cook."

He tucked his phone away and glanced at her. She avoided eye contact and shuffled through her purse while she spoke. She didn't want to be alone and the more people who surrounded her, the better. The guys all nodded, but as he waited for their reassurance, their gazes were caught on the attractive women who'd be under the same roof. He scooped up her hand, stole her attention away from her purse. “We’d love to.”

****

She was right; she lived close. The entire group stopped at the hardware store, like doing anything without each other an impossible task. They were able to cut off the owner in the parking lot on his way to his car and convince him to reopen for them.

He and the guys took the lead, with boxed air mattresses under one arm and their bags over the shoulder of the other. The girls brought up the rear, talking and laughing as they carried bags in, all set for s’mores over the bonfire.

He strolled through the front door, into the kitchen, and froze. He dropped the box and his bag. Broken dishes littered the floor and a towel covered an offensive smell.

This is where it happened.

He clutched his stomach and ran out the door toward the bushes. His name yelled in the distance was somewhat audible through his heaves, but he couldn’t make the reflex stop.

He wasn’t there for her when she needed him.

When the spasms subsided, he knelt down on the grass and slumped forward.

“Here, drink.” Katherine handed him a glass of water and a of couple pills. “These will help with the nausea, Izzy swears by them. Sorry about the mess. It’s all cleaned up now.”

He sat back on the ground, took the water and pills, and glanced back over his shoulder at the house. “I wasn’t here when she needed me.”

She placed her hand on his shoulder and squeezed.

"There was no way to predict what happened. We *were* here and didn't, so don't beat yourself up. No matter where you were, there still would have been nothing you could do." She sat down beside him and he, too, got comfortable next to her. She put her hand on his leg. "It was scary shit. No one deserves to see that. You dropped everything to come for her. Now that's something."

He met her gaze. "I love her."

The ache that weighed him down lightened when she swayed into him, as if it was no surprise. He'd hurt Isabelle. Which should impact Katherine's feelings about him, but even these beautiful friends of hers were perfect—like Isabelle.

"I know you do, and when she wakes up, she will tell you the same. We've all had enough heavy for today. Let's go to the backyard and relax by the fire. I don't know whether you have a sweet tooth, but I make a mean s'more." He placed his hand over hers; he was right where he was meant to be.

Chapter Twenty

Dear Diary,
You never know when you will find what you were never looking for in the first place.

He paraded down the hall, refreshed from a warm morning shower, and a coffee in his hand. People gawked at them, the effect of no disguises and bold tattoos. He glanced at Carol, who shook her head when the girls took advantage of it and snuggled up to their sides for dramatic affect. While they laughed and poked fun at one another, panicked voices sounded and doctors ran for the ICU.

"Isabelle." Cole threw his coffee at the nearest trashcan and took off. The many footsteps behind matched his pace. The doors swooshed open, a sound he would never forget, and a bed, her bed, was rolled out of the ICU in a hurry.

"What's wrong? Where are they taking my daughter?" Carol yelled her questions at the closest nurse.

"Her brain is swelling. They're taking her back into the OR to do a procedure that will help relieve the pressure. It's a simple operation, but they need to get it done now. The doctor will come see you when he can."

They stood, frozen in place while the rush of scrub-covered bodies bustled to the end of the hall; the noise faded with them. He took her into his arms. He didn't know what to say. What could he? The doctor was clear the next forty-eight hours were crucial. This must be what he meant.

They made their way back into the waiting room, same seats as yesterday. No one spoke. Their coffees sat on tables, untouched, cold. An hour later, the door opened and Dr. Harris took one step into the room. Everyone stood and stared at him.

"I see the whole gang is here again."

Yes, his emotions ran high, sensitive, and on another day he'd question the use of the word "gang", but today he just required answers. "Well?" He sneered.

"We managed to get the pressure relieved. We hope the swelling will go down in the next twenty-four hours. Any longer could result in permanent damage. She is still in the coma and will be brought back up to the ICU soon. I will have one of the nurses come and get you when she returns, so you can see her." He scanned the group. No one had questions, so he left.

"We'll go get more coffee." Brett looked at Zander and raised his chin toward the door.

He sat in a chair. He hadn't expect it to be this hard.

Drew sat beside him and put his hand on his back. "She's gonna make it, man. She has to."

"I don't know how to wait, Drew."

He was grateful the guys hadn't let him make the trip alone. He argued with them over it and having reflected on it now, if it were possible to kick his own ass, he would.

"Are you all sure you aren't going to lose jobs by being here? She would never want that," Carol surveyed the reactions of everyone in the room.

The girls laughed and bumped shoulders with each other. Taryn caved first. "Our bosses are all fans of theirs." She tipped her head toward the men. "We promised autographs and concert tickets in exchange for indefinite leaves of absence."

She shook her head and raised her eyebrows at the men, waited with the same expression they've often seen from Derek.

"We've cancelled shows and, without a doubt, pissed off fans. They will be rescheduled and any inconvenience will be compensated, don't worry. Our manager gets paid well enough to know better than to give us a hard time." He bumped fists with Drew. They loved to give Tony a hard time and were good at it.

The door opened. "The family may see her now, one at a time."

Everyone smiled at the nurse, haunted with reluctance to stay behind.

"Carol, please." He motioned for her to go first. He was anxious to get to her, but needed more time.

The way she smiled reminded him of the vibrant woman he loved. He couldn't wait to be a permanent part of their family, to have a wife and a mother. Her list revealed many firsts he never imagined for himself.

Time stood still for the next twenty minutes. The use of distractions stretched beyond their usual limit.

He glanced up at her when she returned. He and the large group of beautiful women and tattooed rockers littered the waiting room floor, cross-legged around a board game.

They took turns, all day. Everyone else played games. They were a competitive bunch. The hospital staff popped their heads in during a few heated moments to quiet them. Like children, they just nodded and smiled each time, and then laughed after the door closed.

When darkness shaded the only window in the room, the games were set aside and the group paced. No one spoke of the day's end. He kept them encouraged with the pictures he snuck, creative ones. He wrote bubble notes on paper and held them beside her head, as if she poked fun at the people she loved. Carol even managed quite a few giggles at his antics. The bubble quote that resulted in a laugh with a light slap was the one saying *Cole rocks my world on stage and in bed.* Katherine asked him to forward all the pictures from his phone to hers for the album she told him about and he couldn't wait to see.

****

The following week of days had the same routine. Drew brought in a couple of guitars, and the hours they didn't spend in comical dispute over games, they wrote. Tony was at least thankful they made their time away from the stage productive. The sheets of music they sent in were sure to make the next album number one on many charts.

Every day Dr. Harris and Dr. Peterson visited, with updates. Day seven, the day to reverse the coma, came with a lot of anxiety. Again, coffee sat on tables untouched and the games were piled at the side of the room.

"Don't expect miracles, folks. She still may be out of it for a few days, at least." He looked from Carol to Cole and cocked his head with a smile. "Do you have a recorder on the phone you've used to, ahem, take pictures?" He tilted his head as an annoyed father would. Only, the doctor couldn`t remain firm. "Record everyone's voice. It's now that we need to offer her everything we've got to urge her back to us. The familiar voices will help."

Heat rose to Cole's skin, as if he'd just gotten caught with his hand in the cookie jar. Which he had as a child, lots. When the doctor left, he gave everyone a lesson on how to work his phone. Each individual took their turn out in the hallway for privacy, while they spilled their heart out to her. It took a while.

He studied everyone in the room. "How do you guys want me to do this? Do you want me to set it beside her and leave while it plays?" He needed to know he wasn't going to hurt anyone if he listened. They all shrugged. Being together the last seven days had allowed them a lot of time to reminisce, convincing him even more that she was the one for him.

When he edged into her curtained-off area he stopped, his hand still gripping the curtain. She had fewer tubes. *Must be a good sign.* He slid his mask down and kissed her forehead. The nurse on duty today told him she was a long-time fan, so he got away with quite a bit. He'd never forgive himself if she lost her job for being so kind.

He sat in the chair and rested his elbows on the side of her bed. "It's time, honey. No more sleeping. You can come back to us. I have a surprise for you." He searched through the recordings on his phone. Katherine was first. She held it together, somewhat.

While on tour, Isabelle described her position as mother hen of the group. She was right. The way she stared at the pictures each day told him it stressed her beyond words not to be at Isabelle's side, insisting she recover faster. She did now. He laughed at her demand for Isabelle to wake her lazy ass up.

The messages from the girls he'd expected. The ones from the guys, no. He sat back in the chair and ran his fingers through his hair with one hand, held his knee down with the other. They cracked jokes about how much of an ass he was after she left, about the shows she missed. All of their messages ended with, *I love you.*

He sat on the edge of his chair and took her hand when the last of the messages played. "No pressure…okay, lots. I need you. Since the moment you walked into that airport…my life has never been so complete. I hadn't even spoken to you and was already jealous of the dude who hit on you at the baggage claim.

"Mine. Remember that, I meant it."

****

Gah. It's cold in here. Wait, where am I?

****

"Dr. Harris, it's been two days. Shouldn't she at least show signs that she hears us, hand twitches, or something?" He paced along the window beside her bed and threw his hands in the air. Carol sat in the chair on the other side of the bed with her fingers laced and shoulders alert and ready.

The doctor stood at the end of her bed, his arms crossed. "There is no way to tell. I said at least three days, remember. We will give her another twenty-four hours. If she doesn't start to come to tomorrow, we will send her for another scan. All the pictures so far show she is on the mend, but the brain is tricky to understand."

"Thank you, Dr. Harris. We know you have done everything possible. It's just a little hard to be patient." She wandered over to Cole, wrapped him in a hug, and offered her motionless daughter a gaze filled with hope. "We will wait some more."

****

Cole? I can smell Cole. Mmmm. Mom? I'm so tired...

****

"So you need to relieve me, Abby, and Taryn of this macho fest before someone gets hurt. They are so competitive."

Cole laughed as he played the last of the messages, again. He needed her. Every time he returned to the waiting room he shoved his phone at them, demanded they talk to her. He could tell from the eager smiles on their faces, the insistence wasn't necessary; they could all relate. The guys poked fun at him, said even in love he still had moody days.

He couldn't argue, so he left the waiting room for where his strength lay, unconscious. "My love, this is tough. I don't know what else to do. It's been two weeks since our last night together, and those pretty blue eyes of yours filled me with so much joy. I need them back."

He resorted to a desperate plea to her. The rocker lifestyle, after so many years, had conditioned him. He got what he wanted, when he wanted it. And now, she needed to wake up, dammit.

The nurse covered her with a heated blanket before she checked her vitals once again.

****

Aw, it's about time. Seriously people, turn the heat up. Cole. I can hear you, why won't my eyes open?

****

"What time is she going down for her scan?"

"Fifteen minutes, Mr. Davies."

"You can't take her sooner?" He scrubbed at his face when the nurse glared at him. Yes, he was an ass, just couldn't stop it. Isabelle slept too well, him, not so much. A healthy glow had returned to her skin, healthy. The only tubes in her were the IV in her hand and the catheter. Now he just needed to see those beautiful blue eyes.

He sat on the edge of the chair, again, held her hand tight. To cause her physical pain would be okay at this point, right? Heck, if it woke her, it would only be a blessing.

Weeks out on the road with the guys held no comparison to the exhaustion that consumed him now. Through bloodshot eyes, he stared at her bed for a moment, hunched forward, and placed his forehead down beside her. He was so worn out.

Carol stood behind him, her hand on his back. She treated him like a son. With his eyes closed, he sighed at the gentle gesture. The night before, she confided in him about her anxiety when Isabelle had left. How it faded now that she'd come to know the compassionate group of men with her and the other women. She told him she couldn't wait to have him as a son-in-law.

"Look."

She hit him on the back, startled him just as his body relaxed. He raised his head and strained to open his eyes. Her excitement stopped him mid-yawn, to follow her pointed finger. His eyes opened wider than they'd been in days. It was heaven.

Isabelle's fingers twitched, several times.

She ran and got the nurse, yelling, "She's waking, she's waking," the entire way. Words he'd fix to his memory, and his heart, from that point on.

The doctor and nurses rushed to the side of the bed. They smiled.

****

Geez. Where is that blanket? Mom? Cole? I'm here. Can you see me?

****

"Isabelle. Sweetheart."

His gaze snapped up from her fingers to the doctor. He spoke with enthusiasm. About time.

"Honey, it's time to wake up."

He scowled. *She's my sweetheart pal, back off.*

"Isabelle. Come on, you have a lot of people here waiting for you to open your eyes."

****

Hello? I'm trying, jerk off.

****

He shook his head, glanced down at her face, and leaned close to her ear. He chuckled. "Hello, my love. Can you please open those beautiful eyes? I'll share my cookies with you."

****

Mmmm, cookies, and his laugh. Oh how I've missed you.

****

"Did you see that? I really don`t want to know what you said, but it did make her smile."

He beamed with the thrill of hope at Carol, and then back to her. "Always about the cookies, hey?"

A deep breath, so full, it gave him the energy of a thousand men, overruled his exhaustion. Nothing would ever be the same again. His knee bounced. He didn't hide it.

"Isabelle? You have a very impatient boyfriend here to see you and a whole roomful of men and women down the hall. Come back to us, honey."

He didn't miss the tear that fell down Carol's face.

He leaned into Isabelle's ear again and everyone gasped when her chest rose with his nearness. He didn't want to have to resort to this, but what the hell, he was desperate. "I read your journal, baby. Mmmm, we are good together aren't we?"

"Nooo," she groaned with a raspy voice.

Cheers and claps of joy filled the room. Carol hugged the doctor and spun back to her daughter with happy tears. He closed his eyes and sat back and let his own tears fall as well, no longer concerned about being tough. She could reduce him to weakness anytime, as long she was there, alive. When he opened his eyes, he was hit in the heart, hard.

She lay there, facing him, and stared. "You are in trouble, mister."

He smiled, his tears poured at the low whisper of her scratchy words. He couldn't wipe them away fast enough. "Baby, as long as you're here with me always, you can give me all the shit you want. I can handle it."

The doctor stepped up. "Why don't you two go fill in the rest of the group while we examine her? If everything checks out, we'll have her moved into another room, where they can all visit her. No more than two at a time, of course. She is still going to be weak and need rest."

Yes, they needed to know, but to leave her now seemed impossible. The corner of her mouth rose and she lifted her hand to him. He grasped it and held on tight.

"It's okay." Her voice grew stronger, music to his ears.

He kissed her, on the lips this time, without a care what others said about it. "I love you," he whispered and kissed her again.

"I love you, too."

He grinned so big, a spark only she ignited, coursed throughout his entire body. *She said it.* He touched his forehead to hers and let his eyes drift closed with relief.

****

They paced. The hallway was sure to be covered in scuffmarks by the time everyone got to see her. Two at a time sucked, not conducive to his mood swings when forced to wait. He itched to be back with her, and they made fun of him. The opportunity didn't come often enough, so he let it go for now.

"So?" Drew smacked him on the back. "If she happens to *forget* she loves you, 'cause you know, amnesia, can I make a play for her?"

He laughed and nudged him with his shoulder. "Not a chance man. She's mine."

****

Visitors arrived daily and the girls returned to work, autographed pictures and VIP tickets in hand. Their time away from work was still spent in the hospital, and the guys were more at ease leaving her side to explore the city. She'd be there when they returned.

He never left her side and became quite the annoyance to the nurses. He fussed over her, even had a bed brought in for him to sleep on. Carol just shook her head and said Isabelle's father would have done the same for her.

They talked about everything, even Alexis.

"I'm sorry I left you. I had no idea."

He shrugged his shoulders. "No one did, other than the guys. That was the point, to keep her from embarrassment in the tabloids. My life is an open book most of the time. It's hard to keep secrets with professionals, like *Katherine*."

She laughed. "She is ruthless."

"My dad always told me if I found the woman of my dreams, to fight for her. You weren't getting away from me that easy. I can't wait for you to meet him, and my brothers."

The pride on his face sent a warm, familiar sensation, through her body. She caught herself glancing at him often.

How did I get so lucky? Maybe next year—wow, next year—I will go to New York with him. Maybe.

She smiled at him. It'd been a while since she'd imagined a future for herself, but that didn't mean she'd make nice with his ex-girlfriend just yet. His dad and brothers—that she could do.

Her mom stayed as often as Cole, but left at nightfall to sleep in her own bed. Every time someone new stopped in to say hello, she glanced at her mom, hugging herself and happy. A sight she would never tire of.

When she and her mom demanded time alone, Cole pouted but complied. She enjoyed the delight in her mother's voice as she explained, in private, how the guys and girls insisted they stay until she got home.

It took a few days before she could ask about *that* day. Tears streamed down her face at the pain in her mother's voice; she didn't like the gaps in her memory. Offers of apology for the panic she created didn't go very far.

At the end of the five demanded days of hospital rest by the doctor, her room was filled with cards and flowers from everyone, even her students. She didn't see herself as that important to others, but this obvious display changed that. Cole told her every few minutes he loved her. The smile on his face when she said it back each time was priceless, as if she'd just said it for the first time.

****

"She will be on bed rest for another week while at home. A nurse will check on her each day and change her bandage. I am sure the girls can help her come up with an attractive hairstyle to cover the slight scar she will have."

The doctor laughed. "Someone still needs to be with her at all times to monitor for signs that she needs to come back in, such as dizziness, blurred vision, and vertigo. She will continue to have mild headaches for a while but they should be nothing compared to what she suffered through before."

She sat in the wheelchair, and tapped her fingers with a glare at the doctor while he gave the discharge instructions to her mom and Cole, not her. She took a deep breath and smiled at Cole, who took notes with actual pen and paper.

Many nurses, doctors, and hospital staff stood in

the hallway as Cole wheeled her to the elevator. She'd beaten odds that amazed many people. He fussed over every bump and people snickered at his expense. Bedrest with him by her side sounded like the most excellent kind of heaven.

"What's funny, baby?"

She extended her hand over her shoulder, to touch his. "Nothing. Just excited to get home." Her gaze drifted to the open hospital door. Bed would be nice, too.

"You, my darling, are trouble." He leaned over to kiss the top of her head.

****

Carol and Cole each held an arm as she eased her way through the front door to loud claps and cheers. Katherine, Taryn, Abigail, Drew, Brett, and Zander smiled, ready to pounce in with hugs. They didn't. They each took turns and told her they loved her, even the men. Her heart swelled.

The crowded house and enormous amount of tattooed individuals would make anyone think a wild party occurred. Nothing of the sort. They all sat and talked, just spent time together. Carol did her usual—feeding everyone until they couldn't possibly eat anymore.

She scanned the tiny sitting room, all the tired faces around her. Most of them stood since there were only a few spots to sit, and air mattresses littered the much larger living room on the other side of the wall. "Go to bed already, I'm fine. Cole will help me."

"I'm sure he *will* help you."

Carol smacked Brett, but not soon enough.

They all hugged her again before they made their

way to bed. The quiet of the room calmed her. She snuggled into the small loveseat, closed her eyes, and listened to him shuffle around the room. The sound of a zipper sparked her attention, and then he sat beside her. His scent filled her nose when he put his arm around her and huddled in closer.

"I missed this." He kissed the top of her head.

"Me too."

She opened her eyes, and he handed her a book, her journal. "Would you like it back?"

She grabbed it from his hands. "I still can't believe you read it. Weren't you ever taught a woman's journal is sacred property?" She hugged it to her chest and glared up at him.

"Honey, I grew up in a home full of rowdy men, remember?" He laughed. "We were only concerned about getting into a woman's sacred property." He squeezed her tighter when she wiggled to get away. "There's something in there."

She glanced down at the book and up at him again when he nudged his chin in the direction of the book. Eyebrows raised, she opened the journal slowly and flipped through the pages until she revealed the last one, covered in his handwriting.

Dear Diary, <—lol

I have met her...the woman of my dreams. She is beautiful, intelligent, sassy, caring, and MINE. I never knew what to expect when I made that offer, the one that would change my life forever. Her desired experiences gave me hope that I could love in a healthy way. Although I may convince people otherwise, life isn't easy on the road. It gets lonely. I have always dreamed of the day I'd have someone to call after a show to say I love you to—when drunk of course. That probably won't change, Isabelle, just so you know.

I will slur my love in a barbaric manner and always hope the next day she will forgive me for any wrongdoing. I want my knee to bounce as I, not so patiently, wait for the plane to arrive home to her.

I want to share my love with her, with you, Isabelle. As well as my bunk, my cookies, my passion...my children. I have never felt so complete and your strength to survive only makes it clear we were meant to be.

I only have one bucket list item—to see you walk down the aisle to me. Marry me, Isabelle? Make my bucket list complete and I will move heaven and earth to get that last item on your list complete. <—I would anyway...

I love you. Say yes....

Isabelle's vision, blurred with tears, made it difficult to see Cole's face. She scrambled for a pen and tissue from the table. She wiped her eyes and held the opened book close. Out of the corner of her eye, his knee bounced while his finger tapped his leg. Although she was done writing, she pretended to scribble and glanced up over the top of the book. When he seemed like he'd crawl out of his skin if she didn't hurry, she handed him the book and smiled. He glared at her. She laughed and snatched it out of his hands. "Fine then."

"Oh no you don't." He tackled her and stole the book.

A rush of excitement filled Isabelle. She bit her lip as he read her words, or word. A smile spread across his face, one she would remember forever. Now that she had forever.

Dear Diary,

Yes.

He set the book down and lowered himself to the floor in front of her. She scooted to the edge of the couch with her legs on either side of his body. He cupped her face with his hands, caressed her cheek with his thumb, and stared deep into her eyes. Like nothing in the world would compare to this moment. He guided her in for a kiss.

With her guard no longer in place and her emotions available to him, it swept her away. The kiss grew forceful.... desperate. As if he promised to make up for the many hours they've spent apart. The days they'd fought against the current.

He swayed into her. His hard shaft grazed against her already swollen nub, and she moaned. She was just as weak for him as he seemed for her. She loved him. Loved the effect they had on each other. She placed her hands on his shoulders and used just enough pressure to get the distance she needed. "The doctor said—"

She had very little time to catch her breath before he cut her off with the smack of a playful kiss. "I know what the doctor said, baby. As long as I have forever, I can wait."

He wiggled his eyebrows up and down. "Just don't be alarmed when you feel me rub up against you with a hard-on that will never go away. Get better so we can go back to *your* house, and I don't have to defile you under your mother's roof. My dick has a mind of its own. When it comes to you, I have no control."

She covered her inhale with her hand, embarrassed, and glanced at the open doorway to where the girls slept.

"Don't bother Izzy, we heard it all," Katherine yelled from the living room on the other side of the wall. "And I'm pretty sure you're engaged now, congrats."

"I'll make celebratory drinks soon," Taryn yelled and then giggled.

"I am totally helping with the plans," Abigail pitched in.

He tucked an arm under her knees, braced the other around her back, and stood. "If you ladies don't mind, I think I am going to take my fiancé to bed in the spare room tonight."

She snuggled into his chest and inhaled the scent once temporary. Not anymore.

"No bucket list items yet, Cole, doctors' orders," Carol lectured from her bedroom.

She gasped at her mother's voice, fully aware of what they'd done on tour.

"And, welcome to the family."

He fell asleep with a smile the second his head hit the pillow and she held him tight, all night.

****

Isabelle sat out on the swing with Katherine and sipped her coffee. The early morning dew made the green grass, and all of her mother's hard work sparkle. Birds sang and the high-spirited banter from the men and women inside, as they enjoyed her mother's feast, warmed Isabelle's heart.

Her chest had tightened when she sat at the table earlier. Katherine, good at sensing her need for diversion, explained to everyone she needed some alone time with her best friend and gave them a glare that said back the fuck off, when they protested. The guys now made fun of her motherly tone; it was priceless.

Isabelle crossed her legs, lifted her mug to her nose, and inhaled. Her mind wandered as she admired the colorful flowers. She pictured the many days to come alongside her mom and her best friends as they worked in the garden and drank anything cold that mixed well with liquor.

She was right all along. His friends matched well with hers. She couldn't see any romantic notions, but friendships had kindled.

She let her head fall back on the cushion with her contented gaze on Katherine. "Thank you for being there for me and Cole."

Katherine shrugged her shoulders. "I'll admit," she sighed. "It wasn't easy letting you go. The list made it feel like there was an end, one I didn't want to face." Katherine adjusted in her seat with a subtle cough and directed her somber face to the garden. She took a sip of her coffee, held it close to her mouth, and spoke softly. "Your list brought you the love of your life. Maybe there's something to it."

About the Author

Denise Marie lives in Canada with her husband, and two children. She divides her time between family, a day job, and writing, while also trying to sneak in a little break for a steamy read. She enjoys the trials and tribulations of life, often catching herself imagining the sizzling story she could make of it.

Visit Denise at
https://www.facebook.com/denisemarieauthor

To chat with Denise Marie and other Wild Rose Press authors of erotic romance, join us at www.groups.yahoo.com/group/thewilderroses.

Also Available

Angel's Addiction

Rockin' Hard, Book One

by

Nese Lane

http://amzn.com/B00FZ1O1HM

his angel...

Gabriella Blanchett can't seem to resist the addictive lure of another pleasure-filled night with the smoldering rock star. He'd be perfect except for the sudden and mysterious disappearances in the middle of the night. His ability to sense her every need, coupled with the secrets he harbors, leave her head spinning, her body humming, and her heart in jeopardy.

her addiction...

Rock star Auro Moretti tours the world with a goal that's two-fold. He hopes his music is inspiring, but as an empath, he also heals tortured young souls in the audience with his gypsy gift. Protecting his family's secret and Romani heritage proves as difficult a task as keeping Gabriella in his bed.

She fills his soul with light...he feeds her craving for love...and a stalker threatens to destroy both.

Chapter One

Gabriella

Sweat trickled between my breasts as I yanked on the door to the amphitheater. For six months, I'd craved his touch, a lifetime of replaying each moment of our short time together. I shouldn't have come. Being with him was like a drug to me. Addiction in any form was dangerous. But how do you rehab yourself from a person? How do you insist to your inner voice, making love to a rock star who appeared to sense your every desire was bad for you? You don't. Or at least, I hadn't been able to. So much for being a strong, intelligent woman. Oh, well, they say the meek shall inherit the earth.

Yeah, right. I am so screwed.

The music and energy hit me full in the face when the door swung open. I straightened my shoulders and made my way through the throng of people standing in the aisle. The time before, I'd come with friends. This visit was all on me. I searched the stage for his presence. His voice alone could send me into mini-orgasms, but he wasn't singing now.

Instead, I caught sight of a blond in ragged jeans, crooning into the microphone. Jasper Lyons, lead singer for the opening band, Twisted Talons. His voice was sweet and sultry, almost every woman's wet dream. Just not mine. He was all kinds of yummy, but too cocky for my tastes. The fans on the floor next to the catwalk observed, completely enthralled.

I wandered to the side of the stage, the laminated badge hanging from my neck, and cut through people and security like a warm knife through butter. All Access Pass. I snorted. If people only knew what it gave admission to.

I had received it three days ago in a pretty box with a single piece of white card stock. Elegantly written in a masculine hand were five little words—*Angel Eyes, I need you.*

My world had tilted. My first thought was, *yes!* Then, *holy crap, he found me. Now what?* It was supposed to have been a fling. How had he found out my name? Discovered where I worked?

Decorator's Walk, the exclusive store I owned, provided unique items for interior designers. Located in The Houston Design Center, the boutique was away from the bustle of downtown. And I'd made sure to be vague during our time together. I thought back, to figure out what I might have done to give myself away.

The night had started out normal. I went with friends to a local restaurant for dinner and drinks. The week had been long and hard, so I decided to let loose and relax. The parmesan-encrusted filet mignon was to die for. I sipped a glass of cabernet, listening to the joking banter among the other women at the table. They were all hardworking ladies who loved getting together. My group kept me grounded.

Lisa called a waiter over and whispered her order into his ear. Crazy heifer, always an instigator. We'd been friends since grade school. Either of us would do whatever it took to help the other.

The server returned with a round of tequila shots for all six of us, accompanied by a tart lime slice. I shook my head, lifting my wine glass.

Lisa stared at me, the fire from her Latina heritage reflected in her eyes. "Give it up, *chica.* We're all doing this. Roxy has the company limo for the evening so designated driving isn't an issue."

"Oh, what the hell." I picked up the small glass and licked some of the salt off the rim. It couldn't hurt to live a little.

"On three," Lisa said, with a smirk. "One…two…three!"

We all downed the smooth *agave* at the same time. When I bit into the small wedge of citrus, the flavor exploded on my tongue and I licked my lips savoring the taste. After my initial reluctance, more liquor followed. A little reckless, why not? I deserved to let go. Three of the others called it a night and left me, Lisa and Roxy discussing various options to extend our evening out.

"We could go to a club. Neon Nights is supposed to be the new rage," Roxy said.

"They're having a party down at East Beach. Sand, warm fire, hot guys. What's not to like?" Lisa chimed in.

I rolled my eyes. Galveston? I mean, was she serious? In my opinion, it was a tad juvenile for twenty-something career women to crash a beach party. But before I could express my reluctance, the owner of the restaurant, Michael Rand, a friend of Roxy's, walked up to our table with an envelope in hand. "Ladies, I hope you enjoyed your dinner."

We all made the right noises, oohing and ahhing

over what we'd consumed. I commented on the filet and raved about the asparagus salad. I turned to ask Michael if I could beg the chef for his recipe and noticed him watching Roxy. A look of desire flashed in the depth of his gaze before he cleared his throat. "Would you lovelies be interested in taking in a concert tonight?"

The roar of the crowd chanting "Encore! Encore!" brought me back to the present. Michael Rand. He had to be the connection. The night of the concert, he mentioned he had been given the passes by a friend in the band. Roxy's buddy must have handed over the information needed to track me down. Mr. Rand had some explaining to do, though to be honest, I hoped this night would bring a status change from ex to current lover.

Michael may have given my info, but I'm the one who couldn't stay away, definitely a glutton for punishment. Hello, I'd walked out last time because he wouldn't come clean about why he left me hanging at the hotel. There were so many things about him I didn't know or understand. And now I had chosen to return to his chaotic world. I shoved the irritating inner voice to the back of my mind. The addict in me hoped for the best.

I glanced at the platform once more. Jasper Lyons took his final bow, then exited the stage to screams of "I love you, Jasper" and "I want to have your baby." Some girls didn't have a clue. Maybe I was one of them. The roadies scrambled to reset the dais for the headliner, Empathy, *his* band.

The feeling of a small winged creature trying to fight its way out of my stomach made me pause and reevaluate my decision. Most people got butterflies. I got bats. *What am I doing?* I'd been back and forth for the past three days. My resolution slipped.

I pivoted toward the aisle to make my escape when a familiar voice rang out. "Angel? My god, it's you! Auro is going to freakin' flip!"

I glanced over my shoulder to see who'd recognized me. The rumpled appearance of the mastermind behind the sound and lights portion of the show made me smile. His curly, light brown hair was in disarray, evident from the fact he was running his fingers through it while we spoke. The wire-rimmed glasses balanced on his nose made the geek in him more apparent.

"Hey, Chad. How's it hangin'?" A slight blush tinged his cheeks. He was way too easy to tease. "Auro shouldn't be too surprised. He sent me the pass."

"From what I hear, he wasn't sure you would come."

"I almost didn't." Derision hardened my voice.

He ducked his head. "Well, I gotta head to the S&L board in the back and make sure things are ready to go. The crowd is getting restless." He gestured to the mass of bodies in the mosh pit. "Go on upstairs. I'm sure he'd rather you be in the wings than standing down here in bedlam. Why didn't you come in through the back entrance?"

I shrugged. "You know, it never even occurred to me." Only having been to a concert once before, it hadn't crossed my mind. I was so bad at this rock star's lover thing. That explained the odd look from the guy taking tickets at the door.

"Big Lou is handling security on this side. Go on

up and get settled in for the show." With a wave, he headed to the back of the arena and slid behind the immense control panel.

I drew a quick breath to bolster my courage and climbed the metal stairs. At the top, I stopped when a massive body blocked my path.

His head was completely shaved, his arms and neck covered in tribal tattoos. The sleeves on the black security T-shirt he wore stretched taut, trying to cover the enormous biceps. "No groupies allowed in this area."

I kept my head down not meeting his gaze. "Not even with an All Access Pass?"

He snorted. "Try another one, missy. Those only go out to family and sponsors."

I chuckled at his response. This was going to be fun. Big Lou looked scary as hell, but I knew better. "What about close personal friends of Auro Moretti?"

The weight of his gaze began at my hair and traveled down the entire length of my hourglass figure. I had dressed sexier than my norm, but it was still a far cry from fan girl attire. I'd settled on a see-thru navy blouse with a dark lace bra underneath. I wore my favorite crushed-velvet pencil skirt with a slit up the front left side that showed flashes of my black stockings but didn't go high enough to show the garters holding them.

My one sexy indulgence was a pair of four inch, platform, peep-toe, fuck-me heels in black patent leather. Observing discreetly from under lowered lashes, I smothered a giggle when his gaze hovered there briefly before coming back up to my face. I tilted my head back, staring straight at him. The realization of who I was registered on his face. "So does the package meet with your approval Big Lou? Or should I turn around and show you my ass as well?"

A prickling sensation at the back of my neck was the only warning I had before—

"Now that is a vision few men could give the proper appreciation."

I shivered when the sinfully seductive notes of *his* voice skidded across my senses, causing an immediate dampness between my legs. I turned, searching for the source, gasping when my gaze locked with the decadent chocolate eyes of my former lover.

For a moment, I thought the mind kept memories a little fuzzy as a coping mechanism. I'd remembered his gorgeous face and lithe form, imagining it was him while I pleasured myself. The image before me now was so beyond my paltry musings. He leaned negligently against the metal truss layered with multi-colored lights.

"Ro," I whispered.

"*Occhi Angelichi.*"

Angel Eyes, his nickname for me. I hesitated, my body warring with my mind. The physical urge to touch him was excruciating, but inside my head, I was screaming… *He will make love to you and move on. Can you deal with that?*

Quit lying to yourself. You were the one who left last time…remember?

Got it. Shut up!

My indecision must have shown on my face, because he raised a single brow in question, shoved away from the support beam, and sauntered my way.

His hair was longer than I remembered, the straight

ebony tresses hung over his shoulders. The ends flirted with the play of muscles in his chest as he drifted my way. Oh hell, yes, I was doing this. Dealing with the fall out would have to come later.

I gulped down a moan. The passion in his gaze brought back a flash of the night we met.

He'd entered the after party, ignoring the jovial greetings and compliments, perusing the room until he fixated on my face, as if he'd been searching for me, which was crazy since we'd never met. He strode my direction, his actions dripping raw power. It took everything I had not to back away. His breathtaking form towered over me. Strangely enough, he was actually of average height and build. Watching him perform on stage was minimal compared to his charismatic force in person.

Eye candy didn't come close to describing what stood before me. Holy-shit-hot just about covered it. He was almost effeminate in his beauty. The harsh planes of his cheek and jaw kept his masculinity apparent, but the overall sight made my breath catch.

I will never forget the first thing he said, his Italian accent thick with sentiment. "You have stolen my soul with your angel eyes."

It took a second or two to process his statement. I laughed and then covered my mouth with my hand to try to disguise my disbelief. Was this guy for real?

"So, is that a standard pick up line for a rock star? Sorry, I really enjoyed the show, but I'm not groupie material." The snarky comment fell from my lips before I could stop it.

His confusion showed plainly on his face. "You laugh at my emotion?"

I couldn't believe he was serious. "Don't you think soul stealing is a little strong for someone you haven't even met?"

"Auro is my name. And yours is?"

"Irrelevant."

He raised his brows sardonically. "If you will not tell me your name, I will just call you Angel. It seems appropriate considering the color of your eyes. They are so grey they appear silver in the light. I was held spellbound through most of the set by their radiance."

I wondered if this smitten routine worked for him with other women? Not really impressed with the conversation, I turned to look for Lisa or Roxy, hoping to make my excuses. "Um, thanks for the compliment, but I need to find my friends."

When I turned to go, he wrapped his fingers around my wrist. "Please do not leave. I just want to talk…to know you."

His touch electrified me, and the sizzle coursed from my arm straight to my clit. I bit down on the inside of my lower lip to keep a whimper from escaping. I glanced back, first, to where he held me in his grasp, then up to see the imploring expression on his stunning face. My reaction to the contact of his hand had my senses reeling. If we were ever head to toe, skin to skin, I'd implode.

Of course, that never happened, but eruptions of passion, followed by mind-blowing orgasms did. And the promise of those explosions reflected now in his gaze.

With Big Lou in front of me, Auro stepped behind. He gripped my hips and eased me back against his solid frame. One arm slipped around my waist, and his fingers slid under my blouse to play with my belly button ring. I jolted at the contact, my nipples tightening, my clit swelling.

He nuzzled the side of my neck, placing a feather light kiss at the base of my ear. "I have missed you, *cara*."

He breathed the words against my skin, causing me to tremble and close my eyes. My pulse accelerated, producing a flutter in the hollow of my throat. He nipped and laved that point, then growled as he spun me in his arms.

With the unexpected movement, I fell forward, my frame resting against his from knees to hip, my hands gliding up his chest. The full contact of my body against his hard muscular build amplified my desire.

He lowered his head and brushed my lips lightly, then teased the bottom one with his teeth. His tongue soothed away the slight pleasure-pain before delving into my mouth. The black currant flavor that was uniquely Auro exploded across my taste buds, feeding my addiction.

His tongue sought then intertwined with mine, the silkiness teased and retreated, then teased again. My core pulsed with arousal, and I squeezed my thighs together.

While he plundered, I moaned, skimming my hands around his shoulders and burying them in his glorious hair. At the slight tug of his raven locks, he smoothed his palms down to cup both ass cheeks. He squeezed, pressing my cunt against the hard ridge of his cock, and slowly rocked his hips. The slight friction sent waves of pleasure to the tiny bundle of nerves nestled there. My juices trickled from my pussy saturating my panties.

Big Lou cleared his throat.

Auro broke the kiss and rested his forehead against mine, his breathing harsh. "*Merda, cara.* You make me forget myself."

I licked my lips drawing in his taste. His eyes darkened at the action. He gave my backside one last caress and reluctantly turned to the security guard with instructions to escort me to the VIP seats.

Before I could gather my wits enough to follow, he tucked an errant curl behind my ear then traced my jawline with his thumb. "Know this my *tesoro*, when the show is over, I will be taking you to the hotel. No parties, no press, just you and I. I am going to make you come three times before we ever hit the bedroom. I can't wait to see your soft pink mouth slide back and forth over my cock and the ends of that long sable hair pooled around my thighs. Do you understand?"

The intensity of his expression had me nodding in assent. He visibly relaxed, as if he hadn't been sure I would agree. He grazed his lips over mine one last time and headed back to the dressing room.

I followed Big Lou to a roped off area of seats located on the left wing of the platform. He pointed to a chair on the first row with a clear view of the stage. Positioned in the center of the seat was a small box wrapped in silver. I scooped it up, placing it in my lap as I sat. My heart raced along with my mind, and I rested my head in my hands to ease the pounding.

His apprehension was my fault. The last time we'd been together, I'd called him an overbearing possessive jackass during the huge fight we'd had. Okay, so it wasn't one of my better days. He'd wanted me to take more time off from my "work" to travel with him and the band.

Owning my own decorators boutique, I found it relatively easy to adjust my schedule. I had just finished a large project for a client so I'd rescheduled my appointments from the prior week.

Reality had come crashing in with a phone call from my customs broker. He informed me the antique mirror commissioned from Paris was being held at U.S. Customs due to improper paperwork. The subsequent calls kept me occupied for over an hour.

Auro had become irritated at my apparent distraction and dismissed my concerns by suggesting I let whoever was in charge handle it. He rambled on to say he would take care of me, and my job, whatever it may be, was no longer necessary.

My temper snapped. I'd been floored by his caveman attitude, considering he'd been unnervingly sensitive to my moods and needs for the preceding days. He had no idea I ran my own business, but his predilection for the Ozzy and Harriet lifestyle was more than I could accept.

We exchanged heated words, but he'd calmed me with promises to be less demanding and acknowledged I could take care of myself. Two days later, I'd packed and left. His disappearance from the hotel room in the early morning hours and failure to show for our planned outing had been all I could take.

The opening strains of Empathy's most recent number one song filtered through my consciousness, and I forced my attention to the musicians on the main rostrum.

From where I sat, I could see Auro as he prepared

to enter the stage. His eyes were closed, his body relaxed. He leaned against the wall, lost in deep meditation.

I greedily took in his exquisite countenance. All harsh angles under golden bronze skin, his dark lashes fanned on high cheekbones, a perfect combination.

Sensing my perusal, his lids raised, and his coffee gaze met mine. I inhaled, and my hard nipples cinched tighter, triggering a spasm low in my belly with the barely leashed lust apparent in his stare.

I shuddered, and his lips quirked, letting me know he'd noticed. He blew me a kiss, settled the sound monitor in his ear, turned, and raced to the edge of the platform. The crowd roared at his entrance, the sound bringing me to my feet.

"He is such a hottie! Don't you think?"

I ripped my gaze from the stage to take in the young blonde next to me. I couldn't fault her opinion, considering I had been thinking the same thing, albeit a little more graphically. Playing dumb, I asked. "Which one?"

"Auro, he's the one out front singing," she said with an enamored sigh.

I turned in the direction she indicated and watched him sway to the beat of the ballad he sang. Each movement he made was a sensuous tribute to the creator of man. His skintight russet-colored pants showed the contraction of each muscle in his thighs when he shifted his weight from one leg to the other.

The soft leather affectionately cupped his perfectly rounded ass like a lover. Sheer turquoise-silk stirred with the motion of his torso, and the shirt gave flirty glimpses of his rock-hard abs.

He stepped to the edge of the stage serenading the front row. As the song ended, he threw his head back and belted out the closing refrain. The exertion to reach and hold the final note had him raising the microphone high, his spine arched, his long ebony locks brushing that luscious ass.

The tail of his shirt lifted, showing the trail of hair running from his navel into the low-slung waistband of his pants. The vision before my eyes, coupled with the memory of licking my way down the luscious path… He was sin personified.

"Definitely a hottie." I dropped into the chair behind me, thankful for the support.

Empathy cruised into their next song. Overheated, I brushed my sweaty bangs from my eyes and realized I still held the gift-wrapped package. Auro had a penchant for surprises.

With shaky fingers, I tugged the bow and gently ripped away the shiny paper. The box inside was beautiful. Hand-carved, dark cherry wood with a mother of pearl inlay in the form of a pair of wings graced the lid. Angel wings. I gasped at Auro's symbolic choice. *Major brownie points*.

"Oh, how pretty! What's inside?"

I blinked back the tears that threatened to fall and looked up at the girl. I swallowed past the lump in my throat and finally managed to croak, "I'm not sure. I haven't opened it yet."

"What are you waiting for?" Her youth was apparent by her impatient statement, and in the way she bounced up and down with excitement for me.

I lifted the top of the tiny ornamental chest. Inside, nestled in sapphire velvet sat an old-fashioned skeleton key. Made of pewter, the bow in the shape of a heart, the patina suggested it was very old. The smooth texture of the ornament hinted that the previous owner lovingly wore it close to the skin.

With closer examination, a long luminescent silver chain spilled out. The necklace threaded through the center, dainty yet secure. I ran a finger along the delicate links then slid it over my head. After adjusting my hair, the pendant rested in the cleavage of my breasts.

"Wow, very nice. It reminds me of Empathy's song *Salvation*. There is a verse that mentions how every person will find, if they search hard enough, another soul who holds the key to their salvation."

"I don't remember that one." Through a shimmer of tears, I fumbled with my clutch purse and wrenched it open to store the box inside.

"Auro wrote the song and the band released it about two years ago."

"I've only been listening to them for about a year. I guess I should check out their older stuff." In reality, I hadn't made the time. With my comment and a feeble smile, I returned my attention to the show.

Auro strutted across the platform. I admired his lithe form while I pondered the thoughtfulness of his gift. What could I do for him in return? The idea of pampering him for his kindness struck me as an excellent place to start.

I motioned Big Lou over. "Are the reservations for tonight's suites the same as last time?"

He deliberated for a moment, and then nodded. "You'll have to ask Cameron for the keycard."

I rolled my eyes at the mention of the band's

manager. He'd been polite to me last time but made it very clear he considered me one of the masses. "Which way?"

Big Lou jerked the walkie-talkie from his hip and spoke into the mic. He located Cameron and sent me off to search for the office at the back of the stage.

I weaved in and out of the roadies and other technical staff. The amount of people it took to run a show of this size was astronomical. I slowed my pace, entering the back hallway. Big Lou had directed me to the last entryway before the exit.

I hesitated before knocking. Since Big Lou had called to locate him, he knew I was coming, but with Cameron's prior dismissal of me, I wasn't sure he'd welcome the interruption. Squaring my shoulders, I shook off the apprehension and pounded on the thin metal, hoping to be heard above the roar of the music.

With no immediate answer, I turned the knob and opened it to an interesting sight—Cameron seated in the chair behind his desk and a curvy blonde on her knees with his cock buried deep in her throat. Her head bobbed as she licked and sucked her way up and down his swollen shaft. Before I could react and retreat from this private scene, Cameron threw his head back and shouted his release.

I stumbled out and quietly closed the door. I leaned against the frame, praying I hadn't been noticed. *Wow, way too much in the way of visuals.* Collecting myself, I settled on the speaker case propped against the wall.

About five minutes later, the office opened, and the voluptuous woman walked out, tugging her dress back into place. She glanced in my direction with a smirk, then turned and walked away. So much for not being noticed. She obviously knew she'd had an audience but wasn't in any way concerned about her performance.

Well, maybe Cameron would still be basking in the afterglow. I jumped to my feet and entered the room, this time without knocking.

He stood at a small bar, pouring dark liquor over ice in a glass. At my entrance, he turned my direction. "What can I do for you, sugar? You know you could have joined us. Nadine wouldn't have minded."

His lewd tone sent my temper soaring. He assumed I was an easy mark because I'd slept with Auro. My first instinct was to tell him to go screw himself, but I decided to let it slide in order to get what I needed.

"Thanks, but sharing is something I only do with my lover. You guys had it all under control without my help."

"Guess so, but if you change your mind…"

"Believe me, I'll take it under advisement." I shook my head at his arrogance and got straight to the point. "I'm going to surprise Auro with a little pampering. I need the keycard for the penthouse suite in order to get things set up before he finishes the show."

His calculating expression had my instincts on alert. If there was any way the man could turn this situation to his advantage, he would find it. My skin literally crawled while he looked me over. "Sure, but it will cost you a kiss," he said as he leered at my breasts.

"I am very particular about who I give kisses to," I said flippantly, trying to diffuse the situation. This guy was crazy if he imagined I'd ever willingly touch him. Feigning a haughty demeanor, I held out my hand and demanded, "The key Cameron. You know Auro will be upset if you spoil my surprise."

He studied my face for a fraction of a second before he crossed to pick up a large manila envelope. Assuming I had won this round, I relaxed while he sorted through the contents. He extracted a card and held it out for me to take.

I'd grasped the corner when he seized my wrist and jerked, dragging me forward, flush against his frame.

Pain radiated the length of my arm from his vice-like grip. He snaked his other arm around my waist, drawing me in tight. The ridge of his arousal pressed into my belly, and it took everything I had not to cringe in disgust. His bourbon soaked breath filled my nostrils, and I leaned back staring into his hooded gaze.

****

Auro

"How is everyone here in Houston, Texas tonight? Twisted Talons rocked the start of our night here with you. Are you ready for Empathy's ass kickin' finish?" The wave of excitement and euphoria from the crowd hit me full force while I sang the opening line of our first number one hit. A fan favorite, we saved the tune for later in the set to bring the crowd's enthusiasm back to a fever pitch. With my mind's eye, I drew the energy in and allowed it to boost my jubilant mood.

On autopilot, I let the words of the song flow from my mouth while my mind drifted. *Angel Eyes. She is really here.*

The vision of her standing with hands on her hips, yanking Big Lou's chain, had me hard in three seconds flat. I observed her playful teasing as I drank in her appearance. If possible, she looked more beautiful than she had six months ago.

Dressed to kill and wearing a pair of heels that

made her legs go on for days, I had to tamp down my desire to grab hold, and fuck her against the wall.

Long sable hair flowed down her back almost touching her succulent ass. She smirked, her soft pink lips etched in a perfect bow, then bowed her head and allowed her gorgeous tresses to hide her face. A wave of mischief brushed across my senses. Her playful ploy to mess with the stoic security guard brought home how much I'd missed her.

A single curl snuck over her shoulder and wound around the curve of her breast. My mouth watered at the sight, and even when I sensed her slight hesitation at my appearance, I had been unable to stop from wrapping myself around her soft curves.

A flicker of pain slipped past my mental guard and jerked me back to reality. I tamped down my desire and attempted to focus on the sea of faces below the stage.

Nothing. Everyone appeared to be enjoying the show. I stepped to the side and grabbed a towel to wipe my face. Behind the cover of the terrycloth, I reached out with my gift and concentrated on the separate energies.

Features faded to points of light. Shades of blue and green sparkled in my field of vision. I panned the arena and spotted a tiny flicker of red at the back.

My target in sight, I strode to the end of the catwalk and entertained the mass of fans who had the less expensive seats.

As I sang, I covertly studied the youth huddled next to the merchandise booth. I reached out to his energy and lowered my mental shields. Hurt and rage swamped my senses. This young man teetered on the edge between lashing out and giving up.

Damn, I hated to have to deal with this tonight of all nights, but emotions were fragile things, and tomorrow might be too late. I prayed Angel…no, *Gabriella* would forgive my delay.

Years of family conditioning kicked in. My empathic abilities were a gift passed down from my Romani heritage, and I had been raised to believe I was duty-bound to help.

I motioned to my guitar player to lead off with a solo while I danced to the back of the stage. Once out of sight, I used the monitor in my ear to signal the sound and lights guy. "Chad, hey bud, you copy?"

"Loud and clear, bossman. What's up?"

"Do you see the kid leaning against the back of the T-shirt shack?" I grabbed a bottle of water and downed it.

"Black hoodie, blond, heavy on the attitude?"

"Yes, that is him. Send someone over with a pass." I tossed away the empty and turned back to the crowd.

"You got it. Consider it done."

I glanced back at the guy while I made my way back to the front of the stage. Attitude aside, he would receive a coveted invitation to the after party.

I drew a sigh of relief when we finished the second set and strode to the hallway behind the stage to relax and catch my breath before the encore. Resting against the wall, I closed my eyes. A jolt of fear and pain slapped across my senses, and I jumped forward. "Big Lou!"

The massive bodyguard hurried over with a questioning look. "Auro?"

I met his gaze. "Where is Angel?"

He shrugged. "She might not want you to know. I

think she is planning a surprise."

I brushed past him and headed for the back rooms. "Something is going on, and it is not good."

He stepped in front of me and blocked my exit. "You have a concert to finish. I'll go find her and…handle it."

I dragged my hand down my face. "If I do not hear from you via com in five minutes…to hell with the encore.

****

Gabriella

"Release me this instant."

"Not on your life, sweet cakes. I've wanted to get my hands on your sexy ass since that first night."

Now what? No one would hear me if I screamed. The bass beat of the concert filtered through the walls, causing a vibration beneath my feet. He was only of medium stature, but his strength was still superior to mine and I didn't think I could fight him and win. I needed to stall for time, and come up with a way out of this mess.

Contrary to my screaming instincts, I compelled my muscles to relax into his hold and melt against his frame. With a coyness I didn't feel, I fluttered my lashes and met his lascivious gaze. "Cam, you know I appreciate you're a strong virile man, but at least pour a lady a drink before getting up close and personal." I laughed, trying to make light of the circumstances, but it came out flat, even to my ears. I stood, not moving a muscle, waiting to see how he would respond.

Indecision crossed his expression. I could tell he didn't want to relinquish control but worried about the fallout with Auro.

“Sure thing, doll.” He released me and stepped toward the bar.

I waited until he crossed the room before I backed to the door. With his attention diverted, I cracked it open. I should have left but refused to let him ruin my surprise.

My resignation didn’t slow the wild beating of my heart against my ribs or stop the salty sheen of sweat I licked from my upper lip. I suppressed a shudder and eased back toward the center of the room.

Tremors from the music made the lamp on the desk shake. The vibration caused eerie shadows to fall on Cameron’s already disturbing mug. I recognized one of Empathy’s most popular numbers pounding through the walls. They were getting close to the end of the encore.

Against my better judgment, I tried once more to coax the key from Cameron. “So where did you meet Nadine?”

He peered up from the cocktail he poured and gave me a nauseating smile. “Is that what I said her name was? I usually don’t remember them for long.”

Well, subject number one, big mistake. I struggled to think of a neutral topic. “How many more shows are scheduled on this tour?”

Cameron sauntered toward me, my requested beverage in his hand. “Six. Why?”

Determination held me in place when the compulsion to retreat screamed in my head. “No particular reason. It’s just last time the band was in town, they took a two week break.”

“Not happening this time, sugar. We have three sold out shows this weekend, and then we move on to LA.”

I took the highball he offered and sipped the pungent alcohol with a straight face. I might not enjoy the taste, but it bought me some time. "Sounds like you have a full schedule." I calmly walked over to the bar and set down my glass, then picked up the card he'd set on the edge. "I guess I will have to make the most out of the time I have with Auro."

I turned and strode to the door. His failure to intercede with my departure had me both relieved and confused. I grasped the knob and glanced over my shoulder at Cameron. Goosebumps rose on my arms. His face held a mixture of hate and lust. "Thanks, Cam," I muttered as I stepped across the threshold and quickly shut the door behind me.

I gulped much needed oxygen into my lungs. The sight of Big Lou headed down the hall in my direction filled me with relief. "Where can I find a taxi to get me to the hotel?" I asked, impatient to leave before Cameron exited of the office.

He stopped and took in my flustered appearance. "You okay, Angel?"

"Of course."

"You look a little worse for wear. Did that sniveling bastard give you a hard time?"

What an understatement. The jerk had some serious issues. I drew in a deep breath and nodded. "Yep, but nothing I couldn't handle. Thanks for your concern, though. You're really sweet."

Big Lou eyed the entrance to Cameron's workplace and then studied me. "I don't think it is a good idea for you to be alone with him again. I have a gut feeling something ain't right with that one."

"I agree. I plan on steering clear of him in the

future. In the meantime, where can a girl catch a cab?"

He shook his head, the disapproval clear on his face. He yanked the walkie from his belt then requested a limo be brought to the South exit. "Auro would skin me alive if I let you leave without proper escort. The car will take you anywhere you like."

"Okay, thanks."

Big Lou hesitated, focused on something over my shoulder and said in a softer tone, "Auro sent me, you know. He does that sometimes, gets a sense about someone. He had an uneasy feeling about where you had gone. He cares for you, Angel. You get that, right?"

I leaned forward and gave him a quick hug causing him to tense. I smiled at his sudden discomfort and kissed his cheek. "Thanks for your help, Big Lou. I appreciate it, and between me and you, I'm pretty crazy about him, too."

He pointed to the illuminated sign at the end of the hall. "Out you go then. The chauffeur should be there waiting by now."

I hurried outside with the card clasped tightly in my hand. I glanced at the key suspended on the beautiful chain around my neck and reaffirmed my desire to make this a night Auro would never forget.

Also Read

She Likes It Irish

by

Sophia Ryan

http://amzn.com/B00BIW8Q3C

Kristin DeMarco vows to protect her broken heart and swear off men until she finishes her degree and starts her career. Survival sex—a vibrator and a sizzling-hot roommate—eases urges that can't be ignored, until her craving for a man propels her from the arms of Mr. Wrong to the door of Mr. Right. Irishman Sean O'Neill forces her to consider what she really wants. And what she wants is him in her bed. Too bad he's not cooperating.

Sean is only in America for six months to complete his degree and an archeology field school. He's as serious about his education as he is about keeping his sex life casual. When Kristin knocks on his door asking for condoms, the encounter forces him to rethink that single-minded focus. He wants Kristin for more than one night, but their secrets may end the relationship before it begins.

www.ingramcontent.com/pod-product-compliance
Lightning Source LLC
Chambersburg PA
CBHW070804030726
47504CB00003B/692

* 9 7 8 1 5 0 9 2 0 2 6 7 6 *